KT-385-061

CATHERINE FERGUSON

FOUR WEDDINGS & A FIASCO

LIBRARIES NI
WITHDRAWN FROM STOCK

avon

This novel is entirely a work of fiction.
The names, characters and incidents portrayed in it are
the work of the author's imagination. Any resemblance to
actual persons, living or dead, events or localities is
entirely coincidental.

AVON

A division of HarperCollins*Publishers*
1 London Bridge Street
London
SE1 9GF

www.harpercollins.co.uk

A Paperback Original 2016
3
Copyright © Catherine Ferguson 2016

Catherine Ferguson asserts the moral right to
be identified as the author of this work

A catalogue record for this book is
available from the British Library

ISBN-13: 978-0-00-816361-7

Set in Minion by Palimpsest Book Production Limited,
Falkirk, Stirlingshire

Printed and bound in Great Britain by
Clays Ltd, St Ives plc

All rights reserved. No part of this publication may be
reproduced, stored in a retrieval system, or transmitted,
in any form or by any means, electronic, mechanical,
photocopying, recording or otherwise, without the prior
permission of the publishers.

MIX
Paper from
responsible sources
FSC www.fsc.org **FSC® C007454**

FSC™ is a non-profit international organisation established to promote
the responsible management of the world's forests. Products carrying the
FSC label are independently certified to assure consumers that they come
from forests that are managed to meet the social, economic and
ecological needs of present and future generations,
and other controlled sources.

Find out more about HarperCollins and the environment at
www.harpercollins.co.uk/green

ACKNOWLEDGEMENTS

Hugs and thanks for my lovely and supremely talented friend, Victoria Robinson, whose success as a wedding photographer inspired me to write this book. Truly, research has never been such a good laugh!

And big thanks to my agent, Heather Holden-Brown, who does such a marvellous job of encouraging me and sorting out all the necessary practical details that my brain (with its tendency to drift off to another world altogether) can sometimes find hugely perplexing! Thanks so much, Heather.

And, of course, the wonderful team at Avon Maze – especially Natasha, who did such a fantastic job on the manuscript before bowing out to tackle an even more important assignment of a family nature! Also, my lovely new editor, Ellie, who arrived part way through the process but has nonetheless managed to pick up the reigns so seemlessly. A special mention for Helena, whose incredible flair and enthusiasm for social media never fails to astound me. And the multi-talented Helen, who has always made me feel so welcome and so much part of the team – thank you!

Thanks to my fantastic family, especially Matthew, who does a great job (as teenagers tend to do) of keeping my feet firmly on the ground! And Viv and Mick, who've had their trials recently but have come through fighting fit, thank goodness.

Patricia, I'm finally out in paperback! I know you enjoyed reading my books on kindle – but I hope this one is extra-special for you!

And finally, all those lovely people who make me laugh and give the sort of unstinting support that's so vital for keeping me relatively sane – Ian & Krysy, Dave, Carole, Helen, Angela, Pamela, Phyllis, Margaret, Maxine . . . love you all!

For my lovely Dad, who would have been so proud

Prologue

Some moments in life stay with you.

A vivid memory, full of colour and texture, which, years later, still has the power to make the breath catch in your throat thinking of it.

Of course, they're not always the moments you'd *expect* to live on in your mind.

I can't remember a thing about my first kiss, for example. Nor can I recall what I ate for breakfast the morning I turned twenty-one. And as for my first day in the job as a shy, newly qualified photographer at the advertising agency all those years ago? Well, stomach-churning nerves probably crowded out the details of that particular milestone.

But that moment with my sister, laughing and clinging onto each other, jumping up and down like five-year-olds who've over-dosed on gummy bears?

That was one of those moments . . .

I'd called in at our local printer's in Willows Edge on the way home to collect the glossy leaflets we'd designed for our brand new business. The brown package lay on the passenger seat, one of the leaflets taped to the front, and every time I glanced over and saw the words, Sister Act Photography, printed in that elegant, curly script we'd chosen, a little bubble of excitement rose up in me.

1

When I arrived home, Sienna's car was parked outside. My sister – at twenty-one, almost a decade younger than me – was still living at home with Mum. But we'd decided to use my house as our business headquarters, so she had a key.

I let myself in, yelling, 'I'm back!' and I was about to run upstairs when Sienna appeared in the hallway.

'Got a surprise for you,' she said, her eyes sparkling.

Curious, I followed her through to the living room.

'To celebrate you starting up the business.' Stepping to one side, she gestured with a flourish. 'Ta-dah!'

I could hardly believe my eyes.

There was a piano in my living room.

'What do you think?' asked Sienna eagerly, beaming at my amazed delight. 'You always said you wanted to learn how to play. Well, now you can!'

'Wow. Thank you.' I shook my head and laughed. 'But how could you afford it?'

Sienna was fresh out of college where, like me, she had studied photography. Hardly Miss Moneybags. A lump rose in my throat.

She shrugged. 'A friend wanted rid of it so I persuaded him to sell it to me for a ridiculously low price. Do you like it?'

'Like it? I love it!' I said, attempting 'Chopsticks' through slightly blurry eyes and hitting the wrong notes entirely.

'Bloody hell!' she groaned. 'You definitely need lessons.'

I shrugged. 'Even Chopin had to start somewhere.'

'Are they the leaflets?' She pointed at the package under my arm.

Nodding, I opened it up and passed one to her. She stared at it with glee. 'You know, you really are a chip off the old block.'

We smiled at each other, remembering Dad and his various business ventures, some a great success and a few frankly disastrous.

'You, too,' I said, but Sienna shook her head.

'I'd never have the balls to go it alone. Not without you taking the lead, Big Sis!'

I leaned over her shoulder and we read the leaflet together, poring over it as though we didn't already know the words off by heart.

'Oh, my God, Katy. It's official.' She turned to me, her eyes shining. 'We *are* Sister Act Photography!'

'Yeah, watch out world, here we come,' I grinned.

We looked at each other, mad-eyed, and squealed in unison.

I grabbed her arms and yelled, 'We're going into business!' At which point we started jumping up and down, singing raucously, 'We're going into business! We're going into business!'

I caught a glimpse of us in the mirror above the fireplace.

Two sisters.

Two blonde heads.

Sienna's hair so pale it was almost white, chopped in a short style that highlighted her porcelain skin, blue eyes and small, delicate features. She had a look of Dad when she laughed like that.

And me.

The protective big sister. Taller than Sienna and not quite so fine-featured. My own hair a darker, caramel blonde, shoulder-length. The image of Mum, in photos from the Seventies, with my almond-shaped green eyes, larger nose and fuller lips.

Both of us laughing, almost hysterical with excitement, high on the feeling that we were balanced on the brink of something really special . . .

I grabbed my camera and captured the moment with a selfie.

It's a brilliant photo, if I say so myself.

But it's packed away in a box now with other photos of my sister.

Back then, life seemed so full of promise.

We'd lost our lovely dad six months earlier and it had been tough for us all, especially Mum. I'd long had dreams of setting up on my own as a wedding photographer, and Dad's death was the catalyst for me handing in my notice at the advertising agency

3

in London and moving back to Willows Edge, the village where I'd grown up. I needed to be there for Mum and Sienna. It felt odd leaving the bustle of the capital for the rather sleepy village of my childhood but it was only an hour's drive from London, so I could easily stay in touch with all my friends there.

Planning my new venture had given us all something to occupy our minds. It even brought the occasional sparkle back into Mum's eyes, especially when Sienna took up my offer to join me in the business.

And so Sister Act Photography was born.

It felt like a healthy new start.

We were beginning a new adventure together. Two sisters, as close as siblings could possibly be.

Blissfully unaware that our happy optimism wasn't going to last.

And that a catastrophic blow, which I could never have foreseen happening in a million years, would soon tear our relationship apart . . .

Two years later . . .

A Spring Wedding

ONE

'Ooh, this is cosy!' says Andrea, simultaneously adjusting her bra for better effect and getting her stiletto stuck in the lawn.

Her enhanced cleavage has Ron's eyes out on stalks.

I have to admit, I'm grateful for the reprieve.

I've been dodging Ron's slightly moist clutches from the moment I walked into their house and followed them out into the back garden.

Ron is the original Space Invader.

Not that he goes around blasting aliens to smithereens in a very 1970s computer game sort of way. He just *crowds* you, so you spend the entire time (subtly) backing away until you eventually find yourself in the next room.

Ron and Andrea live in my cul-de-sac. Despite being well past the first flush of youth, they're known around here as a couple who like to have fun. And their snowdrops are definitely looking perky today.

I glance around the garden, looking for the best place to get down to it.

'Can we do it against the fence?' I instruct, aiming as always for 'friendly but firm'.

As they obligingly reposition themselves, I compliment Andrea on her dress and laughingly suggest that Ron might be boxing a little above his weight there. (I'm only half-joking about this. And I know Ron won't take offence. He has an ego the size of a small Baltic state.)

The point is, couples can be quite shy about throwing off their inhibitions, so a joke can really break the ice.

I'm trying to relax and just go with it, but it's not easy when my mind keeps drifting to the backlog of work I need to tackle when I get home.

'It's like that dress Lucy Mecklenburgh wore at the Baftas,' says Andrea, breaking away from Ron to do a little twirl. It's a strapless mini, heavily embellished with large silver and bronze sequins. A little over the top for a bleak, parky February afternoon, but Andrea does have the figure for it.

I nod, pretending I know what she's talking about.

But Andrea is not fooled. (I probably should have looked more impressed.)

'Lucy Mecklenburgh?' She frowns. 'You know, the Towie girls? Jess Wright? Ferne McCann? Danielle Armstrong?'

I look at her, confused, feeling like I'm in an exam I haven't revised for.

I shake my head apologetically. 'Sorry, no. Is Towie an area of London?'

Even Ron laughs at that. It's clear I need to get out more.

The thing is, if it's not on the nine o'clock news, I tend not to know about it. I force myself to watch the news, just so I know what's happening outside the narrow confines of my world. But work consumes practically every other waking minute in my life these days – mainly because I really need the money.

I think of Dominic's recent, late-night phone calls and a dark cloud descends. His tone is friendly on the surface but the sense of threat is all too evident. I've started letting the phone go to answer machine in the evenings, even though I know from experience that he's not going to give up that easily.

Suddenly aware Andrea and Ron are staring at me, awaiting instructions, I force a jolly smile. 'Right, can you put your hand on Ron's chest? That's right. Lovely!'

There's a peculiar intimacy to these open-air encounters with my clients, Ron and Andrea being a case in point. Peculiar in that generally, we're not much more than friendly acquaintances.

I place my hand on Ron's leg. 'Could you move slightly sideways so Andrea can . . . that's it. Lovely!'

He gives me a full-on, teeth-whitened smile that's obviously designed to render me helpless with lust but actually makes me want to giggle. 'Would you like *my* hand on *her* chest?' he growls suggestively, leaning closer.

'Ha-ha! That won't be necessary, Ron.' I leap nimbly away.

I've never been keen on threesomes in the back garden. Not since the time a wasp landed on the bloke's ear, just as the woman was moving in to nuzzle his neck. The insect did its worst, which resulted in the man being carted off to hospital, suffering mild anaphylactic shock.

The shock to my bank balance was much worse.

No engagement photo. No payment.

I cross the lawn and ask them to stand under the willow tree, which I think will provide a perfect frame. Having snapped a dozen or so, I study them in the camera's viewfinder.

Great. Job's a good 'un. I can now dash home to finish the photo editing I was working on until the early hours. Plus, I need to take delivery of a completed album, which the print company promised would arrive in today's post, so that I can send it off to the bride as a matter of urgency. Rose, the bride, is lovely, but during the wedding preparations, she had a tendency to get very stressed if everything didn't go exactly according to plan. She's apparently organised a party so that everyone can see the photos for the first time – and I really don't want a hysterical bride shouting down the phone that her family gathering is ruined because she didn't get the album in time.

9

Andrea offers me a coffee and normally, I'd stay to chat out of politeness, but I have too much to do. Also, because it's a freebie session, I don't feel quite so bad having to rush off.

When they asked me to take their wedding photographs, I invited them round and showed them some of my sample albums.

'Ooh, lovely,' enthused Andrea. Then she said something that sounded like, 'We're having a Cayman Cannier wedding.'

'Oh?' Cayman Cannier? It sounded swish. And expensive. 'Is he your wedding planner? This – er – Cayman person?'

Andrea looked at me blankly. 'No. *Kim* and *Kanye,*' she said, enunciating the words very slowly for the benefit of the idiot in the room.

Light dawned. 'Oh, Kim Kardashian and – erm—' I frowned, clicking my fingers. 'Kanye Thingy!'

'Kayne West, yes.' She beamed. 'Everyone's coming dressed as a celebrity.'

'Gosh. Right.'

'My dress is to die for. Just like Kim's.' She clasped her hands over her chest. 'And Ron's going to look *ever* so sexy.'

She twinkled at Ron, who merely grunted. (I couldn't tell if he was agreeing or just expressing weary resignation.)

I nodded as my mind went into boggle overdrive.

Rapper Ron? Now there was an image to conjure up.

A disturbing vision flashed into my mind. Ron. In dropped-crotch trackies and dark glasses. Alarming grannies and flexing his 'swag' to the max.

Should make for an interesting album.

I'd gone out of the room to turn up the heating, at which point Ron oozed into the kitchen after me and started telling me about his new camera and how he'd love me to give him a few pointers. Then he'd 'charmed' me into agreeing to take some engagement photos as a little extra freebie.

Actually, it wasn't his 'charm' that swung it.

He'd been wafting garlic over me as he waxed lyrical about his camera and I'd flattened myself against the fridge freezer. I'd watched in queasy close-up as a bead of perspiration wobbled at his hairline then broke loose. I'd only said yes so I could slide away before it skidded down his face and landed on me . . .

Now, engagement shoot done, Andrea says she'll fetch me the list of wedding photos they'd like, so I stand awkwardly in their living room as Ron busies himself putting Frank Sinatra on the music system. 'I've Got You Under My Skin' fills the room. Ron gives me a wolfish grin and, to my alarm, starts swaying in time to the music.

I plaster on a smile, wondering if he's expecting me to join in.

I can't help being fascinated by his relationship with Andrea. It's a second marriage for both of them and, on balance, I think Ron's getting the better end of the deal. Andrea is fun, slim and glossy-haired; a great advert for being fifty-something. But I'm struggling to pinpoint what she sees in Ron. Looking beyond the paunch, 'disguised' by a loose shirt, and the dyed brown hair brushed forward to hide the bald patch, you can tell he was probably good-looking in his younger days.

But Ron's problem is he still firmly believes he's the Milk Tray man. His sexual confidence is astounding. (If it could be bottled I'd order a weekly supply immediately.)

Luckily, Andrea shimmies back in at that moment, her fourteen-year-old daughter in tow.

'Hi, Ron. How's it hanging?' Chloe asks, with a sly grin at me. She takes out her chewing gum, frowns at it and pops it back in again. 'Still determined to marry Mum instead of just living in sin?'

Andrea gives her a warning look.

'You're damn right I am,' declares Ron in a cringy American accent, grabbing Andrea in a showy embrace. 'Hello, soon-to-be-Mrs-Watson.' He winks at me. 'Am I not the luckiest man in the world?'

Andrea pushes him away but I can tell she's chuffed.

Behind them, Chloe crosses her eyes and does a vomiting mime, and I try not to smile.

'Not quite the luckiest, Ron,' Chloe remarks. She gulps down some juice from the fridge then scrabbles in her patchwork bag and throws a magazine onto the table. It falls open at a double-page spread, featuring a newly engaged celebrity couple. He is chisel-jaw handsome, and the woman's crimped blonde hair and scarlet, figure-enhancing dress are pure Hollywood glamour.

'Oh, is that Blaze Jorgensen and her man?' says Andrea, clipping over in her fluffy mules to have a look. She turns to me and says proudly, 'They're getting married the same day as us, you know.' She does an excited little clap.

I try to look enthused. 'Lovely! I didn't even know Blaze Jorgensen was engaged.'

In fact, who the hell's Blaze Jorgensen?

Chloe darts me a puzzled look, as if I've suddenly grown thick facial hair and a pair of antlers. 'But they're Hollywood royalty,' she says.

'Are they?' I shrug cheerfully.

'Er, ye-es! Crikey, what planet exactly do you live on?'

Andrea laughs. 'Don't be so rude, Chloe.' She purses her lips at her daughter, although I can tell she's thinking exactly the same.

Chloe shrugs. 'But *everyone* knows she's marrying Dieter Hanson.'

'I wouldn't worry too much, Katy,' soothes Andrea. 'Dieter Hanson's a very *minor* celebrity.'

The conversation moves to Blaze Jorgensen's acrimonious divorce from her previous husband, also a very minor celebrity apparently. She seems to specialise in them, possibly to make her own star shine more brightly? Actually, I haven't got a clue. I'm not into all this celebrity gossip.

Ron is staring out of the window, letting the girl talk wash over him, and for a second, I feel a pang of sympathy for him. He was chairman of a big software company until he retired last year, used to rubbing shoulders and intellects with a veritable 'who's who' in the industry. The only *who's who* in his world now is likely to be *who's* marrying *who* in *Hello!* magazine.

'Chloe's going to be an actress,' says Andrea, stroking her daughter's hair proudly. 'Aren't you, darling?'

Chloe squirms away. 'Yeah.' She glances at me. 'I'm playing the lead in the school play just now. And Mum and I are going to start a drama group in the community centre. We'll be putting on our first show at Christmas time.'

'Really? That sounds great fun,' I say, gathering up my things, hoping she's not going to ask me to become a member. I'd rather eat my own toenails than stand up on stage in the spotlight being stared at.

'You can join if you like,' says Chloe.

I grin at her. 'Thanks but I think I'd be a bit wooden to be honest. I'm far more comfortable *this* side of the camera.'

Andrea gives me the list of wedding photos they'd like. As I leave, she and Chloe are discussing the merits of *Cinderella* over *Snow White and the Seven Dwarves* for their Christmas show.

'But where would we get all those *little people*?' frets Andrea, clearly going down the *heigh-ho, heigh-ho* route.

'I hope you're not being politically incorrect there, Mother,' comments Chloe.

'What on earth do you mean? You know I'm not into politics. I didn't even vote at the last election . . .'

Back home, the next hour is spent at my computer screen, editing photos and waiting for Rose's album to arrive. She's been on the phone three times this week to double-check she'll have it by tomorrow.

The pressure is huge. I feel like a sumo wrestler is taking a nap on my head. A little knot of anxiety has been sitting in my stomach since yesterday afternoon.

Apart from the thought of having to deal with a horrendously upset client if I don't deliver – and getting paid late, which frankly would be disastrous – I really don't want Rose to be disappointed. I always feel honoured when a bride trusts me with her special day, and I'll do anything necessary to make sure I don't let her down.

When the doorbell rings, I rush to answer it. It's the postman with an album-sized parcel and I can't decide whether to throw my arms around his neck or weep with relief.

I check through the album, holding my breath anxiously, hoping nothing has gone wrong. But, thankfully, it looks fantastic, so I parcel it up to send off to Rose.

The phone goes just as I'm about to dash out of the door. I hesitate for a moment, then pick it up. It's a business call – an enquiry from a girl called Bethany, whose friend's wedding I photographed last year. She's phoning to ask about my prices and whether I'd be available to shoot her wedding. Being newly engaged, she's brimming over with excitement about her forth-coming nuptials, even though it's still almost a year off.

Hopeful of securing a new client, I don't want to cut her off in mid-stream, so I chat for a while.

Her happiness is infectious. That's one of the nicest things about my job.

Okay, the brides can sometimes get very stressed as their Big Day looms. And the grooms can be a bit stern about shelling out the cash. But mostly, I'm dealing with people who are at an incredibly joyful stage in their lives. And in spite of my own marked lack of bliss on that front, I still love to talk weddings.

Bethany and her groom are flying to Italy for the ceremony but they're having a church blessing on their return, and they would like me to take the photographs. We have an excited discussion about the venue in Italy and how marvellously romantic it will be to sip cocktails with her wedding guests on the rooftop terrace as the sun goes down over the Bay of Naples. I can't help sighing inwardly at the thought of such a glorious setting. I haven't been abroad on holiday in years. But maybe one day . . .

I get a shock when I look at my watch.

Bugger! I've got precisely eighteen minutes to get to the post office in the village – a five-minute walk away – before it shuts. I'd take the car except it packed up again yesterday and it's at the garage being fixed. (I'm bracing myself for the damage – of the financial kind.)

I used to have a lovely new Toyota Corolla but having failed – despite my best efforts – to keep up the payments after Sienna left, I was forced to give it back to the lease company. I bought this old Fiesta at a car auction for a few hundred pounds. But sadly, it's far from reliable.

I apologise to Bethany, grab the album and flee from the house, slamming the door behind me so that the whole house shakes.

And then, just as I'm thinking I'm finally home free, a big white van draws up and a guy shouts through the window, 'We're here to collect the piano?'

My heart sinks. For a number of reasons that I don't particularly want to examine.

'I thought you said after five?'

He shrugs and climbs out with his mate. 'Sorry, love, we need to take it now.'

Oh God, all I need now is for the gate to stick . . .

'Can you get the gate open?' I call.

They walk through without a problem and look at me like I'm mad.

Thanking God for small mercies, I dive back in the house, moving bits of furniture I think might impede their progress with my ancient upright piano. Having shown them where it is, I find myself retreating to the kitchen so I don't have to watch it go. I'm annoyed at myself for feeling so emotional about it. I haven't even touched the damn thing for well over a year.

I lean back against the sink, arms tightly folded, listening to their huffing and puffing as they heft the piano about, and wincing as it bashes against the doorway on the way through to the hall.

I remember the day it arrived and how my sister was pink-cheeked with excitement, anticipating my reaction. A wave of nausea washes over me. Resolutely, I push the image away.

And then finally, *finally*, it's gone and the men are carting it off to the van.

And then, of course, I can't get out myself with the parcel because the gate is wedged shut. I try to wrench it open but it's obviously determined to sabotage my day.

Aaargh! Bloody thing! Must get it fixed.

Honestly, the whole bloody house is falling down around my ears.

I've got seven minutes before the post office shuts.

I yank the gate one more time, feeling the panic rise.

Oh, to hell with it.

It's a fairly high fence and as I clamber over, it catches me in an awkward place.

I yelp in outrage.

Then I howl again as, safely over, my right shoulder whacks into someone racing past the house. The impact jolts the album parcel out of my arms and I watch in dismay as it skids along the grimy pavement and lands in the gutter in an oily puddle.

Breathlessly, I turn, wondering what just happened – and find myself staring up into a pair of icy blue eyes beneath drawn-together beetle brows.

The man they belong to is tall and dressed in running gear.

He must have been pounding the pavement at a fair old rate because his chest is still heaving beneath the white Aertex top and his dark hair is slick with perspiration. (But not in a Ron way. This man's sweat is the impressive, vigorous exercise sort.)

'Gosh, sorry,' I blurt out, trying not to look at his lean, muscled legs in the black running shorts.

'You all right?' he demands, still breathing strongly, hands on hips, as – somewhat unsettlingly – he stares at my nether regions.

I glance down.

I'm still grasping onto my crotch, casualty of the mean picket fence.

I laugh, a bit hysterically if I'm honest, and fold my arms. 'Fine, thanks. Just – er – scaling the fence. Always good to keep active.' I nod at his running shorts, hoping to indicate a common interest.

'Active?' His grin is incredulous and I feel myself blush. 'I think you might need a bit more practice.' He indicates the fence. 'Unless you want to go around *actively* maiming pedestrians.'

He rotates his right foot, a little gingerly, then tries putting his weight on it.

Oh, shit! He's obviously injured.

'Did I do that?' I wince. 'Sorry.'

He dismisses this with a little shake of his head. Then he bends to retrieve my parcel and I swear I hardly notice his bum and his long, beautifully flexed thighs.

He hands me the brown bundle, which is now a water-logged, soggy mess. 'Hope it's nothing too important?' His expression softens into a smile.

I smile back as a surprising feeling trickles through me, making my eyes widen in a 'hey, I remember that sensation' sort of a way. (It's been a couple of years, at least.)

I'm vaguely aware I should be upset about the album, but what comes out of my mouth is, 'God, no. It's nothing. Absolutely nothing.'

'That's a relief.'

'Yes, isn't it?' I swallow hard, imagining how horrified Rose would be if she could see her album now.

'Nice piano.' He nods as the men slam the back doors of the van and climb in, preparing to move off. 'Are you selling it?'

'Yes. Do you want to buy it?'

He frowns at me. 'No.'

I give myself a swift kick in the shins. Metaphorically speaking. *Do you want to buy it?* Chrissakes, where did *that* come from? No

17

wonder he's looking at me like I'm one leg short of a baby grand. Apart from anything else, I've already sold the bloody thing. It's currently bouncing on its merry way to a Mrs Turner in Easthaven.

'Right,' I mumble, feeling escape is my best bet. 'Got to pet to the ghost office.'

'Sorry?' His brows knit in further confusion.

'*Post office!*' I yelp. 'Got to get to the post office.'

Bloody hell, what's wrong with me?

Cheeks well alight by this time, I raise my hand and march off with the soggy parcel under my arm, painfully aware I've left him bemused. Probably wondering what sort of a halfwit climbs over the fence instead of using the gate like most normal people.

It's only when I've turned the corner at the bottom of the street that it occurs to me I can't possibly send the album off in this wrecked brown paper packaging.

But I can't just do a U-turn. What if Runner Man is still watching? What if I have to cheerfully explain that I actually hadn't noticed the shagging dirty marks and the wodge of something revolting that's completely obscuring the address?

I sidle back to the corner and, feeling like a total fruit loop who's been allowed out for the day, peer furtively along the street, clutching my damp parcel.

Phew! The coast is clear.

He must have run the other way.

'I'd use the gate next time,' says a voice behind me, making me jump.

Runner Man speeds past me with a cool, backwards wave, and slows to cross the road.

He half-turns his head and grins. 'A fence can get caught in all *sorts* of tricky places.'

TWO

It's almost March.

Every day this week, the residents of Willows Edge have awoken to blue skies and a silvery frost on the trees at the edge of the village green and on the roof of the cricket pavilion.

But as I walk the familiar route to the little row of shops that borders the green, I can see signs that spring is on its way. Little clumps of crocuses, in brilliant shades of violet and egg yolk yellow, are bravely defying the cold snap, and the daffodils are beginning to push through.

As a child growing up in the idyllically pretty village of Willows Edge, I took my surroundings completely for granted.

I wasn't especially interested in the way the houses in the village centre were ranged so picturesquely around the village green and how the row of stylish and colourfully painted shops lured customers in with their tempting window displays. People came in from neighbouring villages to shop for their weekend croissants and Danish pastries at the family-owned bakery; to sip hot chocolate in the welcoming warmth of Rosa's coffee shop; eat their ploughman's at The Bunch of Grapes, just off the main street; and to wander into the pretty church with its ancient bell tower and low porch, set back from the green and shaded by willow trees.

The greengrocer's on the main street was forced to close when people started shopping at the new express supermarket, but apart from that, the village has managed to retain all its charm.

It wasn't until I moved away, first to college then to London for work, that I started looking at Willows Edge in a new light and realising how special it actually was.

This afternoon, my destination is the florist's.

The shop owner, appropriately named Daisy, greets me with a cheerful smile.

Daisy is about my age with long dark hair in a ponytail and her one-year-old, Luke, almost permanently welded to her hip. Like the bakery, the florist's is a family-owned business and Daisy recently took over the reins.

'Hi Katy. How's things? Are you doing Ron and Andrea's wedding?'

'I am indeed.' I smile at her. 'Three weeks on Saturday. You?'

Daisy has a crack of dawn start on wedding days, driving up to the London flower markets to buy her blooms dewy-fresh.

She nods and hoists Luke higher on her hip. 'It's going to be a wedding with a difference by all accounts.'

Luke gurgles and holds out a pudgy fist towards me.

'It certainly is, Lukie,' I say in a sing-song voice, bending towards him and tickling his cheek.

He biffs me smartly on the nose. It takes me by surprise and makes my eyes water.

'Celebrity-style, I hear,' says Daisy, after gently reprimanding Luke. 'Are you going in fancy dress?'

I grin. 'No, thank goodness. I'll be blending into the background, as usual.'

'Well, what can I do you for today?' She places Luke in his bouncy chair and clips him in.

I glance around at the floral displays, breathing in the heady mix of scents and wondering how much a small bunch of freesias will cost. I hate having to skimp when it comes to my best friend's birthday, but I know Mallory understands. In fact, she'd tell me off if I spent too much on her.

Mallory is similarly strapped for cash and her motto, as regards gifts, is always brisk and practical. 'It's the thought that counts.' (Her thoughts usually originate in charity shops, but that's fine by me because she's great at hunting down amazing birthday presents that you'd never, ever guess were second-hand.)

Not only is Mallory a great friend, she also assists me at weddings, gathering folk together so all I have to think about is taking the photos. For a while, after Sienna left, I struggled on alone, trying to manage without an assistant. But then Mallory stepped into the breach, offering to help out when she could. (She runs her own on-line vintage clothing business, so she can generally be fairly flexible.)

Mallory lives at Newington Hall, a huge and draughty cavern of a place belonging to her parents, Roddy and Eleanor Swann. They're practically never there, so she rattles around it on her own. The house was quite clearly magnificent in its heyday but now the roof leaks into buckets dotted around the place and many of the window frames are sadly rotting.

Taking my freesias, I get in the car and set off to see the birthday girl.

Even though my temperamental little Fiesta has been fixed, I find I'm still tensing up as I drive along, waiting for the dreaded knocking sound that led me to the garage in the first place. But so far, so good . . .

Newington Hall is situated five miles outside the village of Willows Edge, and as I turn in and bump along the potholed driveway, I can't help wondering how on earth Gareth, the gardener, manages to keep the fairly substantial grounds from running completely wild. A much younger man would struggle, never mind someone in his fifties, however fit and strong he might be.

I park up and get out of the car, walking round to the back entrance, which everyone uses, and bracing myself for the challenge of gaining entry. The doorbell there doesn't actually work, which means that unless Mallory is in the kitchen, or at least in one of the ground-floor rooms, you haven't much chance of being heard. Unless you graze your knuckles knocking and yell 'hello-o-o!' through the letter box. Which is what I do.

Today, the door opens almost immediately and Mallory appears.

'No need to shout, darling,' she laughs, tossing back her long, strawberry blonde hair and wiping her hands down the front of her flower-sprigged dress.

I grin and open my mouth to say, 'Well, actually, I do.' But my words are drowned out by a vast sucking sound coming from somewhere in the chilly depths of the house. The noise is getting louder and angrier by the second.

'Blast! The coffee.' Mallory rushes off to rescue the ancient stove-top beast, and I follow her down the flagstoned corridor into the huge kitchen.

Despite the enormously high ceiling, it's cosy in here after the biting March wind outside. Actually, it's the only warm room in the house. The rest of it is like a massive, twelve-bedroom fridge that instantly freezes your breath and gives you ice-encrusted eyebrows. Okay, I exaggerate slightly – I think there might be eight bedrooms –- but not much, believe me.

'Crikey. Happy birthday to you.' I gaze at the banks of lilies arranged in family heirloom vases on various ancient dressers and work surfaces. And the extravagant display of exotic blooms in the centre of the weather-beaten wooden table that's had one shortened leg propped up on a pile of books for as long as I've been coming here.

Mallory gives a bark of laughter. 'I know, darling. You'd quite think someone had died.'

I raise an eyebrow. 'All from Rupert?'

She smiles. Her floaty, floral-sprigged dress and burnished hair make her look like a heroine from a Barbara Cartland romance. 'What are brand new fiancés for if not to spoil a person?'

She got engaged to Rupert just after New Year and I'll be photographing their wedding in December.

I'm really happy for her, although I can't help thinking that it's been a bit of a whirlwind. But she seems certain Rupert is the one for her, and I'm the last person who should be judging people's compatibility in the romance stakes. My own track record hasn't exactly been brilliant.

I hand over my birthday card and gift.

'God, I'm thirty-four,' Mallory groans.

Then she smiles and sniffs the freesias. 'Thank you. They're perfect!'

'You're welcome, Granny.' I grin.

'Oh, ha flipping ha! You'll be just as ancient as me in six months' time, darling.'

Mallory is pretty much the same age as me but she turns older first. Not that I'd point it out, of course. Well, not often. (Rub it in? Me? Never!)

'Coffee?' she asks.

'Go on, then. But I can't stay long.'

'Meeting with Miss Polar Ice Cap?'

I giggle. 'No, that's tomorrow's delight.'

She frowns in sympathy and reaches for the ancient stove-top coffee pot.

'Cressida is a perfectly nice client,' I say, grinning. 'Not terribly warm or friendly, I grant you. But she can't help being a complete control freak who will actually kill herself if the raisins in the wedding cake aren't all exactly the same shade of chocolate brown.'

Mallory pours coffee into mismatched floral china cups. 'You do realise you took your life in your hands when you agreed to do her photos?'

I sink down gloomily at the table. 'True. If they're not perfect, she'll probably sue me for ruining her day.'

'So why are we doing it?'

'Silly question. I can't afford not to.'

'I know the feeling. Thank God I met Rupert, that's all I can say.'

I flash her a dubious look and she grins. 'Joke, darling.'

I laugh, thinking she's probably only *half* joking. Mallory has a decidedly practical attitude to relationships that I actually rather admire. She thinks romance is highly overrated.

She puts a cup and saucer in front of me then sits down, lifting her dainty feet in ballet pumps onto a chair and flicking back her hair.

'Come December, money is the very last thing you'll have to worry about,' I murmur.

She frowns. 'His family aren't *that* rich, you know. I mean, obviously they're a lot more affluent than *my* folks, but then Daddy probably qualifies as the poorest baronet in the history of the aristocracy.'

Two hundred years ago, the Swanns were wealthy landowners, but a succession of heirs with a liking for booze, gambling and women chipped away at the money – and now, Mallory's parents are probably even poorer than the mice in their basement.

Newington Hall swallows cash as eagerly as kids breaking out their chocolate eggs on Easter Sunday.

They're always having to auction off paintings to cover the cost of repairs to the house.

I don't know why they don't just sell it.

But Mallory says it's all to do with pride. Her father couldn't forgive himself if he failed to hold on to the family seat for future generations.

I glance sideways at Mallory. 'Speaking of your dad . . . have you heard from them?'

She barks out a laugh. 'What do *you* think, darling? I'm lucky if they remember to phone me every alternate Christmas. I've given up expecting a *birthday* miracle.' She takes a sip of coffee, her eyes clouding over, and we're silent for a moment.

I really feel for her. I can't imagine my lovely mum ever forgetting to include me in her Christmas plans. It would be unthinkable.

Mallory flicks a glance at me. 'On the subject of wealth . . .' She hesitates. 'Did you manage to sell the piano?'

My heart lurches. 'Yes. Some men came and carted it off.' I glance down at the table. 'Should have got rid of it a long time ago.'

There's a pregnant silence as I continue to stare at the table, seeing its scratched surface through a blur.

Like Mum, Mallory knows that certain subjects are out of bounds and that this is one of them. I'm grateful for her silence.

And in the same vein, I know not to probe too much about her parents.

Roddy and Eleanor Swann are obsessed with travelling the world. It was what drew them together in the first place and the passion has never faded. Mallory, their only child, comes a pretty poor second to their treks in the foothills of the Himalayas and their voyages into the jungles of Borneo.

Her father, a botanist, is currently writing a book on the lesser-spotted haggis or something, and has decamped with Mallory's mother to their converted bothy in the Highlands of Scotland. They're tough, I'll say that for them. It must be pretty chilly up there at this time of year.

Mallory once told me that her middle name, Beatrice, means 'traveller'. She flicked her eyes to the ceiling and snorted. 'Isn't it marvellous? They name me "traveller", then they bugger off on exotic trips and leave me behind. You can't fault their brilliant sense of irony, though, can you?'

How these hardy adventurers made Mallory is a bit of a mystery. She's very much a townie. Wouldn't know what a ridge tent was if it climbed into bed with her and made her a sausage sandwich. The most pioneering she ever gets, at her own admission, is trekking along Willows Edge main street, searching out bargains in the two upmarket charity shops.

She trained in fashion and design after leaving school, and it was always her dream to have a shop selling vintage shoes and clothing. But the reality turned out to be a Saturday job in a vintage boutique, which eventually became a full-time career in retail.

Then, three years ago, Mallory finally took the plunge and – having saved a little money – set up her vintage clothing shop. On-line.

She works really hard, sourcing items from all over, and makes a modest income. But her dream is that one day, 'Vintage Va-Va-Voom' will hit the big time and become a household name.

The fact that she works for herself now, means she's usually free to help me out at weddings, which is great. I can't afford to pay her much but she enjoys the work and, as she keeps telling me, every little helps.

Which reminds me . . .

'Are you still okay to help me at Ron and Andrea's wedding?' I ask.

'Of course.' She laughs. 'Wouldn't miss it for the world. Good old Kim and Kanye. What a hoot! Are you sure we can't dress up as the 118 boys? We'd just need curly black wigs and shorts.'

'No! We're there to do a job. Don't you dare!'

She snorts. 'Spoilsport.'

'We have to look professional.'

She grins. 'I know. But I do think it's time you stopped working quite so hard. You never have any juicy tales for me these days.'

'Aha!' I smile triumphantly. 'Well, that's where you're wrong. As far as the gossip goes, anyway.'

She shuffles her chair closer. 'Ooh! I'm all ears, darling.'

So I tell her about my close and rather bruising encounter with Runner Man. She listens with avid interest. Any mention of a man – even those who are ancient or infirm or living several continents away – and Mallory is alert to the cheering possibility that I might start having sex soon. (She has a very practical, down-to-earth view of sex, believing that for a balanced mind, it's almost a

26

medical necessity. I don't think she quite understands that I don't even think about stuff like that unless there's someone fanciable right there in front of me.)

'And I've just remembered,' I say forlornly, as my humiliating tale draws to an end. 'I made him limp. I *actually made him limp*.'

I've been trying hard not to think about my encounter with Runner Man – without much success, it has to be said. It was all *so* embarrassing. Clambering over the fence, getting my private parts wedged, talking a load of drivel then heading off to post a pile of shite. I mean, it doesn't get any worse in the humiliation stakes.

I failed to make the post office before it closed. Obviously. And in order not to disappoint my bride, I had to shell out a small fortune – and go even deeper in debt – to have the album couriered all the way to Essex.

My stupidity is gnawing away at me.

'Oh, never mind, darling. It could have been worse,' muses Mallory.

I stare at her questioningly and she gives a light shrug. 'You might have damaged a lot more than his foot, if you know what I mean. I'd be thankful for small mercies if I were you.'

I bark out a laugh. 'Well, that might possibly be relevant if I actually had designs on the man. But obviously, I don't.' My cheeks catch fire as I'm saying this. Probably because of Mallory's piercing look.

'Really? Why on earth not?' she asks. 'He sounds simply scrummy to me. And it's been an *awfully* long time since you – ahem – hoisted the flagpole, darling, correct me if I'm wrong.'

'Well, that's as may be, but I'm not like you, remember? I can't just shag a man for practical purposes then forget all about him.'

'I resent that,' says Mallory indignantly. But the laughter in her pale grey eyes tells a different story.

A voice calls from upstairs. 'Where's my darling birthday girl?'

'In the kitchen, Rupie.'

A minute later, the door bursts open and 'Rupie' makes his entrance.

It's a fairly impressive sight.

Rupert has the look of an Italian stallion – all sleek black hair, Greek-god body and permatan – although he hails from a small village in Sussex.

He stops in the doorway, smiling broadly and holding out his arms. 'Katy! Baby! Great to see you.'

I get up for a hug. He smells of ozone, like a day at the seaside.

Rupert's always like this – rather theatrical, fond of extravagant gestures, right at home as the life and soul of every party. But none of it is forced, for effect. It's just the way he is, and everyone warms to him. His pleasure at seeing me is, I know, absolutely genuine.

'The shirt looks good,' says Mallory, giving him a thumbs up.

I nod, enthusiastically, and he looks pleased. The shirt's pretty colourful, patterned all over with exotic birds. It suits him perfectly.

He comes into the room and spins round so we can admire the full effect. Then he gyrates his way over to the coffee pot, singing, 'I'm too sexy for my shirt, too sexy for my shirt, so sexy it *hurts*.' His tight butt in the pale, paint-spattered jeans moves perfectly in sync.

Rupert is an artist. He paints watercolours of hills that all look the same to me, although I'm probably doing him a grave injustice. My art appreciation skills are dubious, to say the least. For instance, I've always thought the Mona Lisa was a little bit boring. She's famous for looking mysterious and 'enigmatic'. But frankly, the only mystery to me is why on earth she didn't get some body into that lank hair before she sat for the great Leonardo. (I mean, you would, wouldn't you?)

Anyway, enough said. I wouldn't know a masterpiece if it fell from outer space and landed on my head. For all I know, Rupert's paintings could be truly magnificent.

His artistic nature has certainly come to the fore with the

28

wedding plans. He's created this beautiful 'mood board' of colours and fabrics. I've never known a groom be so interested in the finer details and Mallory couldn't be happier – practically all that's left for her to do is choose the dress.

I can't believe I'll be photographing their wedding in December. It's all happened so fast.

It was his mum, Serafina, who first introduced Mallory to Rupert.

Mallory and Serafina met several years ago, just after Mallory had set up Vintage Va-Va-Voom. There had been a mix-up with an order and as the customer lived locally, Mallory had offered to jump in her car and deliver the dress in person. Apart from anything else, she was curious to meet the person who'd fallen in love with the lilac jacquard silk fitted evening gown, elegant enough to grace the red carpet at an Oscars ceremony.

It turned out to be Serafina Lorenzo, whose striking dark looks and willowy frame complemented the dress perfectly. By the time she'd offered Mallory a martini and tried on the gown – declaring it perfect for her charity midsummer ball – the two had bonded over the wonders of Chanel and YSL, and were on their way to being firm friends. Their families moved in the same circles, so they even had acquaintances in common. (Although while the Lorenzos holidayed on their private island in the Caribbean, the financially stretched Swanns could barely afford a week in Bournemouth.)

It was almost a year later – last summer, in fact – that Mallory finally met Rupert. She'd known *of* Rupert, of course, through Serafina. His mother always spoke so proudly of her artist son, who she'd given birth to at the relatively young age of nineteen, after conceiving on honeymoon. She and Rupert's father enjoyed a strong marriage and always planned to have a large family. But after their daughter, Arabella, was born, there were no more children. So Rupert was their only son. (And spoilt rotten, according to Mallory.)

Rupert, who's seven years younger than Mallory, was entranced by her style and her laid-back attitude to life, and they quickly became a couple, much to the delighted approval of his mum and sister.

In a relatively short space of time, Mallory has almost become one of the family. She meets Serafina and Arabella for coffee, and they've treated her to a few totally indulgent spa weekends, from which Mallory always returns happy and glowing. I'm really pleased for her. I can't help thinking the lustre to her complexion is less to do with creams and potions, and far more a result of feeling she belongs.

After a lifetime of playing second fiddle to her own parents' wanderlust, I can totally understand this. I just sometimes wonder if maybe the lure of being part of a 'proper family' isn't colouring her judgement slightly. But she's clearly very happy with her new fiancé, so I should probably stop worrying . . .

Rupert gives Mallory a lingering kiss, while I try not to look, and he teasingly refuses to tell her where he's taking her for her birthday dinner.

They're so sweet together, I'd probably throw up if she wasn't my best friend.

'Right. Toodle-oo, ladies!' Rupert blows kisses at both of us and disappears off to check out some art studio in a local crafts complex he's thinking of renting. And Mallory and I kick off our shoes and settle in for a gossip.

It's getting dark by the time I leave.

On the drive home, I reflect on how amazing it is that Mallory and I met only a little over eighteen months ago. I honestly feel like I've known her for years.

We met when I was shooting a wedding at the Greshingham, a five-star country house hotel just a few miles from Willows Edge.

It was a bad time for me.

Sienna had buggered off to Paris a few months earlier, leaving me completely in the lurch. I was doing my best to keep the business going on my own while trying to cope with the aftermath of our traumatic fallout.

I knew I would have to employ someone to help me at the weddings, but my head was all over the place. I was finding it hard enough to get through the days, never mind trying to focus on finding an assistant I knew I could trust.

The wedding that day at the Greshingham was proving a challenge, to say the least. The wedding party were in fine spirits – quite literally. (The groom's Uncle Bob was breathing a particularly fine whisky spirit all over me from pretty much the word go, joking around in a harmless but distracting way.)

Trying to corral a group of 'well-refreshed' guests onto the lawn for the photos, I began to feel a new appreciation for sheepdogs. I'd get ninety per cent of them there, then a small group would break away and start wandering back to the bar. My voice was hoarse from cajoling.

At one point, I thought grimly: *Come back, Sienna, all is forgiven!*

Except it wasn't, of course.

And it never would be.

I was close to tears by the time the outdoor photos were done and I'd scuttled into a dark corner of the bar to take stock.

I sat there, trying to check down my list, terrified I might have missed something vital.

But there was a woman with a loud, plummy voice on the next table who kept barging into my thoughts, messing everything up. She was all, 'Oh, *totally*, darling!' and 'I say, how absolutely *awful* for you!'

It seemed I couldn't get peace anywhere.

Then, the crowning glory, Uncle Bob found my hiding place and plonked himself and his whisky breath down right beside me.

I had an urge to run off screaming.

But I took a deep breath and did my best to be polite and smile, turning down his repeated offers of a drink on the grounds that I was working.

At some point, I made accidental eye contact with Plummy Voice over Uncle Bob's shoulder. She pointed at my half-cut companion and made a revolted expression.

Bob tried to swing round to see who I was grinning at and nearly fell off his chair.

I bashed my forehead to mime how fed up I was and she burst out laughing then turned to murmur something to the woman beside her.

Bob, meanwhile, had shuffled his chair so close, he was practically sitting on my knee.

'Show me how it works,' he slurred, making a stab at picking up my camera and knocking over his whisky glass instead.

As he apologised earnestly and attempted to mop my list with his sleeve, someone said, 'I say, darling, you didn't tell me you were the official photographer at this shindig!'

I glanced up in surprise. Plummy Voice was smiling down at me.

'Could I have a word?' she asked cheerfully.

I blinked. 'Er . . . yes, of course.'

Giving Uncle Bob the benefit of her smile, she leaned down and pressed his shoulder, murmuring sweetly, 'So sorry to drag her away from you but it's really very important. I'm fresh out of tampons, you see.'

Even Uncle Bob, in his alcohol-soaked haze, knew when it was time to make a sharpish exit.

Plummy Voice sat down and we watched him stagger off, narrowly missing cannoning into a large-breasted woman in an even larger wedding hat.

My rescuer's name was Mallory and I felt bad about my earlier grumpiness. I thanked her for frightening Bob away and giggled when she said the tampon emergency was just a ruse. We hit it off immediately, swapping stories about men who wouldn't take no for an answer and she told me about the 'frightful chap' she'd been unable to escape in a bar one time, until she mentioned she had to get back to her five children who were at home, being baby-sat by her lesbian lover.

'Worked like a charm. He was orf like a shot,' she grinned, flicking back her amazing, strawberry blonde hair.

Mallory was proof to me that you should never judge someone by their voice. Because while she might *sound* posher than the Queen, she was actually far more Sarah Millican by nature, with her earthy humour and slightly irreverent take on life.

I warmed to her no-nonsense approach to life and her ability to make a joke out of everything, even the bad stuff. We swapped business cards and I dashed off for the next round of photos, feeling so much more cheerful and energised than before.

I wasn't expecting her to phone, but she did, a few days later.

She said if I needed an assistant, she was available. 'No pressure, darling. Obviously. But you'd be a first class chump to turn me down.'

I had a feeling she was probably right. So we arranged to meet at Rosa's coffee shop to discuss it, and we haven't stopped talking since.

Mallory likes to try and sort out my life.

Sometimes I listen, sometimes I just laugh. She doesn't seem to mind either way.

And she's a great wedding assistant . . .

THREE

When I arrive home and slide my key into the lock, I hear the muffled sound of the phone ringing.

My heart lurches. Few people call me on the landline these days.

Dominic does, though.

It must be him.

For a second, I'm caught in limbo, heart slamming against my ribs.

I could just let it ring. Hurry back to the car and drive round to the safety of Mallory's house . . .

But if I run away, I'll just be playing into the hands of a bully.

Taking a breath, I push the door open.

The jolly ringtone is deafeningly loud now, slicing through the darkness.

I close the door softly behind me and stand in the shadows of the hallway, holding my breath, wating for it to stop.

Perhaps this time he will hang up without leaving one of his messages.

'Katy, love? Are you there?'

For a stunned second, I can't take it in.

Then I run through to the living room and dive on the phone.

35

'*Mum?* Is that you?'

She laughs. 'Of course it's me. Sorry, were you busy, love?'

'No. No.' Blissful relief courses through me, and a laugh bursts out. 'It's just so great to hear your voice.'

There's a brief silence.

'But I only saw you last week,' she murmurs. 'Are you all right, Katy?'

I flop down on the sofa. 'I'm fine, Mum. Honestly. Everything's great.'

'Are you sure?' Her sharpness takes me by surprise. I thought I'd been doing a pretty good job of shielding her from the mess that is currently my life.

'It's just you looked so exhausted when you were over last Tuesday,' she says. 'I've been thinking about it, and I'm worried about you. Did you know you nearly nodded off when I was telling you about Venus's demonic entity fright.'

I lean my head back, aware of my heart rate gradually subsiding. 'Venus? Demonic entity fright?' It does ring a vague bell from last time. I think I just switched off, it was so preposterous.

'Yes, Venus. You know. That nice but slightly batty woman who's started coming to yoga?'

I nod, still feeling weirdly spacey.

Ah yes, the yoga class.

It's been a bit of a turning point for Mum.

In the time since Dad died – coming up for three years now – she's really been through the mill. For a long time, she refused to even consider selling the family home, even though it was clear she couldn't go on paying the huge mortgage herself. Then about a year ago, I took her for a drive to Clandon House, an old country estate that had been modernised into apartments. And incredibly, she loved it.

Since she rented her two-bed flat there and moved in last March, she's actually started to get back some of her joy in life, which is a huge relief for me.

Two of her new neighbours, Grace and Annabeth, have become

36

good friends, which seems to have really perked her up. And they've introduced her to yoga, which she loves.

Last Tuesday, when I was at Mum's for afternoon tea, they were all talking about someone called Venus. They kept referring to her as 'the new girl in class', which made me smile, bearing in mind their average age must be about sixty.

'Katy? Are you still there?'

'Yes. Sorry, Mum. Go on.'

'Forgotten what I was saying now.'

'Venus. And her – um – demonic entity experience?'

'Ah yes. Nice woman but decidedly odd. Claimed she was just minding her own business, shopping for kitchen roll and kippers, when this huge force entered her and she felt she was being possessed by Satan. I mean, really. Have you ever!'

'It does sound a bit unlikely, Mum.'

'You're not wrong there, love. But anyway, when I was telling you about it on Tuesday there, you were actually drifting off. You know, you really are working much too hard these days.'

'Mum, when it's your own business, you *have* to work all the hours.'

Not that she needs reminding of this. She was, after all, married for thirty-six years to a serial entrepreneur. Dad, bless him, was forever pursuing one business idea or another, with varying degrees of success.

Mum sighs. 'I know, love. But it must be so difficult having to do absolutely everything yourself. Now that your sister . . .'

My grip on the phone tightens.

Mum trails off, knowing she's straying into forbidden territory.

'You're very precious to me, Katy.' There's a break in her voice. And her unspoken subtext hangs in the air: *Especially now that your sister is living so far away.*

Tears prick my eyes and, for once, I don't dash them away.

It's so hard for her, I know. She must miss Sienna terribly, and the last thing I want is her worrying about me, too.

Mum thinks I work silly hours because it's my business and I love the work, which is partly true. But she knows nothing about the stomach-churning fear that dominates my life; the debts that hang over me and routinely keep me from sleeping properly at night; and why working seven days a week is something I just have to do, because then at least I'm in with a chance of keeping my head above water. A chance to avoid the thing I most dread – losing the business and having my little house repossessed.

I open my mouth to try and reassure her again that I'm perfectly all right, but nothing comes out.

There are times in life when nothing but a hug from your mum will do.

And for a second, I find myself wishing desperately that Mum were here. Sitting on the sofa next to me, absently playing with the lump of rose quartz on the chain round her neck and delving in her homemade raffia bag for the little bottle of foul-smelling anti-stress tincture that Annabeth gave her to 'balance her system'. I don't know if she uses it, but it goes everywhere with her. (It smells like something died in her handbag, which makes her slightly embarrassing to go shopping with.)

I stand up, as Mum talks on, and walk through to the small conservatory, which is bathed in an eerie semi-light from the full moon.

I know it's a mark of how concerned she is that she bravely brought up a forbidden subject and risked me hanging up on her. I just wish she could understand that the days of Sienna and I being as close as sisters could be have gone forever.

I do *not* need Sienna's help. We may have worked together for the first six months, but I've managed to keep the business afloat all by myself since Sienna left, almost two years ago.

And as far as I'm concerned, the day she left for Paris, leaving me with an avalanche of debts, was the day she relinquished all rights to being my cherished baby sister. Let alone my business partner.

I will do this alone.

Without help from anyone.

I know that Mum has weekly phone conversations with my sister and, at times, I can tell she's itching for me to ask her how Sienna's getting on. But I don't because I'm really not interested.

After Mum says her goodbyes, I stand there in the conservatory, staring out into the inky blackness, clutching the handset to my chest. I feel silly now for having reacted so violently to the ring of the phone.

Angry tears prick my eyes.

I will not live in fear of Dominic!

An owl hoots and my heart leaps into my mouth.

Suddenly the shape of the hawthorn tree, in my little patch of back garden, looks ghostly and sinister – a black, looming figure with clutching hands reaching out towards me . . .

I close the door on the darkness beyond the windows. Then I go round the rest of the house, swishing curtains shut and turning on lights until the place could seriously outshine Blackpool Illuminations.

But only once I've unplugged the phone and checked that the doors are locked can I finally breathe easily.

Barricading myself in makes me feel safer.

But as I kick off my shoes and start chopping salad for supper, the spectre of Dominic and his threats still hangs over me.

Turning a key in a lock is not going to banish him from my life. If only it were that simple . . .

Next morning, I've got my meeting with Miss Polar Ice Cap, aka Cressida and her groom-to-be, Tom.

They're getting married in June.

So far, I've only spoken to Cressida on the phone. But today I'm meeting them in person to get to know them and chat about the wedding arrangements.

Cressida made it clear that strict schedules – and people being *on time* – were a top priority of hers. Which means spotting the white meter van out in the street just as I'm about to leave for our meeting fills me with double panic.

I can't possibly leave now and risk having my meters read, so that means I'll be late for Cressida.

Feeling sick, I scamper up the stairs before meter man has a chance to spy me through the glass in the front door. Then I rush into the bathroom and peer cautiously out through the frosted glass.

Evading meter readings is a vital part of my life. It's not that I don't pay my gas and electricity bills. Of course I do. But the thing is, my direct debit amount has been *way* too low ever since I moved here.

Before I arrived, there was an oldish lady living here who obviously didn't use much power because the estimated monthly bill was very small. And some glitch in the system meant I carried on paying this tiny amount each month, while thanking my lucky stars for old Mrs Jennings and her frugal nature.

I always knew they'd catch up with me eventually but I sort of kept brushing the thought away. (I was having to cope with other, more pressing demands for money.)

And then they did. Catch up with me. A couple of months ago, a stern official letter arrived.

I read it in the car before I set off for an appointment with one of my brides. I was running late, as usual, but seeing those stark words requesting up-to-date meter readings as a matter of urgency sent a bolt of cold fear through me. I thought I was going to be sick. I had to put my head back and do the breathing exercise Mum's friend, Annabeth, taught me until I felt well enough to drive. I've been on high alert ever since, dreading a second letter demanding the readings.

Now, I take another peek out of the bathroom window. The white van's gone. Phew! I dive downstairs, grimace at my reflection in the hall mirror to check for lipstick on teeth, grab my briefcase, coat and keys and hare out to the car.

Of course, all that furtive hiding malarkey has made me late.

I turn on the engine and roar off, managing – by some miracle and obliging traffic lights – to screech to a halt outside Cressida and Tom's only two minutes late.

She answers the door before I ring the bell, and I get the distinct impression she's been pacing and checking out of the window since first thing.

'Ah, you found us!' she exclaims with a tight smile and a pointed glance at her watch.

Cressida is tall and very thin. She's wearing a dark grey tracksuit and her brown hair is cut in an angular bob that makes her rather broad face seem even more so.

She ushers me through to the living room.

'Do sit down, Miss Peacock. Coffee?'

'Er, yes please.'

She nods and disappears, and I hear her calling sternly up the stairs. 'Tom? The wedding photographer is *here*.'

I glance around the room. Everything is immaculate. Just like its owner. I open my briefcase and get out my sample wedding albums and my notebook and pen.

Minutes later, I hear a tray clanking in the hall. '*Tom?* Could you *come down*?' An icy pause. '*Now please?*'

I wince slightly, feeling vaguely sorry for the groom-to-be. It's fairly clear who wears the trousers here. Already, I'm picturing how she'll be on her wedding morning.

Normally a nice chilled glass of champagne is enough to calm everyone down. For Cressida, I'm thinking horse tranquilliser.

Tom, who was apparently upstairs working, proves to be an amiable Geordie with a wicked sense of humour, the complete opposite of his fiancée.

We drink our coffee as Cressida perches on the edge of her seat and goes on and on about the absolute 'deal-breaker' of having people with their eyes closed in photos. 'So I'm thinking at least fifteen takes of *every group shot*, just to be on the safe side,' she concludes.

41

I nod reassuringly at them both. Lots of brides are anxious that I might not take enough shots, and I get that. I'd probably feel exactly the same if it was my wedding. 'Don't worry, I'll make sure you have plenty of choice. I always take multiple shots of everything, from different angles and distances, so that we end up with as near perfect a photo as we can possibly get.'

She eyes me sternly. 'Yes, but *near* perfect isn't quite good enough, is it?'

Tom, who's been lying back in his seat, taking it all in with a look of mild amusement, obviously catches my panic. 'I wouldn't worry too much, pet. I get that every night.'

Cressida glares at him like a teacher warning a naughty pupil.

Totally unfazed, her husband-to-be leans forward, takes her hand and gently kisses it with a smile that's full of affection. 'I'm joking, like.'

Cressida bats him away but I can tell she's pleased.

Not that she's ready to let it go. 'But I'm right, aren't I, Tom?' she snaps. 'We expect the best. The *very best.*'

'Eeh, calm yer tits, pet!' He smiles and rolls his eyes at me. 'It'll be all right on the night. I'm sure our Miss Peacock here will do a marvellous job.'

I leave an hour later, feeling as if I've sat a theory exam and only just scraped a pass mark.

And I've still got the practical to go . . .

FOUR

A flurry of weddings over the next few weeks keeps me even busier than usual – so much so that I start to feel I'm neglecting Mum.

But at last, a few days before Ron and Andrea's wedding extravaganza, I finally grab an hour or two to pay her a visit.

Driving south out of Willows Edge, after a few miles the road climbs steeply and that's where you get the best view of Clandon House. It was a familiar landmark in my childhood. When Dad was driving us back from days out, I always looked out for it as we crested the hill because that meant we were nearly home.

It seems slightly surreal – but somehow perfectly natural – that Mum should now be living there.

It's a lovely country house, built in the nineteenth century and developed ten years ago into eight apartments. The adjacent stable block has also been renovated into flats and Mum rents a bijou, two-bed place. I had grave reservations when she first decided she wanted to move there. The rent would take a large chunk out of her modest income and now that Dad was no longer here, I wanted her to have the cash to be able to socialise. Make new friends. Not be stuck in admittedly lovely surroundings but without the finance to enjoy her life.

I agreed to take her for a tour, hoping she'd change her mind.

But in the end, the big smile on her face – as she happily planned where her furniture would go and we took an amble around the leafy grounds – actually changed *my* mind.

I hadn't seen my mum smile like that in two years – not since Dad died.

Now, a year later, I'm heartily thankful for Clandon House.

I didn't even need to worry about a social life for Mum. The country estate is popular with retired people – and in the year she's been here, Mum's been made to feel right at home, especially by Grace and Annabeth who both have apartments in the same block.

Driving through the main gateway, I catch sight of Gareth and wave. He's removing an overhanging branch from a tree near the entrance and I wind down my window, noticing he's had his dark blonde hair cropped shorter than usual. It suits his tanned complexion.

Gareth and his small team take care of the gardens here at Clandon House, as well as at Mallory's Newington Hall.

'Is the lady of the manor at home today?' I ask, smiling at him through the car window.

He wipes his forehead with the back of a huge, well-used gardening glove and grins at me. 'She is, as a matter of fact. But I'd try over there first.' He indicates the woodland area to the right of the main hall.

'Was she in her tracksuit?'

He nods. 'She disappeared into the trees with a couple of the other ladies about twenty minutes ago.'

'Thanks, Gareth. How's the shoulder?'

He was single-handedly moving a dresser for Annabeth last week and he ended up tearing a ligament. It must have been agonising, but to hear him talk, you'd think he just had a nasty bruise.

'Ah, nothing wrong with it.' He brushes off my concern. 'But don't tell the doc I'm still at work,' he adds with a mischievous wink.

Laughing, I tell him I won't.

I carry on up the winding driveway and park outside The Stables.

Gareth is another reason I'm so glad Mum lives here. He's the sort of bloke who'll go out of his way to help. He's already fixed a leaky tap for Mum and climbed in through a window when she locked herself out once. His easy manner and strong physique have many of the Clandon House ladies coming over all unnecessary, as Mum would put it. But he's too modest to ever pick up on the signals.

A widower in his early fifties, he retired from the police force when his wife died five years ago and turned his lifelong hobby into a job. I doubt he needs the money. I suspect he set up his gardening company to keep himself busy, and because physical work in the open air really suits him. Actually, it was me who got him the job at Clandon House.

I first met him at Newington Hall, where he gardens for Mallory's folks, and when Mum said the gardener here was retiring, I had no hesitation in recommending Gareth and his small team.

I joke that his real job is to keep an eye on Mum when I'm not here. And he jokes that really he's only here to stop himself falling off his perch now he's retired. Although from the healthy tan and the twinkle in his eyes, I'd say he's a long way off that. It's lovely to know he's on hand if Mum ever needs him.

I shrug into my parka against the chill of the March day and walk across the gravel at the front of The Stables then along a path that takes me into the little wooded area.

The first person I spot is Annabeth. A tall, auburn-haired woman in her late fifties, she's looking trim in navy track pants and a pink T-shirt and as I watch, she bends to the grass and performs a carefully controlled headstand against the trunk of a horse chestnut tree. My eyebrows rise in admiration. The last time that I did a headstand was in the school playground. I'd probably need a crane lift to get my legs up there now.

Then I spot Mum, several trees away, psyching herself up to do

45

the same. I have to hand it to Annabeth. Under her influence, Mum seems game for anything these days. She's exercising much more, and even her fashion sense has undergone a make-over. Today she's wearing the peculiarly youthful, bang-on-trend grey and white patterned tracksuit she picked up a few weeks ago on eBay. Since being forced to tighten her belt financially, Mum's turned bargain-hunting into something of a hobby. I grin to myself. Today's edgy outfit is rather more 'Snoop Dogg at the O2 Arena' than 'lady of a certain age'. I love that, at sixty, she doesn't care a jot.

For her first attempt at a headstand, her legs get no higher than a foot off the ground, and the second is not much better.

Mum scrambles up to remove her glasses and passes them to silver-haired Grace, who's standing nearby, hands on hips, watching their antics with a mixture of amusement and incredulity. To be fair, despite being slightly older – she turned sixty-three last year – Grace is just as fit, and would probably be joining in if she hadn't recently had keyhole surgery on a painful knee joint.

On Mum's third attempt, just as her legs are about to come back down to earth, Grace springs forward, grabs her ankles and hoists them up so that her feet actually make contact with the tree trunk. Their precarious balance is short-lived, however. I'm not sure if it's the shock of suddenly seeing the world upside down, but Mum starts to list to one side, and she and Grace end up on the grass, shrieking with laughter.

Mum spots me and waves.

'I haven't done a headstand since I was about ten,' I laugh, joining them. 'What on earth are you up to?'

Grace snorts and murmurs, 'Ask Annabeth. This is her crazy idea.'

'Shh!' whispers Mum, with a quick glance over at Annabeth, who's still upside down, her eyes closed, I suppose in a sort of meditation.

'We're rebalancing our energies by communing with nature,' Mum says loudly, so Annabeth can hear, but winking at me.

'It's the rush of blood to the head I worry about,' says Grace. 'Look at that one.' She nods at Annabeth. 'She'll be there for ages, and it's all in aid of a better sex life.'

'No, it's not,' calls Annabeth calmly. 'It's to relieve stress.'

'Why would you need stress relief?' calls Grace. 'You lead a charmed life.'

'I live next door to you, don't I?' replies Annabeth.

Mum laughs and gets to her feet, then helps Grace up. 'You probably think we're bonkers,' she says to me.

I grin. 'Must be something in the water here.'

Her eyes sparkle with mischief. 'Oh, do I embarrass you, darling?'

'Of course. But isn't that your job?' I joke. 'As a parent?'

To be honest, she could prance around on the lawn doing the dance of the seven veils stark naked and I'd cheer her on. It's such a relief to see her so happy and upbeat these days.

'Come on. Hurry up,' says Annabeth, passing us at speed. 'That programme's on in a minute.'

'What programme?' I ask, as we follow her back to The Stables.

'It's about Princess Anne,' says Mum.

'You mean *The Princess Royal*,' calls Annabeth sternly.

'She thinks we're related to royalty,' mutters Grace, rolling her eyes. 'It's a story that's been passed down the generations and, for some reason, Beth's bought into it.'

I stare at her. 'Hang on. Are you two related?'

'They're sisters. Didn't I mention that?' says Mum.

I shake my head in bemusement and Grace laughs. 'I know. You'd hardly believe it, would you? We're like chalk and cheese in everything.' She pauses. 'Well, maybe not everything.'

Something in her tone makes me glance over. Her sunny expression has vanished.

But before I have time to wonder, she smiles at me. 'Did your mum tell you she's coming for a spa weekend with us?'

'Oh, lovely. Can I come?'

I'm only jesting but Mum looks at me in delight. 'Of course you can, love. That would be wonderful.'

Feeling bad for getting her hopes up, I put my arm round her and give her a little squeeze as we crunch our way across the gravel to The Stables' main entrance. 'I'd love to, Mum. But I can't. I'm just—'

'Too busy. I know.' She smiles at Grace. 'This daughter of mine . . .'

The pride in her voice makes me feel emotional. But also guilty. Yes, I am too busy to take a weekend off. But it's more than that. I simply don't have the spare cash. But Mum knows nothing about my dire financial state. And while I tell myself I'm only keeping it from her so she doesn't worry about me, deep down I know it's also because I'm too ashamed to tell her.

'You could come to the séance instead,' says Grace matter-of-factly. 'You must be able to take an evening off?'

'Séance?' I look from Grace to Mum in bewilderment. 'What séance?'

The two of them glance at each other and grin.

'It's Annabeth's idea,' murmurs Mum as we climb the stairs to Annabeth's first-floor flat. 'Venus at the yoga class in the village fancies herself a bit of a psychic and she offered to conduct a séance here for free.'

Grace chuckles. 'She's hoping Venus might be able to conjure up the spirit of our dear departed Great-Aunt Edna.'

'But why?' I ask, mystified as to why anyone would want to try and summon dead people.

'Oh, Great-Aunt Edna was a practising psychic herself. And Annabeth's convinced she might be able to confirm whether or not we have royal blood.'

Grace grins. 'It should be a laugh. Venus is nutty as a fruitcake with extra pecans.'

'I'm not sure I like the sound of it,' whispers Mum to me and I make a face in agreement.

'In here,' calls Annabeth, and when we walk into the living room, she's perched on the edge of her chair, eyes riveted to the TV screen.

'Shall I put the coffee on?' asks Grace.

Annabeth waves her hand impatiently at Grace. 'Just look at that chin.' She points at the screen where the Princess Royal is making a speech at some charity gala. 'Doesn't that just prove it?'

'Prove what, Beth?' asks Grace.

'Well, I've only just realised her chin is *exactly like mine*. Look.' She sticks out her chin, angling her head helpfully.

As one, we all transfer our baffled gaze from the Princess Royal's chin to Annabeth's.

'Well, what do you think?' The action of thrusting out her chin makes her sound like she's just had heavy dental work.

Mum tips her head thoughtfully to one side. 'They're very, um, *similar* chins, Annabeth.'

I nod. 'Very similar. As chins go . . .'

Annabeth nods at Grace in a *told-you-so* sort of way.

Grace snorts. 'If we're related to royalty, I'm a bloody corgi's auntie.'

After sitting through the chin programme, trying to keep a straight face, and drinking coffee made by Grace, Mum and I take our leave and go back to her flat.

'Did I tell you I'm doing Ron and Andrea's wedding on Saturday?' I ask, knowing she'll be interested.

She frowns. 'Really? Well, you take care. When that man has a drink in him, he's more slippery than a wet fish. And he does like his drink.'

I laugh. 'It's his wedding day, Mum. I'm sure even Ron can be trusted to stay sober and keep his hands to himself on the day he marries Andrea.'

I'd like to think so, anyway.

Mum shudders. 'Do you know he once propositioned me in the supermarket?'

I nod, smiling. I've heard this story a thousand times before. 'I was a toddler in the trolley and he asked you how to judge a melon's ripeness.'

Mum nods, looking affronted but enjoying it all the same. 'When I showed him how to press the end, he waggled his eyebrows at me and suggested we continue the lesson back at his house!'

I grin. 'If you'd said yes to the melon-pressing, I bet Ron would have run a mile.'

She purses her lips. 'That's not the point.'

'What's this?' I ask, noticing a hardback book with a black cover on the side table. Thinking it's a thriller, I pick it up and my eyebrows rise at the title: *Talking to the Dead: Seven Ways to Successful Communication with the Other Side.*

I hold it up and Mum waves her hand. 'Oh, nothing. Just something Venus left behind. She thought I might be interested, what with the séance and all.'

'She's been here?' I ask, surprised Mum hadn't mentioned it.

'Oh yes. Annabeth and Grace were coming for tea anyway, and Venus sort of invited herself along.'

I run my hand over the glossy cover. 'Have you read it?' I ask curiously. Mum's always dismissed such things as utter tosh.

'No,' she scoffs. 'As if. I just took it to be polite. I'll get it back to her at the next yoga class. I think she's a bit New Age nuts to be honest.'

I laugh. 'And doing headstands on the grass is normal behaviour?'

'Touché.' She smiles ruefully. 'But that's just a bit of fun to please Annabeth.'

I get up reluctantly. 'Right, I'd better go. Tons to do.'

'Well, don't work yourself into the ground.' She cups my face in her hands and plants a kiss on my cheek. 'And listen?'

'Don't be a stranger,' I chant with a grin.

This is Mum's motto. She even said it to the postman once – to which he remarked that since her gas bill was due, there was a distinct possibility he'd be back as large as life the next day.

She opens the door and gives me a playful push.

I catch something red and sparkly out of the corner of my eye.

It's a key fob, dangling in the door.

I stare at it. It's a cheap thing with a big sparkly letter 'S' on it. '*Where*—?'

Mum's eyes slide away. 'I was clearing out the spare room and I found it in a box.' She shrugs and adds, a touch defiantly, 'I like it. And I needed a key ring.'

I turn to go but Mum grabs my arm.

'Katy,' she murmurs. Her tone is tinged with pity, which only makes things worse. 'When it was you two girls running the business, you seemed to have such fun. It almost didn't seem like work at all.' A pause. 'Don't you think things would be so much better if Sienna were still here?'

A little bolt of shock zips through me at the mention of my sister's name.

There's a pleading tone to Mum's question, and I can understand her bewilderment. Often, I wonder if she blames me for not trying to get Sienna to come home.

She's aware we had a major falling out which was why Sienna left, but she has no idea what we rowed about. I've certainly never told her and I'd bet my house and all its contents that Sienna will have remained silent on the subject.

On the way home, I think about Mum and her constant hope that Sienna and I will eventually be reconciled. I wish she'd stop it and realise, once and for all, that as far as I'm concerned, that's never going to happen.

I suppose if Mum knew how precariously I'm living – always looking over my shoulder, in fear of yet another demand for money

I can't pay – she might understand why I still can't think of my sister, two years later, without feeling sick and shaky.

Sienna is the reason I now struggle daily to keep the wolf from the door.

At first when Sienna left, Mum – grieving over Dad's death a year earlier – was devastated and tried her best to smooth things over between us. I know she had long talks with Sienna on the phone, although I can only imagine what was said. And she tried to convince me that family was everything. We'd lost Dad. Did I really want to lose my baby sister as well?

But sunk in my own grief and despair over Dad's death and all that had happened with Sienna, I was in no mood to forgive. My life was in ruins. She'd left me high and dry, committed to paying off the loan I'd taken out to buy equipment all by myself. The loan payments were pretty hefty. Shared with Sienna, they were manageable. But paying it on my own – on the last day of every month – kept me constantly on edge, worrying whether this was the month I'd be forced to admit I couldn't cope and throw in the towel.

But while the business ended up being a millstone around my neck in many respects, ironically, I think it also saved my sanity.

By the time Sienna left, we already had ten or so weddings in the diary, so I absolutely couldn't back out, even if I'd wanted to. I could never have let my clients down. So I just dived right in, doing the best job I could, learning as I went along all the particular skills needed to be a good wedding photographer.

I pour everything into giving couples a great service and a beautiful album at the end of it all. I'm busy from early in the morning to late into the evening and I collapse into bed at the end of each day, glad of the oblivion. And working hard does have some advantages. It occupies my mind and keeps the nightmare thoughts at bay.

I know Mum thinks I should put the past behind me. That I should care enough about the baby sister I once loved so much to hold out an olive branch.

On occasion, when I've felt especially low, I've been tempted to pour out the whole sorry mess to Mum. Tell her exactly what happened to wreck our sisterly bond forever.

But something always stops me.

I think it's that I know Mum would immediately set out to try to make things better between us.

But as far as I'm concerned, her efforts would be useless . . .

FIVE

Walking through the front door at home, I hear the buzz of my mobile signalling a new message.

It's Bethany, the bride I spoke to recently, confirming she'd like me to take the photos at her wedding.

Angrily dashing the tears from my eyes, I push all thoughts of my sister out of my mind and immediately return Bethany's phone call so that we can sort out dates for future meetings.

Afterwards, I stand at the kitchen window, staring out at my small patch of garden without really seeing it, thinking about Bethany and how she's embarking on a whole new happy chapter in her life.

I'd thought that's what Sienna and I were going to do.

We'd always had a special bond, even though I was nine when she was born. And once she was grown up, we weren't just sisters, we were the best of friends, too.

When she left school, she decided she'd like to go and work abroad for a while, so she took a course with TEFL and ended up being qualified to teach English as a foreign language. I supported her in this, even though I knew we'd all miss her. But then, to my delight, she changed her mind and decided she wanted to follow in my footsteps. And it seemed entirely natural that she should join me in the wedding photography business.

I was just in the early stages of setting the business up, so the timing was perfect. And for a while, everything was brilliant. We were starting this exciting new venture together but it wasn't as scary as it could have been because we had each other to talk things over with, make plans and iron out any teething problems.

But then everything went pear-shaped. And Sienna reverted to her original plan and moved to Paris.

Everything changed after she left.

There was a time, in the early days of the business, when landing a new booking filled me with excitement. The creative cogs in my brain would immediately start to whir into action. I'd picture the venue, recalling the layout of the hotel and the gardens, dreaming up perfect settings and imagining bringing together the results of the bride and groom's big day in a glorious keepsake album.

Now, though, there's only ever one thing on my mind.

Money.

As soon as the booking is in the bag, my head goes into mathematical somersault mode as I feverishly figure out how much profit I'll be able to set against my credit card debt once I've covered the mortgage and the bank loan repayments. Sometimes, if it's a lean month for work, there isn't even enough to cover the basic household bills. So then I have to stall paying the bank loan so that I can keep up with the mortgage.

After a lot of agonising, I decided that I'd have to sell my house. But in the six months that it's been on the market, there's been no firm interest. Viewers probably take one look at the old-fashioned kitchen and slightly sad bathroom and decide their pockets aren't deep enough to give it the care and attention it badly needs.

The threat of losing my house to the building society hangs over me constantly. However hard I try to get myself out of the mess, I don't seem to make any real progress. It always seems to be two steps forward, three steps back.

This house – compact though it is – means everything to me

and it devastates me to think I will have to hand over the key to a stranger.

It's in the same street as the larger family home I grew up in. An ancient milestone protrudes from its tiny patch of front garden, 'Willows Edge ½ mile' carved into the stone. It used to fascinate me when I was a kid, traipsing past it every day to school and back. Dad said the stone was probably a century old and I used to wonder about the man who carved the letters all those years ago. It seemed odd and a little creepy to think that he'd be dead now.

I often wonder if some weird, sixth sense was telling me that one day, I'd live there. What I didn't realise was that in the end, I'd face losing it.

Of course, I never stop praying for a miracle. Hoping that a flood of new business might transform the situation.

But I've got no money to advertise in the big, glossy wedding magazines. So I'm relying on word of mouth and recommendations, while still only clocking up around fifteen weddings per year. Although, to be honest, without a full-time assistant, I'm not sure I'd be able to take on more work and retain the level of quality I will absolutely not compromise on.

Something happened just before Christmas, though, that gave me a little spark of hope.

I was shooting another wedding at the Greshingham Hotel, and as I waited to take photos of the first dance, Corinne, the hotel's new weddings co-ordinator, came over to chat.

'Katy Peacock, isn't it?' She smiled. 'I remembered because it's such a lovely name. You were the one who hijacked the cherry-picker truck.'

'Yes, that was me.' I laughed, remembering that wedding.

The groom had unexpectedly requested I take a shot of him and his new wife out on the bridal suite's first-floor balcony. I'd wanted to get the angle right. I'd have even climbed a tree if there had been one nearby; it wouldn't have been the first time I'd resorted to such measures. While I was pondering what to do, someone suggested they'd seen a cherrypicker truck at the bottom of the drive and maybe that was the answer. And as it happened, it turned out to be the perfect solution.

Corinne smiled. 'How you managed to persuade that guy to hoist you up in his truck, I can't imagine. Brilliant!'

'It was a bit risky,' I confessed. 'When I realised you'd seen what I was doing, I was convinced I'd be banned from taking any more photos here.'

She shook her head. 'Not at all. The bride and groom were absolutely delighted with your efforts. *Above and beyond the call of duty* was how the groom put it. So well done.'

'I was glad to help.'

'You've shot quite a few weddings here, haven't you?'

I nodded, wondering where all this was leading.

'The thing is, I've been putting together a file of information for bridal couples to take away with them. Hints and tips on how to organise their big day, that sort of thing, with a few recommendations for sourcing wedding cars and flowers.' She smiled. 'And photographers.'

'Oh?' My heart started beating very fast.

'It's nothing definite,' she murmured, 'but if I wanted to give our couples the name of a good wedding photographer, would you mind me mentioning you?'

I felt my cheeks start to flush. 'Mind? No, of course not. I'd be absolutely thrilled!'

Oh my God! This was just the break I needed!

Then I cleared my throat and said in a much more professional manner, 'Thank you for thinking of me. I really appreciate it. Do let me know what you decide.'

When she left, my legs were actually wobbling on the way to the car. I couldn't believe it. This was the sort of magical opportunity I'd longed for, and if I hadn't been in professional mode, I'd have done a little dance right there on the lawn.

That was over two months ago now, and although Corinne has

my number, I've heard nothing at all. With each week that passes, my hope fades a little bit more. But next week, I'll be back at the Greshingham Hotel for Ron and Andrea's wedding.

And maybe – just maybe – Corinne might have good news for me.

It's the night before Andrea and Ron's big day and I'm in full panic mode.

Not about the wedding.

But about something far more critical.

'Chill, darling,' advises Mallory, from her flaked-out pose on my sofa. She's watching me with mild amusement as I tear around, ransacking the house. 'Stop looking and it'll turn up.'

'I can't stop looking!' I yelp. 'If I don't find it, the whole day will go pear-shaped!'

Mallory examines her nails. 'It's a piece of jewellery,' she murmurs. 'Not some magical talisman.'

'But it's not just any old brooch. It's my lucky charm,' I call, running upstairs to check my bedroom drawers for the twenty-seventh time.

'Which jacket were you wearing at your last wedding?' calls Mallory.

Her question stops me in my tracks.

'Brilliant!' I yell, diving for the wardrobe. Sure enough, there it is, pinned to the lapel, and I breathe a sigh of relief.

Dad bought me the beautiful ceramic brooch years ago. It's a single, perfectly formed daffodil and the yolk yellow petals are so vibrant against the pale green stem, they cheer me up just to look at them. Dad said the brooch reminded him of the first ever photograph I had framed for him and Mum. It was a black and white shot of a daffodil in a slim vase and it hung on the living room wall ever afterwards and – much to my complete mortification – was pointed out fondly every time we had guests.

Usually, Mum did the gift-buying in our house, so the brooch from Dad was really special. I've had it for ages but it's in perfect nick, except for a tiny stress fracture running down the centre, which is barely noticeable.

I wore it when, filled with butterflies and nervous excitement, I shot my very first wedding. The day turned out to be perfect, so now I *have* to wear the brooch to make sure things go smoothly. (When things do get hairy occasionally, Mallory will remark wryly, 'So much for the lucky charm.' But I counter that by pointing out how much worse things could have been without it.)

Apart from anything superstitious, the brooch makes me feel I've got my dad close by.

Dad worked as an accountant when he left college, but he always dreamed of being his own boss. And when he was forty, he took the plunge, left his job and started up the sandwich business he'd long been planning and scheming in his head. Of course we had to downsize because selling sandwiches didn't bring in nearly as much as Dad's steady nine-to-five job. So there were no more holidays to Spain or nice meals out. But even though he had to work crazy hours, I think that was the happiest I ever saw him. He'd have been so proud of what I've managed to achieve, all by myself, slowly building up a solid reputation in the industry.

When things are tough and I've got a headache trying to juggle money, robbing Peter to pay Paul, I think of Dad's favourite saying: 'Courage is being scared to death but saddling up anyway.'

That always spurs me on.

When I wake next morning, I feel hung-over. Which is a bit unfair since I didn't have anything to drink.

I'd stayed awake until the early hours, practically propping my eyelids open with matchsticks, getting my accounts up to date. (Numbers aren't my thing so balancing the books regularly taxes my brain to its limits.) As a result I was in the deepest sleep ever when the alarm went off and it felt like only ten minutes since I'd crashed into bed.

I pour strong coffee down my throat while making last-minute checks of my equipment. I once ran out of batteries in the middle of shooting a wedding for an extremely uptight bride. Not an experience I ever want to repeat. If it hadn't been for a junior guest, who apparently kept a supply of triple AAAs in his pocket at all times in case of a gaming controller emergency (no, I didn't understand it either), I'm pretty sure the bride would have spontaneously combusted.

Needless to say, I now have spare batteries on me at all times.

I'm meeting Mallory at the venue.

In theory, I like to arrive twenty minutes before we're expected so that we can park up and take our time checking out the lay of the land for the photos later.

The reality tends to be a little different.

Like this morning.

Just as I'm opening the front door, the house phone rings.

I pause, thinking I'll let it go to answer machine. But then there's always the thought that it could be Mum in trouble, so I close the door and go to check.

It is Mum.

We chat for a few minutes then I say I have to go but I'll call her later.

'If you could, love. Because I've got something to tell you.'

'Tell me now.'

She hesitates. 'No. It can wait till later.'

'Mum?' A feeling of foreboding prickles my scalp.

I straighten up. 'What is it?'

I hear her sigh at the other end.

Then she says, in a low voice, 'Sienna's coming back.'

SIX

Sienna's coming back.

Mum's words swim around in my consciousness.

I'd always wondered how I'd react if Sienna returned. Actually, I feel quite numb.

Gently, I place the phone in its stand. And when it rings a few seconds later, I'm already closing the front door behind me.

I drive to the venue in a daze, almost missing the turn-off. I have to brake suddenly and the driver behind me slams the horn three times and races furiously past me. Trembling, I pull into the side of the road and turn the engine off, then I sit there, staring ahead, grasping the steering wheel as if it's a lifeline.

A cold feeling settles in my heart.

Then an ambulance hares past, its siren blaring, bringing me to my senses.

For a few seconds, my mind is blank. *Where was I going? What was I doing?*

I glance at the clock.

The wedding!

I set off, driving almost as fast as the ambulance, determined not to be late for Andrea.

The sight of Mallory, jokingly flagging me down in the car park and pointing accusingly at her watch, brings me back to the present. Mallory is actually really laid back about this sort of thing. She's only doing the watch thing because she knows *I'll* be anxious to get going.

'Chill, darling,' she says when I emerge from the car. 'They're probably not even ready for you yet. You know what these fussy brides are like.'

'Hey, don't be so hard on brides. It'll be your turn in December.'

In stark contrast to my plain navy suit, crisp white shirt and navy heels, Mallory's wearing a floaty, mauve dress, cream fake fur and little pixie boots. All charity shop, of course. Anyone else would look appalling in this ensemble but Mallory has the personality to pull it off.

'Great tree,' she points out.

I look across at the old, gnarly oak whose magnificent branches look like they've been arranged precisely with us in mind. 'Perfect backdrop for the bride and groom shots,' I agree.

I glance up at the hotel. Behind one of those gorgeous Georgian windows, Andrea and her bridal entourage will be in a state of nervous excitement, talking Kim and Kanye. And hair, make-up and veils. And probably quaffing far too much champagne.

It always feels a privilege to be there, among the bride's family and friends, on this most intimate of occasions.

Some families embrace me like they would a family friend, which is lovely, while others regard me as simply the professional photographer, who's there to do a job. Either way is fine by me.

Sometimes my role expands to become the chief calmer of nerves, hanky provider or bridal car arrival checker. I can even be called on to help a bride choose between two shades of lipstick – obviously a decision of vital importance, so no pressure there, then. I take it all very seriously because I know how important it is that the bride feels beautiful on her special day.

I usually enjoy every aspect of it.

But today, with my legs still shaky from that phone call, all I want to do is get through the work and go home.

I draw in a breath of bracing March air. 'Right. Better get in there.'

'Are you all right, darling?' Mallory peers at me. 'You seem a bit queer.'

That almost makes me giggle. Sometimes Mallory seems to have been born into the wrong century. And the sort of day I'm having, 'almost a giggle' is quite a result. It reminds me why Mallory is my best friend. One of the reasons, at any rate. She has this knack of being able to perk me up instantly – whether her remarks are intentionally funny or otherwise.

'I'm feeling better by the minute,' I tell her honestly.

I leave Mallory scouting round the grounds while I head up to the bride's bedroom.

Squeals of delight greet me when I enter – mainly from Chloe and Sophie, her cousin. Both are bridesmaids and both are already high as kites with excitement.

Andrea, slim and newly fake-tanned in cream satin bridal underwear, is standing by a free-standing mirror, holding in front of her The Dress.

'Hi, Katy. What do you think?' she squeaks. 'Isn't it just Kim's dress to a tee?'

'Gosh. Yes. It's amazing.' I've no idea what Kim Kardashian's wedding gown looked like but there's no denying it, Andrea's dress is stunning.

'It's a mermaid silhouette gown,' she says proudly, swishing it in front of her. 'See the fishtail?'

'Put it on, Mum,' orders Chloe. She grins at me. 'I'm Kourtney and Sophie is Kendall.'

She sees my knitted brow.

'Kardashian?'

'Ah. Right. Well, you both look sensational,' I say honestly. They do. They're wearing identical white dresses. Long and figure-hugging with posies of white roses.

Andrea's dress, when she's eventually in it, is quite simply jaw-dropping.

White with long lace sleeves, it's quite modest from the front.

But when she turns and looks back at us with a coquettish little smile, we all let out a gasp.

The gown is daringly backless, plunging down almost to Andrea's waist, with a long train stretching out over the carpet. Neither is the veil a shrinking violet. It's quite simply the longest I've ever seen, swooping right to the floor. With her deep tan, Andrea carries it off perfectly. Ron really won't know what to do with himself.

'Ron's getting a buzz cut,' says Chloe, raising one eyebrow. 'So he'll look the image of Kanye.' She looks at Sophie and they both burst out laughing.

Andrea seems totally unperturbed. She's too busy swishing this way and that in front of the mirror. And to be fair, the girls' merriment is probably far more to do with the excitement of the occasion, than deliberately taking the mickey out of poor Ron.

Andrea turns suddenly. 'You'll never believe it, Katy. The wedding's off.'

'*What?*' I stare at her, confused.

She laughs and waves a hand at my daftness. 'Not *our* wedding, silly. Dieter Hanson's wedding to Blaze Jorgensen.'

'Oh. Right. I see.' To be honest, I'd forgotten all about it.

'It was meant to be today? The same day as ours?'

'Yes. I remember now.'

She nods at the open tabloid newspaper on the bed. Dutifully, I go over and glance at the headline. Sure enough, there it is. The whole story with a picture of Dieter Hanson emerging from some building with his head down, looking understandably devastated.

I must still be feeling fairly wobbly after hearing about Sienna's imminent return, because his plight suddenly strikes me as incredibly sad. The breakdown of a relationship once so full of promise. All those dashed hopes and dreams. One person left to pick up the pieces of their life . . .

My throat is suddenly thick with emotion. I'm no stranger to the trauma of love gone wrong. I know exactly how Dieter Hanson must be feeling today.

'I felt so sorry for him, I sent him an invitation to *our* wedding,' says Andrea.

Her announcement is so unexpected, it instantly catapults me out of my sudden gloom.

We all stare at the bride for an incredulous moment. Then Chloe and Sophie burst into gales of laughter.

Andrea purses her lips. 'Well, that's not very nice, I must say. The poor man must be absolutely devastated.'

'Oh, Mum, we're not laughing at him being jilted.' Chloe looks guiltily at me. 'It's just do you really think he's going to want to come to *your wedding*?'

Andrea shrugs huffily. 'Probably not. I just thought it might cheer him up to be asked.'

Chloe looks at me as if to say, *A film star at my mum's wedding? I think not!*

But when Andrea glances at me for support, I find myself nodding. 'Absolutely. You need all the support you can get at a horrible time like that, when you feel as if nothing makes sense any more and all the colour has been bleached out of your world.' I swallow hard. 'And your guts are being slowly dragged out through your mouth by an alien force . . .'

All heads whip round to me. I suddenly remember where I am and my cheeks grow warm with embarrassment.

'Right, let's get some shots of this amazing dress,' I say hurriedly, moving round to find the perfect angle.

Bloody hell, it's not like me to overreact like that. Especially in a professional setting. Mum's bombshell news about Sienna coming home has knocked me completely off-kilter.

Andrea fills a glass with champagne, which she shoves into my hand, clearly thinking I need it after my bout of emotional leakage. A glass of delicious fizz would definitely help. But after taking one sip, I set it firmly down.

I've learned from experience.

At one of my first ever weddings, the champagne in the bride's room was flowing freely and I was so nervous, I drank two glasses on an empty stomach then spent the next three hours trying to enunciate my words and keep the camera from wobbling. I have no memory of taking the photographs, although strangely, it turned out to be one of the best albums I've ever produced. What it lacks in formal group shots, it more than makes up for in candid, relaxed photos of all the guests, which suggests I was snapping away happily as if I was on my holidays.

Thankfully, the bride and groom loved that album. Even if I did have to delete an unsually high number of blurry images and photos of nothing but feet.

I'm very aware it could have been a different story altogether.

I steer clear of the champagne now, tempting though it is. One sip is definitely enough.

The girls are admiring themselves in the mirror and chattering away about the cancelled wedding.

'I feel dead sorry for poor Dieter,' Sophie says, thrusting her face close to the mirror to apply more lip gloss. 'It was bad enough when Ryan dumped me last year, but imagine how horrible it would be having it splashed across the front pages like that.' She nods at the tabloid newspaper on the bed. 'I'd absolutely want to hide away forever.'

'I hope it's not a bad omen,' says Andrea with a nervous giggle. 'Ron had better show up.'

Chloe laughs. 'Don't be daft, Mum, of course he will.'

Andrea smiles fondly and reaches for her daughter's hand. 'Oh, isn't this lovely?' Her eyes are misty. 'You know what I wish? I wish I'd thought to bring a notebook and pen so I could have written down the whole story of our wedding day – all the tiny little details that are so special to me, then I'd never, ever forget them.'

'If you were writing all day, you'd have no time to get married,' giggles Sophie.

'Oh, God,' exclaims Andrea. She looks up, opens her eyes wide and blinks furiously. 'My eye make-up's going to smudge.'

I whip out a paper hanky from the stash I carry for emotional emergencies.

Andrea carefully blots her under-eyes, then all three stand by the elegant, free-standing mirror so that I can take some shots of their reflection. Then I take some of the two girls fixing Andrea's veil before saying, 'Right, come on, everyone, pick up your glasses and let's do a toast for the camera!'

Finally, I position Andrea next to the tall sash window, holding her bouquet and looking out dreamily over the lawns, the perfect showcase for her incredible dress.

Everyone goes silent. My own throat is suddenly thick with emotion again.

'Oh, Mum, you look absolutely stunning,' breathes Chloe. 'Have you got another hanky, Katy?'

I dig one out for her.

Then I leave them to finish off getting ready, and go off to find Mallory and check out the room where the ceremony is to be held.

The official part of the day takes place in a purpose-built annexe a few yards from the main hotel, and several intriguingly dressed guests are already lingering outside the room, waiting to be allowed in.

The Queen and Prince Philip are chatting to Posh and Becks about the traffic on the bypass.

'Posh' looks model lean and elegant in a figure-hugging black dress, cut an inch or so below the knee, with impossibly spindly heels and what I suspect is a shiny black wig in a sleek, geometric cut. Her 'Becks' is standing, arms folded, looking extremely awkward in his sarong.

'Mind, I don't know how she does it,' the Queen says. 'I've had this thing on for less than an hour and already it's irritating the life out of me. Plus it's too big.' She shakes her head and the gem-studded crown slips down over one eye.

Posh, seeing me – and therefore an audience – straightens up, takes David's arm and slinks into a catwalk pose, staring poutingly into the distance with a bored look on her face.

A helpful male member of staff opens the door for me and I go inside. I've photographed many a wedding in this room, but it's always good to double-check the venue in case anything has changed.

Satisfied I'm familiar with the layout and have some idea where I'll position myself for the photos, I go outside to find Mallory.

Standing at the hotel entrance, I survey the scene.

The car park is filling up.

A scent of damp trees and woodsmoke hangs in the clear, cold air as guests climb out of their cars and head for the wedding annexe. I spot a variety of Queens and Prince Philips, two Sonny and Chers in ridiculously big wigs, and a Marilyn Monroe with a man in glasses who I suppose is meant to be Arthur Miller. It strikes me that it's generally the women who have gone that extra mile in the dressing-up stakes. (With the exception of the man dressed as an inflatable vibrator, emerging from a Vauxhall Corsa with his other half, the Battery Bunny.)

My attention is caught by a tall man in jeans and a well-worn casual jacket, standing at the entrance to the car park. He seems vaguely familiar although I'm struggling to place him. Every now and again, he stops a group of guests, charms them into posing and quickly takes a few shots.

Great. Just what I need. A guest who fancies himself as another David Bailey.

Well, just as long as he doesn't get in my way . . .

I spot Mallory crossing the lawn to join me.

'Who's *that*?' I nod at the man.

'Whoever do you mean? Sexy Hugh Jackman over there?'

I laugh. 'He doesn't look in the *least* like Hugh Jackman.'

'How not?' asks Mallory, lingering on the view. 'Dark hair, broad shoulders, great smile, *very* nice.'

I shrug. 'He's far too tall.'

'Well, Hugh Jackman's tall. At least six foot, I'd say, wouldn't you?'

'Yes, but I bet he'd never go to a wedding looking like he just rolled out of bed ten minutes ago. He's not even wearing fancy dress.'

'Hmm.' Mallory takes her time considering. 'You do have a point. Sexy, though, that dressed-down jeans look. *Exceptional* bottom—'

The penny suddenly drops. And I swear it's absolutely nothing to do with the exceptional bottom.

'Oh God, I don't believe it,' I mutter. 'It's him.'

SEVEN

'Who?' demands Mallory. 'Who is it?'

'It's that man,' I say faintly. 'The one I maimed, leaping over the fence.'

'Really?' Mallory stares intently. Then she scrabbles in her bag and brings out her glasses.

'What are you doing?' I demand.

'Having a closer look, darling. What do you think?'

'Mallory!'

Terrified he'll spot her ogling him, I hurry off to the wedding annexe, pausing once to beckon for her to follow me. And doesn't she choose that very moment to call helpfully, 'He doesn't seem to be limping now.'

My face flushes the colour of a ripe tomato.

I don't dare look back to see if he heard.

Mallory gives me a funny look as if I'm making a mountain out of a molehill but I just ignore her. Sometimes I wish she wasn't quite so tuned into my emotions.

The room where the wedding ceremony is taking place has a peaceful, soothing effect. I force myself to take in the sumptuous details – the rich fabric of the wine-coloured chairs, set out theatre-style, the log fire burning in the grate, casting its reflection in two of the most spectacular crystal chandeliers I've ever seen. At either end of the aisle, a glowing church candle sits atop an ornate holder entwined with foliage and white roses.

The place is filled with a delicate floral scent, and I stand at the back of the room, taking a few deep breaths to help me focus on the task in hand. It's proving to be quite a challenging day, what with Mum's news about Sienna and now Runner Man turning up out of the blue to shake my composure by reminding me of the fence incident (*so* embarrassing). But I have a job to do and I will *not* allow anything to distract me.

'Are you all right, darling?' asks Mallory, appearing at my elbow. 'You look a little distracted.'

'I'm fine.' I plaster on a smile to prove it. 'Actually, I was just wondering what's behind those curtains,' I say, quickly improvising, and walking away from her curious looks.

Every time I've photographed a wedding here, the curtains have been closed, I suppose to enhance the warm, candlelit ambience of the room.

I peer behind the heavy red and gold drapes at the window nearest the altar. Patio doors lead out onto a terrace and instantly I'm thinking about the natural light that would flood in and how, from a position on the terrace, I could get some lovely shots of the bride and groom signing the register at the table in the corner.

But a quick word with the manager, who's hovering nearby, reveals that those patio doors are never opened during the winter months.

'Guests would start wandering in and out,' she murmurs confidentially. 'The carpet would be ruined.'

'I'd only be a moment,' I say.

But she shakes her head apologetically. 'Sorry. Hotel policy.'

Feeling slightly frustrated at the wasted opportunity, I nonetheless smile and nod. Rules are rules.

I scan the room. There's a low hum of conversation and an air of contained excitement as guests file into the room in small groups and settle themselves into seats. A string quartet is playing at the back, and Ron is there at the altar, looking surprisingly dapper in his plain black tuxedo and white shirt. And buzz cut.

As I take some shots of him, the groom's best man cracks a joke and Ron gives a strained laugh. He's clearly very nervous. He keeps running his hand over his head as if his buzzed hair might have somehow grown back.

I catch Mallory's eye and we retreat to the back of the room for the entrance of the bride and her father.

And that's when I notice Runner Man sitting slumped in his seat at the end of a pew, arms folded, one long leg encroaching on the aisle. He looks oddly out of place wearing jeans among all these 'celebrities', especially as he's sitting next to an elaborately dressed Elton John in his powdered wig party phase. (The wig is so massive, it's blocking everyone's view and probably required a wedding invitation all of its own.)

In the same row I can see Wallace and Gromit, a couple of Oompa Loompas and a Derek Zoolander with a pink bandana round his head.

They've all gone to so much trouble with their costumes – and it just highlights Runner Man's complete lack of effort in the dressing-up stakes. And lack of effort in the staying awake stakes as well, I reflect a minute later. He looks worn out, as if he might topple off the end of the pew at any minute.

And then the doors open and in walks Chloe, with Sophie a few steps behind her. They look like fairy-tale princesses. Chloe looks around, spots me with my camera and gives me a wink, which I manage to snap.

Runner Man turns in his seat at that point to take in the scene and to my horror, his eyes travel around the room and land on me. I look away immediately, praying he hasn't recognised me as the loon who bashed into him.

But a second later, he looks over again and I realise he has.

75

It's just a brief glance. But the amused twist to his mouth suggests he's rumbled me all right.

Bugger. But I suppose it had to happen eventually. You can't exactly hide away when you're the chief photographer.

Andrea enters a second later in her dramatically backless dress, smiling radiantly on the arm of her dad. Her stunning train glides along the carpet as they make their way up the aisle to the strains of The Wedding March, played by the quartet.

The whole room seems to swell with the emotion of the occasion.

I spot Princess Fiona laying her head on Shrek's shoulder. And a middle-aged Pamela Anderson, in leopard print and blonde wig, snuggling closer to her *Baywatch* lifeguard. Keith Lemon gives his nose a trumpeting blow.

The ceremony turns out to be beautifully simple, which quite surprises me. I suppose with her love of all things celebrity, I was expecting Andrea to go slightly overboard with the bling and the extravagant gestures. Perhaps a dove or two flying up the aisle to deliver the matching rings? But there's none of that. Just Andrea and Ron promising to love each other.

I slip up the side of the room to the altar, feeling horribly self-conscious knowing that Runner Man could be watching me – and having a good chuckle to himself about me snagging my privates on the fence and bizarrely asking him if he wanted to buy my piano.

A blush creeps into my cheeks at the memory.

Mind you, it's him who should be ashamed of himself, turning up at a wedding dressed in scruffy jeans and T-shirt. If I were the bride, I'd feel quite insulted. At least he's no longer attempting to muscle in on my patch by posing as the *un*official photographer! I suppose I should be thankful for that, at least . . .

I'm suddenly aware of Mallory gesticulating to me on the other side of the altar.

Oh, shit!

I dart forward and manage to snap the 'I do' kiss just in time. And as Ron and Andrea break apart and share a joke, I keep on snapping, to make up for the fact that I almost missed the main event.

I'm hot and sweaty all of a sudden. And annoyed with myself. I *never* lose concentration like that.

Taking a deep breath, I force myself to focus on the task in hand.

Andrea and Ron move to the little table in the corner, and as the guests chat amongst themselves, I take shots of the happy couple signing the register.

I'm so busy, at first I don't notice that the light falling on my subjects has altered slightly. When I turn, I see that the hotel manager has swished back the curtain and is now opening the patio doors. Then she turns with a smile towards . . . Runner Man!

I stare in stunned disbelief.

He's walking out onto the terrace and nabbing the shot I wanted!

What the hell's going on?

She wouldn't open the doors for me. So how come *he* gets preferential treatment?

I'm tempted to walk away in disgust but that would be shooting myself in the foot, so I make sure I get out there and take *even more* shots from the terrace than Runner Man does. Ha! That will show *him* . . .

'The light's great from out here,' he has the nerve to point out.

I smile stiffly and check out his camera.

Expensive.

He's obviously one of those amateurs who thinks buying the best equipment will make him an expert in no time.

I take a few more shots of them signing the register, then walk to the back of the room in order to take the all-important shots of Ron and Andrea walking back down the aisle together.

Mallory sidles up and says, 'What's up?'

My frown deepens. '*Him.*'

She grins. 'But all he's done is take a few photographs. In common with about ninety-nine per cent of the other guests in the room.'

'Yes, but how come *he* gets the shot *I* wanted?' I snap. 'I *hate* bloody amateur photographers at weddings!'

She gives me a puzzled look and I know what she's thinking. Normally I'm fairly gracious and understanding of happy snappers at weddings. It's just most of them don't rub me up the wrong way like Runner Man.

I move to the centre of the aisle, ready for the perfect shot. And Runner Man finally stops flirting with the manager, making her giggle like a silly schoolgirl, and goes back to his seat.

Who is he anyway? Probably a friend of Ron's. This often happens. The bride and groom start to worry the professional photographer might cock it up, so they appoint a friend or relative to take back-up photos. *Just in case.*

Andrea and Ron are walking happily back down the aisle towards me.

And then – *oh, here we go!* – Runner Man is back on his feet, snapping away, totally blocking my view.

Probably sensing my daggers look, he turns a brief apologetic glance my way. And I might have forgiven him had it not been for *The Hand.*

The Hand is held aloft, in my direction, and says, very firmly: *Hold it just a minute, please. This is important. Your little snaps will have to wait.*

I'm fuming.

Honestly, who the hell does he think he is? Doesn't he realise I'm the official photographer and there's an etiquette to this sort of thing?

I'm so mad, I feel like marching right over there and wrestling him to the ground. Not that I'd win the bout. Those tree-trunk denim legs are so solidly planted, it would take a force ten gale to shake them. Not that I've been ogling them, you understand.

I'm starting to really panic now that I won't get the shot.

Blissfully unaware, the happy couple are walking back down the aisle to 'God Only Knows'. I can think of a different version. God Only Knows why Runner Man is acting like a self-important tit!

Then – Hallelujah! – he has a brief word with Andrea and Ron, obviously about me because they all look over. Then he steps back and summons me forward as if he's the one in charge here.

I suppose I'm meant to be grateful to him now for letting me do my job! Gritting my teeth, I paste on a cheery smile and start clicking as they pause happily in the aisle for my benefit before moving on, no doubt relieved to have made it to the pre-lunch drinks stage.

I'm just checking a photo in the viewfinder, when a deep voice says, 'The name's Gabe.'

I look up. It's Runner Man, holding out his hand. The very one he used to stop me in my tracks earlier.

He has long fingers, lightly tanned, and clean, manicured nails.

Still simmering with resentment, I shake the hand and say pointedly, 'I'm Katy. The *official* photographer.'

As soon as I've said it, I wish I hadn't. It sounds so petty. And it must be perfectly obvious that's what I am.

'I know.' He looks a little sheepish. 'Sorry for encroaching on your patch. Force of habit, I'm afraid.'

His apology takes the wind right out of my sails. He does actually look genuinely sorry.

'I managed to get the photos I wanted,' I say, thawing slightly. 'That's the main thing.'

He stifles a yawn. 'Sorry. Jet lag.' Then he smiles, his eyes crinkling rather attractively at the corners. 'Nice of you to take it so well.'

I shrug. 'Everyone takes photos at weddings.'

'Yes, but they don't all accidentally compromise the job of the professional.' He smiles ruefully. 'Andrea asked me to take a few snaps and I couldn't say no.'

Ha! It's just as I thought, then. Gabe is the back-up. *Just in case.*

I glance at him curiously. 'Have you known Andrea long?' *Old girlfriend, maybe?*

'All my life. She's my cousin.'

'Oh.' Mentally, I size them up. There's definitely a physical similarity. Thick, dark hair, almost black, although I'm sure Andrea's gets a little glossy help with that. Strong, handsome features. Nose a little too prominent. And they're both really tall.

A piper starts up in the background.

Gabe winces. 'Am I alone in thinking bagpipes should be banned in all public places? Sounds like a spooked bloody cat.'

'I quite like them, actually. I think they add a touch of ceremony to the occasion.'

'They add a touch of something, that's for sure,' he remarks dryly. He points at the door. 'I think you'd better go.'

'Sorry?' I frown up at him. *Is he trying to get rid of me?*

He laughs. 'You don't want to risk missing *the* shot of the day.'

Turning, I find to my horror that all the guests have disappeared. 'Oh bugger, right. See you!'

I hurry out, face burning, wondering what the hell is happening to me today. I'm not usually so disorganised. So thrown off course. I blame my sister.

The next half hour is spent mingling with the colourful array of 'celebrity' guests at the pre-reception drinks stage, and putting them at ease so I can help them shine in a series of natural shots. That's the theory anyway. It isn't always the easiest thing to do. In my experience, not many of us – apart from trained models, obviously – find it easy to relax in front of the camera. And a lot of people consider themselves to be horribly unphotogenic. They've seen so many unflattering pictures of themselves over the years that they tend to assume that's how they're going to look in my photos. It's part of my job to get their true personality to shine through and produce a great shot.

I'm relieved Gabe hasn't yet appeared to put me off my stride. For some reason, he makes me feel really self-conscious and I want to feel relaxed so I can get the best out of my subjects.

The fact that most people have entered into the spirit of the 'Kim & Kanye Wedding Extravaganza' has added a huge sense of fun and frivolity to the day. Even as I'm taking a photograph of a man in a plain white T-shirt that's straining ever so slightly over his belly and the most high-waisted trousers I've ever seen, another interesting sight enters the room.

It's actually worth putting the camera down for. A long, six-foot orange oblong, with a rectangular opening near the top for a face and holes for arms and legs. The colourful and rather restricted guest has a quick look around the room then retreats back into the corridor.

'Who on earth is he supposed to be?' I murmur. 'A giant carrot?'

The man in the embarrassing trousers, who's obviously meant to be Simon Cowell, grins and nods his head over my shoulder. 'He's with him over there.'

I turn to see. A man in a braided navy uniform, with huge white whiskers and a stuffed parrot on his shoulder, is deep in conversation with the younger and more shapely of the Marilyn Monroes.

'Captain Birdseye?' Light dawns and I point into the corridor. 'Oh, and a fish finger!'

Simon Cowell winks. 'Cod it in one!'

I groan and head over in the direction of Captain Birdseye himself to ask him if he wouldn't mind . . .

These are certainly going to be one of my more interesting sets of wedding photos.

Obviously, there are a lot of shots that will be instantly discarded – including the one of Ron leering down the cleavage of a leggy blonde in glamorous cream chiffon, who I guess is supposed to be Dolly Parton. He's clearly been on the champagne since breakfast and seems to be growing louder by the second.

Right on cue, across the room Ron bellows with laughter and prods the Queen he's talking to with such enthusiasm, I'm amazed she manages to remain upright. At least he's a happy drunk. I catch Andrea's glance from the other side of the room. Not too sure *she's* terribly happy, though.

I've just nipped out of the room to change the batteries in my camera, fumbling in my bag for a coin to open the back-up battery slot, when someone says, 'Problems?'

I turn. And come face to face with the man-sized fish finger himself.

'Batteries.' I return his smile. All that's visible is his eyes. 'Have you lost your friend? He's in there.'

'Captain Birdseye? That's my brother, George.' He grins. I can tell that because his rather nice grey eyes crinkle up slightly. 'This was his idea,' he adds, 'and I think I got the raw end of the deal.'

'It can't be very comfortable in there.'

'It's a new experience, that's for sure. I was actually wanting George's help adjusting my T-shirt. It's riding up at the back and I can't get to it without taking the whole bloody contraption off.'

Automatically, I find myself saying, 'Oh. Would you like me to . . . ?' I tail off awkwardly. *No, of course he wouldn't! And anyway, how would I get in there? That fishy costume looks pretty impenetrable.*

'Nice of you, but no. I'm a bit hot under this mountain of polyster and I wouldn't want to subject you to that.' His eyes crinkle up again. 'So how long have you been a photographer?'

'Since I left college. Many moons ago.'

He smiles. 'Can't be *that* many moons. You're no older than me and this is only my second year in the business.'

'Oh? How old are you, then?'

'Twenty-four.'

I laugh. 'Then I'm *considerably* older, believe me. So you're a photographer, too?'

82

'I like to think so.' He grins. 'I was looking for you so I could introduce myself. But then the T-shirt rode up and I chickened out.'

'Haddock costume malfunction, did you?'

He groans. 'Salmon get me out of here. Her jokes are rubbish.'

We chortle for a moment at our great wit.

'Not much opportunity for networking dressed like this, though,' he says at last. 'I'm Harry, by the way.'

'Katy.' We shake hands. Then over his shoulder, I spot my arch rival in his scruffy jacket and denims, walking our way.

'I won't offer to take your photo,' Gabe says to me with a rueful smile as he passes us, on his way in to the party. 'Hi, Harry. Talk to you later?'

'Yeah. Great.' Harry grins at me. 'I'm Ron's nephew, in case you're wondering how I got my invitation.'

I nod. 'And that's how you know *him*?' I ask, watching Gabe stroll confidently into the room.

He laughs. 'Yeah. Amazing, isn't it? I'm actually sort of related to him by marriage now. I only met him today.'

I stare at Harry curiously.

Why it should be so amazing to find yourself related to Gabe, I really can't imagine. Each to his own, I suppose.

Without warning, the bagpipes start up with a great wail of noise, making me flinch, and Harry has to raise his voice to be heard. 'Is it your own business?'

I nod and he shouts, 'I'd like that some day. But for now, I just want to learn as much as I can on the job.' He nods at the piper, who's just visible through the doorway, blowing his lungs out. 'Great sound.'

I can see Gabe, lounging against the wall with his camera slung round his neck. He's chatting to a tall blonde, who's laughing herself hoarse and grasping his arm. I snort. I really can't believe his jokes are *that* funny. 'Not everyone would agree with you,' I comment sourly. 'I have heard bagpipe music described as sounding like a spooked cat.'

Harry frowns and follows my gaze. 'Well, whoever said that has no taste in music whatsoever. Personally, I think a piper is perfect at these events. Adds a sense of occasion to the whole thing, don't you think?'

I glance at him in pleased surprise. 'Yes. That's exactly what I think.'

EIGHT

I can't believe I'm standing here, having a serious conversation.

With a fish finger.

Mallory arrives. 'Oh, there you are! Shall I start gathering everyone outside for the group shots?'

She grins at Harry and I give her a thumbs-up.

'Yep, I'm just coming. This is Harry, by the way. Harry, this is Mallory, my assistant. You've got something in common,' I tell them, as they shake hands.

'We both like rolling around in a nice, crispy crumb?' hazards Harry.

Mallory giggles. 'No, we're both in love with the lovely Captain Birdseye.'

'*Cap'n* Birdseye, please,' says Harry in a terrible Cornish accent.

'Ha-ha. No, I meant you're both good photographers.'

Mallory flicks her hair back. 'I'm not sure "good" is the right word. "Passable" maybe.' She grins. 'My favourite saying is *I'll fix it in Photoshop*!'

Harry laughs. 'Thank God for computer software, eh?' he says, winking at me.

I smile back, wondering idly what he looks like when he's not being a fish finger.

We spend the next hour focusing on the bridal group shots, which I've decided to take on the lawn in front of the hotel.

Mallory does her usual great job, seeking out aunts and uncles, and prising from the bar friends of the bride and groom – whoever is needed, in fact, for the next photo on my list. It would take three times as long if I didn't have Mallory rounding everyone up efficiently but with unfailing charm.

The reception is due to kick off at one o'clock, which means I'm rushing to get this round of group shots finished super-fast. But Ron, who has a drink permanently welded to his hand, is proving hard to manage. He keeps interrupting the line-up to chat loudly to his best man and I spot Andrea holding onto his jacket sleeve to stop him wandering away. Then when I call out to him to focus on me, he looks around as if he has no idea where the voice is coming from.

'Ah, isn't it lovely?' sighs Mallory in my ear at one point.

'What?'

'Finding that one special person you want to annoy the hell out of for the rest of your life.'

I laugh. 'Does Andrea know what she's letting herself in for?'

Mallory shrugs. 'Well, he's not a bad man, is he? He just likes a wee drinkie. And he must be worth a bob or two—'

'Mallory!' I can't help feeling shocked when she says things like this.

'Listen, darling, answer me this. Penniless or comfortably orf? Your choice.'

I don't answer because it's obvious.

'There, you see. So if a groom is wealthy, it has to be better than if he's not. That's all I'm saying.'

'And love?'

Mallory nods. 'Well, that's nice, of course. But it's certainly not the be all and end all.'

'So where does poor Rupert stand in all of this?' I ask innocently, but she just laughs and shakes her head at me.

At last all the shots on my list are done, apart from the giant group photo – of all one hundred wedding guests – that we've agreed will be taken from a tiny first-floor balcony. Mallory sails around, gathering everyone up, but I suddenly realise we're missing a family member.

Gabe.

I spotted him snapping a group of kids over by the big oak tree. The one I'd earmarked as a background for some intimate shots of the bride and groom later. I glance over. He's still there.

I've had some bad experiences in the past with brides upset because someone vital has been missed off their photos. I really don't want that happening today. So as Mallory assembles the group, I slip over the grass to fetch Mr Snap Happy.

He's got the kids sitting along a branch for the photo. It's fairly low to the ground but some of the kids are quite small.

'Are you sure you should be letting them climb trees?' I ask. 'I'm pretty certain that's against hotel regulations.'

He turns from where he's crouched down on one knee on the grass and studies me calmly. 'It's only out of bounds if you get caught.'

I raise one disapproving eyebrow, while feeling a prickle of irritation that he got there before me. The kids lined up along the branch will make a great shot.

He laughs. It's a deep, rich sound, loud enough to disturb two blackbirds, which rise up squawking from the tree. 'Do you always abide by the rules, then?'

'I find it helps when I'm doing my job.' Even to my own ears, I sound horribly prim. 'You're needed for the group photo.'

He nods. 'Just let me get this and I'll be over.'

Turning back to the children, he encourages them cheerfully. 'Right. Big smiles. Come on, that includes you, Jack!'

They say you should never work with kids or animals. And I know from experience how hard it can be sometimes to persuade children to perform when you want them to. But over the years,

I've learned a few tricks. I'd better help out – otherwise, at this rate, by the time I get him over for the group photo, the bloody sun will have set . . .

So I lean down and murmur, 'Try saying, "Right, I want everyone to smile, *except Jack*!" Works every time.'

Gabe gives me an odd look. Then he shrugs. 'Okay, let's give it a go.'

Of course, it works beautifully, as I knew it would.

He springs to his feet, towering over me. 'Hey, thanks.' He looks impressed. 'You know what you're talking about.'

'I should do.' I smile modestly. 'I've been in the business for years.'

He nods. 'Any more tips? I'm always keen to learn.'

He's smiling broadly and for just a second, I wonder if he's joking with me. But he's looking at me intently, with those piercing blue eyes, as if he's genuinely waiting for more pearls of wisdom.

So I shrug and say, 'Tuck your elbows in. If you do that, your camera will be more stable. Oh, and make sure you don't cut off their feet. That's a common mistake.'

'What about their heads?'

Now he *is* kidding. Isn't he?

I laugh and say, 'Well, yes, that just happens to be another no-no.'

He gets the kids ready for another snap.

'Tell them to shout "purple pizza" instead of cheese. Their smiles will be much more natural,' I suggest, and he sticks his thumb in the air.

Someone calls my name and I turn to see Mallory flitting over the grass. 'We're all ready.'

The kids shout 'purple pizza' and Gabe clicks away. Then he springs to his feet and gives Mallory the benefit of his pearly whites. 'My fault for keeping her. I was getting some tips.'

Mallory looks from Gabe to me and back again with an odd

little smile. Then she shakes his hand. 'Hi. Pleased to meet you. She's awfully good, isn't she?'

He nods and says solemnly, 'Very professional.'

I shoot him a suspicious look, still getting the feeling he's somehow having a joke at my expense.

'Well, *he's* rather nice,' says Mallory, in a tone loaded with meaning, as we walk back to join the group.

'Not always,' I snap. 'He can be a real pain in the butt with that camera of his.'

Mallory laughs.

'What?' I demand.

'You don't know, do you?'

I stare at her in confusion. '*What* don't I know?'

She turns to look at Gabe. 'I thought I recognised him from somewhere and it's just clicked. He's that—'

I dig her sharply in the ribs. '*Don't look!* He'll know we're talking about him.'

'Okay, darling, keep your wig on. Anyone would think you cared.'

I quicken my step and leave her behind as colour flares in my cheeks.

There are some days you wish you'd never got out of bed. And this is definitely one of those.

A few minutes later, when I go out onto the tiny balcony to get my group shot, my eye is drawn immediately to Gabe – but only because he towers over everyone else in the back row. He's chatting to that blonde woman again. Honestly, her laugh is so shrill, it's a wonder her champagne glass hasn't shattered.

After I've taken enough shots, I call out my thanks to everyone and I'm about to suggest they make their way to the reception when the bagpipes scream into action from somewhere below me and I almost drop my camera over the balcony wall. It actually wobbles horribly for a moment in my hands, as if I'm watching in slow-motion, and I feel my stomach plummet. I manage to grab it. But the shock washes a wave of dizziness over me and I have to lean back against the doorjamb and close my eyes.

I have a vision of my precious camera flying through the air and smashing into pieces on the gravel below. It makes me feel quite nauseous, thinking how much it would cost to replace it. A pain is beating at my temples.

But there are photographs to be taken so I pull myself together and head downstairs, where Mallory and I gather everyone on the hotel's beautiful solid oak staircase for one last group shot.

When the guests start drifting through to the reception, I'm there in a flash. Andrea will never forgive me if I don't get shots of all the guests in their costumes (and in many cases, wigs) as they line up to congratulate the new Mr and Mrs Hargreaves.

'You'll be pleased to hear I've put the camera down,' says a voice at my shoulder, and turning, I find myself staring up at Gabe. He looks more relaxed now. Maybe he's getting over his jet lag.

I give him an arch look, hoping my silence says it all.

'Do you just do weddings?' he asks, waiting for the woman in front of him in the line – Cher, as it happens – to stop shrieking with delight over Andrea's new wedding ring.

I nod, clicking away. 'For now.'

'Interesting.'

I shoot him a look. What does he mean, *interesting*? Why does it feel like a criticism?

Not that I *care* what he thinks.

'Come on, move it along there, Mr Harlin,' jokes Ron, raising his glass and depositing some of it on the floor. 'Our lovely Katy is not impressed by celebrities.'

I stare up at him, confused. *Celebrities?* How much has Ron had to drink? He's not making much sense.

Gabe laughs. 'I'm not terribly impressed myself.' He winks at me. 'Make sure you get my best side,' he quips, before kissing Andrea on both cheeks and strolling in to the reception.

I glower at his bum in the scruffy jeans.

Suddenly realising I've missed a few vital shots – including Andrea's best friend hugging her in the line-up – I rush to catch up. But I can't help speculating on the celebrity tag. He certainly doesn't look familiar to me. And let's face it, with his height and brooding dark looks, he's not exactly the sort of celebrity you'd forget in a hurry. He's probably a bit-part actor. Or a musician in a band no one's heard of.

Once everyone has eaten their prawn cocktail and spring lamb, and the speeches have been done, Mallory and I retreat for a quick break to a quiet corner of the hotel lounge. She lies back in her plush chair with a little sigh of happiness and studies the ornate mosaic-patterned ceiling, while I start flicking through the bank of photos on my camera, already mentally picking out my favourites for the album.

'Do you *ever* take a moment off?' sighs Mallory.

I smile grimly. 'No. Because every moment counts.'

A waiter approaches our table and Mallory orders herself a gin and lime then raises her eyebrows at me.

'Water, please. Still.'

'Oh, have a cocktail, darling,' she says when he whisks off, between tables.

'Hey, I'm trying to make a profit, not drink it away. A cocktail in here will cost a small fortune.'

Mallory shrugs. 'So put it on your expenses.'

'I need to stay sober.' Actually, I'm really tempted. A glass of wine would slip down a treat right now. It might just help me forget all the bad stuff that's pressing down on me today, like a vice squeezing at my temples.

But no, I'll stick with water.

'By the way,' says Mallory. 'I meant to say. That man you apparently injured? Gabe?'

'Yes?'

'You've really got it in for the poor guy, haven't you?'

91

I feel myself redden. 'No.'

'Just because he happened to get in the way of one of your photos. It's not like you to get so uptight, darling. What's wrong?'

I shake my head.

She sits forward. 'Come on. Tell your Auntie Mal.'

So I do. I explain about Mum's phone call this morning and how it's totally knocked me off balance.

Mallory listens anxiously. Then she reaches for my hand and squeezes it. 'It'll be fine, you know. It will. It's high time you two made peace.'

I force a smile and rise to my feet. She hasn't got a clue. But why would she? I've never told her the grim details of what happened. 'That drink sounds like a good idea.'

I head for the bar, but at the last moment, think better of it and swerve off towards the Ladies. However helpful a drink might be in calming my nerves, I don't want to start down that slippery slope. Not while I'm working. And besides, it would only make my headache worse.

As I push open the door, my phone pings. A message. Probably Mum wanting to know how the wedding's going. I open it up.

Avoiding my calls won't make the problem go away. I want my money back. Make sure you have it ready for when I come round to collect it. Dominic.

A shock, almost like an actual physical punch, slams through me.

I stand at one of the sinks, my whole body trembling, staring at my stricken white face in the mirror.

Oh, God, no!

Dominic at my door?

Demanding money I don't even have?

I'm not in a position to pay him back. Not immediately, which is what he wants. I only have a few hundred in the bank – and even that's about to be swallowed up by the monthly mortgage payment.

Dominic loaned me some money to do up my house when I

92

first moved in. I didn't feel right about taking it. I'd heard all the stories about relationships gone sour over money. But he laughed and said I was far too cautious for my own good. We were madly in love then and I remember him saying, 'What's mine is yours,' and hinting that pretty soon we'd be living together anyway. In the end, I told him I'd borrow the money – but that I'd start paying it back immediately, a regular amount each month. And that's what I've been doing ever since, slowly eating away at the debt and looking forward to the day when it will all be paid back.

My eventual break-up with Dominic, six months after I moved into my house, was horrendous and I cut off all contact immediately. But naturally, I kept up my monthly loan repayment to him. I suppose I'd assumed that in a year or so, I'd have paid it all back and that would be that. The end of a not-so-beautiful friendship . . .

But then, just before Christmas, I bumped into him outside the post office. He acted all friendly, wanting to know how I was and telling me how much he regretted what had happened between us.

I just wanted to get away. Dominic was history. I had no desire to stand there making polite conversation. When he suggested going for a drink to chat over old times, I couldn't believe what I was hearing. I told him I was too busy with work for a social life and walked away, my heart hammering unpleasantly.

The following week, he phoned late one night. All pretence at friendliness had gone. His tone, as he informed me he was calling in the debt, was cold and distant. I knew Dominic of old. When I snubbed him in the village, I'd dented his pride. Now, he was out for revenge . . .

Immediately, I started planning how I could get the money together. It was a few thousand pounds, which might not seem a great deal to some people – but to me it's a small fortune.

It broke my heart to think of selling the house. But I knew enough about Dominic's personality to know that he wouldn't let up on the pressure until he had his money back. I was really worried what lengths he would go to if I didn't pay him back quickly.

I thought if I put the house on the market, he would see that I was serious about paying him back – and maybe, just maybe, he'd give me time to get the funds together.

In the meantime, I started selling stuff online. Items of furniture. Bric-a-brac that I didn't want but other people did. Good clothes from the days when I worked in London.

The piano, which I'd been wanting to get rid of for ages anyway, was the first thing to go. I put the money I made from my sales straight into Dominic's account. But it wasn't enough.

When he phoned for the second time, a couple of weeks ago, he made it clear he wasn't waiting and expected the entire sum I owed him in his account within a fortnight. I asked him why he needed it, thinking maybe he was in trouble. But he laughed and asked me what business it was of mine what he spent his money on.

When Dominic and I were together, I'd seen how he would hold a grudge for ages, unable to see the other person's point of view and let things go. He'd stubbornly refuse to see sense, whatever I said. And now he had a grudge against me, and I knew I wouldn't be free of him until I'd paid back every penny.

Sagging over the washbasin, I stare at the gold-coloured taps, wishing I had the money to pay him back right now and be done with it.

A little spurt of anger rises up in me. I'm paying back the debt as fast as I possibly can. Barring robbing a bank, there's nothing else I can do. And Dominic knows that. Why should I allow him to terrorise me? I have a job to do right now and I can't let him get in the way of that.

But just as I'm making for the door, a sound – like a hiccup – catches my attention.

I freeze and there it is again. Except it isn't a hiccup. It's a full-blown sob. Someone breaking their heart in one of the cubicles.

'Hello?' I call, a little timidly, all my worries forgotten. 'Are you all right in there?'

There's a brief silence, then the rattle of the loo roll and the sound of someone blowing their nose.

I wait uncertainly. Perhaps whoever it is would prefer me to go away. But next second, the bolt is drawn. And out comes Andrea.

'Oh my God, what's wrong?' I gasp.

She stands there, in her beautiful Kim Kardashian rip-off gown, mascara tracks down her cheeks, unable to speak for a second. A far cry from the perfect, composed woman of earlier. Then she sits down carefully in the pink chair, puts her face in her hands and gives in to a strangled sob.

'Hey, hey, it's okay.' I crouch down beside her and lay my hand on her back. 'What on earth's happened? Is it Ron?'

The sobbing intensifies and I flick my eyes to the ceiling. *Oh great, what's he done?*

NINE

I hold Andrea's hand as she cries some more. Then I dig out a clean paper hanky and she gets herself under control. Finally, she looks up at me with mournful eyes, her make-up a complete train wreck, and whispers, 'Ron hasn't done anything. It's me. I'm just not good enough for him.'

I almost laugh, it's so not what I expected. I stare at her, wondering how I'm going to word this. 'I can't believe you think that,' I tell her at last.

'But it's true,' she wails. 'Ron's handsome and funny. And he's so *clever*. I'm just a total thicko by comparison.'

'Hey, don't be silly,' I soothe. 'Of course you're not. Ron thinks the world of you.'

'But he's far more cleverer than me. I mean, how can I talk about what's happening in foreign countries? I don't even know the capital of Spain.' She looks up, her brow knitted. 'Actually, I think I do.' She clutches my arm. 'It's Benidorm, isn't it?'

'Erm, well, you're *close*,' I say encouragingly. It's true. Benidorm isn't *that* far from Madrid . . .

'So it's *not* Benidorm?' She looks so utterly crestfallen, my heart goes out to her.

I put my arm round her. 'Well, if it isn't, it bloody well *should* be,' I say firmly. 'Andrea, you're beautiful and kind and great company. And best of all, people really warm to you. Who cares whether you can do complicated sums in your head or pontificate on the situation in the Middle East?'

'Ponty-what?' She looks up, startled.

I shake my head and give her arm a squeeze. 'You're a lovely person and that's what counts. That's *all* that counts, actually.'

She still looks uncertain but at least she's stopped breaking her heart.

'What brought this on, anyway?' I ask gently.

She sniffs loudly. 'He's been drinking way too much lately, but I've been putting it down to the stress of organising the wedding. I never thought he'd get drunk today, though, so I told him off and he got all huffy with me.'

She pauses and blows her nose hard.

'Then he heard me talking to my friend, Jackie, about Ryan Gosling and how fit he is. Well, honestly, you'd think I'd said I was going to divorce him and marry Ryan instead! He got all shirty and started going on about his own fitness and did I want him to climb that tree outside the main entrance to prove he wasn't completely over the hill. So I laughed and told him not to be so ridiculous and that he wouldn't even reach the lowest branch, especially after the amount of alcohol he'd got through. At which point, he shouted, "Christ, I think a man's *entitled* to have a drink on his wedding day when he's just married the world's biggest bloody nag!" And he stormed off to the bar.'

I shake my head. 'Men.'

She nods and gives a giant sniff. 'But I feel terrible now. I shouldn't have attacked his manhood like that.' She gives a giggle that could be a sob. 'Not that I kicked him in the goolies or anything. I just meant—'

'I know what you meant. You dented his pride, questioning his tree-climbing fitness.'

She covers her face with her hands. 'I always thought it was too good to be true when Ron chose me,' she moans, her voice muffled. She looks up at me, her eyes brimming with tears all over again. 'Oh Katy, what if he's having regrets about marrying me?'

'Of course he won't be.' I hand her a clean tissue. 'Andrea, for what it's worth, I think *Ron's* the lucky one here. He fell on his feet when you agreed to marry him. And I'm sure I'm not the only one to think that.'

'Really?'

I nod firmly. 'Absolutely.'

She thinks about this then she gives me a watery smile.

'Now, how about we repair that make-up and get you back out there? Otherwise Ron might think you've done a runner.'

'Thank you, Katy.' She honks into her tissue. 'Thank you so much.'

'Hey, you're welcome.'

'You might have just saved my marriage. Maybe I can return the favour one day.'

'Maybe you can,' I murmur.

'And here's an *actual* favour to be going on with,' she says, digging in her little cream satin tote. She pulls out a pink chiffon drawstring bag and hands it to me with a shy smile. 'Sugared almonds.'

'Ooh, lovely, thank you.' I can't stand the things, but that's beside the point.

'A *favour* while you're waiting for the *real favour*,' she exclaims, delighted by her own wit.

I laugh with her and we set about dabbing and reapplying, to rescue her make-up.

When we're satisfied, I take her hand and say solemnly, 'You ready, Mrs Hargreaves?'

She smiles. 'I'm ready.'

'Good. And just remember that man of yours is *very* lucky to have you.'

She laughs and tosses her head. 'He is, isn't he? Right, wish me luck.'

I watch her go, with a sort of motherly pride.

Mallory is waiting for me in the lounge. 'Can we go now and grab a sandwich? I'm absolutely starving.'

'Yes, sure. I just need to check something, then we can be off.'

'Super. I'll meet you out at my car.'

Mallory heads for the main hotel entrance, while I go back through to the reception room to make sure Andrea has made up with Ron.

But while Andrea is sitting in her chair at the top table, chatting to her mum, Ron's nowhere to be seen. I'm just about to go in search of him when a member of the bar staff comes up to me and says, 'Excuse me but we're having a bit of a problem with one of the guests. Kanye West is stuck up a tree.'

'Oh, no,' I groan, a vision flying into my head of Ron crashing to earth and having to be carted off to hospital.

A second later, I'm bolting out of the room and running outside. Sure enough, there's Ron, jacket thrown on the ground, endeavouring to tackle the oak tree. He's managed to get onto the first branch, where the kids sat earlier when Gabe was taking their photo. Another bar staff member is trying to coax him down. But he's staring up into the tree, apparently planning his next move.

As I watch, he reaches up and grabs onto a higher branch then swings his leg up, miraculously managing to find a foothold. But when he hauls the other leg up, he slightly loses his balance and I hold my breath as he does a terrifying wobble.

'It's against the regulations to climb that tree, sir,' shouts the barman 'helpfully'. 'Can you come down now, please?'

Ron ignores him and looks up for a higher branch.

I step forward, in front of the barman, and stare up at him. He's a good ten feet off the ground. A fall now would be nasty.

'Ron?' I call gently. 'Andrea's looking for you. She's really worried about you. It's nearly time for the first dance.'

Ron glances down. And he freezes. I can see the panic in his face.

'It's okay.' I keep my tone light. 'Just come down the way you went up.'

Agonisingly slowly, Ron makes his descent. In his inebriated state, he might as well be abseiling down The Shard. But as he's lowering himself to the bottom branch, his foot slips on the mossy bark and he loses control. He does a sort of weird roll over the branch before falling off, grabbing for me as he goes. The weight of his body cannoning into my side sends us both sprawling onto the grass.

I lie there for a moment, winded. Then someone is crouching over me asking if I'm all right.

Gabe.

God, why does it have to be *him* who finds me sprawled on the ground? (Or diving over a fence.) It's more than a little humiliating.

Helping me up, he says, 'I wondered where you'd run off to.'

I attempt a smile, feeling a little wobbly but grateful to have his arm wrapped tightly around me.

'Are you all right, Ron?' I ask, as the barman helps him stagger to his feet.

He grins over at us rather sheepishly. 'Sorry. Don't know what came over me.'

'Never mind. No bones broken,' says Gabe. 'That's the main thing.'

'Does Andrea have to know . . . ?' Ron frowns, looking thoroughly defeated. 'That woman could have anyone she wants. I don't know why she chose a stupid old duffer like me.'

I really feel for Ron. Andrea's clearly not the only one who worries she's not good enough.

'Hey, there's life in the old dog yet,' grins Gabe. 'Why don't you get back in there and make her glad she married you.'

'She doesn't need to know you didn't make it past the second branch,' I smile, trying to work out why I'm still feeling a bit dazed. It can't have been the fall. I'm not injured in the slightest. Gabe is holding me tight to his side and I can feel the heat of his skin through his shirt. I've got the oddest feeling that if he lets me go, I might just sink to the floor.

He laughs. The deep, rich sound tingles through me deliciously. 'Yeah, we'll tell Andrea you were halfway up the tree and we had to talk you down.' He leans over and pats Ron on the back, while keeping his arm clamped firmly around me.

We start walking back to the hotel.

'Hey, what about your jacket, Ron?' says Gabe suddenly, turning back for it. And letting go of me.

I watch him jog over to pick it up, feeling oddly bereft. The cold March wind is blasting at my side now that I'm no longer being sheltered by the warmth and strength of Gabe's body. It's an odd feeling. But then, this whole day has been weird – one that in many ways I'd rather forget. And it's not over yet . . .

Andrea is waiting for us by the hotel entrance and when she sees Ron, she runs over towards him, hitching up her gown, apparently not caring about her extravagant train getting covered in grass stains.

'You silly old bugger,' she laughs as he envelops her in a hug.

Gabe grins at me as we walk away, leaving them to make up for lost time. 'You do realise you missed a great photo opportunity there.'

I laugh. 'I'm not sure Ron would want his mad, tree-climbing adventure to be fixed for all eternity in the wedding album.'

He rubs his nose and pushes the door open for me. 'You've got a point. Well done, though, for rescuing their day. Your face was a picture when you raced out of the reception.'

I glance at him curiously. 'Well, thank *you* for coming out to help.'

His eyes crinkle in a disarming smile. 'No problem. See you later.'

I watch him walk away, with mixed feelings. I haven't exactly been overflowing with bonhomie towards him today, and yet he saw the concern in my face and rode to my rescue. I feel oddly humbled somehow. It's a good lesson in not judging a book by its cover.

Andrea and Ron appear, arms around each other, looking blissfully happy.

Seeing me, she rushes over.

'Thank you. *Again!*' She beams at me. 'We're okay now, thanks mainly to you.'

I shrug. 'Glad I could help. I'm just pleased you're both smiling now.'

'I saw you chatting to Gabe. I hope you didn't mind him showing up today, taking photos?' She peers at me anxiously. 'I couldn't believe it when he phoned first thing to say he'd be able to make it.'

I stare at her. I'd assumed Gabe would have received an official invitation. 'No, of course I didn't mind. But isn't he your cousin?'

She nods, her face breaking into a warm smile. 'Yes he is. I've got dozens of cousins but Gabe has always been my sneaky favourite. He was invited, of course. But we thought he'd still be in New York today.'

'In New York?' That explained the jet lag.

Now it's Andrea's turn to look puzzled. 'At Blaze Jorgensen's wedding?'

'But why would he be at Blaze Jorgensen's wedding instead of yours? Is he a friend of hers?'

'Well, no, she's a client. Or she *was* a client, before the wedding was suddenly cancelled. Gabe was booked to take the photographs.'

I stare at her. My poor, befuddled brain is having a hard job assimilating this news.

At last I find my voice. 'Wait. Gabe's a *photographer*?'

Andrea looks at me like I'm a battery short of a complete set. 'You didn't know? I thought *everyone* knew . . .'

Suddenly, it dawns on me. Ron called him 'Mr Harlin'. 'Oh God, he's *Gabe Harlin*?'

She nods. And I stare at her, open-mouthed.

I feel such a bloody idiot. Because even *I've* heard of the great Gabe Harlin. Who hasn't? He's built up quite a reputation over the past few years – ever since he staged his remarkable photographic exhibition of African tribesmen. I remember hearing about the TV documentary, following the six months he spent in Africa, living among the people he was photographing and highlighting their plight. I'd always meant to buy the DVD but never got round to it.

So yes, I'd definitely *heard* of Gabe Harlin. But I failed miserably to actually recognise him.

'He'd already been booked to do the Jorgensen job when we set the date,' Andrea is saying. 'So we thought he wouldn't be able to come. But when he realised he wasn't needed after all, he got on a plane and came straight here to catch our wedding instead.'

Heat rushes into my cheeks. My face must be an absolute picture.

Frantically, I race back over our conversations. It really can't be that bad.

But seemingly it is.

I groan silently. He might have *told* me who he was. I try to ignore the little voice in my head currently insinuating that in my hellishly snippy mood, I actually didn't give him much of a chance to reveal himself . . .

But oh God, I should have *known*. How utterly bloody mortifying.

Mind you, thinking about it, Mallory struggled to place him too. Not that this makes me feel vindicated in the slightest.

'You didn't know he was coming, did you?' says Andrea, clearly misreading my agonised expression. 'I meant to tell you first thing, but then it completely slipped my mind what with everything else that was going on . . .' A shadow crosses her face and we exchange a sheepish look, remembering her crisis in the Ladies earlier.

I sigh feebly, too weak with shame to even formulate a sentence.

Today will haunt me for ages to come. I can feel it in my water.

The great Gabe Harlin, creative genius and world-renowned humanitarian, was taking photos at the wedding today. And did I approach him with the respect he so obviously deserves? Did I study him at work, in the hope of absorbing something meaningful that would emerge in my own creative output? Did I perhaps try to seek out a little friendly advice about my own career in the business?

Er, none of the above.

I actually told him how to hold his camera properly.

And how to avoid cutting people's heads and legs off.

Brilliant . . .

TEN

I wake next morning to a heart-stopping crash from downstairs.

Heart pounding, I sit up, clutching the duvet around me. Then I hear a cheerful whistle outside my window and the repeated click of someone attempting to shut my broken gate.

Postman.

I collapse back against the pillows with relief.

Then I remember my humiliation of the day before and let out an anguished groan.

I can't believe I failed to recognise Gabe Harlin. Among all the bloody 'famous' people at the Kim and Kanye wedding, he was actually the only one who'd be recognised in the street. And there I was, blithely passing on handy photography tips to the master himself.

I want to crawl back under the covers and never come out.

Oh, God! He must have thought I was a total moron. Being a photographer myself, yet completely missing the true expert in our midst!

My temples, already delicate after yesterday's chaos, start to pulse painfully at the memory. Oh well, I suppose I'm unlikely to ever bump into him again.

I smile grimly. Unless he happens to be pounding the pavement past my gate, of course. Then it's a distinct possibility.

I think of Andrea and Ron, waking up as man and wife in the bridal suite of the Greshingham Hotel. I'm probably not the only one with a headache. I briefly wonder if Ron's escapade up the tree will come up over their full English.

The morning is spent trying to catch up with paperwork, aided by large quantities of own-brand instant coffee. (I feel the usual pang of regret, remembering my much-loved coffee machine, which is now living with a very nice Welsh couple in Guildford. Much like a pet, I couldn't have let it go if I'd thought they might mistreat it, which could have led to a rather awkward doorstep encounter.)

Despite the caffeine, my concentration is poor.

Snippets from the day before keep rising up and interrupting my train of thought. Well, one snippet in particular. Every time I think about my 'helpful' advice to Gabe Harlin, I just want to dig up a floorboard and slide right under.

My shame does serve one useful function. I'm so busy blushing over that hideousness, that there's barely any headspace left to worry about Sienna's imminent return. In any case, I've already made up my mind that if my sister calls me or has the temerity to come to the house, I will refuse to speak to her.

All the same, when the house phone rings five minutes later, I almost jump into next week.

'Good morning,' says a man's voice. 'I'm conducting a survey and I'd like to ask your opinion on fish?'

My heart sinks. Great, a marketing call. Just what I need holding me up when I've got so much work to get through.

'I'm not a great fish eater, to be honest with you,' I say, hoping he'll strike me off his list and move on to the next call.

'What about fish fingers?'

'Nope. Can't stand the things.'

'Not even fish fingers in a nice, crispy crumb?'

I stare at the phone. Weird. But I suppose he's just doing his job, reading from a script.

Then, to my surprise, he laughs. 'Don't you recognise the voice, then?'

'Give me a clue.'

'Sweaty orange man-made fibre and a fondness for an old sea cap'n?'

The light goes on. 'You're that fish finger at the wedding! Harry, isn't it?'

'The very same. I got your number from Uncle Ron. I hope you don't mind. He wasn't going to give it to me, but I said my mate was getting married and needed a photographer.'

I laugh. 'Very enterprising. I take it your mate's not really getting married?'

'Sorry, no. But I'll definitely recommend you when he does.'

'Well, thank you.'

'So I hear you live in Willows Edge?'

'Yes. Just up the road from your uncle, actually. It's the house with the milestone in the garden.'

'Oh, yeah. I know it. By the way, I'm very glad you survived Uncle Ron crashing out of the tree and landing on top of you.'

I laugh. 'Well, it wasn't quite that dramatic. How did you find out?'

'Oh, *everyone* knows. The bar staff were all talking about it. Ron's quite famous apparently. They've never had a groom behave so disgracefully.'

I laugh. 'Good old Ron.'

'Gabe said you were brilliant talking him down, as it were.'

Colour floods into my cheeks. 'He did?'

'Oh, yes. I had quite a long chat with him later. Andrea knew he was looking for an assistant so when he turned up at the wedding, she suggested I talk to him. He's a really cool guy and he seemed interested in what I'd done so far.'

'Did he ask to see your work?'

Harry laughs. 'He did. And I'd taken my portfolio along in the car, just in case.'

'Wow, good for you.' Privately, I can't help but think Gabe Harlin is the very last person I'd like as my boss. Those intense blue eyes can be so full of warmth one minute, stormy as the North Sea in winter the next. But maybe Harry will cope. 'So do you think you're in with a chance?'

'I think so. He wants to arrange a more formal interview.'

'Fantastic.'

Something clicks in my head. Of course. That's why Harry, a photographer himself, was so amazed at finding himself related to Gabe by marriage. I couldn't understand it at the time, but it all makes sense now.

I groan inwardly, not relishing being reminded of my huge faux pas with Gabe the day before.

There's a pause.

Then Harry says, 'Actually, I was really phoning to ask if you'd like to continue our photographic discussion over a meal?'

'Oh. Right. Gosh.' I suddenly realise I'm being asked out. By a man who seems very nice. Last time I saw him he was dressed as dinner, but I can at least recall his lovely, smiley grey eyes, which is a good start.

True to form, though, I immediately start assembling reasons why I can't possibly go out with him.

Over the past few years, I've constructed a sort of invisible force field around me to keep men away. This makes me sound like I'm a latter-day Pied Piper of Hamlin, dancing tunefully through life with a posse of hopeful men trailing in my wake. Which is obviously far from the truth. But on occasion, at a wedding, there will be a brother or an uncle who's had a bit to drink and fancies his chances (possibly enjoying my schoolmarm way of ordering people about for the photos). They never get very far.

'We could just go out for a drink if you don't fancy dinner,' says Harry, and I suddenly realise he's nervously awaiting my answer.

I'm about to say no but I hesitate. Both Mum and Mallory are in my ear, telling me to throw caution to the wind because it's high time I had some fun.

'Dinner would be lovely, Harry,' I tell him. 'Although it can't be this week. I've got so much on.' *That's a good compromise, isn't it?*

'Great!' Harry sounds relieved. 'Fantastic! Possibly next week, then?'

I close my eyes, feeling the pressure. Then I tell myself it's no big deal. It's just a meal out in good company. And since there doesn't seem to be a shortage of conversation with Harry, it might even be fun . . .

So to my surprise, I find myself saying, 'Yes. Next week. That would be lovely.'

'Good. Right, I'd better go and return the costume. Funny, but I've gone right off fish fingers.'

I laugh. 'Beans on toast from now on?'

'Looks like it.' He pauses. 'I'll phone you about next week. Take care, Katy.'

I'm smiling as I disconnect the call.

Back at my desk in the conservatory, I stare out across the garden, at my display of daffodils beneath the hawthorn tree. It will soon be April. In a month or two, the sleeping bulbs in my little plot will have burst through the soil into a riot of colour.

I think of the hopeful note in Harry's voice as he asked me out.

Perhaps it's time for me to burst forth, too . . .

I've been invited to afternoon tea at Annabeth's, and as I drive in the main gates and head up to the main house and converted stables, I find myself appreciating afresh the little community at Clandon House. It's such a beautiful, peaceful place. Very soon, the woodlands will be richly carpeted with April bluebells.

Mum's left a note on her door telling me they're already at Annabeth's, so I take the stairs up to the first-floor apartment.

111

The door has been wedged open for me so I walk straight in.

Annabeth herself emerges from the living room and greets me with a lily-of-the-valley kiss on each cheek. She looks cool and elegant in neutral tones – well-cut linen trousers and a long-sleeved cream blouse with delicate drawstrings at the wrists.

'Come in, come in.' She ushers me through to the living room, where Grace, in a tracksuit, is sitting in the lotus position in the middle of the floor.

Annabeth shakes her head good-humouredly at her sister. 'Do you have to do that right now? We've got guests if you hadn't noticed.'

'Not guests,' says Grace firmly, moving smoothly into a downward dog position, bum stuck in the air. 'Dorothy and Katy are family.'

I smile. 'What a lovely thought.'

Grace gives me an upside down grin. 'So since you're family, could you go and put the kettle on? I'm parched.'

I laugh. 'Will do.'

But Annabeth grabs my arm. 'Dorothy's still in there with Venus.' She casts a worried look at Grace.

Grace snorts. 'I'm only glad that bloody woman's not staying for tea. I'd probably choke on my fruit scone.'

I frown. 'Has something happened?'

They exchange a look.

'Your mum will tell you,' says Annabeth lightly, which only makes me feel more anxious.

I pop my head round the kitchen door, not meaning to disturb them if they're talking. Mum is sitting at the table, her eyes cast down, and a small, dark-haired woman, who I assume is the mysterious Venus, is perched on a chair opposite, holding Mum's hands.

'It's up to you, Dorothy,' she's saying, as she gently kneads Mum's fingers. 'It's entirely your choice. But whatever you decide, I'm there for you. All the way, okay?'

Mum looks up and attempts a smile. And that's when she sees me standing there.

'Katy, love,' she exclaims, getting up and coming to give me a hug. 'Meet our friend, Venus.'

We exchange a polite smile.

'Venus, this is my gorgeous daughter,' says Mum and we shake hands.

'So pleased to meet you at last,' Venus murmurs, giving me a head-to-toe flick of her eyes. 'But I really must be going. Remember what I said, Dorothy.' She gives Mum an intense look. 'Give me a call any time.'

She glances fleetingly at me then back at Mum. 'I'll just say my goodbyes to Beth and Grace.'

When she's gone, I look at Mum, waiting for some comment about the odd little scene I've just witnessed.

But she just smiles brightly, puts her arm round my shoulders and gives me a little squeeze. 'So glad you could make it, love. Let me put the kettle on and we'll go back through.'

'Are you okay?' I ask, as she bustles about collecting cups and saucers on a tray, almost as at home in Annabeth's kitchen as she would be in her own. 'You looked upset. Is something wrong?'

'No, no.' Then she turns and sees my face, and her smile slips. 'I had a bad morning, thinking about your dad, that's all. Venus was cheering me up.'

'You should have phoned me,' I say, dismayed.

She gives me a sad little smile. 'Thanks, love. But if I phoned you every time I was missing your dad, you'd be sick of the sound of my voice.' She rubs my arm briskly. 'Anyway, I'm fine now. And I've just thought. I've got some whipped cream in my fridge. Can you go and ask Annabeth if she'd like it for the scones?'

'What's going on with Mum?' I ask worriedly, when I return to the living room. 'She won't say.'

They exchange another look.

113

I laugh incredulously. 'Will someone please *tell* me? I can't help if you keep me in the dark.'

'Tell her. She needs to know,' says Grace simply.

My heart starts beating fast.

Annabeth gives a little shrug. 'We had the séance the other night. In my apartment. And Venus – well, she claimed to have contacted a spirit . . .'

I grin. 'Don't tell me. Your Great-Aunt Edna?'

Annabeth shakes her head. 'It wasn't Great-Aunt Edna. It was your dad.'

A shiver runs through me.

Grace snorts. 'And if you believe that, you'll believe anything.'

'Shush, Grace. We're not all as cynical as you,' chides her sister. 'And Dorothy might just happen to believe in it.'

I laugh to cover my shock. 'What? That my dad was trying to contact her with a message? I don't think so. Mum's as cynical about that kind of thing as the next person.'

'That bloody woman ought to be strung up,' says Grace. 'I can't believe she did that to your mum.'

Annabeth shrugs. 'Venus didn't force us to be there. We all took part willingly. Including Dorothy.'

Grace sighs. 'Yes, but I thought it would just be a bit of fun. You know. Spooky. Like riding the ghost train. I didn't expect things to turn so – well, *sinister*.'

'What happened?' I ask.

'Well, we were sitting in the dark,' explains Grace, 'doing all that stuff and nonsense with the glass, and Venus asked if there was anybody there. And suddenly a voice started coming out of her mouth, saying Dorothy wasn't to grieve because he was fine and that he was always there by her side, watching over her and protecting her.'

'*He?*' I repeat.

Grace backtracks. 'Well, when I say *he*, I mean Venus made her voice sound like a man's.'

114

A shiver goes through me. I wish I'd been there. I can't imagine how Mum must have felt, listening to all that. Even if Venus made the whole damn thing up – and I can't help thinking that's highly likely – it would still have been a big shock for her.

'I tried to make your mum see that it wasn't real. That Venus had obviously fabricated the whole thing,' says Grace, putting into words what I'm thinking.

'But you don't know that she did,' says Annabeth gently.

Grace snorts. 'Pardon me but I *do*. That woman is a charlatan of the first order.'

'Yes, but it's not that simple, is it?'

'What do you mean? It's perfectly simple. Dorothy should have told her where to go with her stuff and nonsense.'

'Yes, but you're not Dorothy, are you?' says Annabeth gently. 'And think about it. Would you be quite so calm if Venus had claimed she had a message from *Michael*?'

A silence descends.

Annabeth reaches out to touch her sister. But Grace jerks away from her and goes to stand by the window.

I look from one to the other.

Who's Michael?

'Right, that's the lamp working.'

Startled, we all turn to find Gareth standing in the doorway.

'Oh, Gareth, thanks ever so much. You're an absolute angel,' says Annabeth.

'No problem,' he grins, looking down modestly at his big, workman's hands. 'Any time.'

He smiles at me. 'Hi Katy. Listen, could you tell your mum that I managed to get her a ticket for that Chopin concert?'

'Oh, brilliant. Yes, I will.'

I notice Annabeth and Grace exchange an interested glance.

But if they're hoping for some gossip there, they'll be disappointed. Apart from the fact that Gareth is much younger than Mum, I know for a fact that this concert outing is born out of

115

their shared interest in music, nothing else. Gareth is into classical music in a big way, and Mum used to play the accordion many moons ago.

Dad played the fiddle and they'd sometimes join other musician friends on Sunday lunchtimes in a back room of the local pub. When Sienna and I were young, we'd often sit drinking coke through a straw, listening to them play all the old favourites.

Since Dad died, Mum hasn't touched that accordion.

I found it once in a box at the back of a cupboard when I was helping her with a clear-out. I was about to suggest she play something, but the look on her face stopped me. It's been gathering dust ever since.

After Gareth's gone, Mum comes in from the kitchen with a tray of tea and scones. Her face is still quite flushed but she seems back to her normal self, joining in when the other two start talking excitedly about their forthcoming spa weekend.

Later, when Mum and I go back downstairs to her apartment, she asks me to come in for a minute.

'More tea?' she asks, going through to the kitchen.

I shake my head. 'No, thanks. I'm all tea-d out.'

'Well, just go and relax for a bit while I get changed.'

'Mum, who's Michael?' I've been intrigued ever since Annabeth mentioned him.

She frowns. 'Michael was Grace's husband. He died about ten years ago, I think. Why?'

I shrug. 'His name was mentioned and Grace's reaction was really odd.'

'I get the impression they don't like to talk about him.'

'Oh.' I stare at her curiously. 'But why? What happened?'

Mum shakes her head. 'All I know is that Grace adored him but he died. They never talk about him to me and I don't ask.'

She disappears off to her bedroom and automatically I start on the breakfast dishes sitting in the sink. I'm so not used to doing nothing.

'Leave those,' shouts Mum, obviously hearing the chink of crockery.

Smiling to myself, I do as she says and retreat to the living room, sinking onto the sofa. It's warm in the room – Mum likes her heating turned right up – and my mind starts to drift. It would be so nice just to fall asleep, right here, but I've got an album to finish when I get home so I need to get going.

Yawning and stretching, I make a mental note to phone the weddings co-ordinator at The Greshingham Hotel. I looked for her yesterday but she didn't seem to be around, and I haven't heard from her since she said she might consider recommending my services to her clients. I don't want to be pushy but I don't want to lose the opportunity by not being proactive, either.

Whenever I'm faced with a problem like this, I tend to think of Dad and imagine what he would do. Now, I can almost hear his voice, in the room with me, saying, 'Give it a fortnight, love, and if you haven't heard anything, give her a ring.'

That's the problem with working solo. There's no one to bounce ideas off. When I worked at the advertising agency, things were very different. I was part of a team and I enjoyed the benefits of holiday and sick pay, and a good pension scheme. Now, if I'm ill, I carry on working, regardless. I have to because with Sienna gone, there's no one else to take up the slack. I haven't had a proper holiday in years and Sundays are spent catching up with paper-work. The sad thing is, with all the day-to-day tasks involved in running a business, I no longer have the time or the energy to challenge myself creatively the way I used to.

Paying off my debts is now my main priority.

Growing the business so I no longer have to worry about money is my dream. At the moment, though, with bills piling up and Dominic on my back, that's more of a pipe dream than anything else . . .

There's a book on the coffee table in front of me called *101 Ways to Relax*.

Smiling, I reach for it and when I open it up, a piece of paper slides out. I recognise Mum's loopy handwriting. I'm about to tuck it back in the book, when three words catch my eye.

My darling Ralph.

My heart misses a beat.

Dad?

I stare at the paper in my hand, confused.

Is it a letter Mum wrote to Dad while he was alive? But why would she be writing to him? There would have been no need. He and Mum barely spent a night apart in all their thirty-five years of marriage.

I glance at the door, aware I shouldn't be looking at her private letter but unable to stop myself. Heart banging, I start to read.

My darling Ralph,

The TV is on the blink again! Either that or I'm even worse than I thought about understanding how that satellite box thingy works! Katy set it up for me, bless her, and she took me through it but I promptly forgot what she said.

I know, I know, electronics stuff just goes in one ear, out the other! But in my defence, that was always your province. Do you remember the time I thought broadband was an *actual band* – like a hair band – that you connected to the telephone? I was searching in the box they sent and I couldn't find it! We had a good laugh about that, didn't we?

But before you get big-headed, just remember how much better I am at other things, like crosswords. No, don't argue! My word power and spelling were always far superior to yours!

I miss you, you lovely, infuriating, wonderful man! More than you can ever know.

Your Dorothy

The lump in my throat feels as big as a snooker ball. I open my eyes wide to stop the tears brimming over.

Mum walks in right at that moment, joking that she thinks Grace might have a bit of a thing for Gareth.

She sees my stunned expression, glances at the letter and quickly crosses the room to whisk it out of my hand.

'Mum?'

She sniffs and forces a laugh. 'Silly, really. But when he was working away from home before we were married, we wrote to each other all the time, and I'd chatter on about all the little, inconsequential things that were happening at home. He kept every single one of those letters. I found them after he died in an old trunk in the loft. So I started writing to him again. I don't know. It sort of keeps him . . .' She gives a little helpless shrug.

I watch her go off to put the letter that she will never send in her bedroom. The ache in my heart is almost physical.

It sort of keeps him with me.

I miss Dad so much myself. Not a day goes by when I don't think of something he used to say or do. At first, each memory was like a stab, deep in an old wound. But the more time that passes, the more often I can recall little things and actually smile to myself. Sometimes a song will set me off, though, and my heart will break all over again. If it's been that much of a struggle for me, I can barely imagine the terrible void that's opened up in the centre of Mum's life.

Coming here to Clandon House and making friends has perhaps taken the edge off the ache, and the passage of time will have made it less raw. But I suddenly understand that she will never be the same again without Dad.

Now is definitely not the time to ask about Sienna.

She bustles about, putting some home-baked biscuits in a box for me, and it's clear the subject is closed.

I hug her for longer than usual at the door, and I can feel her giving in to it.

Just before we part, she murmurs, 'As for Annabeth and Grace thinking I might be after Gareth . . .' She shakes her head sadly.

The subtext is clear: No one will ever replace her beloved Ralph.

ELEVEN

My dad was never the kind of man to be satisfied with a routine office job.

I only began to understand this when I was at college, debating my own future. Dad always dreamed of being a successful entrepreneur. He was forever scribbling ideas on scraps of paper and disappearing off to his study for hours on end. I have a vivid memory of being at the breakfast table, ploughing bleary-eyed through my cornflakes one school morning, and Dad eagerly telling us about the sandwich-delivery business he was working on (or it might have been the scaffolding rental idea). Mum kept telling him to eat his eggs before they got cold. But he was clearly on a high, with breakfast way down his list of priorities. Anyway, he must have been swinging back excitedly on his chair as he talked because all of a sudden, in mid-sentence, he fell backwards and landed with a surprised shout on the kitchen lino.

We laughed ourselves silly. And so did Dad.

A few of his business ideas came to nothing. But on the whole, Dad had a good instinct for what would work. I realise, looking back, that he was lucky to be married to someone as understanding as Mum. She was always really stoical about the long hours and the many nights he'd be closeted in his study, working on his latest project.

It was truly a hammer blow when Dad died.

He'd been on his way to Guildford to check out a new location for his chain of sandwich shops. Instead of driving there, he'd left his car at the station and taken the train, I suppose so he could do some paperwork on the way. But he never made it to the meeting. As he got off the train, he collapsed with a massive heart attack right there on the platform.

It cuts me up to this day, the fact that we weren't there with him when he died.

I try not to think what his last moments must have been like. But there are nights, when bleak thoughts can seem even more frightening, that it haunts me.

Especially when I think about the financial pressure he was under.

It emerged soon after he died that he'd been fighting to keep the sandwich business afloat. He must have thought that by expanding his little empire (two shops, one local and one in Brighton) with premises in Guildford, he'd have more chance of survival. It was a risk. But my dad thrived on risk of that kind. He was the kind of man who talked about 'challenges' not 'problems' and if he had an obstacle to surmount, it seemed to fire him up even more with attack and enthusiasm.

But he kept the financial details from all of us. So it was only after he died that we discovered he'd let his life insurance policy lapse, which meant there was no financial cushion for Mum at a time when she really needed it. We managed to sell the business as a going concern but that gave us barely enough to pay off the business loan Mum had inherited. The shops were rented, so there was no property to sell. He'd also remortgaged the family home to finance the shop in Brighton, assuming, I suppose, that he had many years of working life left in which to build up the capital again.

It was a dire situation. Mum was left with a sky-high mortgage and very little income. But, inconsolable with grief, she refused point blank to put the house on the market. So, soon after Dad died, I gave up my job with the London agency and moved back in with Mum and Sienna briefly, before buying my own place. Having us both home to support her, Mum's spirit gradually started to revive.

It was then that I started planning the photography business, and Mum found herself getting swept up in my excitement, which I think helped a lot to distract her from her sadness. For a while, things were looking brighter for all three of us – especially when Sienna started working alongside me. I really thought we were building something fantastic together that would provide us all with a future.

But Sienna, it seems, had different ideas.

When she left for Paris, everything changed completely. But at least, by then, Mum was practically back to her old self and finally acknowledging the need to sell the family home and downsize to something a lot smaller.

A year ago, we found Clandon House. She moved in straight away and – to my huge relief – has never looked back.

I drive home, thinking all the way of Mum writing those letters to Dad.

I can hardly bear to imagine her loneliness. And the level of anguish that would prompt her to do such a thing.

When I eventually pull into my road, I have to park a little way off, and as I'm hurrying along the pavement, the thought of entering the dark house alone snaps me right out of my fug of sadness. My hand clutching the cold bunch of keys is shaking slightly. Then, just as I reach my gate, a tall figure looms out of the shadows. I gasp and my legs turn to jelly.

'Katy, it's me,' says a man's voice. 'Harry.'

Harry? *Oh, Harry!*

I peer up at him through the gloom as my heart rate steadies. 'Hi, there.'

'Hi.' He pushes back a lock of floppy blonde hair and I study him properly for the first time. Minus the fish finger outfit, he's really quite cute. 'I'm honestly not in training to be your chief stalker.' He smiles apologetically. 'I wasn't even going to ring the doorbell. I was just going to put this through your letter box.' He hands me a postcard-size white card.

It's an invitation to a photographic exhibition.

'Sounds intriguing. Do you want to come in?' A blustery wind is tugging relentlessly at my hair. It's very cold out here. But it's not just the temperature that's making me keen to go in. The idea of actually being accompanied by someone when I open my front door and step into the empty house is suddenly very appealing.

Once inside, I go round switching on all the lights and Harry, who's standing in the living room, hands in pockets looking around a little awkwardly, laughs and says, 'Blackpool Illuminations have nothing on you.'

'I'm not keen on the dark.'

'Yeah, you never know what monsters might be lurking.'

I think of Dominic and frown. 'Ain't *that* the truth!'

'The only monster worrying *me* right now is my bank manager.' Harry looks serious for a moment. Then he laughs. 'But that's another story.'

'Student loan to pay off?' I ask.

'Something like that.'

I nod in sympathy, only too familiar with the struggle to stay afloat financially. It's obvious he doesn't want to talk about it and I don't blame him in the slightest. Some details are best kept private.

'Have a seat. Coffee? Glass of wine?' I offer.

'You don't have beer, do you?' He looks apologetic. 'It's just I've never got into wine.'

'Sorry, I don't.'

'Tea, then?' He looks very young, sitting there on my sofa, still in his buttoned-up jacket. The stripy scarf gives him the look of

124

a student, even though I know from what he told me at the wedding that he's already graduated and has been working as a photographer for the past year or so.

I smile warmly, hoping to put him at his ease. 'Coming right up.'

When we're sitting with our drinks, I say, 'So where's this exhibition?' I glance around for the invitation.

'It's in London. And you know the photographer.'

I glance at him. 'Oh? Who . . . ?'

He grins. 'A mutual friend. Gabe Harlin?'

'Oh.' Colour shoots into my face for some reason and I make a show of going back into the kitchen to fetch the invitation, then studying it. Sure enough, there's Gabe's name in gold letters. 'I'm not sure I'd call him a friend.'

'Well, acquaintance, then,' says Harry. 'And soon-to-be-employer. With a bit of luck.'

'Really? Oh, wow. Do you think you'll get the job?'

Harry nods. 'Hope so. He sent a note with the invitation saying he'd like to talk some more when I'm there. It's not in the bag yet. But it's looking good.'

'Are you sure you don't want a glass of wine? We could toast to "not quite in the bag but almost".'

'Go on, then.'

So I fetch us a glass of chardonnay.

Harry takes a gulp and says, 'Mm. That's quite nice.'

But he's obviously just being polite because after we've done the toast, he sets the glass down and forgets about it.

'So you'll come?' he asks me. 'To the exhibition?'

'Erm . . .' I study the invitation as if I'm trying to work out if I'm free on that date, in a week's time.

I have no desire to see Gabe Harlin again in my life after embarrassing myself so thoroughly at the wedding. But I'm getting the impression Harry isn't about to leave until I agree to see him again. Which is really rather flattering.

So I pass back the invitation and say, 'Thanks, Harry. I'd love to come to the exhibition with you.'

'That's great. Right. I'd better leave you to, er . . .' He stands up, looking around him for inspiration.

'I've got an album to finish tonight otherwise the bride will *not* be happy,' I say, leading him to the door. 'Actually, I've already done the album but according to her, all the pictures are in the wrong places.'

He groans. 'Let me guess. She works as a dentist but thinks she knows far more than you do about creative layout?'

I laugh. 'She's a solicitor but yes, you're absolutely correct.'

At the door, he turns and tightens his scarf against the wind. 'And of course the customer is always right.'

I nod solemnly. 'Goes without saying.'

'Even though they might sometimes benefit from a kick up their right royal arse?'

Laughing, I say, 'Well, I'd never advocate physical violence, but . . .'

I'm expecting some more banter. So it takes me by surprise when Harry suddenly leans forward and kisses me briefly on the mouth.

It feels nice.

'I'll phone you to make arrangements,' he calls back, walking away into the darkness.

'Okay.' Then to give myself a sneaky get-out (old habits die hard), I shout, 'I'll double-check my diary.'

I stand with my fingertips to my mouth, listening to his departing footsteps and cheerful whistle on the night air until they fade away into nothing. Then I glance quickly up and down the street before shutting and double-locking the front door.

Suddenly, the house feels a whole lot emptier . . .

TWELVE

I'm sitting beside Mallory on a train bound for London.

We're on rather different missions, though.

I'm going to see a client who lives in the capital but is getting married locally. And Mallory is meeting up with Rupert's mum and sister to go shopping for a wedding gown. Serafina has offered to buy the dress, and the three of them have been excitedly planning this tour of the bridal boutiques ever since Mallory and Rupert got engaged.

'Are you sure I look all right, darling?' she asks for the second time since we left the car at Willows Edge station and boarded the London train.

I smile, a little surprised at this glimpse of vulnerability. 'Honestly, Mallory, you look fabulous.'

She does. She's wearing a jade green wrap dress and cream heels under her vintage mac. Her hair has been pinned back into an intricate up-do, with little plaits at each side, and I can tell she's spent time carefully applying her make-up. The whole effect is stunning.

The man sitting opposite us, a mature student type with a beard and horn-rimmed glasses, seems to agree. He's hunched into the window seat opposite Mallory, the movement of the train rocking him to sleep, but every time we bounce over points, his eyes spring open and he stares right at her.

She's oblivious to this, of course. And having recovered from her temporary lapse of confidence, she's now chatting away, trying to organise my love life.

'You have to go to Gabe's exhibition,' she's saying. 'You absolutely *must*. Otherwise poor Harry will feel *traumatised*, poor pet, after plucking up the courage to ask you along.'

I snort. 'Traumatised is a bit of an exaggeration. And is it really Harry you're thinking of? Don't you just want me to go on a date? *Any* date?'

She smiles wryly. 'Oh God, am I that obvious?'

'Frankly, yes.'

'Well, darling, it *is* time you got yourself out there. Do you know what actually happens to women who go without sex for months on end?'

The man opposite opens his eyes. But this time he's looking at me.

I flush. 'No. Do tell,' I murmur. 'What does *actually* happen to women who – you know . . .'

'Well, the thing is, I'm entirely the wrong person to ask, darling, because it never *ever* happens to me.' She smiles smugly, no doubt thinking of Rupert and his enthusiasm in bed. And according to her, on occasion, the kitchen table. And up against a tree. And round the back of House of Fraser one time.

'So what's Rupert doing tonight?' I ask.

'Oh, watching that film for the twenty-ninth time. Honestly, he's obsessed. What's it called?' She clicks her fingers. '*Mamma Mia!* That's the job. Never seen it myself. Is it good?'

'Er, yes, very good.' I catch the man opposite doing a 'so-so' expression.

'I thought it must be. Rupe's in floods of tears at the end. Every single time.'

'Gosh. Really?'

'Oh yes. He's the same with all musicals. Can't watch that thing *Glee* without virtually howling the house down.'

'That's nice, though, isn't it?' I murmur, thinking the man opposite could at least *pretend* he's not listening to every word. 'A guy who's not frightened to show his feelings?'

'Yes, it is. Bless him. Now, let's get back to you and Harry. What are you going to do?'

I shrug. 'Still deciding. I like him but I don't want him to think I want anything serious.'

'Oh, stop debating and just *go* for it, darling! Life is short. I mean, when *was* the last time you had a bit of glorious rumpy pumpy, no strings attached?'

'A one-night stand, you mean? Erm, *never*?'

She frowns at me. 'What, *never* never?'

I laugh. '*Never* never.'

Well, maybe one or two, but, I'm not going to admit it with that man ear-wigging every gory detail.

She sighs and stares out of the window at the fields and trees rushing by. 'Not even with the pool boy when you were holidaying in Sardinia? Or with a man you'd just met on a residential course and it was pretty exciting sex because you knew you'd never see each other again?'

I give her a sideways look. 'Er, that would be "never" on both counts. And by the way, I've never been to Sardinia but I believe you have? Nice time, was it?'

'The pool boy?' She smiles dreamily. 'Oh yes. The most heavenly thighs. I suppose from all that very manly graft, humping sun loungers about and saving people from drowning.'

I laugh. 'Did a lot of humping, did he?'

'Actually, he was rather sweet. Asked me out on a date and I said yes. Then we spent the entire evening doing sign language because he barely spoke a word of English. Awfully exhausting in the end.'

'I bet.'

'But it has to be done.'

'Does it?'

'Yes! And you have a lovely, attractive twenty-four-year-old just pining to go out with you. So get on with it, darling. Incidentally, what does he look like when he's not a fish finger?'

I glance at our fellow passenger. Even though his eyes are half closed, I just know he's riveted.

'He's quite tall,' I say slowly, recalling Harry kissing me on the mouth, taking me by surprise, 'with floppy blonde hair and nice grey eyes. And he's quite wise and self-assured, too, for a younger guy.'

'Well, there you are, then. Shag him.'

'*Mallory!*'

'Okay, well *don't* shag him, then. Not straight away. Get to know him first. And then shag him. But don't leave it too long.'

She swings around. 'And don't even *think* of chickening out of going to that exhibition! You are, aren't you?'

'No, I'm not!' I protest furiously.

Although if I'm being totally honest here, my indignation stems largely from the fact that she's hit a nerve and this is *exactly* what I was planning to do.

Gabe Harlin has been interfering with my concentration far too much lately. Every time I recall what a complete tit I made of myself, not recognising him at the wedding, I close my eyes and moan softly.

'Has Rupert sold any paintings lately?' I ask, to change the subject.

'Oh, God knows. He's a bit secretive about his art, to be honest. He rents a studio somewhere nearby and he goes there every day but I've never seen it.'

'Really? Have you asked him?'

'I did once and he said he'd take me there, but somehow it's never happened.' She smiles. 'Actually, I think his studio is the equivalent of a man's shed. And as we know, women enter sheds on pain of death.' She makes a disgusted face. 'Let's face it, darling, what they get up to in there is *anybody's* guess.'

The man opposite shifts his position, his mouth quirking up at the side. Clearly a shed man, then.

'I also think he doesn't want me to see his works in progress.'

'Why not?'

'Probably worried I'll tell him exactly what I think.'

I laugh. 'Which of course you'd never do.'

'Of course not, darling.' She sticks her tongue in her cheek. 'But to be honest, I don't really take Rupert's art terribly seriously. I mean, it's a hobby rather than a profession.' She shrugs. 'His folks are fabulously wealthy, so it's not as if he has to earn a crust churning out those watercolours of his.'

'Are your parents going to meet Rupert's folks before the wedding?'

Mallory frowns. 'Suppose so. If Ma and Pa can be bothered to drag themselves home for five minutes at a stretch. Can't say I'm particularly bothered.'

I glance at her with a little pang of sadness. She always pretends she doesn't care, but deep down, I know she must.

I've never actually met them, but from what I've heard, I'd dearly love to give them a piece of my mind. When Mallory was sent off to boarding school at the age of seven, they'd send her exotic parcels, all the way from Timbuktu. And I mean that literally. Mallory once remarked that receiving a parcel full of exotic gifts for Christmas was not quite the same as knowing your parents would collect you for the holidays. When I probed further, she told me that one year, she'd found out the day before Christmas Eve that they wouldn't be coming for her until Boxing Day. They'd been unexpectedly invited to spend the big day itself on an island in the Caribbean and felt they couldn't say no. I was aghast. 'But what did you *do* on Christmas Day?'

Mallory smiled. 'Oh, pulled some crackers with the other four poor unfortunate abandoned kids. And counted down the minutes till Boxing Day, I imagine. It wasn't so bad.'

My heart went out to Mallory when she told me that. I'd long known they were cold fish (except with each other) but this lack of parental feeling was astounding.

It's no wonder she's excited about Rupert's family welcoming her into the fold. I just wish I were sure she was marrying Rupert for the right reasons. Because sometimes I do wonder . . .

'Do you think you and Rupert were meant to be?' I ask casually. 'You know, fated, written in the stars and all that. Your one and only soulmate.'

She snorts. 'That's all just a load of old codswallop, darling. The very idea that there's this one special person for you and you alone. Pah! Give me a sodding break.'

The man opposite makes a weird noise and turns it into a cough.

'I think Rupert and I have just as much chance of marital happiness as anyone,' she goes on blithely. 'He accepts me as I am and I accept him as he is. That's the trick. I mean, you know how he just *adores* Dame Shirley Bassey. Every one of her concerts, he's there. In the front row. He's convinced that one day she'll throw her feather boa in his direction.'

I glance at our captive audience. The word 'agog' springs to mind.

I look away quickly. 'She does have a very powerful voice.'

'Quite the diva, I know. But what I'm saying is that it's absolutely fine by me. Just as long as he doesn't expect *me* to turn into a Dame Shirley groupie too . . .'

We lapse into silence, and I get back to the debate that continues to rage in my head: Shall I go with Harry to Gabe's exhibition? Or should I heed the butterflies and give it a wide berth?

THIRTEEN

The evening of Gabe's exhibition rolls around before I can think of a reason not to go.

I sit at my bedroom mirror applying a last touch of pink lip gloss, wondering why I'm so jumpy. Hopefully the butterflies aren't a premonition of doom but rather a slight nervousness over the fact that, for the first time in years, I'm going on a date.

Gabe gave Harry some extra tickets so Mallory and Rupert will be joining us, which I'm really pleased about. The more people around, the more relaxed I'll be, is my reasoning.

The plan is to take the train into London, go to the exhibition, then head off to a nearby restaurant where Harry has reserved a table for the four of us.

I've spent time putting make-up on and blow-drying my hair so that it's sleek and shiny and swishes deliciously around my bare shoulders. And I'm wearing my best little black dress, bubble-gum pink heels and my favourite handbag, a beautiful pink feather clutch that Mallory bought from an upmarket charity shop for my last birthday. It's so lovely, I ended up treating myself – after an awful lot of 'shall I, shan't I?' anxiety – to the pink shoes that match perfectly.

Harry's face, when he picks me up, is a picture. I suppose he's only ever seen me in my plain work suit. 'You look amazing.'

'You don't look so bad yourself.' I smile shyly up at him.

It's true. In his dark suit, open-collared white shirt and tan mock-croc shoes, he manages to look both sophisticated and funky, and definitely more mature than his twenty-four years. In fact, anyone observing us probably wouldn't be able to tell that I'm out with a much younger man.

At the station, Harry stands squarely by the carriage door when the train arrives, letting me on first and murmuring to me, with a cheeky smile, to mind the gap.

Mallory and Rupert get on at the next stop, collapsing into the seats opposite in a cloud of Chanel (and that's just Rupert). Mallory is wearing a long, floaty lilac dress and an exquisite coat embroidered extravagantly with flowers in pinks, purples and greens. Rupert looks effortlessly handsome in jeans and pale blue shirt, which shows off his tan to perfection, and a gorgeously textured pale jacket that looks so soft, I immediately want to reach over and feel the expensive fabric. A five o'clock shadow gives his look an edginess that I have a feeling is deliberately calculated. On anyone else, I'd think they just didn't have time to shave.

I do the introductions, telling Harry that Rupert is an artist, and the two men start chatting away about Rupert's paintings and an art exhibition they both went to last year. I'm surprised how much Harry seems to know about art. For myself, I just know what I like. I'd never have the confidence to talk about perspective or mood or symbolism in painting, as Harry is doing so easily.

I glance at him with an increased appreciation. He's funny, caring and smart. And really rather attractive.

I definitely don't believe I need a man to feel complete. But tonight, with Harry, I'm remembering what it's like to have someone at your side. It's a nice feeling.

He takes my hand and I smile at him. This is my first night off in a long time. I'm determined to make the most of it.

After a while, we all lapse into companionable silence, staring out of the window.

Mallory and Rupert curl against each other as we rattle along, murmuring little private jokes into each other's ears, and generally behaving as if they've been separated for the last twelve years, living on different continents. Whenever I'm with the pair of them, I always gets the impression that the instant I leave the room or turn my back, to put the rubbish out, for instance, they will leap together like magnets and start snogging each other's faces off. Usually I take it all in my stride but today, with Harry here, it's just a little embarrassing, so I'm quite relieved when the train pulls into Waterloo Station.

The exhibition venue is in a smart area of London. A discreet banner outside reads, simply, 'Celebrity'.

Unaccountably, my heart starts beating frantically as we push open the door and go inside. A quick glance around reveals that the photographer himself is nowhere in sight. My shoulders sink with relief and I suddenly realise my butterflies have less to do with first-date nerves and more to do with coming face-to-face with Gabe Harlin again, after my spectacular fall at Andrea's wedding.

But I've probably been worrying about nothing. The exhibition is running for a whole three weeks. He's hardly likely to be here in person every night.

Feeling much more relaxed, I glance curiously around me. I'm struck by the scale of the space. Stark white walls stretch to forever and the lighting manages to be at once flatteringly subtle – casting our faces in a lovely, warm glow – and dramatic where it matters, showing off to perfection the black and white images capturing well-known faces in unexpected settings.

It's a lovely, convivial atmosphere, which helps me relax even more. There must be fifty or so elegantly dressed people here. Some stand at the sides of the room viewing the photographs and some are grouped in the centre, talking, laughing and sipping drinks.

A well-groomed young woman in a skinny red dress makes a beeline for us with a charming welcome, and a second later, we all have glasses of champagne in our hands.

The photos themselves are stunning – without exception – and after a slow walk around, exchanging the occasional remark with Harry about Gabe's creative and technical brilliance, I'm left with a new understanding of just how great a photographer he actually is.

I can even forgive him for taking over my patch at Ron and Andrea's wedding.

My favourite photograph is a candid shot of a legendary model, who shot to fame in the Sixties. She's dressed in old gardening gear, hair in a rough ponytail, kneeling in a flowerbed with her back to the camera. She's just thrown a pile of leaves into the air and they're falling down around her. Her head is turned slightly so we can just recognise her laughing profile.

'I love that,' I murmur.

Harry grins. 'I'd buy it for you if I had a spare few thousand.'

I shake my head. 'I'd prefer a burger. My stomach keeps rumbling.'

'There's food arriving.' He points at a waiter in a long white apron who's gravitating towards us, bearing a large silver tray of what look like canapés.

'Ooh, yummy.'

I catch sight of Mallory and Rupert. They've been welded together ever since we arrived, flirting, kissing and drinking champagne from each other's glasses.

'Look at those two.' I nod over at them. 'Do you think they'll ever notice the photographs?'

Harry laughs. 'Not sure they're bothered.'

The champagne is slipping down a treat. Wonderfully chilled, it fizzes on my tongue, magically warming my insides and causing my head to swim a little. I'm enjoying the sensation, although I'm quite glad I've got Harry to lean against.

And I'm so, *so* glad Gabe Harlin's not here tonight.

I don't know what it is about him, but he makes me nervous. And tonight, I just want to relax and enjoy myself.

The tray of canapés arrives, and I suddenly realise the last meal I had was breakfast. We sample the glorious delicacies which our charming waiter tells us are mini spiced blinis with smoked salmon, tomato and basil tarts and bite-size beefburgers with Gorgonzola cheese.

Harry grabs me another glass of champagne from a passing waiter's tray.

I eye him, half-amused, half-disapproving. 'Are you trying to get me drunk?'

He laughs. 'No. I just think you should relax while you get the chance.'

'Don't you want one?' I hold up my glass.

He shakes his head. 'Gabe wants to talk about the job. Can't afford to screw it up by slurring my words.'

I stare at him.

Oh God, of course. I remember Harry mentioning that. How could I have forgotten? So that means Gabe will be here tonight.

I glance around, already less relaxed than before.

But he's definitely not here. Maybe he's been held up. Or perhaps he's forgotten he said he'd chat to Harry tonight.

I take another slug of champagne. Whatever, I'm not going to let Gabe Harlin spoil my night!

I take Harry by the hand and lead him over to where Mallory and Rupert are locked together. 'Honestly, you two,' I giggle, 'do you ever come up for air?'

Rupert grins and waggles his eyebrows suggestively at me. Then he swings Mallory round to face him, grabs her bum with both hands and does a slow gyrate which makes her shriek with laughter.

A waiter comes round with a tray of desserts. It's a choice between tiny raspberry tartlets and mini chocolate mousse cheese-cakes but my brain is so hazy with alcohol, making a decision is nigh impossible. Noting my anguish, Harry hands me his drink and scoops up three of each onto a napkin.

He grins. 'All yours, if you want them.'

I nod happily, passing back his glass so I can dive in. The chocolate mousse is *so* delicious, I have to close my eyes to savour it. This makes me sway a bit, but Harry's arm is around me. I grin and settle against him, happily surveying the scene. Champagne bubbles rise up, making me burp, and Harry nudges me, grinning.

I smile back at him. This is so bloody lovely! For once, the champagne is flowing when I'm not actually working and having to stay sober. And Harry is so handsome and attentive and getting on *so well* with my best friend in all the world and her incredibly handsome fiancé. I'm feeling completely chilled.

A whole stretch of time has gone by in which I haven't thought about my sister at all. Not even once.

A dark cloud appears, threatening to damp down my happiness.

But resolutely, I push it away and beam up at Harry.

There's nothing at all to stop me having a really wonderful night!

Full of joy and Cristal, I turn and raise my glass to the room in general and a fair whack of champagne slops out over my right shoulder.

I lurch round in surprise to see where it landed and find myself peering at a pair of large tan shoes, which appear to have taken the brunt of the alcoholic shower.

'Oh shit, I'm so sorry,' I mumble to the feet. I bend down with my napkin to mop up the mess but my head swims a bit weirdly so I change my mind. Harry's hold on me tightens.

I linger there a moment, frowning down at the sheer waste of champagne. Then my gaze travels up a pair of long legs encased in dark jeans to a tan belt. This is followed by a washboard stomach and nicely broad shoulders in a fitted white shirt. I'm just about to repeat my apology, more effusively this time, when my eyes finally meander on up to his face.

Oh, bloody hell.

It's him. Of course it is.

Gabe Harlin.

With those piercing and strangely unsettling blue eyes.

I wobble slightly, grateful for Harry's arm around my waist.

Gabe grins at me. 'Watch out. You might catch a fly.'

Huh?

It takes me a second or two to realise my mouth must be gaping open. I snap it shut.

'A stunning exhibition,' says Harry. 'Incredible.'

Gabe nods brusquely. 'Thank you. Can I – er – have a word with you?'

Even in my slightly blurry state, I clock the significance of this. 'Ooh, exciting!' I look from Gabe to Harry. Then I give Harry an encouraging nudge for good measure. Just to show support.

His face looks strained. Bless him, he's bound to be nervous. He lets go of me and nods at Gabe. 'Of course.'

An unnaturally loud laugh rings out and we all turn towards the door.

Jenny, the girl in the skinny red dress who welcomed us, is speaking to a blonde woman, who's just walked in. The woman, who is strikingly beautiful, has clearly been drinking and is causing a bit of a commotion. Jenny's smile is strained as she runs her eyes down the piece of paper in her hand.

I glance at Mallory, who grimaces at me. 'Mustn't be on the guest list.'

The woman's friend, a larger, flame-haired woman, keeps trying to steer her away. But Blondie seems determined. Suddenly, her gaze sweeps the room and lands in our direction. Instantly, her face lights up and she starts tottering over to us on her spindly heels.

I glance at Gabe. He's staring at Blondie with an expression that's icier than a neglected chest freezer at the North Pole. Oh God, she's not going to launch herself on him, is she? Poor misguided soul.

But this she does.

I'm not sure what I was expecting Gabe to do. But it definitely wasn't pulling her into his chest and hugging her back. Everyone's watching as Gabe rhythmically strokes her hair, a faraway expression in his eyes.

I glance at Harry. He raises his eyebrows fractionally and murmurs, 'Let's go and look at some more photographs.' He takes my hand and tries to lead me away but I resist. I want to see what happens.

I'm trying not to stare as Gabe attempts to separate himself from his biggest fan, holding her arms gently but firmly and talking to her in a low voice. I can't hear what he's saying but she keeps looking away from him, a sulky twist to her beautiful mouth. He steers her over to her friend, who tries to talk to her. But Blondie's having none of it. She's clinging to Gabe like a limpet.

Is she an ex-girlfriend? An ex-*wife*?

Perhaps she's not an 'ex' anything. She could be his current girlfriend. They might have argued.

Or maybe . . . maybe Gabe Harlin is the sort who has a few women on the go at once and Blondie's found out and . . .

I catch my rambling thoughts and stare at my half-full glass. Then I plonk it on a nearby ledge. The alcohol is clearly messing with my head in a big way. Why else would I be interested in Gabe Harlin's love life?

It's all kicking off now. Blondie isn't going without a fight, but Gabe is slowly shepherding her towards the door.

Suddenly, she wrenches her arm away. 'Just remember it was me who walked out on you!' she yells in Gabe's face. Then she starts to laugh. Everyone turns to watch in fascinated horror as Blondie's friend bundles her out into the street.

Gabe runs both hands through his hair, still staring at the door. Then he glowers over at Harry, nods in the direction of his office and strides towards it.

I squeeze Harry's hand. He plants a quick kiss on my mouth that tastes deliciously of the exotic strawberry cordial he's been drinking, and he follows Gabe, glancing back at me with a nervous grin.

'I suppose that was the entertainment,' remarks Mallory drolly. 'What a striking woman, though.'

'Not half as stunning as you,' growls Rupert, grabbing her bum with one hand and cupping her face to snog her with the other. I try not to watch but it's too horribly fascinating. It's a bit like watching a cringy afternoon melodrama on TV. You know you should switch off because it's probably going to get worse rather than better, and kill several million brain cells in the process, but somehow you can't tear your eyes away.

Sighing, I pick up my glass and take a large swig. I'm probably just jealous because a man has never swooned over me like that.

Next moment, Rupert heads off in the direction of the men's toilets.

'Gone to cool his ardour?' I ask with a grin.

She shakes her head. 'Drop of champagne on his jacket. Gone to scrub it orf. *I* can't see anything but he insists it's there.' She leans closer and grins mischievously, her lipstick all smudged. 'So. *Harry's* rather nice.'

I smile shyly. 'Yes, he is.'

'So do you think you might . . . ?'

I stare at her, appalled. 'No, of course not. We've only known each other five minutes. And anyway, we're friends, that's all.'

Mallory looks over my shoulder and frowns. 'Oh my gosh, here he is now, darling,' she murmurs. 'And that's not a happy face.'

I turn round. Harry is heading over, and his expression is indeed thunderous.

'I have to go,' he says brusquely.

'What? But why?' I stare at him. 'What happened?'

'Apparently I don't fit the bill. The great Gabe Harlin doesn't want me after all.'

'But I don't understand. I thought it was practically in the bag. What went wrong?'

Harry shakes his head. 'Will you be all right getting home?'

I stare at him in dismay. 'But you can't go now. We need to talk about it. What about dinner?'

He ignores this and sullenly repeats, 'Will you be all right getting home?'

Mallory puts her arm round me and murmurs, 'Of course she will. We'll make sure of it.'

'Right.' He pecks me on the cheek, holds up a hand to Mallory and practically races for the exit.

I stare after him, stunned. 'What the hell's going on?'

At that moment, Gabe himself appears. He doesn't even glance in our direction, so I know he's not looking for Harry. It would seem that he, too, is storming out of the venue without a word of explanation.

He makes straight for the door, stopping only to exchange a few words with a group of stylishly dressed people by the window.

One of the women grabs his arm and says something to him, and he throws back his head and laughs. It's a real belly laugh. And I think of poor Harry, who he's just sent packing into the night for whatever reason.

Harry's not laughing . . .

Suddenly furious that he's enjoying himself after so clearly upsetting Harry, I swig down the remains of my champagne to give me courage and march on over.

'What did you say to him?' I demand, shaking because I'm no good at confrontation.

He's still laughing. But at my question, the shutters come down. Those blue eyes are hard, like chips of ice. He shrugs. 'I had to tell him it wouldn't have worked.'

I glare at him, full of alcohol-fuelled indignation. 'What do you mean it wouldn't have worked? Of course it would have worked. You might think you're the greatest photographer since . . . since photographers were invented.' My words are slurring into each other but I can still just about form sentences. 'But I'll have you know, Mr Harlin, that Harry happens to be *huge* . . . erm . . . *huge* . . .' My brow furrows in consternation. I know what I want to say, but mysteriously, the champagne has made my lips too big and unwieldy to actually form the word.

'He's *huge?*' Gabe peers at me, mystified.

'No, no, no.' I shake my head impatiently and say it slowly, to get it right. 'He's *huge-ly tal'nted.*'

Gabe goes back to scowling. 'Well, that's as maybe, and I admire your loyalty, but there's no way Harry is going to be my assistant.'

'But why not?' I demand, drawing myself up to my full height then ruining the effect with a very loud hiccup.

'Ask him yourself,' barks Gabe, as he strides towards the door. 'But I'm not sure you'll get a straight answer.'

FOURTEEN

When I wake next morning, my head feels as if there's a mini fairground going on in there, complete with jarring noises, squealing kids and one of those old-fashioned games where you hit something with a hammer and try to get the dial to rise up as far as possible.

Not pleasant.

I have to get up, though, because I've got a pile of photos to edit, then – horror of horrors – another meeting with Cressida and Tom. It's the final time I'll see them before the actual wedding in a fortnight's time and as Cressida's stress seems to be rising at a frighteningly exponential rate as her Big Day approaches, I truly fear for my safety. It would be hard enough at the best of times to convince Cressida I have everything under control, without having a head that might explode at any moment.

Hangover cure. That's what I need.

Finding a pack of bacon in the freezer cheers me up no end. But then the fraught business of trying to defrost it in the microwave and prise off some rashers leaves me so weak and shaky I have to sit down and moan for a while.

I will never drink again. And I mean that. Never!

On second thoughts, what about hair of the dog? It's worth

a try. There's definitely a bottle of chardonnay in the cupboard somewhere.

Aha! Here we are. Oh God, no, it's a bloody cork, not a screw-top. I really haven't got the strength.

Instead, I settle for a generous swig straight from the Christmas sherry bottle, bought three years ago with Mum in mind. Can't stand the cloyingly sweet stuff myself but desperate measures . . .

The result is a hangover that's even worse. Because now I feel really sick too.

I keep thinking about the events of the previous evening and experiencing grave regrets.

As in: *Must have shifted my weight in champagne* (groan).

Made a complete tit of myself in front of Harry (bigger groan).

Emptied most of my glass onto Gabe Harlin's shoes then yelled at him like a mad-eyed fishwife (inconsolable whimper).

Harry hasn't even bothered phoning to apologise for storming off last night. So I still don't know what he and Gabe were at loggerheads about.

If this is what happens when I allow myself to 'let my hair down', suffice to say I will not be doing it again. There's far too much at stake – from my pink fluffy bag to my lovely heels (which, you never know, could fetch a small fortune on eBay) and my professional integrity.

At the ping of the microwave, my heart lurches.

Rising in slow motion from the table, so as not to jar my head, I set about the tricky business of frying up the defrosted bacon, while trying not to gag at the cooking smells.

Mallory phones as I'm licking tomato sauce from my fingers, feeling fractionally better after my grease-fest. She pretends it's work, but I know she's really calling to check I'm okay. After Harry departed, leaving us all open-mouthed with shock, she and Rupert took me to a local restaurant to soak up the alcohol (ha!) and made sure I got home safely.

'Christ, my head feels like a football,' she says.

I laugh. 'What, twice its normal size?'

'No, it's being *used* as a football – by a team of tiny but enthusiastic Sunday leaguers.' She pauses, clearly trying to stop the riot in her head. 'Rupert's pissed off to his studio, so I'm free if you need any help this morning.'

'Thanks for the offer but it sounds like you could do with a lie-in. And if it's any consolation, I'm feeling like shit, too.' I remember her 'pissed off to his studio' comment. 'Have you two had a row?'

'Oh, it was nothing really. He'd got theatre tickets to see *The Sound of Music* and instead of being perfectly *orgasmic* with delight, I laughed my socks orf. So then of course the darling boy went off into a major huff.'

'Oh dear.' A vision of Maria running gaily over a hill whooshes into my mind.

'I know what you're thinking, darling,' trills Mallory.

'You do?'

'Yes. And you're absolutely right. I should start appreciating my gorgeous Latin lover a whole lot more.'

'Right.' That wasn't *quite* what was preoccupying me.

'And I will,' she says suggestively. 'Starting tonight. After Serafina, Arabella and I decide which spa we're going to.'

'Everyone's going to spas these days,' I point out. 'I have a feeling I'm missing out.'

'Who else is going?'

'Mum. With her friends on the estate. So is this a pre-wedding treat, then?'

'Yes. Should be enormous fun. They're going to smuggle in bottles of Bolly.'

I laugh. 'Stuff the healthy option, then.'

'Oh, absolutely. So have you heard from the boy?'

'Harry? Not yet.'

'Hm. He seemed so keen, I assumed he'd be on the phone first thing to apologise about storming out and leaving you in the lurch.'

'Seems not,' I say non-committally. 'And actually, he didn't leave me in the lurch. He made sure you'd get me home.' I'm surprised myself, though, that Harry hasn't phoned. I really thought he would.

'That was obviously some clash of swords last night,' Mallory's saying. 'Although I get the impression it was Gabe Harlin, not Harry, who emerged outright champ. And who on earth was that *woman*?'

'Blondie on a mission, you mean? God knows. She wasn't giving up, though.'

'I suppose a man like Gabe must have women launching themselves at him all the time. But she was enough to put the wind up a Buddhist monk. What was going *on*, darling?'

'No idea.'

Back at my desk, I find myself pondering the very same question. She was obviously an ex of his – hence her shouting that *she* left *him*. (Bet he was glad.) But perhaps she's turned into what's sometimes termed a bunny boiler? She did have an air of chaotic desperation about her, like she wanted to get her claws into Gabe and never let go.

My mind goes into overdrive, trying to imagine what murky secrets Gabe might be hiding from his fans. With the result that very little work gets done . . .

FIFTEEN

By the time Friday rolls around, Harry still hasn't been in contact. I sent him a light-hearted text on Wednesday, saying I hoped he was okay and that Gabe Harlin was enough to make anyone want to flee the area. But he didn't reply.

I have to admit, I'm feeling more disappointed than I thought I would. Until Harry disappeared so abruptly from the exhibition, I'd been having a surprisingly good evening. It's a long time since I've enjoyed the attentions of an attractive man and Harry is most certainly that. Plus he's clever and funny into the bargain.

But to keep the vague disappointment at bay, I keep telling myself it's probably for the best. Harry's far too young for me. It was always going to be a bit of a non-starter.

Then on Friday night, as I'm coming out of the late-closing supermarket in the village with my meal-for-one, I spot a familiar figure across the street.

A group of young guys have just ambled out of the pub, looking very much 'refreshed'. One of them is balancing on the low stone wall of the graveyard, wobbling badly and looking as if he won't be upright for long.

'*Harry?*' I call across the road but he doesn't hear me.

He's too busy shouting, 'Fuck Gabe Harlin! Why would I need his help? I'm fucking brilliant *anyway*!'

He flings his arms in the air, slips about for an agonising few seconds, then sort of rolls backwards off the wall. The guys all cheer, clearly thinking it's hilarious, and only one of them bothers to stagger across to peer over the wall.

I get there just before him. Harry is sitting on the grass, rubbing his ankle. He looks confused at the sight of me. Then his face breaks into a huge grin. 'Katy.'

I climb over the wall and hold out my hand to steady him as he hauls himself up. Then, limping, he allows me to lead him to the nearby gates and back onto the street. His mates are all whistling and cheering, and Harry laughingly tells them to shut up before introducing me. There's a hint of pride in his voice as he carefully enunciates my full name.

'Katy Peacock,' repeats one of his mates. 'Pleased to meet you. Heard a lot about you.'

I smile and solemnly shake hands with him, although I know it's unlikely he'll even remember what I look like in the morning.

I turn to Harry. 'You'll never get home on that foot. Here's a taxi. Come on.'

He grins but doesn't object as I flag it down and guide him inside.

'Ooh, you'd better do what Mum says,' jokes one of the guys, as I get in too.

The driver wants to know where he's taking us but I can't get any sense out of Harry, so I give him my address.

As the taxi pulls away, his mates are already ambling down the street, having forgotten all about us. The taxi bumps over a pothole and Harry lurches to the side, ending up sprawled across the seat, grinning sheepishly at me.

I grin back, shaking my head.

'Thought you'd never speak to me again,' he says after a pause, during which I'm sure he's about to fall asleep to the rocking motion of the cab.

I frown. 'Why wouldn't I?'

He shrugs. 'I barged out of that expedition.'

'The ex*hibition*?' I laugh.

'Swat-I-said. Did Gabe tell you why he sent me packing?'

I shake my head. I'm waiting for him to explain but he just frowns and closes his eyes.

Back at mine, he flakes out on the sofa, cheerfully rubbishing my attempts to be sensible and look at his ankle.

'It's fine,' he keeps repeating. 'Come and sit down beside me.'

Eventually, I give in and sit beside him. He hooks his arm round me and kisses my forehead. Then he flops his head back against the sofa and falls fast asleep in seconds, mouth open, snoring loudly.

Carefully, I extract myself from his arm and manoeuvre him gently so he's lying flat on the sofa, a cushion for a pillow. Then I remove his shoes and cover him with a couple of throws, studying his face affectionately for a moment as he snores gently. In sleep, he looks very young indeed. Further proof that it could never have worked.

Smiling sadly to myself, I retreat upstairs.

SIXTEEN

Next morning, I wake from a deep sleep with an awareness that I'm not alone in the house. I smile and shake my head, remembering Harry's drunken adventures of the night before.

Tying my dressing gown, I go downstairs. The sofa is empty, the two throws folded neatly on the arm.

I follow the sound of whistling to the kitchen.

Harry is standing by the toaster, fully dressed except for his socks, waiting for it to pop up. He's been having a good root through my cupboards, by the looks of things. Making himself right at home.

'Aha! The sleeping beauty,' he says, pouring boiling water into a mug. The smell of coffee drifts over.

'Good morning, Harry. How are you feeling?'

He butters the toast and spreads marmalade on it. I watch him, thinking how much I hate that marmalade. Dominic bought it because he likes big chunks of peel. It must have been sitting there, at the back of the cupboard, all this time.

'Head feels like someone's jumping up and down on it,' he says, 'but apart from that . . .'

'Never thought of marmalade as a hangover cure,' I comment dryly.

He stirs the coffee and puts it on the table with the plate of toast. 'Not for me. I was going to bring it up to you. Breakfast in bed.'

He smiles and warmth trickles through me.

'What a lovely thought. Thank you.'

Feeling guilty for misjudging him, I sit down at the table and glance at the toast. Marmalade. With chunks in. Well past its sell-by date. Yuk. But since Harry has made such an effort, I make myself eat it, washing it down at regular intervals with gulps of coffee that scald my mouth.

Harry sits down opposite. 'What can I say? I've got a lot of apologising to do.'

'On you go, then,' I tell him, only half joking.

He sighs. 'I shouldn't have left Gabe's exhibition last week without giving you some sort of explanation. And I should have phoned the next day to apologise.'

'Yes, you should.'

He hangs his head. 'I thought you'd never want to hear from me again.'

'Yes, but you should at least have given me the chance to *tell* you that I never wanted to hear from you again!'

I'm being mock stern but half grinning at the same time.

Harry winces. 'I'm mortified I was drunk and fell off that graveyard wall.'

'Yeah, your balance is rubbish.'

'Thanks for bringing me back here last night. Honestly, I'm really grateful.'

'No problem.' I smile at him, relenting. Then I finish my toast and push my plate away. 'Thanks for that.'

'Have you forgiven me?' He looks winsomely sheepish. 'I honestly thought you'd be glad to see the back of me.'

I tip my head on one side, pretending to weigh it up. 'Okay. Forgiven.'

He grins. 'Right. Well, in that case I've got a suggestion to make.'

'What's that?' I laugh.

'It's Saturday. So even *you* can legitimately take the day off. And we are going to have fun!'

'Fun?'

He laughs. 'Yes. Fun. Remember that?'

I shake my head. 'Too much work to do.'

'I know. But it won't run away, you know. It'll still be there, waiting for you, when you get back.'

I frown. 'I'd need to get my accounts up to date first.'

'I'll help.'

'No, no, that's fine. It won't take long,' I say hurriedly, not wanting him to clap eyes on my rather basic accounts which I enter into a cheap notebook. 'So what do you have in mind? For this – er – fun thing?'

He gives a mischievous grin. 'We're going to forget official wedding line-ups and portrait photos. And we're going outside with our cameras to snap anything we like.'

'But I can't!' My automatic response kicks in. The one that warns me if I don't work from dawn till dusk every day, the business will definitely fail.

He narrows his eyes at me. 'When did you last have a day off?'

I look away to think. Then I click my fingers triumphantly. 'I didn't work at all on Christmas Day. Or Boxing Day, come to that.'

He snorts. 'You've just proved my point. You've got to have time off, Katy, otherwise you'll dull the old creative processes and you'll find your work will suffer.'

I frown. He's got a point, I suppose. My 'creative processes' are probably as fertile these days as a dried-up old riverbed.

'All right,' I sigh. 'After I've done the accounts. And on one condition.'

He cocks his head.

'You tell me what the hell Gabe Harlin said to make you storm out of the exhibition like that.'

155

His eyes cloud over. 'I'd rather forget about it, to be honest.'

'No, tell me, Harry. Please. You never know, I might be able to help.'

He looks at me, debating, and I say, 'If it's any consolation, I'm on your side already and I don't even know what it's about.'

He grins. 'I'll tell you at the park.'

'The park?'

'Yeah, that's where we're going first. So come on, get busy, then we can go.'

I speed through my work and within the hour, we're charging around the local park, having a contest to see who can snap the most variations of flowers and shrubs in ten minutes. Luckily, the park is deserted so there's no one to observe our slightly weird antics.

'Do blades of grass count?' I yell at Harry, who's over by the swings, crouched down by a crop of dandelions.

'Only if they're good at maths,' he yells back.

We sit on a bench and count our photos, and it ends up being a draw. Then Harry gets up and starts walking back to my car.

'Come on,' he calls, turning to face me and walking backwards. 'We're off to Brighton.'

Again, my head says no. But this time, it's more of a whisper in the background. I haven't laughed so much in ages. It has to be doing me the world of good.

'What are we waiting for?' I get up and walk over to him with a big grin.

Harry drives and when he fills up with petrol, he refuses to allow me to pay. 'I'm in charge of this day. You sit there and enjoy.'

I smile across at him, happy to do just that. But there's just one thing and my curiosity won't let it be . . .

'You said you'd tell me about Gabe when we were at the park.'

His smile slips.

'Come on, a deal's a deal.'

He takes a deep breath and blows it out. 'To cut a long story short, he found out I have debts.'

'Debts? But don't a lot of people have debts these days?'

His mouth curls up at the corner. 'Yes, but I'd hazard a guess that most people's aren't so bad that they've had their car repossessed by the rental company.'

He glances across at me.

My mouth has fallen open.

'I know. Terrible, isn't it?' he says, totally misinterpreting my reaction.

I shake my head. 'I'm just amazed because that's what happened to me, too. I couldn't keep up the payments so my lovely car had to go back. And that's why I now drive a rusty old tin can that keeps on breaking down.'

His eyebrows shoot up. 'Really?'

'Yeah.' I grin at him. It doesn't seem so bad, knowing that Harry's been through the same thing and knows how it feels. 'So how did *you* end up there?'

He shrugs. 'I first got into bad spending habits when I was a student in London. I was sharing a flat with three other guys – out most nights, partying, getting shit-faced. I look back now and think how incredibly stupid I was. But it set a pattern that I couldn't seem to get out of, and I ended up with a whole wallet full of credit cards, trying to juggle everything just so I could pay the rent.'

He looks over and I frown in sympathy. 'That's tough.'

'The thing is, I'm a reformed character now.' He grins. 'No, honestly, I am. I'm doing my best to pay off all the cards and get back on my feet. But it's not as easy as it sounds.'

'Tell me about it,' I say, with feeling.

'So how did you . . . ?'

I shake my head firmly. Talking about my financial troubles would mean talking about my sister. And I never, ever talk about Sienna to anyone.

Harry lets it go and we drive along, deep in our own thoughts for a while.

Thoughts of Sienna are like a dark cloud passing over the sun. And since Mum's news about her return, they've become even more difficult to ignore.

Why couldn't she have stayed in Paris?

Just knowing there were hundreds of miles and the English Channel between us made me feel safe. She couldn't hurt me again, not from so far away. And it meant I never had to worry about bumping into her and having to explain why I returned her letters unopened.

In the months after Sienna left for Paris, there was a flurry of communications from her. Emails, which I deleted without reading. And at least five letters, one arriving almost every week, which I immediately readdressed and sent back to her. I didn't want to hear her pathetic excuses because there could never be any justification for what she put me through. The hurt ran so deep, I knew I'd never get over it. A few letters were never going to help me get out of the mess Sienna had created for me.

'Are you okay?' Harry's looking at me with concern.

'I'm fine,' I say, shaking off my bleak memories. 'I haven't been to Brighton for years.'

'You're in for a treat, then.'

Smiling, I settle back in my seat, determined not to let Sienna spoil my day.

'What I don't understand,' I say, resuming our chat about Gabe, 'is how Gabe found out about your debts in the first place.'

'From Andrea.' He grimaces. 'I really like her and she'll be the making of Uncle Ron. But her mouth runs away with her at times. She was mortified when she realised she'd landed me in it.'

'What did she say to Gabe?'

'Apparently she told him I was doing a brilliant job of moving on from the mistakes of my past.'

'Oh, God.' I groan. 'So she was actually trying to compliment you.'

He nods. 'But then, of course, Gabe wanted to know what those mistakes were . . .'

I think about this for a while. 'But why would your debts stop you working for him? I mean, it's up to you how you spend your money, isn't it? And I can't imagine you having your car repossessed would have any effect on his photography business.'

Harry shrugs. 'That's what I thought. But he was quite adamant. And angry, too. Like I'd wasted his precious time or something. Said there was no way on earth he'd employ someone who'd let debts pile up and was obviously bad with money.'

'Well, it's a ridiculously hyper reaction if you ask me.' I glance at his profile. 'No wonder you were so disappointed when you found out he wasn't taking you on after all.'

'I was totally gutted. I couldn't believe my past had ruined such a great opportunity.'

I touch his hand on the wheel. 'Never mind, there'll be other opportunities.'

'There will indeed.' He turns to me with a sheepish smile. 'But listen, no matter how gutted I was, I should never have just walked out on you like that. Sorry.' He cranes his head round. 'Shit, was that the sign for Brighton?'

We end up coming off at the next junction and taking a little back road into the city.

It's midday by the time we hit the promenade. I buy us ice creams and we mingle with the tourists ambling along, enjoying the warm May sunshine.

Harry's such great company. He's gallant and thoughtful and he makes me laugh. His blonde hair is slightly too long but it suits his youthful exuberance. And he's also fairly easy on the eye in his faded jeans and well-worn sweatshirt with the one cuff that's unravelling.

I lick my ice cream thoughtfully.

Perhaps Mallory is right and he could be just the man I need for where I am right now.

'Right, we need another contest,' he decides, and pops the remainder of his cone into his mouth. The challenge is to see who can best sum up the seaside in a single shot, so the next half hour is spent on the beach, taking photographs of everything in sight. Then Harry rolls up his sleeves and declares that you can't possibly come to Brighton and not build a sandcastle.

He gets to work near the water's edge, energetically scraping up damp sand with his arms and forming it into a pretty impressive stronghold, while I sit and watch, laughing at his boyish glee and cheering him on.

When he's finished, he flings himself down beside me on the sand and we choose our favourite photos.

Harry's is a rather arty one of the sun catching a wave as it rolls around the moat of his sandcastle. And mine is of two old ladies with their trouser bottoms rolled up, turning to each other in shock as a cold wave rushes over their feet.

We decide it's another draw.

Then we wander through The Lanes, snapping the eclectic array of little antique and gift shops. I'm surprised how much I'm enjoying myself. Being away from the normal, day-to-day worries is so liberating. I'm so glad Harry prised me away from my desk.

'Have you ever been in the Royal Pavilion?' asks Harry, as we're trying to decide what to eat for lunch.

'Can't say I have.' I grin. 'But I have a feeling I'm about to.'

'Yep. Come on.' He grabs my hand and steers me off in the direction of the most exotic building for miles around. I've always been awed by this extraordinary creation, set right in the centre of the city, with its domes and turrets and wonderful gardens. A pleasure palace by the sea built by a king. So romantic. I'll be fascinated to see inside.

We spend over an hour wandering around, looking at the antiquities and exploring the gardens.

'There's a café in here, if you fancy it,' says Harry, looking at his watch. 'It's past two o'clock.

'But won't it be expensive?'

He grins at me. 'Yes, Miss Sensible. You're absolutely right. Pizza from a street vendor it is, then. Pepperoni for me.'

So we head back to The Lanes, buy our lunch and wander round a corner to eat it, away from the busy street where people are milling about in the sunshine.

'I've had a lovely time,' I tell Harry, feeling unaccountably shy.

He grins and sits down on a step nearby. 'Me too. And the day's not over yet.'

He pats the step and I glance up at the building. There's a sign above the entrance in red lettering that says, 'Crystal's Closet'.

Sitting down, I offer Harry a piece of my ham and pineapple pizza. He drops a kiss on my nose then takes the pizza, folds it over and pops it into his mouth.

'Excuse me,' says a gruff voice behind us.

'Sure,' I say, squishing closer to Harry along the step to let the man past.

To my surprise, a man in a silky, flower-patterned dress and pink heels swishes past us, down the steps, in a cloud of delicious perfume. He hesitates a moment, looking back at the entrance and hitching his bag over his shoulder. Then he starts to walk away, slowly, in the direction of the main street.

'Nice shoes,' I murmur, thinking how nicely they'd match my pink fluffy evening bag.

A second later, someone follows him out – a man in jeans and a Hawaiian patterned shirt. He runs down the steps next to us, calling, 'Hey, Terry, hang on!'

The man in the dress slows and waits for him, a big smile on his face beneath the swishy blonde wig. They loop their arms loosely round each other and walk off, into the crowd.

Something about the man's shirt is oddly familiar. I'm sure I've seen someone wearing one exactly like it . . .

At that moment, the pair turn a corner and I catch a glimpse of their profiles. My eyes widen in surprise. Of course I've seen that shirt. And I know the man who's wearing it.

It's Rupert . . .

SEVENTEEN

By the time we get back to mine, it's nearly seven, so I decide to invite Harry in for a bite to eat.

It's the least I can do after the fabulous day I've had.

I chop onions, peppers and garlic, and put together a sausage and tomato pasta bake while Harry downloads the day's photos onto my computer then searches through my CD collection.

I'm about to suggest he nip out and get us a bottle of red wine to go with the sausage pasta, then I remember he doesn't like wine. So I ask him to pick up some lager and he goes off, whistling, to the supermarket.

When he's gone, my mind drifts to Rupert. Who was that man he was with? And more to the point, does Mallory know about her fiancé's trip to Brighton today? Something tells me probably not, although I might be completely wrong. Maybe she knows all about 'Terry', Rupert's transvestite friend.

I'm so deep in thought, wondering how I can broach the subject with her – or whether I should just leave it alone – that I nick my thumb with the knife as I'm chopping salad.

When Harry gets back, he insists on washing the wound and applying the Elastoplast himself. I surrender happily. It feels surprisingly good having him fussing over me.

Later, after we've eaten, we sit on the sofa and channel flick for a bit, and it feels really nice and companionable. I watch him examining my book shelves, taking out a thriller or two and reading the blurb on the back.

He's such a decent guy. It's a shame he's so young. Not that Mallory would think that was any kind of objection. Quite the opposite, probably.

When he sits back down, much closer to me on the sofa this time, I smile at him, wondering if he got up deliberately so he could do just that.

'I've never fancied anyone quite so ancient,' he says, grinning broadly, his thigh touching mine.

'*Ancient?*' I stare at him in mock horror. 'Haven't you heard? Thirty-two is the new twenty-one.'

'Can I kiss you?' He looks serious suddenly, and a little vulnerable. Which is quite attractive, really.

Yet I hesitate.

A number of thoughts race through my head. Do I really want to spoil this new friendship by taking it to the next level? Or is my hesitation down to fear? I know it's a cliché but I really don't want to get hurt again. On the other hand, he asked so nicely, how can I possibly say no?

I smile at him. 'Yes, you can.' After all, one kiss does not a relationship make. And it might be nice.

So he lowers his mouth to mine and kisses me. And I kiss him back. And actually, it feels good.

Soon, we're lying on the sofa, and apart from the fact that his weight on top of me is making it quite difficult to breathe, I'm really enjoying being part of the human race again. This is what other people do on their Saturday nights and now here I am, back in the saddle as it were, which is quite a cheering thought. It's like riding a bike, really. No matter how long since your last snog, you never forget how to do it . . .

Harry raises himself up to look at me. 'Would you like me to stay?' he asks, his grey eyes locked onto mine.

Would I like him to stay?

Oh, bugger. That's a lot more than a kiss. And I'm not at all sure I'm ready for anything more than that.

He sees my hesitation and levers himself up. 'Sorry, Katy. Obviously misread the situation.'

Dismayed, I struggle to a sitting position. 'No, you didn't. I think you're great, Harry. But I just think it's perhaps a bit too soon?'

He smiles at me and there's a touch of regret in his grey eyes. 'I'd better go.'

'No, please don't. I'll make some coffee. We can – listen to some music . . .'

But he's on his feet, collecting his jacket and heading for the door.

'I had a fantastic day,' I tell him earnestly, hating the thought that I've hurt him somehow.

He pauses at the door and gently brushes my cheek. 'Me, too. See you, Katy.'

And before I can try again to persuade him to stay, he's disappeared into the night.

I stand at the door after he's gone, feeling suddenly bereft. It's been so good having his company, but I've obviously offended him without meaning to.

How sad that the day had to end so abruptly . . .

It's now Tuesday, three days since my Saturday with Harry in Brighton. And I haven't heard a single squeak from him.

I've been really busy preparing for the wedding of Cressida and Tom at the weekend, so I haven't had a lot of time to think about him, as it happens. But I can't help feeling disappointed that he hasn't rung.

We'd had such a gorgeous day and I was sure he'd enjoyed it as much as I did. But then, the circumstances of our parting that evening were so horribly awkward, what with him expecting to stay over and me not at all sure I wanted him to.

I've also been putting off phoning Mallory, telling myself I'm busy and I'll see her on Friday for a catch-up before the wedding.

But deep down, I know it's partly because I'm still not sure what I actually saw when I was in Brighton.

If Mallory knows about Terry, and he *is* just a friend, then obviously I'm worrying about nothing. But what if there's more to it and Rupert has another life she knows nothing about?

But every time I think this, it just seems so utterly unlikely. Rupert is devoted to Mallory. Anyone with eyes can see that.

Eventually, I convince myself I'm making a drama out of nothing. Although I will casually mention that I saw him in Brighton, and see what she says.

In the end, I phone her on Friday morning – and she's so stuffed up with cold, I can barely make out what she's saying.

'Ba dose is all blocked up,' she wails. 'I really think I'm dying, darling.'

'Oh, poor you. You sound terrible.'

'It's dot dice.'

'Sorry?'

'Dot dice. It's dot dice feeling so bloody ill,' she grumbles. 'I bade Rupert spend last dight in the spare room, so I could bake as much doise as I deeded to. Coughing and everything.'

'Oh, dear. But I'm sure he's looking after you, bringing you chicken soup and everything?'

She groans. 'Dot really. He's a rubbish durse. Scared stiff of germs, would you believe. So he's practically camped out at his studio.'

'Really?' Warning bells start ringing. But I'm probably just imagining things.

'Yes, he crashed out there last dight on the sofa, as a batter of fact, and reappeared this borning. To be truthful, darling, I was rather glad. Meant I could cough and splutter to ba heart's content.'

'Does – er – does Rupert have any friends in Brighton?' I ask, casually, my heart thudding uncomfortably fast.

'Brighton? Doe, I don't think so. Why?'

'Oh, just I was there with Harry on Saturday and I saw Rupert coming out of a shop with someone.'

'Really? Bale or female?'

'Er – male?'

'Oh, that's probably Terry,' she says. 'He lives in Brighton.'

My whole body slumps with relief.

She clears her throat loudly. 'Yes, he did bention he was picking up painting supplies. There's a little shop in Brighton he goes to.'

'Oh, right. That's great. Fantastic.' It was all perfectly innocent. I *knew* there was nothing to worry about.

'Didn't you speak to him?' she asks.

'No, he – er – was over the other side of the road and didn't see me,' I say, crossing my fingers.

I feel bad about lying. But I don't want to tell her that I was so taken aback to see Rupert with a man dressed as a woman that I was rendered temporarily speechless . . .

'So, you and Harry, eh? Hope you had a lovely time, darling, and I want to hear all about it.'

There's a great sneeze explosion in my ear followed by the sound of Mallory blowing her nose furiously.

'Listen, just you get yourself better and don't worry about the wedding.'

'Thanks, darling. Can't stop this wretched sdeezing. *So* sorry I'm letting you down. Tell the happy couple I wish them well.'

'I will.'

Mallory met them at our last meeting. She thought Tom's Geordie accent was really sexy and that Cressida was punching well above her weight.

'I wouldn't care but I was really rather looking forward to the duptials of Sexy Tob and his Scary Stressida,' she says.

'Don't call her that,' I giggle guiltily. 'She's paying me a lot of money, you know.'

'Just as well, darling. You deed *danger* buddy going anywhere near that woman. She's got bore sharp edges than a smashed glass. Oh hell, I've rud out of tissues. And where's my fiadcé when I deed him? Orf doing God dows what!'

I recall Crystal's Closet and grimace.

Then I tell myself to stop being so ridiculously dramatic.

Everything's fine. Mallory obviously knows all about Terry and her fiancé's trip to Brighton, so it's clear Rupert's not keeping anything secret from her, thank goodness.

Hanging up, I turn my mind to the wedding. With Mallory out of action, I'm going to need to find someone else.

Last time she was ill, I phoned an old friend, Louise, from college, who was happy to stand in for the day. But then I promised I'd keep in touch and I haven't. Not because I didn't want to but because the sad fact is, I have no time at all these days for things like socialising. So I'm reluctant to call Louise in case she thinks I've got a bit of a cheek, only phoning when I need a favour.

By next morning, I still haven't decided what to do.

I keep thinking Harry would be perfect. But we parted on such awkward terms . . .

My only feasible option is Mum. She'd gladly help, I know, but I'm not sure how great she would be at rounding people up for the photos. Still, any help would be better than none at all. So I pick up my phone to call her – and right that second, it starts to ring.

Harry.

I force myself to sound upbeat. 'Harry! How are you?'

'I'm good, thank you.' He sighs heavily. 'Look, I just wanted to apologise – *again* – for leaving so suddenly last Saturday night. I felt . . . I don't know . . . embarrassed, really. I should never have assumed you wanted me to stay. Bad mistake on my part. Very bad mistake.'

He sounds so regretful and apologetic, I can't help taking pity on him. 'Hey, don't worry about it.'

There's a brief silence.

Then, in a much lighter tone, he says, 'I suppose I was hoping for more than you were offering.' He chuckles. 'But I'll get over it.'

I feel terrible. 'Listen, Harry, I'm really glad you phoned. I'd like to at least stay friends . . .'

'Yeah, yeah, of course.'

'We could maybe go out for dinner some time? See what happens?'

'If you like.'

'Just enjoy each other's company?'

'Yeah, sure.'

I have a feeling he's acting deliberately cool. He must have felt really rejected.

'So how are you?' he says.

'Good, thanks. Got that wedding tomorrow.'

'Oh, yes. The scary control freak and her Geordie groom. Brilliant. Let's hope you don't have to rescue *him* from a tree.'

'Oh, don't,' I groan. 'It has to go smoothly because I don't have Mallory. She's ill in bed.'

'Oh.' A brief pause. 'I'm free tomorrow.'

'You mean you could help?' Hope soars in me. It's the perfect solution.

'Yeah, why not?'

'Oh Harry, that's brilliant. You're a star. A total life-saver. I'll pay you, of course—'

'No need.'

'There's *every* need. And I'm treating you to dinner afterwards, okay? If you haven't got other plans, that is.'

'Well, we'll see. So shall I meet you at the church?'

'Yes. The one in Broomhill village. Then it's the Broomhill Hotel and Golf Club for the reception.'

'Right,' he says cheerfully, sounding more like his old self. 'Haven't been in the Broomhill for ages. Might check it out tonight. Have a pint. Get the lay of the land, so to speak.'

169

I laugh. 'Great idea, Harry. Have a drink on me.'

I hang up with a big smile on my face. Problem solved.

And Harry and I are still friends. I'm so relieved, I feel like celebrating. A nice bottle of dry white wine, I think, shrugging into my jacket and grabbing my keys. I haven't treated myself in months.

It's a gorgeous, balmy evening in early June, and as I park near the supermarket and stroll in, I'm feeling more hopeful about life than I have in a long time.

In the past week, I've taken on two new clients and the deposits they've paid me are tucked away in my savings account, along with the money from various things I've sold on auction websites.

I also haven't heard from Dominic in a while. Not since that text he sent me when I was at Andrea and Ron's wedding. Another reason I'm feeling more optimistic. Soon, I'll be able to pay Dominic what I owe, and get him off my back for good. And then I can start afresh, pouring all my energies into paying off the bank loan and building up the business, with nothing dragging at my heels and holding me back.

I choose my wine and sling a large bar of chocolate in the basket for good measure. Heading along to the checkout, I'm in the bakery aisle when I spot something that stops me dead in my tracks.

A slim young woman with blonde hair in a neat ponytail has just joined the queue with her basket of items. She looks casual but chic in dark blue jeans and a pink silky top with tan moccasins.

I stand there, barely breathing, eyes fixed on her back, waiting for her to turn her head so I can see her face. A woman with a trolley passes by and gives me a funny look. But I'm unable to move from the spot. Part of me wants to abandon my basket and hare out of the shop as if a pack of wolves were after me. But another part of me has to know for certain.

Then it happens.

The woman behind her in the queue must have accidentally

bumped her with her trolley and apologised because she turns to smile at her.

And then I *do* know for certain.

Panic grips me. A cold hand is squeezing my insides. I've been dreading this for so long.

My sister is back . . .

EIGHTEEN

Driving back from the supermarket, my hands are trembling so badly I have to grip the steering wheel really tightly.

Halfway home, I give in and pull into a bus stop. I switch off the engine and lean my head back to try and calm myself and shake off the horrible queasy feeling in the pit of my stomach.

Seeing Sienna again after so long has sent my whole system reeling.

For some reason, an image of her as a baby lodges itself in my mind. Until I was nine, I was Mum and Dad's little princess. An only child. Completely secure in their love and attention.

And then Sienna arrived.

At first, I was enchanted by the little scrap in a blanket that Mum and Dad brought home from the hospital. She had a perfect rosebud mouth, the smallest fingernails I'd ever seen, and a tiny little tuft of soft, white blonde hair. Some babies are born with blonde hair then over the months, it darkens. But over the years, Sienna's hair remained as light as the day she was born.

Mum, obviously feeling it would be a good thing to involve me from the start, told me I'd be her little helper, and I changed nappies, fed Sienna her bottle and helped Mum push the pram when we took her out for walks at the weekend. While she was a baby, it was a bit like having a doll, I suppose.

It was only when she hit the 'terrible twos' and became a real handful – for Mum especially – that I started to slightly resent her presence. It wasn't that I wished her any harm. Far from it. If anyone had threatened her safety, I'd have dived in to protect her, no question. Because even at that young age, I was aware of the importance of family. Sienna might have taken up all of Mum's time, but I loved my baby sister nonetheless and it helped that Mum was always at pains to emphasise that she loved us both equally.

When I hit my teens, like most people my age, I was typically self-obsessed, focused on my stuff at the expense of everyone else's. I tolerated Sienna. She was just my little kid sister. She could be quite sweet at times, the way she followed me around and was forever trying to copy me. But it made me mad that Mum always took her side in arguments, claiming I was the mature one and should know better.

Then, when Sienna was five, something happened that changed everything. She contracted bacterial meningitis. I don't remember much about what happened in the run-up to her being taken away in an ambulance. It all seemed to happen so fast. But I have an abiding memory of sitting by her hospital bedside, horrified by all the machines surrounding her, and the tubes going into her tiny body, all pumping fluids that the doctors thought might or might not succeed in keeping her alive.

I remember holding her hand and willing her to live. And talking to her all the time she was unconscious because the doctors said she'd still be able to hear me and I felt somehow that I had to keep her attached to this life, otherwise she might just slip away. She needed to know how much we needed her to pull through. So I chatted about her friends at school and told her that My Little Pony, her all-time-favourite toy, couldn't wait for her to come home and play.

I felt so bad for all the times I'd got annoyed with her for making a noise or getting into my cupboards and pulling all my things out. Or told her to go away when all she wanted to do was play with her big sister. I vowed that if she could only pull through, I'd make sure I was a much better sister.

When she turned a corner, we all cried. Even Dad. He must have been staying strong and stoic for me and Mum. But that day, he broke down and sobbed – these strange strangled sounds that seemed barely human – which was somehow more horrifying than anything that had gone before. Then he hugged Mum and me so tightly, it felt like he might crush our ribs.

I was so grateful Sienna had got better and I silently promised myself I'd always be there for her.

But that was before she left . . .

I open my eyes and hold up my hand. The tremor is not so bad and the nausea has abated slightly. I start the engine and drive home slowly, feeling as though I'm in a bad dream, reliving my frantic escape from the supermarket.

When I realised it was Sienna, I placed the basket on the floor and left by the far checkout, squeezing past a line of customers, praying my sister wouldn't see me. Hurrying back to the car, I kept checking back over my shoulder, convinced she'd seen me and would be following.

Driving along, I glance in the rear-view mirror for the umpteenth time.

No sign of her.

Back home, I pour myself a large brandy and down half of it in one go. Then I take it through to the living room, where I sink down on the sofa and stare, without seeing, at the opposite wall.

I'm so stunned, I can't even cry. I just sit there, staring into space, as images of Sienna's later years flood through my mind.

When she got out of hospital, things returned to normal, and naturally the little irritations crept in again.

At fifteen, I was starting to have boyfriends and when I invited them back to the house, you could bet your life that my six-year-old terror of a sister would embarrass me somehow. She'd go up to them and ask, 'Are you going to marry my sister?' or 'Do you love

Katy?' Or 'Do you like my doll? She does proper wee-wees.' (And guess what? She did. All over Malcolm's best trainers.)

I remember a boy called Sam I was particularly struck on. He came to the door and Sienna managed to answer it. From upstairs, I heard her say in an indignant, high-pitched tone, 'Who are *you*?' Like he had no business being there.

'I'm Sam, Katy's friend,' came the reply. 'And you're Sienna.'

There was a pause. Then, as I hurtled down the stairs, she said firmly, 'I liked Malcolm best.'

After her illness, she was clingier somehow, and she was left with a real fear of doctors and hospitals. But remembering how we almost lost her, I found I had more patience with her than before. She followed me around and tried to be like me in every way she could (Mum drew the line at lipstick and pierced ears) and I was like her number one protector.

By the time she left school and followed me into a career in photography, studying at the local college, we were good friends as well as sisters.

I was upset when, on leaving college, she decided she wanted to work abroad for a while before settling to a career at home. But I nonetheless backed her up in the inevitable arguments with Dad, who didn't want her to waste her photography skills. In the end, she trained with the TEFL organisation so she could teach English as a foreign language, and managed to land a job in Paris.

Then, just a month before she was due to go off on her French adventure, tragedy struck and Dad died.

We were all totally devastated. But I think Sienna felt it even more keenly because she'd argued with Dad so much in recent months and felt really bad about it.

She told the French language school she wasn't coming, and it seemed like the natural next step that she should join me in the business.

At first, it all seemed to be working brilliantly.

Then something happened that completely disrupted the happy

status quo. Sienna's boyfriend, Daniel, who she absolutely worshipped, dumped her. For his ex-wife.

It was totally out of the blue.

And looking back, that's what started the whole disastrous chain of events that brought our hopes and dreams for the future crashing down around our ears.

A Summer Wedding

NINETEEN

When I wake next morning, I feel like I've been hit by a truck.

I stagger to the bathroom and frown at my peaky complexion in the mirror. Dosed up with brandy, I'd been expecting to crash out and sleep, but no such luck. I tossed and turned, finally falling asleep as the dawn was creeping through the curtains, only to wake an hour later after a horrible nightmare in which a vampire was chasing me through a dark forest.

I've had approximately one-and-a-quarter hours' sleep.

And I seem to have developed a weird eye twitch.

I splash cold water over my face again and again, determined to stay strong, despite the shock of seeing Sienna the day before. I have a wedding to do today. Cressida and Tom are relying on me. I will not let my focus slip just because my sister has decided to waltz back across the Channel.

It's a perfect June morning with a clear blue sky and a tinge of apricot on the horizon. First hurdle over, then. It will be dry for the photos. So no dodging the showers with Cressida hyperventilating over her hair frizzing up. The very thought makes my eyelid reverberate like a washing machine on 'spin'.

A bath. That's what I need to revive me. I'm too exhausted for a shower. All that moving about. Unfortunately, the bath is so relaxing, I fall asleep, then end up having to race around at high speed, completely undoing any sense of relaxation I'd achieved.

All set, I grab my gear and head out to the car. Cressida is expecting me at ten for the 'getting ready' photos at her parents' house, where she spent last night.

I put my foot down and get there only a few minutes late.

I ring the bell.

And then a realisation hits me. It's like a stinging punch to the stomach.

Bugger!

The batteries!

I should have recharged them last night. The shock of seeing Sienna has knocked me right off course.

A wave of panicky heat washes over me and my eyelid twitches into overdrive.

A figure appears in the frosted glass of the front door.

Stay calm, stay calm!

A tall, very thin woman, who I assume is Cressida's mum, opens the door. (I'm assuming because she's practically a carbon copy of Cressida. Even down to the tight smile that goes nowhere near her eyes.) She's wearing a cerise skirt and jacket, and has the same dark brown helmet of hair as her daughter.

She observes my equipment. 'Photographs? Excellent. I'm Mrs Wilson. Go on through. First door on the left.'

'Thank you.' I plaster on a smile and make for what I guess is the living room, my brain ticking over feverishly.

If I'm very lucky, the batteries I've got might see me through this session at the house. But there's no way they will last the whole day. I'll have to phone Harry as soon as I can and ask him to buy some on his way to the church.

I do a couple of swift deep breaths and tell myself to get a grip.

Cressida is sitting on a stiff-backed chair in front of a gilt-framed wall mirror, having her veil arranged. 'That's not how it looked in the bridal boutique,' she points out.

Her bridesmaid, who I know is the groom's sister, has a go at repositioning it and stands back. 'What about that, then, pet?' She's been condemned to wear an interesting lavender creation over her ample curves. It has a ballooning skirt and equally bulging puffed sleeves that really only a stick insect could pull off. She turns and gives me a warm smile. 'Eeh, hello, pet, I didn't see you there. You must be Miss Peacock. Lovely name.'

'Katy.' I smile back.

'Well, I'm Sally. Pleased to meet you, Katy.'

It's obvious she's Sexy Tom's sister. Same slightly naughty twinkle in her eye. Same broad Geordie accent.

Cressida clears her throat pointedly. 'That's definitely *not* how it looked in the shop,' she repeats, sending an icy smile of welcome my way. 'Sally?' She waves her hand. 'Sally!'

Sally jumps to attention, performing a mock salute and winking at me.

'Not *that* far back!' Cressida snaps. 'I look ridiculous now.' She pushes Sally's hands away. 'Here. Look. There. How's that?'

'Eeh, it's lush!' Sally beams, as Cressida gets to her feet. 'You'll be a proper bobby dazzler at that altar. What do you think, Katy?'

'You look amazing, Cressida,' I say truthfully, aware I need to phone Harry as soon as I can. 'Could I possibly use your bathroom?'

Sitting on the lid of the loo, I try Harry's mobile, followed by his landline, then his mobile again. Recorded messages every time. Why the hell isn't he picking up? I try him once more on the mobile, knowing it's useless.

Perhaps his phone is out of charge? Maybe he's on his way to the church already? I said I'd meet him there just before eleven, so if worst comes to worst, I suppose he could always slip off then to get the batteries.

Taking a deep, calming breath, I head back in to the bridal party and start on the photos. Cressida wants them all done in the precise order she's listed them, so they're all fairly formal.

183

'What about a picture of you perched on the windowsill,' I suggest at one point, 'looking out for the cars arriving?'

She peers at me. 'Is that on the list?'

Despite Sally's efforts at lightening the mood, the tension in the room is palpable.

The bride's necklace falls off at one point, and her scandalised reaction is completely over the top considering it's essentially just an easily remedied wardrobe malfunction. You'd seriously think she'd just discovered the church had been taken over by aliens.

'I'm all fingers and thumbs,' mutters her mum, trying to fasten it back on again, clearly feeling the pressure. 'Can you do it?' She turns to Sally.

'For goodness' sake, here, let me!' snaps Cressida, her tone growing more high-pitched by the second. She grabs the necklace and checks her watch for the nine-hundred-and-forty-fifth time since I got here. It's gorgeous. A silver face with a delicate lavender strap, which I guess is meant to tie in with the wedding's silver and lavender theme. 'The cars will be here in three-and-a-half minutes.' Her eyes are wide and a little scary. 'And we're nowhere near ready!'

Her anxiety only makes mine worse. My heart is in my mouth and my palms are sweating. What if the damned batteries pack up before I can get through Cressida's list?

Thankfully, though, I'm still clicking away by the time the cars have arrived and the bride's dad has come downstairs and clapped eyes on his daughter in her dress for the first time. He's all misty-eyed and proud, which brings a lump to my throat. For the first time this morning, Cressida's stern exterior slips, and when she gives him a hug (and it's not even on the schedule), it looks like her mascara might be in danger.

Sally and I exchange an 'Ah, bless!' look.

After I've waved them off in their posh cars, I leap into my own tin can and phone Harry again. Still no reply. *What the hell is he doing? Surely he can't have forgotten saying he'd help me out today?*

Feeling sick, my eyelid twitching manically, I hare along to the church, arriving just in time to take pictures of the bride stepping out of the car, assisted by her dad.

I pause for a second to admire the dress. It's a white princess creation with bead-encrusted bodice and the most glorious full skirt, multi-layers of net and frothy organza flowing out from her narrow waist.

Cressida poses for two shots, as per the list. Then it's into the church for more photos.

Please let my luck hold out!

But while Harry might be absent without leave, my guardian angel is thankfully by my side. I manage to take all the required photos of the ceremony, and the bride and groom emerging to a shower of confetti, with no battery calamity whatsoever.

The group photos will be taken at the Broomhill Hotel & Country Club before the reception, which means I've got a small amount of time in which to race back to Willows Edge and buy new batteries.

Arriving at the supermarket, I have a bad feeling. But I know it's only because I'm reliving the shock of seeing Sienna there last night. The chances of bumping into her again are pretty small . . .

I grab the right batteries, pay for them and rush out to the car, missing colliding with a male jogger by about a ninetieth of a second. He just gets past and I feel the rush of air in his wake.

He slows down and turns.

And my heart gives an enormous thump.

It's Gabe.

'In a hurry?' he asks, sauntering over, all manly sweat and muscles.

'I am, actually. I'm due at the Broomhill for a wedding.'

He nods at the shop. 'Emergency dash for batteries? Or a quick snack before the fun begins?'

'Batteries.'

'No Mallory today?'

'She's not well. I'm being helped by – erm . . .'

I tail off lamely, some instinct telling me it's probably best not to mention Harry having gone AWOL. He's already in Gabe's bad books. I don't want to make things worse between them.

I shrug. 'Someone else.'

He nods thoughtfully, and I get the impression those startlingly blue eyes of his haven't for a moment missed the awkward nature of my reply. Why does it always feel like Gabe Harlin can see right into my mind?

'Anyway, better get on,' I say, feeling the colour rush into my face.

Putting his thumb up, he starts running backwards.

I dive into the car and turn the key. The sound it makes is not encouraging. Panicking, I try again. But I still can't get it started.

Aaaargh! No! Please don't do this to me! I close my eyes tightly for a second, then try again.

Still nothing.

I want to fall over the steering wheel and sob my eyes out. Except I can see Gabe wandering back over. He raps on the window. It won't wind down, so I open the door, which sometimes sticks so you have to give it a really good shove. Naturally, today, it flies open with ease and almost does the poor man an injury.

'Sounds like the battery's dead,' he remarks helpfully, bending down to me.

I'm about to reply rather scathingly that I'd figured that out for myself, when he adds, 'I can give you a lift if you like. My house is just five minutes up the road.'

It hadn't occurred to me that he might live so close. I stare at him in surprise and my eyelid reverberates.

Oh God, he probably thinks I'm winking at him!

So then, of course, I have to go through the rigmarole of blinking really obviously and fiddling with my eye to let him know it's a physical affliction not a come-on.

'Something in your eye?' he asks.

186

I nod, still fiddling.

'Do you want me to have a look?'

'No!' I squeak, ridiculously panicked by the thought of Gabe coming nearer me and staring deep into my – er – *eye*. Just the thought is making my heart beat like a trapped bird's wings. What the hell's wrong with me?

Taking a swift breath, I amend my answer to: 'Thank you but no, I'll be fine.'

'Lift?' he reminds me.

'Are you sure you've got time?'

Surely the great Gabe Harlin must have many demands on his time?

He grins. 'Sure. Why wouldn't I?'

I shrug. 'Oh, I don't know. I suppose I assumed you'd have lots of pressing photography assignments to carry out. Very important meetings to attend. Big celebrities to shoot.' I twist my lips to let him know I'm not entirely serious, and he laughs.

'I've met a few celebrities I'd like to shoot, although I'm generally not a violent man.'

I grin. *Touché.*

'Sit tight and I'll be back in five.' He taps the roof of the car and sprints off along the high street, weaving neatly between passers-by. I watch him go, admiring his running style – fast with an economy of movement – and, I have to confess, admiring a great deal more besides . . .

Less than ten minutes later, a car pulls into the space in front. I peer at the driver, who's facing me, and find myself returning Gabe's broad smile. An odd little shiver wriggles through me. But I haven't got time to wonder about it. I have to get to the Broomhill Hotel. Pronto.

We load my gear into Gabe's car and I get into the passenger seat.

'Toss me your keys,' he says, and locks my car before sliding in himself.

187

Then we speed off to the wedding venue.

On the way, I try to contact Harry again to find out where he is. But it goes straight to answer machine. Gabe glances over as I'm speaking but I deliberately don't mention Harry by name.

'No luck with your assistant?' he asks.

I shake my head. 'He's probably there already. I'm hoping his phone is just out of charge,' I say, sounding far more optimistic than I actually feel. *Where the bloody hell has Harry got to?*

Gabe pulls into the car park at the Broomhill and brings out my bag. I thank him and go to take it from him but he nods across at the hotel and says, 'I'll come in with you.'

'Oh, thanks, but there's really no need—' I begin.

But he's already striding across to the hotel's main entrance.

I watch him for a second, wondering at his surprising transformation into Mr Nice Guy. Then I set off after him, half-running to catch up.

Guests are arriving in their cars from the church and wandering into the hotel for pre-reception drinks. But the bridal party themselves are not here yet. My plan is to take a quick look around the hotel and grounds, try to track down Harry, then position myself at the main door to await their arrival.

Harry isn't in reception, which is a bad sign. If his phone wasn't working, he'd surely wait for me there.

Gabe sees my confusion. 'No sign of your assistant?'

I shake my head.

'Who is it, anyway?'

Those unsettling blue eyes are boring into me. It would be ridiculous to lie.

'It's – erm – Harry, actually,' I tell him, a slightly defensive edge to my tone.

His eyebrows rise. I can tell what he's thinking. *Bad with money. And irresponsible in other areas as well.*

I glance around, hoping to spot Harry's shock of blonde hair and prove Gabe wrong. 'He'll be here.'

'You think so?' He looks doubtful, to say the least.

And right now, there's nothing to prove him wrong.

'Look, why don't I help?' says Gabe suddenly. 'Until he shows.'

I stare up at him. *Is he joking?* The great Gabe Harlin, prize-winning photographer and celebrity sex symbol (according to my quick investigation on Google) is offering to be *my assistant*?

'But I can't expect you to do that,' I tell him. 'Although it's really very kind of you.'

Apart from anything else, it would be *mortifying* having *the* Gabe Harlin watching my every move, both of us knowing he could do a far better job. I'm just not sure my pride could take it.

Then I remember whose wedding it is. Cressida and her beautiful silver and lavender timepiece will explode if I dare to fall behind the schedule she's drawn up. But without Harry assembling people for the shots, I haven't a hope in hell of finishing in time.

I take a deep breath. 'You really don't mind helping?'

'I'm all yours.' He holds out his arms. 'Completely at your service. Do with me what you will.'

I open my mouth to speak but somehow the words slither away from me. A tell-tale glow rises in my cheeks.

Gabe stands there, eyes crinkling at the corners, having just offered to be my male escort for the day. I should be joining in with the joke, but instead, I find myself completely overwhelmed by the devastating combination of boyish humour and powerful masculinity.

We lock eyes and the smile slips from his face, and for a shocking second, all I want to do is walk into those arms and lose myself forever. The silence seems to go on forever . . .

Then my bloody eyelid winks at him.

I laugh nervously and after a second, he smiles, too, running a hand through his hair, looking a little awkward.

I swallow hard and force some words out. 'Excellent. Right, I'm going to check out the venue.' Hopefully, a display of cool efficiency will offset my scarlet face. 'Would you like to wait by the main door and check for the bridal party's arrival?'

'Your wish is my command.' His smile is less certain now but still tinged with innuendo, and I flee to get my breath back.

Oh God, where are you, Harry?

Taking the shots of the bride and groom arriving is quite an ordeal, knowing Gabe is standing a little way off, observing me. I'm terrified I won't be able to hold the camera still because my hands are trembling. I can't believe how self-conscious I feel.

But I start to relax when I begin the group shots and Gabe starts doing his bit, rounding the guests up for me. He's amazingly good at coaxing people away from the pre-reception drinks, and there are thankfully no hold-ups at all.

I'm finding it quite amusing, watching how people react to him. He's not famous in a celebrity sense but his face is clearly familiar to some of the guests, because every now and then, I spot someone peering at him intently, then nudging whoever they're with and pointing, looking for confirmation that he really is that man who's famous for taking photos. What's his name again . . . ?

I'm in the middle of photographing the groom's close family when a message pings through on my phone.

It's Harry.

So, so sorry. Feeling terrible. On my way now. With you in five minutes.

I slide my phone back in my pocket and continue with the photos. An hour ago, I'd have given anything to pick up that message from him and know he was finally on his way. But now, I'm not that bothered. Gabe is helping me. And if Harry can let me down like that at the very last minute, do I really want him here anyway?

I quickly text him to say not to worry, I'm managing fine and that if he's not feeling great, he should stay at home. Then I shove my phone away.

190

Gabe is assembling the bride's family for the next shot, and I notice Cressida, her face pink and animated, chatting away to him and actually looking relaxed for the first time that day. I snort to myself. It's obviously the Gabe Harlin effect. He should be available on the National Health Service as a mobile relaxation technique.

We're pretty much on schedule, which is great, and after we've done the bride's family, all that's left on the list is a shot of Cressida's four cousins, and the big group shot of all the guests together.

Gabe brings me the cousins, who all turn out to be teenage girls. Very self-conscious teenage girls. I do the usual jokes, trying to encourage them to relax, but their poses are so stiff, it's proving really difficult. Two of them have braces and are clearly determined to keep their mouths closed, and the other two just look plain sulky.

I glance in the viewfinder at the results. Cressida is not going to like these. And we're running dangerously behind schedule.

Gabe wanders over. 'Never work with animals or teenagers,' he murmurs in my ear.

I frown and glance at my watch anxiously. 'Tell me about it.'

'Want me to have a go?'

I hesitate for a second, my pride at stake. Then I see Cressida peering over at me, clearly wondering why the big group shot is being delayed. It would be churlish to refuse his offer. So I smile and hand over the camera.

'Right, girls!' He rubs his hands together. 'Ever heard of squinching, by any chance?' They shake their heads and he grins broadly. 'Technical term. It's the way the stars make themselves look beautiful in photos.' They look at him like he's nuts and he laughs. 'Trust me. You're going to look gorgeous. And Katy here is going to demonstrate. Aren't you, Katy?'

'I am?' I stare at him in alarm. What the hell is squinching anyway? If it's anything like twerking, he can absolutely forget it.

As it turns out, though, all I have to do is sort of tense my eye muscles ever so slightly while smiling at the camera. Gabe does a 'before' and an 'after', then shows them to me and the girls. And actually, I'm forced to admit that I like the 'squinching' shot of myself much more. When pressed, the girls reluctantly agree. I smile to myself. I can tell they're intrigued.

And sure enough, helped along by Gabe's bad jokes and encouraging comments, all four are soon falling about laughing as they practise their squinching for the camera. From looking like a quartet of cardboard cut-outs, they're now completely at ease. Posing, hands on hips and tossing their hair, like A-list celebrities.

I'm laughing with relief, and even Cressida has a smile on her face.

The resulting photos are great. Possibly the best of the day. Not that I'll be telling Gabe that.

I'm about to tackle the big group photo when I spot Harry walking quickly across the lawn towards me. He looks a bit rumpled, in jeans and a creased pink shirt. 'Katy, I am *so sorry*,' he starts, when he's still several yards away. 'I know I said I'd be here in time for the photos but I was out last night and had *way* too much to drink. Didn't get to bed till about four, and then the alarm didn't go off.'

'Just as well Gabe was here,' I respond briskly, not amused by his excuse.

'Hi, Harry,' says Gabe, coming over. 'I see you finally made it.' Harry gives him a stiff smile. 'Better late than never.'

'Right, well, you don't need me any more.' Gabe gives me a cool glance and starts walking away. 'Hope the rest of the day goes well.'

I stare after him as Harry apologises all over again.

It was all going so well. Why did Harry have to arrive and upset the apple cart?

'Hang on a sec.' I touch Harry's arm and run after Gabe. It suddenly seems vitally important that I talk to him.

I catch up, calling out to him, and he turns. 'I just wanted to thank you properly for helping out,' I say, breathlessly. 'I'm *so* grateful.'

'Hey, no problem. It was fun.' He glances back over at the hotel and says, with a hint of scorn, 'At least he turned up.'

Immediately, I'm on the defensive. 'Harry? Yes, I knew he would.'

'Did you?'

'*Yes!*'

His eyes are suddenly chillier than a dip in Lake Windermere. And to be honest, I'm not feeling altogether sunny myself all of a sudden. He's obviously got a real downer on Harry and I can't understand why.

I shrug. 'He's a great guy. And really, really good at what he does. I've seen his work so I know.'

'So have I,' says Gabe shortly. 'And I agree. Harry's a talented photographer.'

'So why on earth reject him just because he's had a few money problems?'

He gives a harsh laugh. 'He told you about that, then?'

'Yes, he did. And I just think it's so unfair of you to deny him a chance.'

His eyes are glinting dangerously but I'm so incensed, I can't help but plough on. 'I mean, I just can't for the life of me understand your attitude. What Harry does with his money is surely nothing whatever to do with you.'

'It's *everything* to do with me,' he barks angrily. 'If there's a chance it could impact on the business. There's also the fact that any assistant of mine must be one hundred per cent reliable. Has Harry shown his worth in that direction today?'

His eyes bore angrily into mine and my heart sinks.

He's absolutely right, of course.

I watch him get into his car, feeling oddly emotional.

He drives off in such a fury, a group of people at the hotel entrance turn and stare after him.

TWENTY

'Christ, what's rattled his cage?' says Harry at my shoulder.

'Oh, nothing,' I say swiftly, not wanting him to know I was discussing him with Gabe. I watch until the black car disappears out of view. 'He was late for some appointment or other.'

'Right, never mind him, we have to get in,' he says. 'The bridal party are lining up to greet their guests, so I think you'll be needed.'

As we enter the hotel, a young woman in uniform passing through the reception area, gives him a bright smile and says, 'Hi, Harry. Fancy seeing you here.'

I glance at him curiously. It was obviously a *really* long night if members of staff now know him by name . . .

'Janine.' He sounds surprised. 'Hi. Yes, I'm feeling much better, thanks.'

I throw him a sharp look as we walk through reception towards the function room. 'Wow, that must have been some night,' I say dryly.

He groans, avoiding my eye. 'The less said the better. I shouldn't have stayed so long. I wanted to check out the hotel in advance of today, that's all.'

'Right, well, I appreciate that, but it shouldn't have got in the way of today. I needed you here this morning, Harry, not just last night.'

He nods sheepishly, then winces and touches his temple.

We arrive outside the function room at the same time as Cressida and Sally, her bridesmaid.

'Come here, gorgeous,' says Sexy Tom, grabbing his bride by the waist and kissing her full on the mouth. 'Where were you? I was starting to think you'd had second thoughts, like.'

'Watch my dress. Watch my dress,' she squeals, pushing him off.

Tom just grins. He's so tolerant. There are many people, I'm sure, who would like to give Stressy Cressy a damn good shake. I mean, if you can't relax and enjoy yourself on the biggest day of your life, when can you?

Sally helps her re-fluff her perfect princess dress to its best effect for the welcome line-up. Then she catches my eye and leans over. 'It's freaky what weddings can do to people. She's usually fairly normal.'

I doubt that, but I smile nonetheless.

Guests begin to drift up to deliver their congratulations before wandering into the reception room.

I glance at Harry, who's doing a great job taking back-up photos for me, just in case I miss a vital shot. He's a really talented young photographer who deserves a break. It was in Gabe's power to give Harry's career a boost. So why didn't he? Surely his debts aren't really enough to stop him getting the job? Couldn't Gabe see that trying to get back on his feet financially meant that Harry needed the job more than ever? It's all very puzzling.

Once the guests are in and the bridal party have been announced by the Master of Ceremonies and taken their seats at the top table, Harry and I move quietly around the room taking shots of the guests, who are seated at large round tables with displays of pretty lilacs and gypsophila in the centre of each.

Cressida is clearly anxious to get going with the meal. She keeps glaring over at the doors leading from the kitchen. And when, finally, a head appears, followed by the rest of the waitress bearing a tray of soup plates, Cressida makes an impatient 'what time do you call this?' sign to her.

The poor waitress, who looks no older than a schoolgirl, hurries in, weaving her way between the tables with her tray, looking as if she wishes the floor would swallow her up. My heart goes out to her.

I've had a look at the menu. The starter is a choice between smoked salmon pâté and gazpacho, a chilled tomato and summer vegetable soup.

The waitress, who's serving the gazpacho, delivers dishes of it to those at the top table who've chosen it, then she moves on to another table. At which point Cressida stands up and says in a loud voice, 'Waitress? We need another gazpacho *here*!'

Everyone turns to look.

The waitress, clearly mortified at having her mistake announced to the entire room, nods and hurries back over.

But in her haste, she gets her foot caught on a chair leg.

She trips and pitches forward, and a bowl of soup flies off the tray and lands right in Cressida's lap.

There's a collective intake of breath and everyone falls silent.

As Cressida slowly looks down at the tomato mess in her lap, you could seriously hear a pin drop.

'Bloody hell,' whispers a woman near me. 'She's going to look like she's just got her period.'

Cressida's mum gets up and rushes over to help, but there's not a lot she can do. The damage is already done. Cressida is sitting, white-faced, in a sort of horrified trance. Everyone is wondering what on earth is going to happen next.

Then Sexy Tom scrapes back his chair and rises to his feet. Everyone stares at him as he clears his throat and looks awkwardly around the room.

'I know it's not speech time yet, folks,' he says sheepishly. 'But I think a word or two is in order here.' He smiles. 'You've all just witnessed me marrying the love of my life.' Without looking down, he reaches for Cressida's hand and takes it between both of his. 'She's taken wedding organisation to the extreme, my missus, and I don't mind telling you, she's tested my patience to the limit too.'

There are a few understanding titters around the room at that.

Tom grins. 'She wanted everything to be perfect. And I get that. I really do. It's an important day, like. But do I care if her dress isn't immaculate? No, I bloody don't. Because all I care about is her and doing everything I can to make her happy.'

A collective 'Ahhhh!' whispers round the room.

He leans down, takes Cressida's face gently in his hands and kisses her. 'I love you, Mrs Taylor. And by the way, what the bloody hell *is* gazpacho anyway?'

As Cressida looks up at him, Tom grins, picks up his own bowl and pours the entire contents – gloopy olive oil, herby tomatoes, the lot – down his white shirt front. Then he sits back down.

There's an astonished silence.

Then everyone starts whooping and clapping at the same time.

Even Cressida is laughing. Big guffaws of glee that might actually be hysteria, but probably aren't because as we all watch, she dives on Tom and snogs him for all she's worth, to more clapping and whistling and stamping of feet.

I've been taking photos throughout this pantomime, while wondering if I should. But now I'm certain it was the right thing to do. Because this was the moment that Mrs Cressida Taylor finally started to enjoy her wedding day . . .

I look around for Harry's pink shirt. There he is by the door, camera poised. I catch his eye and we give each other a thumbs-up. He's obviously been taking pictures of the whole thing, too. Definitely a natural photographer.

I move over to join him. 'I'm glad you made it here today.'

He smiles. 'Any time.'

'Do you fancy a bite to eat when we've finished?'

His smile freezes. 'Er, maybe. Can I let you know?'

'Of course.' I wander away, feeling slightly wrong-footed. That wasn't the response I was expecting. But maybe he's still feeling hung-over from last night.

While everyone starts on their meal, I decide to go outside to eat the sandwich I made up this morning. I've been hired by Cressida and Tom to take photos of the ceremony and reception only. (Some couples, in an effort to trim down costs, get a friend or family member to take photos of the first dance.) So after we've shot the speeches, we'll be free to go. But then there's the knotty problem of how I'm going to get home. With my car abandoned in the village, I suppose I'll have to order a taxi. Or beg a lift from Harry.

But to my amazement, when I go outside, the first car I see is mine. It's parked right outside and at that moment, the girl who spoke to Harry earlier comes up behind me, dangling the keys.

'Mr Harlin brought it back for you. He jump-started it and got a friend to take him back.'

'Thank you.' I take the keys in astonishment.

I can't believe Gabe did that for me. And here I was, having all sorts of dark thoughts about how unfairly he's treated Harry.

Now, I really don't know what to think . . .

TWENTY-ONE

I've been putting off making this phone call. But it has to be done.

Ever since I saw Sienna in the supermarket on Friday, I've been reluctant to leave the house for fear I might bump into her again. I'm honestly beginning to feel there's nowhere I can relax. When I'm at home, I live in constant dread of another threatening phone call from Dominic, piling more financial pressure on me. The fact that he hasn't contacted me in a while just makes me more nervous because I know a call is probably imminent. And then there's having to dodge the meter reader. Plus, every time I leave the house, I'm constantly looking over my shoulder, terrified my sister might be somewhere around. I need to know if she's back for good now.

'She was here for a few days, love,' Mum tells me when I phone. 'She's gone back to Paris to tie up a few loose ends. But she'll be coming home for good on Friday.'

My insides shift uneasily. Five days and she'll be back. Looking over my shoulder is about to become a way of life for me. *Oh God, why couldn't she have stayed in France?*

Mum sighs. 'I wish to heaven you'd let me know why the two of you fell out.'

I swallow hard. 'I keep telling you, Mum, you really don't want to know.'

She gives a groan of impatience. 'But have you any idea what it's *like* for me? You two girls are the most precious things in my life, yet we can never all be in the same room at the same time. It's *crazy*!'

She sounds as if she's on the verge of tears. I know it must be awful for her, but there's nothing I can do about it.

'I have a feeling,' she says slowly, 'that your sister would welcome the chance to talk and sort things out with you.' I grit my teeth.

Yes, I'm sure she would. But for me, it's not that easy. There's a lot to forgive . . .

Mum sighs at my stubborn silence. 'But anyway, it's up to you, love.'

'Yes, it is,' I tell her firmly.

Later, I drive over to see her. As I'm turning into the estate, a small red car is coming out. The driver, a dark-haired woman wearing sunglasses, looks over at me and waves.

Automatically, I wave back, before realising it's that woman, Venus.

'I just saw Venus,' I say, when Mum answers the door. 'Was she here?'

'Er, just briefly.'

'Oh?'

Mum shrugs. 'She wanted that book back that she let me borrow. Come in, come in.'

I peer at the dark circles under her eyes. I haven't seen her for a few weeks because I've been so busy. I'm shocked at how exhausted she looks.

'You lot haven't been to any more of those silly séances, have you?' I ask casually.

Mum laughs. 'Oh God, no. That was all a load of nonsense. Just a bit of fun, really.'

I recall how worried Grace and Annabeth were about Mum

after Venus's so-called communication with Dad. 'It didn't sound like fun. Grace doesn't like Venus much, does she?'

Mum walks off into the kitchen, calling back, 'Oh, Venus is all right. Coffee or tea?'

'Coffee, please. Were you at yoga yesterday?'

'No, I didn't bother. Too much to do.'

I sit down at the kitchen table, watching her fill the kettle. Her hair – which is usually immaculate – looks as if she's just washed it and left it to dry naturally.

'Hasn't Maggie been round this week?' I ask. Maggie, a mobile hairdresser, has been giving Mum a weekly wash and blow-dry for years. It's Mum's treat and she always says life would be infinitely duller without Maggie.

Mum waves her hand dismissively. 'Oh no, I didn't have time, not with the spare room to sort out for Sienna. Maybe next week . . .'

I get up and pop my head round the spare room door. Sure enough, Mum's been busy. There's a new pastel pink duvet cover on the bed and matching curtains, and she's hung a couple of floral prints on the wall.

There's a dead weight inside me. Just seeing the results of Mum preparing to welcome Sienna back has brought it all home to me with a sickening finality.

Soon I'll no longer be able to just jump in the car to visit Mum. Because Sienna will be living here. A wave of misery washes over me at the very thought.

When Mum brings the drinks through to the living room, she turns on the TV and we sit side by side on the sofa, drinking our coffee, watching a documentary about people trying to trace their ancestors. At least, I'm *pretending* to watch it, but I can't stop worrying about how much harder life will be when Sienna is back.

I glance at Mum. She's pretending to watch, too, by the looks of things. Just staring into space. I glance worriedly at her pale complexion. It's really not like her to go without make-up. It's always been part of her morning routine, whether or not she's expecting any visitors. I'd thought she'd be delighted to have Sienna back at home. But the preparations seem to be taking their toll.

As for me, I can't help feeling down every time I think about how my developing friendship with Annabeth and Grace is going to be thwarted from now on. I've loved being able to just pitch up for tea with them all whenever I felt like it. In future I'll have to invite them to mine instead – Mum included – if I don't want to risk running into Sienna.

The doorbell goes and Mum flinches.

'I'll go.' I jump up and open the door to find Grace and Annabeth standing there. They greet me with delighted smiles and hugs.

'Mum, guess who?' I call.

Annabeth catches my wrist and mouths, 'Is she all right?'

I shrug but can't say anything because Mum comes through and beckons them to come in.

'Oh, we can't stop, Dorothy,' says Grace. 'We're off to visit Michael.'

'We were going to try and persuade you to come with us, for a walk round the churchyard and some fresh air,' smiles Annabeth. 'But seeing as you've got very special company, we'll let you off.'

Mum and I stand at the door, saying our goodbyes.

'They're as close as sisters could be, those two,' Mum murmurs, as we watch them walk off, arm in arm.

Back home, I try to push my nagging worries about Mum to the back of my mind.

She's probably been working too hard, preparing for Sienna's homecoming. Everyone responds differently to change. And having Sienna back living with her is clearly going to have a major impact on Mum's life. But things will settle down for her.

I only wish I could say the same for me.

A queasy feeling settles in my gut.

For some reason, I think of the time I spent with Harry, taking photos in the park and driving down to Brighton. It really was a perfect day. I'd been feeling so trapped in a cycle of working all the hours in order to pay the bills, with no time left over for anything else. That day with Harry took me out of myself, and just for a while, I was happy and carefree. *Living*.

Suddenly, I long to see him again. I'll phone him tonight and ask if he'd like to come over for a meal at the weekend. And this time, maybe I won't be afraid to take the plunge and invite him to stay . . .

Decision made, I feel much better. More positive. This is going to be the start of a braver new me.

Settling down at my laptop in the conservatory, I start on the task of editing the photos from Cressida and Tom's wedding. It's always a long job because there are literally hundreds of shots to cast my eye over. It's exciting, though, because you know that however many you might decide to discard, there are always going to be some real gems in amongst them. And the eventual album begins to take shape in your mind.

After a couple of hours hunched over the laptop, my back feels stiff, so I get up and stretch, then wander through to the kitchen to make some tea. I take my cup back to my desk. Seeing my phone lying beside the laptop, I pick it up and dial Harry's mobile. It's time I took steps to change my life. Strike out in a bold new direction. Because otherwise, I will be stuck in this rut forever.

Smiling, I listen to the phone ringing at the other end, still idly flicking through the photos on the screen in front of me. It goes to answer machine. So I end the call and dial Harry's home number.

There's a photo on the screen that I took of Gabe with those four teenage girls. They're all posing like supermodels, squinching away for the camera and having a real laugh. Obviously I can't use it in the album but it's a great shot. Then something in the background of the shot catches my eye. I'd been snapping away merrily, and hadn't actually noticed the couple in a clinch, half-hidden by the branches of a sycamore tree nearby. There's something familiar about the man. That pink shirt . . .

The girl is wearing a plain black skirt and white shirt. She's standing on tip-toe with her arms around the man's neck, drawing him down for a kiss.

I zoom in to get a closer look and my heart does a sickening somersault.

There's no doubt about it.

It's Harry.

And Janine . . .

TWENTY-TWO

I'm not heartbroken. Not really. I didn't know Harry well enough and I certainly wasn't in love with him.

But I'm angry that he lied to me.

All that guff he told me about his alarm not going off, which was why he was late, and how sorry he was – when all the time, he'd been hanging around with Janine.

Feeling like the world's biggest fool, I decide I need to get away from my desk and *that photo*. Slamming down the lid of my laptop, I grab my car keys and head off to check on Mallory.

As I turn into her driveway and motor up the winding, rather unkempt track to the house, I pass Gareth tending to a rhododendron bush. He straightens up and wipes his brow with the back of his hand when he sees it's me, and I stop and wind down my window.

'This must be like painting the Forth Road Bridge,' I laugh, indicating the endless, rambling grounds.

He grins. 'But a bit less dangerous.'

'Is Mallory in?'

'Er, yes, I think she's about.' He runs a hand through his hair. 'Feeling a bit sorry for herself, though. She'll be pleased to see you.'

'Isn't Rupert here, then?'

He shakes his head. 'Joined a baking club, apparently. He's away practising his French fancies.'

I glance at him sideways, not knowing whether to take him seriously. I get the impression Gareth doesn't think a lot of Rupert's artistic leanings. He's more into climbing mountains than painting them.

The mention of Rupert at baking classes gives me a twinge of uneasiness. But I tell myself not to be so ridiculous. Lots of men are good at making cakes. It's not just a female preserve.

'Have you been to the Chopin concert yet with Mum?' I ask, suddenly realising she didn't mention it when I saw her.

He shakes his head. 'She said she couldn't afford it. I told her I'd happily treat her but she wouldn't allow that. So . . .' He shrugs.

'What a shame. Oh well, maybe next time.'

I carry on up to the house, fretting about Mum. I hate to think of her being short of cash. She doesn't have a great deal of income, but she's always been good at making it stretch. I suppose she's had the extra expense of kitting the room out for Sienna's return. I'll have to tell her to make sure Sienna pays her way once she's back.

Mallory greets me at the door in her dressing gown. 'I won't hug you, darling, or you might get this *beastly* lurgy.'

'Poor you.' I follow her into the kitchen. 'Gareth says Rupert's joined a baking club?'

She disappears into the ancient walk-in pantry. 'Yes.' Her voice sounds muffled. 'He's aiming to get more of a rise out of his muffins.'

I wince. 'Is that so?'

I'd pretty much decided my suspicions about Rupert were just a product of my over-active imagination. But now I think I'm back on the fence.

God, why is life so complicated?

Mallory emerges, bearing a bottle of Dandelion & Burdock. 'Can't drink anything else when I'm feeling like shit. Want some?'

'Yeah, go on, then.' After the day I've had, a double vodka would be preferable.

'Has something happened?' she asks suddenly. 'You don't normally pitch up here in the middle of the day unannounced.'

'Can't I come and see my best friend when she's feeling bad?'

'Well, yes, of course. And it's fabulous to see you. Goes without saying. Tell the truth, I'm going cross-eyed with boredom here.'

She sits down and takes a drink which starts a coughing fit.

'It's amazing Rupert hasn't caught it from you,' I say when she's okay again.

'Oh, yes. Mr bloody hale and hearty.' She blows her nose and gets up. 'I got these from Serafina,' she says with a smile, showing me an elegant paper bag (the posh sort with handles) containing three large scented candles. They must have cost a fortune. 'A get-well gift, she said.'

'Oh, they're lovely. How lucky are you to have such a gorgeous mum-in-law.'

'I know.' She smiles. 'So how's Harry?'

'Having fun with a girl who's quite possibly still at school,' I tell her glumly.

'Oh?' Mallory sits down again and pulls her chair up, all ears, and I relate my sorry tale. When I've finished, she frowns. 'Never mind, darling. Plenty more fish and all that.'

'Yes, well, Harry's off the seafood menu altogether.'

'He was just a little tiddler.' She shrugs.

'Yeah, that's the last time I let a fish finger chat me up.'

'*Men.*'

'Yeah. Men.'

'And speaking of the opposite sex, my dear fiancé might just as well move into that bloody studio of his. He stayed there last night. *Again!*'

'Really?' Oh, shit. Now I'm definitely back on the fence.

She shrugs. 'He says his latest painting is his best yet, so he didn't want to stop work.'

'Well, that's understandable,' I say, to reassure her.

Then it occurs to me I'm probably trying to reassure myself as well . . .

In the end, I don't leave Mallory's until after nine. We sit chatting for ages and then Rupert phones and says he's at a crucial stage with his painting and won't be back till later. So Mallory rustles up a pasta dish and we sit and channel flick for a while.

I head out into the drizzly June night, feeling a million times better than when I arrived. The thing with Mallory is that no matter what's happening in my life and how bad I'm feeling, she always cheers me up.

I manage to get a parking space right outside the house and the gate opens first time. I smile to myself. Perhaps things are going my way at last.

Then, just as I'm pushing open the front door, a tall figure steps out of the darkness, right at my side.

'Well, hello, there,' says a familiar voice.

My heart gives a painful lurch.

'Been anywhere interesting?'

I stare up into the shadowy face of my ex . . .

TWENTY-THREE

My heart starts thrumming like a steadily dripping bath tap.

'Dominic. What do you want?'

I transferred another chunk of money into his account only yesterday. I've got nothing left to give him.

'Just to see you,' he says with a lazy shrug.

I feel sick with dread but summon some courage from somewhere. 'Well, I'm actually very busy, so I'd rather you left . . .'

I try to close the door but he steps inside and stops me. My heart is crashing against my ribs. He's a strong guy. Six foot two. I'd be no match at all for him and he knows it.

He grins at me. 'That's not very friendly, Katy. But then, I always quite liked you being mad at me. Very sexy.'

I try to swallow but my throat is bone dry. 'I'm sorry, but I really haven't got time to talk right now, Dominic. I – I've got an important call to make.'

'Aren't you going to offer me a drink, then? We could chat about old times.'

'I don't think so.'

He nods slowly, arms folded, clearly not intending to go anywhere in a hurry.

I take a deep breath. 'Look, Dominic, I'm really sorry I haven't managed to pay all of the loan back yet, but you'll get it soon. I promise. Every last penny. I'm slowly getting the money together, selling things, and the weddings co-ordinator at The Greshingham Hotel has said she'll recommend me to their clients, so business should start to pick up soon . . .'

Okay, it's not happening yet, but it will. Soon. I'm sure of it.

He leans against the wall and folds his arms, a lazy smirk on his face.

'I *will* get your money,' I repeat. 'But I've – er – got a business call to make, so if you don't mind . . . ?'

'No, I don't mind,' he says calmly. 'I'll just wait here. Then we can chat.'

I take a deep breath, hoping he won't see how much I'm trembling beneath my calm exterior.

'What is there to chat about?' I ask lightly.

He smiles. 'Hm, well, let's see . . . how about you start by explaining why you refuse to give us another go?' He shifts his position against the wall. 'I loved you, Katy. Still do, as a matter of fact, even though we've been apart for nearly two years now. But you seem determined to cut me out of your life for good.'

I laugh incredulously. 'Don't you think that's understandable? Under the circumstances?'

He shrugs and looks away. I remember that sulky look of old.

I met Dominic just after I'd set up the business. I fell madly in love with him and life at that time couldn't have been more exciting. But a few months later, the shine had worn off our relationship. Dominic's sulks and silences could last for days on end. And it was always me who had to say sorry.

He says he still loves me, but that's rubbish. I know what this is about. It's his injured pride. He can't stand the fact that I didn't go running into his arms the instant he clicked his fingers. He probably doesn't even need the money. He just wants to get back at me.

Sensing I've momentarily got the upper hand, I force myself

to be strong. 'Look, Dominic, you loaned me the money when I needed it and I'll always be really grateful. But I need you to be patient a little longer. Give me some time to get the rest of the money together and then we can put all this unpleasantness behind us.'

I hold my breath as he continues staring, sullen-faced, into the distance. I've got my fingers crossed behind my back.

At last, he turns and raises three fingers in front of my face. 'Three months. You've got till the end of September.'

I nod, relief washing through me. 'The money will be in your account three months to the day.'

I don't know how I'll do it, but I'll find a way. I have to.

I'm praying he'll leave now. But he glances at the little hall table, where I put mail to be posted. My daffodil brooch is lying there, along with a parcel ready to send off the next day.

He reaches over and picks up the brooch. 'Your dad gave you this, didn't he?' He turns it over and examines it. 'Your good luck charm.' He grins at me. 'Shame your luck ran out.' He tosses it in the air and catches it. Then he lobs it at me.

Taken by surprise, I'm unable to catch it and the brooch bounces off the hard tiled floor.

'Three months,' he repeats. Then he goes out and slams the door behind him.

Trembling, I bend to rescue my brooch. Dropping it has weakened the crack across the middle. My dad's beautiful gift now lies in my palm, broken in two.

That night, I lie awake for a long time, thinking about how I can get the remainder of Dominic's money together. After tonight's unsettling encounter, I know exactly where I stand. If I don't deliver the balance into his account by the end of September, he will be back at my door. Of that I am sure.

So there's no question about it. I need to get that money.

But how?

I'm running out of things to sell on the auction sites. But I have another idea that's been bubbling away in my mind ever since Andrea and Ron's wedding. It was sparked by something Andrea said when she was in her hotel room that morning, getting ready.

She said she wished she'd brought a notebook and pen so she could write down everything that happened. Then she'd never forget the precious little details of her special day.

That set me thinking. Maybe I could offer a slightly different service to other wedding photographers? What if I wrote the story of their day and incorporated those cherished memories into a special wedding book that would contain words as well as photos? It would be the same as a wedding album, except the couple would have an extra element to remind them of their big day. I could offer the story as an extra. And naturally, I'd be able to charge for it. But to convince couples that it would be a lovely addition to their album, I'd have to create a sample. So they could see what they were buying.

Fired up, I spring out of bed, not caring that it's three o'clock in the morning. I grab a pen and paper, take them back to bed, and start writing a fictitious story, based on a wonderful winter wedding I photographed back in December.

Half an hour later, I've got the beginnings of a story:

Oh, the romance of a December wedding! Just the idea of it sets the imagination racing. The feel of cold, bracing air on your cheeks and the glow of lamps in windows hinting at the delicious warmth within. The fairy lights and sparkle of a Christmassy venue. And the best excuse ever for dressing in faux fur.

And the chance it might snow, of course.

A day earlier and The Greshingham Hotel may well have resembled a traditional Christmas card. That week, the first snowfalls of winter had taken the area by surprise and many a guest – not to mention the wedding party themselves – must have wondered if Mother Nature intended to completely mess up their carefully considered travel plans.

But as it turned out, all trace of the snow had vanished by the morning of the wedding, which dawned crisp and still with a hint of blue skies.

The arrival of the wedding transport – two classic cars, organised as a special surprise by the bride's dad – generated a great deal of excitement and it was interesting to note that while the women stayed indoors with the bride, titivating themselves, the men rushed out immediately to examine an altogether different kind of bodywork . . .

When everyone was finally ready, they gathered together in the kitchen for a glass (or two) of champagne. It was agreed that the kitchen – the setting for so many joyful and precious family times down the years – was the perfect place in which to toast the bride's happiness and the prospect of a wonderful day ahead . . .

I read it back, an excited feeling in the pit of my stomach.

Could I be onto something?

I throw my pen and paper onto the floor, put out the light and dive under the covers. I'll talk to Mallory about it tomorrow.

A few weeks later, the first Friday in July, Harry calls me.

I'm working in the conservatory with the doors flung open to the garden, the scent of flowers and barbecues drifting in on the evening breeze.

The last time I saw Harry was at Cressida and Tom's wedding back at the beginning of June so it's a surprise to hear his voice.

'Sorry I haven't been in touch for a while,' he says, sounding – to my ears, at any rate – a little guilty. (Perhaps if I didn't know he'd been hiding something from me, I wouldn't have detected the slight awkwardness in his tone.)

'Hi, Harry. No problem at all. How's the romance?'

A brief pause. Followed by a baffled, '*Sorry?*'

I bark out a slightly bitter laugh. 'You've been rumbled. I spotted you in the background of a photo I took. With the lovely Janine.'

'Oh God, really?' he groans. 'Shit, I'm so sorry.'

'Don't worry about it. Presumably the reason you were late to the wedding was because you'd met Janine at The Broomhill Hotel the night before?'

'Christ, you'd make a good detective.'

He sounds as if he's squirming a bit. No harm in that.

'It was a long night, then, but not with the mates?'

'Yeah. I just . . . well, I know we weren't going out or anything, but I thought you might be upset, so I didn't . . .'

'Hey, it's okay. Really. Are you still seeing Janine?'

'Yeah. She's nice. And she's more my . . . well, we're getting on okay, so far.'

I laugh. 'You were going to say she's more your age.'

'No!'

'But you're right, Harry. She is. And I hope it works out for you.'

I'm surprised to find I actually mean this.

'Thanks, Katy.'

We chat for a while longer and he says he's pleased that he called because he wasn't happy with the way we parted company.

I hang up smiling. I meant what I said to Harry about him and Janine. We were never going to be right as a couple. I can see that now. Harry's a young lad with all his exploring still to do in the world of dating. Whereas I'm . . . well, I suppose I'm past experimenting and content to wait for the right person to come along.

I'm so engrossed in what I'm doing, the time flies by and it's getting dark when I finally switch off the laptop. I'm just putting lights on in the living room when there's a knock on the front door.

I freeze. It's after nine. Who can be calling at this time of night? It can't be Dominic because he's given me three months to come up with the goods. But perhaps he's come back for some reason . . .

216

I open the door an inch or two and my heart lurches at the figure standing there. For a second, I'm convinced it is Dominic.

'Hi, it's only me,' says a deep voice. 'Sorry to call so late. I've only just realised the time.'

Relief floods through me.

It's Gabe.

TWENTY-FOUR

'Hi. I – I thought you were someone else for a minute,' I blurt out.

He gives a wry smile. 'Sounds ominous.'

'Something like that.' I clutch my baggy cardigan around me, suddenly wishing that I could afford to buy myself some chic working-at-home gear instead of slouching around in clothes not even posh enough to do the gardening in.

Not that it's ever bothered me before, so why am I feeling so self-conscious about it now?

'I've got a wedding for you,' Gabe says, without preamble. 'If you'd like it.'

'Oh. Right.' I stare at him in surprise. 'Great.'

'It's friends of mine. They're getting married in a wood and their photographer has cancelled. So I recommended you.'

'Gosh. Well, thanks,' I say, covered in confusion. 'In a wood, you say? That will definitely be a first.'

'They're a great couple. Bryony and Mick. I think you'll like them.' He digs in his pocket for his phone. 'I'll give you Bryony's number.'

The names ring a bell for some reason. 'Is Bryony's surname Williamson by any chance?'

He looks surprised. 'Yes, it is. You know her?'

I shake my head. 'No. But my mum knows her parents.'

'Oh.' He shakes his head. 'Small world.'

'Yes, isn't it? Do you want to come in?'

He nods and steps out of the darkness into the light, and I remember just how tall he is. The hallway suddenly seems tiny with Gabe filling up the space. I usher him through to the living room and pass him a scrap of paper and a pen to write down the bride's details.

'This is nice,' he says, looking around. 'None of your own work on the walls, though?'

I shake my head. 'I always sympathise with actors when they say they cringe if they're forced to watch their own performance on TV.'

He nods. 'Yeah. It can look like you're a bit self-involved if the walls are plastered with your own work.'

'Well, I'm sure *you'd* be forgiven for displaying your own photos.' I intended this as a compliment. I think. But it came out a little aggressively.

He gives me a look as if he's not sure what I meant and I flush an attractive shade of scarlet. There's a moment's awkward silence, then we both start speaking at once.

'Would you like a drink . . . ?'

'There's another reason I came round . . .'

We laugh, and he says, 'After you.'

'Drink?'

'You don't have lager, do you?'

'Actually, I do.' *Thanks to Harry.*

He follows me through to the kitchen. 'It's been on my mind, the conversation we had about Harry. I'm sorry I was abrupt, but I've got a good reason for being cautious.'

I turn. 'You have? Then I'd like to hear it. Harry's just a young kid starting out in life. Okay, he's got a few debts to pay, but refusing to give him a job won't help that situation in the slightest.'

He barks out a laugh. 'It might surprise you to learn that my main aim in life isn't to help Harry dig himself out of debt.'

'Yes, but it does seem rather harsh. Everyone has debts these days. It's not exactly unusual.'

His face darkens. 'Not everyone is in debt. *I'm* not.'

'No, well, that's hardly surprising when you're the great Gabe Harlin and your photos sell for thousands,' I snap, feeling thoroughly judged, even though he has no idea that I'm financially challenged, just like Harry.

He looks away as if he's brooding on how to reply. When he turns to speak, his tone is icy cold. 'What you don't understand is that it wasn't always like that. In fact, there was a time not so long ago when I had absolutely nothing. *Less* than nothing, actually, because I owed people money right, left and centre.'

I stare at him, too surprised to speak.

His face is ashen and two deep grooves have appeared above his nose. His eyes are bleak as a wintry North Sea. Right this minute, he definitely has the look of a man who's been seriously challenged by life. With a heavy sigh, he pushes both hands through his hair.

'Want something stronger than lager?' I ask. 'I've got brandy.'

'Can't stand the stuff. Whisky?'

I nod. 'Coming up.'

When I return with a tumbler full of the amber nectar, he's sprawled on the sofa, long legs stretched out, head resting back on his hands, staring up at the ceiling. He sits up and takes the glass I hold out to him.

Our hands touch and a delicious shock zips through me. His eyes slide up to mine and I shiver. Did he feel it too?

'Thank you. Cheers.' He raises the glass. 'Aren't you having one?'

'I'll have some wine.' I retreat to the kitchen to fetch it, self-consciously aware of his eyes on me. I'm a bag of nerves and when I reach into the cupboard for a wine glass, it almost slips through my fingers.

I'm burning with curiosity to know how a man as powerful and self-assured as Gabe Harlin could possibly have landed in

221

such deep financial trouble. But when I return with my wine and sit in the armchair opposite, he doesn't say anything for a while. We just sip our drinks in silence.

Finally, he says, 'You remember that woman who came to the exhibition?'

'Er, yes, I do. She seemed—' *Oh God, how do I put this politely?*

'Pissed? Yes, she was,' he says softly. 'Sadly, that seems to be pretty much her permanent state these days. When she's not gambling away every penny she can lay her hands on, that is.'

'When she's not gambling away every penny she can lay her hands on, that is.'

'How awful. So who is she?'

'My fiancée.' He smiles grimly. 'Well, *ex*-fiancée. Caroline.'

My heart bumps painfully at his words. For a moment, there's a charged silence.

'Oh,' I breathe at last. 'I see.'

Gabe takes a big slug of whisky, grimacing as it burns its way down. 'She wasn't a gambler when I first met her. Or a drinker.' He laughs harshly. 'Well, she was probably both. But she kept it hidden from me for a long time. I used to wonder why she was always forgetting her purse and how she never seemed to have any money, even though she commanded a high salary from her sales and marketing job.'

His lips twist wryly. 'Anyway, we got together and things were great. I fell for Caroline hook, line and sinker. We were crazy about each other and three months after we met, she proposed.'

My eyes widen with surprise. '*She* asked *you*? How – erm – modern.'

He nods. 'So then a week later, her ring goes missing and however hard we look, we can't find it. So I buy her a replacement – and would you believe it, she loses that one as well. Then she breaks down in tears and confesses that she sold them both to try and recoup some losses at the casino.' He takes another drink. 'Except she gambled that money away, too.'

'Oh God, did she get some help?'

He shakes his head. 'She swore blind she didn't have a gambling addiction. I knew if I couldn't get her to admit it, the future was pretty bleak, but I couldn't bring myself to give up on her.' He's staring into space, lost in the past, and my heart goes out to him. 'We were together three years in total and in that time, she bled me dry. I sold my house to pay off the debts she'd accrued, hoping we could make a fresh start, and she swore she'd never gamble again.'

He looks across at me, his eyes darkened with painful memories. 'But then she was fired for drinking on the job and so, of course, her income stream dried up. And that's when she started shop-lifting to get the money to feed her gambling addiction. In the end, I was forced to declare myself bankrupt.'

'God, how awful,' I whisper. 'Was there no other way?'

He shakes his head. 'I had to start from scratch, building my photography business up again, trying to get people to trust me. There's a stigma attached to bankruptcy. People naturally suspect you must be terrible with money. It took a long time to convince business associates otherwise.'

'So you're . . . not with Caroline any more?'

He shakes his head. 'She broke off our engagement.'

I stare at him in astonishment. '*She* did? But . . .'

'She said I made her feel as small as a slug.' He gives a bitter laugh. 'I suppose that was the guilt talking. But anyway, she left me for some wealthy airline boss she met at the casino. No doubt they gamble their nights away. But at least he can afford to subsidise her. For now.'

'God, that's terrible,' I whisper. He stares into space for a long moment. Then he draws a deep breath and rakes his hands through his hair.

'I only came here to mention the wedding. Sorry for laying all this on you.' He smiles grimly. 'I suppose I'll have to explain myself to Harry, too. The poor guy probably didn't know what was happening, with me raging at him for not revealing straight away the extent of his debts. I mean, why should he? I'm a potential employer, not his keeper.'

He sighs heavily and my heart goes out to him.

That woman, his fiancée, might be clever and beautiful and glamorous but she has a great deal to answer for. The destruction of a man's hopes and dreams, for a start, as well as his whole business and livelihood. With such a liability for a fiancée, I guess his knee-jerk reaction to Harry's money problems was hardly surprising. Debt has ruined his life. Why would he employ someone who might take him down the same path all over again?

There's suddenly a cold feeling in the pit of my stomach.

How would Gabe react if he found out about my own dire financial situation? I'll have to make sure he doesn't find out.

A second later, I'm thinking: *But do I care that much about Gabe's opinion of me?*

I stare into my wine glass. The answer is sobering, to say the least. I do care.

In fact, I care far more than is good for me . . .

'So do you think your ex is hoping you might get back together?' I ask, remembering the dramatic way she clung to Gabe that night at the exhibition. She seemed pretty determined. Woe betide any woman who tried to take her place in Gabe's affections.

He puts his drink down on the side table and stretches out, his head resting back on his hands again. 'Well, if she is, she'll be disappointed. It's never going to happen.'

I nod. 'Not while she's still in the grip of her addictions.'

He rests his eyes on me, and there's an expression in them that I can't quite decipher. 'Not ever,' he says, with a slight shake of his head. 'Those days are over. I've moved on.'

He smiles suddenly and it's like the sun coming out. I smile back, a warm feeling spreading inside me that may or may not have something to do with the fact that he's just consigned his impossibly beautiful fiancée to history.

He glances at his watch and frowns.

'Another whisky?' I offer, suddenly aware I don't want him to leave yet.

Maybe it's because the wine is slipping down nicely and it makes a change to have company. Or maybe it's because Gabe has opened up to me in a way I never expected and I'd like to know more about him. How he managed to claw his way back from disaster to being one of the shining stars in the industry. And even more crucially, whether he runs past my house every morning . . .

'Go on, then,' he says, holding out his glass. 'I'm supposed to be at a meeting. But it's a loose arrangement, so I guess I can be late.'

When I return with our drinks, he's on his feet, scanning my book shelves. He grins. 'There's a high proportion of grisly thrillers among this lot.'

I laugh. 'Yeah, it's pretty much the only excitement I get these days.'

Oh God, what possessed me to say that? Now he'll think I'm a right boring old fart.

'What were you expecting, anyway?' I smile provocatively. 'Lots of girly chick lit?'

'I suppose I was.' He looks over at me, and there's a hint of tenderness in his eyes that makes my heart miss a beat. 'You're full of surprises, you know.'

I laugh. 'Why, because I don't read stories about love and happy-ever-afters?'

'Among other things.' His eyes crinkle at the corners and as he takes his glass from me, our fingers accidentally meet again. A powerful sensation crackles up my arm and through my entire body, making me almost gasp out loud. I whip my hand back and turn away to sit down in my armchair.

'Come and sit over here,' Gabe says casually. 'You're miles away over there. I can't see you properly.'

My heart lurches then starts beating frantically.

'Is there something wrong with your eyes, then?' I ask, laughing far too heartily.

'No,' he replies simply, eyes alight with amusement.

Still I hesitate, as a stern voice warns me it will end in disaster. Gabe Harlin is a gorgeous, talented photographer – *there, I've said it* – who could have any woman he wanted. He couldn't possibly be interested in me.

But he did say I was surprising. And he did pitch up at my door, late at night, to offer me work . . .

'I don't bite,' he says, grinning up at me as I stand there like the indecisive Libran that I am. 'It's just a seat.'

Of course it is. I'm behaving like a coy virgin.

Dear God, the poor man probably thinks he's stumbled across some weird relic from the days of Jane Austen when women sat with their ankles crossed, and being with a man unchaperoned caused such a scandal you had to get married immediately.

I mean, what on earth did I think was going to happen—?

I plonk myself down right next to him to prove I'm not in the least bit coy or virginal. But unfortunately, I misjudge my landing position and lose my balance, swaying into him, my hand ending up pressed on his thigh.

At the touch of those hard muscles beneath my fingers, I leap away, alarmed at what he might think – but even more alarmed by my own powerful reaction to the feel of him.

Bloody hell, never mind a slight electric shock, we're talking national grid here . . .

'You okay there?' Chuckling, he slips his arm around me to steady me.

I turn to protest that I've left my wine by the chair. But those mesmerising blue eyes are gazing down into mine, full of gentle amusement and something else that makes my heart lurch into my throat.

There's a brief second where I know I could escape.

But do I really want to?

Then his mouth comes down on mine and my head starts exploding with stars like a very raunchy version of a Disney movie.

TWENTY-FIVE

A faint whisper in my head is still cautioning me to resist, but it's way too late. My body is in total surrender mode. Crushed against Gabe's broad chest, my fingers moulding the solid muscles of his back and sliding up to entangle themselves in his silky dark hair, I am a total goner, unable to hear anything except the crashing of my own heart.

Things are getting steamier by the moment.

Then from nowhere, a rock band starts blasting out a number, pulsing guitars fighting for space in my head. It's Kings of Leon, I think, puzzled, as I swim reluctantly to the surface.

Gabe pulls away from me and reaches for his jacket. Then he's talking into his phone, still holding me tightly against him.

'Yeah, I know,' he's saying. 'An hour and a half, depending on traffic. I – um – got waylaid.'

He squeezes my waist and I shriek.

'Noise? What noise?' Gabe says into the phone, grinning lazily at me. 'Don't worry, I'll be there.'

He ends the call. 'That was my agent. Wondering where I am.' He kisses my nose. 'So, very regretfully, I'll have to make a move.'

'Of course. No problem.' I get up, straightening my clothes, and start clearing away the glasses, feeling more than a little dazed at what just went on between us.

Gabe comes into the kitchen, where I'm running water into the washing-up bowl and staring dazedly out of the window.

'You're overflowing,' he murmurs, putting his arms around my waist and pulling me against him.

'I'm what?' I squeak, looking down at my shirt.

He chuckles and reaches over to turn off the tap.

'Oh.' I smile and turn towards him.

'Right. I've got to go. Even though I'd much rather stay here,' he murmurs, gazing down at me in a way that leaves no room for doubt that he means every word. 'Are you and Harry . . . ?'

I shake my head. 'We were. Sort of. But we're just friends now.'

He smiles. 'Good.'

My heart lifts.

'So if I were to suggest a little restaurant I know by the sea where we could have lunch and walk on the beach, and get to know each other a bit better, how might you respond?' He says it casually, but I catch a hint of uncertainty in his eyes, as if he's not entirely sure I won't turn him down.

I smile up at him. 'I'd probably say that it sounds heavenly.'

'In that case, are you free the day after tomorrow?'

'Er . . . yup.' I try to sound cool but my big smile probably gives me away.

'Right, it's a date. Haven't been on one of those for quite some time.' He gives me one of his lazy, knee-weakening smiles and my heart leaps.

I laugh. 'Me, neither. Well, apart from Harry.'

'What happened there? If you don't mind me asking.'

'He – er – found someone in his own age group, shall we say? Which was fine by me,' I add, just in case he thinks I'm pining for Harry.

At the door, he sends me a text so I have his number and I

promise to do the same. Then he kisses me hard on the mouth. 'I'll be in touch about the wedding. And that beach walk.'

And then he's gone.

I stand at the door, watching his car lights disappear into the distance, heading for London. Then I go back inside and curl up on the sofa, in the exact spot where Gabe was sitting only minutes earlier. My head is whirling. I can barely take it all in. I've been denying my attraction to him all along, afraid to admit there might be something there because that would mean risking my heart. Opening up to someone for the first time in forever.

It's a scary thought.

But one I can no longer ignore.

Of course, there's always the chance that he's just playing with me. I might let my guard down and be sorely disappointed. Do I really want to open myself up to the possibility of being hurt again?

But the thing is, it felt perfectly genuine when he talked about us spending some time together, getting to know each other. So perhaps I should just go with the flow. Take a chance. That's what Mallory would tell me to do. I can almost hear her voice in my head. 'Just have some fun, darling. You deserve it.'

I spring up from the sofa to go and finish washing the glasses. I'll just go with the flow. See where it leads me. Nothing ventured and all that . . .

But I can't help the nagging thought that getting involved with a man like Gabe can only end in tears.

All of them mine . . .

I spend most of the night tossing and turning, dwelling on everything we said and did, and by the morning I've almost convinced myself that whatever happens is fine by me.

This is rather contradicted, however, by the fact that every time the phone rings, I practically jump into next week, thinking it might be Gabe.

Then at four o'clock, when I've started to wonder if I imagined last night, the phone goes and it's him.

'Hi, Katy. How are you today?'

At the sound of his voice, my heart lifts. It wasn't a dream after all.

'I'm fine. How was the drive to London?'

'Lonely. I was wishing you'd come with me.'

'You didn't invite me,' I say boldly.

He chuckles. 'I will next time. Listen, I'm going to be non-stop the rest of the week, but I'll phone you on Friday night.'

'Okay.' *Perhaps he's regretting last night and he's trying to let me down gently.*

'We can arrange our beach trip then.'

'Lovely.' A little bubble of happiness surges up inside.

'That's if you're still up for it?'

The slight doubt in his tone makes my heart sing. 'Oh, I'm definitely up for it.'

'Good. Great. Excellent. See you, Katy.'

I'm smiling all over my chops when I hang up. And now, of course, I can't settle to anything at all.

So I go upstairs and start rooting through my wardrobe for something nautical but nice that's perfect for lunch at the seaside.

Next day, I phone Mum for a chat. She's seemed oddly distracted recently and I've been telling myself it's because she's engrossed in preparing for Sienna's return.

She sounds better this morning, much more like her usual cheery self. But she's in a rush, she says, because she's getting ready for the yoga class in the village.

'Bet you can't wait for your spa weekend,' I say, aware it's coming up in a few weeks' time.

There's a brief silence.

Then she says, 'I've decided not to go, love.'

'Oh. But why?'

'Well, it's not really me,' she says. 'All that massage and stuff.'

'But I thought you were really looking forward to it,' I say, astonished. 'And Grace and Annabeth will be really disappointed that you're not going.'

'Oh, they don't mind,' she says airily. 'They don't need me there to have a good time, do they?'

'No, I suppose not,' I say slowly.

I can't force her to make the trip. But I do think she'd have had a great time.

'Anyway, got to go, love,' she says. 'See you soon.'

I hang up, feeling vaguely uneasy. But there's nothing I can put my finger on. I must go round and see her, though, before Sienna gets here on Friday.

I spend the rest of the morning designing a flyer to advertise the business. I've included engagement and baby photos among the services I'm offering, hoping to expand my market. And I'm planning to design a dummy wedding book – photos and story – to show to potential clients.

I've phoned Gabe's friend, Bryony, who's getting married to her fiancé, Mick, in September. She sounds really nice and full of fun, and she's amazed when I tell her our mums are good friends. We arrange a date to meet to discuss the details. Her deposit will be very useful indeed, but I need some more bookings – and thus more deposits – in a hurry if I'm going to boost my income and pay Dominic back by the end of September.

At lunchtime, with the leaflet design complete, I decide to go in search of a quality paper. I've just stepped out onto the street, when someone toots their horn and draws up alongside me.

It's Gabe.

My heart goes into happy overdrive.

He leans over and opens the passenger door. 'Hey, sexy. Want a lift? I'm on my way to a meeting but I couldn't just drive past and leave you to walk.'

I lean down to smile at him. I wasn't expecting to even hear from him until Friday night, let alone actually see him in the flesh, so I really feel like I've won the jackpot. 'I'm barely going a few hundred yards.' I point in the direction of the village.

'Well, hop in anyway.'

I shrug happily and slide in beside him.

He leans over to kiss me and it ends up being very thorough indeed. I give myself up to his magical touch and his glorious lemony musky scent. Until the car behind decides we're a road-block and honks his horn impatiently.

We move off and I check my lipstick in the visor mirror. Yup. Plastered everywhere it shouldn't be.

Gabe grins, watching me do a hasty mop-up job.

'I really miss my old car,' I say wistfully. 'It had great mirrors like this one. And built-in sat nav. And Bluetooth.'

'So you didn't always have your old banger? What happened to the other car?'

My heart lurches. 'Er . . . I had to sell it. To buy more photo-graphic equipment.' I bite my lip, hating having told him a lie. I just couldn't tell him that like Harry, I got behind with the payments and the company took it back.

He's nodding. 'Very sensible. Most people would have kept the car and taken out a loan.'

I'm blushing at the lie, crossing my fingers he won't notice.

'I expect you bought this car outright?' I ask lightly.

He nods. 'There's no way I'd pay over the odds to a leasing company. I've learned thrift the hard way.' I glance at the grim set of his jaw. He still bears the scars from the terrible havoc Caroline caused him.

I'll never forget his angry reaction to Harry's being in debt.

What will happen if he finds out about me?

The very thought makes me go cold inside.

I'll just have to make sure he doesn't find out.

TWENTY-SIX

Mallory is over the moon I'm getting some action in the man department at last. Although right this minute, she's panting so loudly, it sounds as though *she's* the one enjoying a close encounter with the opposite sex. I watch her making laborious progress up the grassy bank, her normally porcelain pale complexion beetroot red with the effort.

'When I said a nice country walk.' *Gasp.* 'That's what I meant, darling.' *Gasp.* 'Not a bloody uphill marathon!' *Gasp and a really rather pathetic groan.*

'Nearly there,' I call encouragingly from my perch higher up on a rocky slab. 'Then you can have a rest.'

'Oh, big bloody hoorah! So this date with Gabe . . . ?'

'Yes?'

She gives up and has a minor coughing fit instead, wheezing and bashing her chest like it's next stop, senior citizens' bus pass. I have to say, I was quite amazed when Mallory told me it was time she got fit. I was even more surprised when, next time I saw her, she was wearing jeans and a tight red top that showed a lot more cleavage than usual. The red clashed a bit with her hair but it did look good. When I expressed surprise at her change of style, she got a bit defensive and showed me the label.

'They're vintage, darling. And they're Chloe.' As if that explained everything.

I'd thought a gentle walk would ease her in nicely, but to hear her talk, you'd think I was frogmarching her up the north face of the Matterhorn.

She gulps down water and flakes out next to me, lying flat on the rocky slab. 'Bally heck, Katherine Peacock, what on earth are you trying to *do* to me? That must be the furthest I've trekked in about twenty-five years.'

'At least you've got the gear.'

She certainly has. Although proper climbing boots and water-proof trousers do seem a *little* excessive for a short stroll up to a local monument.

She lifts her leg in the air and examines her boot with disdain. 'They're filthy already. Look.'

I snort. 'They're *supposed* to get dirty in the great outdoors, you pillock.'

She grimaces.

'I mean, you don't see Bear Grylls swinging from tree to tree, looking like he's en route to a royal garden party,' I reason.

Her only response is another groan.

'Is this sudden desire to get fit a pre-wedding thing?' I ask.

'Sorry?' She hauls herself up into a sitting position.

'Is it the wedding that's brought all this on?'

She looks confused for a second. Probably suffering oxygen deprivation at thirty-five feet. Then she nods. 'Oh, yes. The wedding. Got to get in shape for it. Exactly.'

She takes another long glug of water. 'So anyway, this date of yours . . .'

'He's phoning on Friday night.'

'So you don't know where you're going yet?'

'No, but he was talking about lunch by the beach.'

She nods. 'Nice. Just make sure you don't piss him orf the way you did Harry.'

'I'll do my best, Mum.' My heart is doing a funny little dance, just talking about Gabe.

My mobile rings and I fumble in my pockets for it.

'Hi, there,' says the man himself, his deep voice sliding deliciously into my ear. 'I called at the house but you weren't there. Where are you?'

'I'm with Mallory.' My voice emerges as a squeak of delight. He'd said that he'd be busy this week, so it's a lovely surprise to hear from him. 'We're trekking across Britain.'

I'm beaming like a loony so there's no need to indicate to Mallory who it is. She crosses her eyes and clasps her hands to her heart. Grinning, I turn away slightly.

'Out in the hills somewhere?' he asks.

'No, up by the monument at the end of the high street,' I giggle. 'We'll be on our way back down in a minute. That's if I can revive my walking buddy.'

'Ah, right. I'm heading home just now and I'm stopping off in the village. Apparently there's a review of my exhibition in the evening paper, and I want to pick up a copy from the newsagent's. I can give you a lift home if you like.'

'That's nice of you. Although I'm sure we can stagger back okay.'

'That's not the point,' he growls sexily. 'I want to see you. I'm suffering withdrawal symptoms.'

'Ooh, well, we'll have to see what we can do about that,' I giggle, thrilled that he sounds as keen on me as I am on him.

Mallory makes a vomiting sign but I know she's pleased for me. I should probably tone down the ecstatic grin, though. That could get a bit wearing.

'Bloody Nora but he's awfully eager,' she exclaims, when I end the call.

I get up, unable to stop smiling, and she holds out her hand. 'Pull me up, there's a darling.'

The monument is perched on a little hill just beyond the

village, and walking back to the high street, we pass a modern residential area and a little business park that's primarily occupied by craftsmen. There's a ceramics studio where you can go in and buy the most amazing ornaments and jewellery. I think that's where Dad bought my daffodil brooch. And there's an artisan baker that smells gloriously of real old-fashioned bread, the way it apparently used to before it was mass-produced and pumped full of preservatives.

Hungry after our walk, we sniff the air like the Bisto Kids.

'I'm going to start making my own bread,' I announce. 'Imagine if the house was full of that smell . . .'

Mallory hoots. 'Make bread? You've barely got time to tie your shoelaces these days, darling. Where would you find the time for *that*?'

I grin at her. 'There are some things you just have to *make* time for. Hey, isn't that Rupert?'

I point over to one of the studios. A man is getting out of his car. As we watch, he walks over to the building and lets himself in.

'What?' Mallory glances over. 'No. That's not him.'

'But hasn't he just rented a studio to do his painting?'

'Yes, it's somewhere around here.' She looks at her watch. 'Oh Lord, is that the time? I've got a parcel being delivered after five. Can we get a shift on?'

'Haven't you seen his studio?' I'm running to keep up with her. After claiming to be fit for nothing after the walk, she's now a woman on a mission.

'No, darling. Why would I want to? The house is already full of Rupert's landscape watercolours. His studio will just be more of the same.'

She has a point. Rupert's paintings are all so yawningly similar. The only difference, as far as my untutored eye can tell, is that some of his hills have heather on them and some don't. David Hockney can definitely sleep easy in his bed.

It *was* Rupert, though, I'm almost certain of it. Maybe they've had a row and she wants to stay out of his way. Passionate couples like them are always falling out spectacularly.

I'm puzzled by Mallory's reaction. But I'm so eager to see Gabe, I really haven't got time to reflect on it.

As soon as we hit the high street, I spot Gabe's car parked outside the newsagent's and quicken my pace. Mallory says she'll walk back to my house herself to collect her car because she really doesn't fancy being a gooseberry.

'Phone me tomorrow with details,' she orders, walking off.

'What sort of details?'

She waves without turning round. 'Just details.'

'Details about what?' asks Gabe, emerging at that moment from the post office. He grabs me round the waist, then leans down to kiss me.

'Well, *that* would be telling.' I bat my eyelids at him. 'Where's the paper?'

'I'm just going in.' He nods at the newsagent's. 'Back in a sec.'

He starts walking away and I notice he's limping again.

'So what actually happened to your leg?'

He stops and turns. 'That's a story and a half,' he says wryly.

'What do you mean?'

He wanders back, smiling grimly. 'You really want to know?'

I nod.

I want to know absolutely everything there *is* to know about this supremely glorious man.

'Well . . .' He pushes back his hair, obviously wondering where to begin. 'It was one of those team-building weekends, organised by the bank Caroline worked for. I was there as her other half, but it went rapidly downhill the first morning. Literally.'

'Oh God, what happened?'

He sighs heavily. 'She promised she wouldn't drink but she started on the wine at dinner when we arrived on the Friday night. I couldn't embarrass her by ordering her to stop in front of her colleagues. So she went on drinking into the early hours then started on the mini bar in our room before crashing out.'

He relates all this in a grim monotone and my heart goes out to him.

'So anyway, next morning she was still pretty drunk and I tried to convince her to stay in the room and plead a headache to avoid the team-building exercises that were planned.'

'And did she? Stay in the room?'

He shakes his head. 'Caroline doesn't like to be told what to do. I used to admire that side of her when we first met, but it was pretty self-destructive as it turned out. So we joined everyone for the hill walk and she seemed okay at first. That's the thing with drunks; they get used to fooling people into believing they're sober. But the trouble was, we were climbing higher all the time with a steep drop at one side, and she kept straying dangerously near the edge.'

He pauses and I can see the despair in his face as he recalls the events of that day. 'Eventually, I thought, to hell with her colleagues, I need to take her back. But when I took her hand to try and steer her away, she told me to stop fussing because I was just like her dad. Then she pulled away from me with such force, she lost her balance and fell down the slope.'

I stare up at him in horror. 'Oh my God, was she all right?'

He nods. 'She managed to slither down onto a natural ledge about twenty feet below me. I think it was luck more than design that she landed there. Otherwise, she would have fallen God knows how far. The party leader contacted the mountain rescue team, but I wasn't going to wait for them to arrive, so I half-slid, half-jumped down to her. And managed to smash my foot quite badly in the process.'

'When was this?' I ask.

He shrugs. 'A couple of years ago, but it still gives me grief if I've been overdoing the running.'

Something occurs to me. 'Is that why you were limping that first time I – er – bumped into you?'

He grins. 'Yeah, your cannoning into me managed to jar the old wound good and proper.'

I make a guilty face. 'Sorry.'

He leans over and kisses me lingeringly. 'Forgiven. And for the record, crashing into you was one of the best things that's ever happened to me.'

Smiling happily, I ask, 'What were the others?'

'Oh.' He frowns up at the sky for inspiration. 'The day Swindon Town won the FA Cup?'

'When was that?'

'Never. But as fantasies go, it's right up there.'

'Well, I suppose I should feel honoured to be in such fine company.'

He grins. 'You should. They think very highly of you, too.'

He goes off into the newsagent's, and I stand by the window, staring in at the display of old-fashioned humbugs and colourful magazines, thinking what a nightmare he must have gone through with Caroline. Not just the alcoholism but the gambling as well, bleeding him dry so that in the end, he lost everything.

I'm just about to join him in the shop, when out of nowhere, a car hurtles alongside me and screeches to a halt. I turn to see what the commotion is and my heart plummets.

It's Dominic.

He's wound down the passenger side window and is leaning across with a smarmy smile. 'Well, well, if it isn't my favourite creditor. How are you doing getting the readies together?'

I swallow hard as my knees turn to jelly. 'Fine,' I croak.

Dominic nods slowly, clearly doubting me. 'I gave you until the end of September. And I meant it. Please don't disappoint me, Katy.'

'You'll get your money,' I say in a low voice, moving closer to the car, desperate to resolve this before Gabe comes out.

I really don't want him meeting my ex.

But a shout behind me tells me it's too late. 'Got it! And it's a cracking review.'

He emerges from the shop, holding the newspaper aloft, a triumphant smile on his face. Then he registers my grim expression. 'Everything all right?' He comes over and frowns into the car.

Dominic gives Gabe a sullen look. 'Everything's far from okay, mate. But as long as I get my money back, we'll be fine, eh, Katy?'

'You'll get it back,' I repeat, feeling sick to my stomach.

'What's this about?' Gabe demands.

Dominic looks up at him, all wide-eyed innocence. 'Oh, didn't you know, mate? Katy's in debt up to her eyeballs.'

My heart lurches.

I glance, horrified, at Gabe. I've tried so hard to conceal the mortifying truth from him. I would have come clean eventually but I'd have chosen my moment. And now it's too late, because bloody Dominic has just gone and blurted it out.

Gabe is staring at Dominic as if he'd like to kill him.

He wouldn't be the only one.

'Sorry, mate,' says my ex, twisting the knife. 'Thought she'd have told you.' Then he shakes his head regretfully at me, no doubt seeing from my face what a victory he's scored over me. 'Poor Katy. I suppose it also slipped your mind to mention that you had your car repossessed?' He laughs. 'Oops. I can see from your face that you were in the dark about that as well, mate.'

I stand there, feeling sick with revulsion that I could ever have thought myself in love with this man. And filled with desperation, terrified to even imagine what Gabe thinks of me now.

There's no point trying to deny it. My face must be telling the whole story anyway. I should never have tried to hide the facts from Gabe. If he despises me now, it's my own stupid, stupid fault.

'Well, anyway, gotta go, folks. Have a great day.' Dominic winds up the window, gives us a cheery wave and drives off.

There's a silence as Gabe stares after the car until it disappears. Then he turns. 'Is it true, Katy? Are you in debt to that man?'

I swallow hard and open my mouth to speak, but nothing comes out.

'Well?' he demands, his eyes bleak, his face full of fury. I know he's thinking of Caroline. How debt killed their relationship and ruined his life.

'Yes, I owe Dominic money. And yes, they took my car away.' I take a deep breath. I might as well tell him the whole truth. 'And there's a bank loan and two credit cards. But I'm paying it all back.'

He laughs harshly. 'And what about the rest?'

I stare at him. 'No, that's it. Honestly. There *is* nothing else.'

'Really?' His tone is deeply scathing and to my horror, I realise he doesn't believe a word of it.

'But it's true.' I grab his arm but he shakes me off. 'You've got to believe me, Gabe. I wouldn't lie to you.'

He looks at me sadly and shakes his head. 'Funny but that's exactly what Caroline used to say.'

I'm panicking now. I've got to make him understand. 'Look, I might have got myself into a bit of debt, which I admit was really stupid, but I'm doing my best to pay it all back. And I'll never borrow money again in my life. Ever! You've got to believe me. Gabe, I'm *not Caroline*!'

His face darkens at the mention of her name.

'You've already lied to me, Katy. About the car.' His eyes slice through me, cold and piercing as a blade of steel. 'You didn't sell it to buy equipment. It was repossessed. So tell me, what else are you covering up?'

I open my mouth, desperate to say something – *anything* – that will wipe the harsh judgement from his face and make him smile at me again.

But it's too late.

He's gone.

TWENTY-SEVEN

I trail home, too shocked to cry, hoping that by some miracle, Mallory's car is still parked outside my house.

But of course she's gone. She probably nipped off quickly to get her parcel, smiling at the thought of me and Gabe arriving back and getting up to all sorts . . .

If only . . .

I let myself into the house and wander around, opening mail and staring at advertising flyers without reading a single word. There's this frightening emptiness inside me. I feel like I'm just this side of breaking down completely and it scares me how devastated I feel.

I can't stop thinking of the weeks and the months ahead, with this terrible emptiness dragging me down.

I've lost Gabe.

We hadn't even got together properly, which makes it even worse.

If he'd known me better before Dominic dropped the bombshell about my debts, Gabe might have believed me when I told him my spending days were behind me. As it was, I guess he just automatically assumed I was another Caroline . . .

I keep remembering the grim look on his face when I admitted the truth about my car being repossessed. And the loan and the credit cards. The parallels with Caroline are there for all to see. No wonder he took off like a rocket . . .

He's wrong, of course, in thinking I wasn't telling him the whole truth. He's tarred me with the same brush as his ex, but who could blame him? He went through hell with Caroline. If he thinks I'm even remotely like her – with her destructively addictive personality – he's not going to go near me with a bargepole . . .

I spend the evening staring at the TV. But not even the latest goings-on in my favourite soap can distract me from the great slab of misery in my gut.

At nine, I give up and go to bed.

Pulling the covers over my head, I pray for oblivion, as the warm tears trickle unchecked into my pillow . . .

By morning, I've almost convinced myself I really don't care.

I didn't know Gabe at all, really, so the notion that I might have been in love with him was a bit ridiculous, really. He was a shaft of light in my dull life, that's all. No wonder I was so upset when it was snatched away. But there's a lesson there somewhere, if I look hard enough. Relying on a man to light up your life is not a wise thing to do. Friends and family are the only people you can depend on to stand by you.

I'm feeling quite buoyed up by this inner pep talk – until I remember that Sienna is my family and she is the very last person in the world I'd want to comfort me.

What's more, she's due back in the country on Friday. Just a few days away.

I hurl back the covers and head for the shower with some vain hope of washing away the heartache and making a new start. I'm going to need all the strength I can muster, with Sienna coming home . . .

I try to settle to some work at my laptop but it's a challenge because I can't stop thinking about Gabe. I'm clinging to the hope that once he's had a chance to think, he'll realise that of course I'm not the same as Caroline and that he really ought to give me a chance. Maybe he'll still phone on Friday night, as he promised, to sort out our seaside trip . . .

I know I'm fooling myself. I'll probably never hear from him again. But these contradictory thoughts just keep going round and round in my head until eventually, in desperation, I leave my desk, grab the flyers I ran off the other day and go out to deliver them. A good, brisk walk and a purpose is what I need.

To hell with Gabe Harlin. If he can judge me so harshly without really knowing the circumstances, then more fool him. It's totally his loss.

Next minute, of course, I'm having fantasies about him passing me in the car, screeching to a halt and sweeping me into his arms, muttering how wrong it was of him to judge me . . .

Aaaargh!

Stop the mind chatter. I want to get off . . .

In the end, Gabe doesn't phone me on Friday night.

To my complete shock, he phones me at lunchtime on Thursday.

When I hear his voice, my heart starts pounding like a herd of elephants are stampeding after me.

He's phoned early! He wants to talk! There must be a chance for us!

He sounds stiff and formal.

After he's asked how I am, he says, 'Have you had any more trouble from that bloke?'

'Dominic?' My heart feels like a lift, soaring up to the top floor, because Gabe cares enough about me to ask about Dominic. That *has* to mean something.

'Yeah. Has he bothered you at all since . . .'

'Oh, no. No, everything's fine,' I blurt out. Then I decide to tell the truth. Because me not being honest in the first place is mainly why Gabe and I are having this stilted conversation now. 'Actually, it's not particularly fine,' I amend. 'But Dominic has given me some time to pay him back, and I'll do it. I know I will.'

'I'm going to be busy over the next few weeks,' he says, and the lift I experienced earlier begins its slow descent. Before picking up speed and plummeting, when he adds, 'We'll have to take a rain check on that lunch, I'm afraid.'

I swallow hard. Okay, I get the message.

'That's fine,' I reply, mustering all the conviction I can. But my voice still sounds small and desperately sad.

'Right, well . . . take care, Katy. Goodbye.'

There's a lump in my throat. It sounds so horribly, heartbreakingly final.

'Goodbye,' I whisper.

Almost before I disconnect the call, my shoulders start shaking with emotion as the tears start. And that's when I finally face up to reality. Gabe and I had barely even started. But now, we're most definitely over . . .

All the same, when the phone rings again not two minutes later, I dive on it with the thrill of someone on a sugar-free diet being offered a doughnut.

It's Gabe. It has to be. He's decided he can't live without me.

'*Hello?*' I'm all breathless and expectant.

There's silence at the other end.

'Hello?' I repeat, listening intently to – nothing.

Is that faint breathing I can hear? Oh great, a weird phone call. Probably checking if I'm in, to see if it's worthwhile burgling the house.

I'm about to hang up, full of aching disappointment that it isn't Gabe, when a tiny voice says, 'Hello, Cat Ballou.'

My head spins.

I grasp onto the edge of the kitchen table, quite sure I'm about to keel over.

Lowering myself slowly onto a chair, I force myself to take a deep breath.

'I'm at Mum's. Please don't hang up,' begs Sienna. She sounds far away but that's just wishful thinking.

She's arrived a day earlier than Mum said.

Panic rises up, blocking my throat, swiftly followed by an emotion I wasn't expecting to feel.

I haven't heard my sister's voice for so long but it's as familiar as if I just spoke to her an hour ago.

But then anger takes over.

How dare she call me Cat Ballou after all this time? As if I'd remember and be hit in the emotional solar plexus and be totally charmed into forgiving her! As if!

Cat Ballou was Dad's favourite cowboy movie. It stars Jane Fonda as a feisty, gun-toting heroine and it was the first film he ever saw at the cinema. Sienna used to laughingly call me Cat Ballou whenever I was ordering her about, as big sisters tend to do.

'Katy? I just want to talk. Will you please let me tell you my side of the story? Then you can go on hating me if you want to.'

There's a pleading tone to her voice but it has the opposite effect to the one she no doubt intends. It just makes me angry.

'I know you haven't read any of my letters or emails,' she says. 'Mum told me. And I don't blame you. But I want to make you understand how I felt. I went completely off the rails when Dan broke up with me. I loved him so much, I hardly knew what I was doing—'

I knew she'd try to justify her behaviour. But there's no excuse at all for what she did.

'I'm not interested in your excuses, Sienna,' I tell her in a monotone, and end the call.

I wait, biting my thumbnail, for the phone to ring again. If it does, I'll just ignore it. My heart is beating so fast I can hardly breathe.

But the phone remains silent.

I sit and stare at it for a long time, as my heart rate steadies, feeling like everything is crowding in on me at once. Gabe despises me, Dominic's tightened the screws and won't give up until he has his pound of flesh, and now my sister is trying to hold out an olive branch that isn't even hers to give.

Suddenly, I have to get out of the house, away from the pesky phone that just seems to bring more bad news every time I answer it. I'll go for a long walk to clear my head. I'm annoyed that with Sienna returning a day earlier than planned, I now won't get a chance to see Mum on her own.

She looked really run down last time I saw her and I can't imagine why she's cancelled her weekend at the spa when she was so looking forward to it. She even had her case half packed. So what changed her mind?

I slip on my trainers and head out into the warm, mid-July sunshine.

I'm walking through the village when I pass the pretty church at the far end of the high street. I glance over the wall into the church-yard and spot a figure kneeling by one of the graves. She has wavy, auburn hair and is wearing a cream blouse over mushroom-coloured trousers. But it's her posture that's familiar. The way she's kneeling there, back perfectly straight, even though she's staring at the grave with such intensity.

It's Annabeth.

I hesitate, watching her. I'd like to go over and speak to her. Ask her how she thinks Mum is doing and if she has any idea why she's cancelled her visit to the spa. But she looks so wrapped up in the moment. Far away in her own world, thinking, no doubt, of the soul she's mourning. I can't disturb her.

Then a passing bus revs its engine.

Annabeth glances over, sees me and waves.

I wave back and she gets up, brushes herself down and starts walking over. I meet her halfway and we sit down on a bench in the shade of the churchyard's giant horse chestnut tree.

'So how's it going?' she asks.

I smile. 'Not so good.'

'Oh?' Her face falls. 'Your sister?'

I nod.

'Hm. I was thinking about that. It won't be easy, making that decision.'

I look at her in surprise. 'Decision?'

'Whether or not to forgive her.'

'For*give* her?' I give a bitter laugh. 'I don't think so.'

She sighs. 'It's hard, I know.'

We sit in silence for a while, then I ask about Mum.

'It's been a while since we saw her,' says Annabeth. 'She's been really busy, getting everything ready for your sister coming home.' She smiles. 'I miss her company. So does Grace. It's strange but since your mum arrived on the estate, Grace and I have been getting along better than we ever have. Not that we ever fell out, but . . .' She trails off and looks over at the grave she was tending to.

'Whose grave is that?' I ask.

She gives a fond smile. 'It's Michael's.'

'Grace's husband?'

She nods. 'I was bringing him freesias. They're his favourite flower.'

Her eyes suddenly seem over-bright and she turns away quickly.

'Were you fond of Michael?' I ask gently.

She turns to look at me. Her expression is as gentle as ever, but she's moulding a tissue in her hands, tearing it up into tiny pieces.

'I loved him,' she says simply.

I stare at her, trying but failing to keep the surprise from my voice. 'But what about . . . ?' I tail off. It's really none of my business . . .

'What about Grace?' prompts Annabeth softly.

'Yes. Did she know?'

She nods sadly. 'It's hard to keep something like that a secret, especially from someone so close. And Grace and I were really close, despite being so different. We still are.'

'So Grace knowing you loved Michael never altered your relationship as sisters?'

She smiles wistfully. 'It did for a while. But thankfully, Gracie came to terms with it. She knew I'd have done anything not to feel the way I did. But you can't help falling in love, can you? No matter how hard you try not to.' She looks over at Michael's grave. 'And I tried. My God, I tried.'

'He must have been a lovely man.'

'He was.' She glances over my shoulder and smiles. 'Wasn't he, Grace?'

I turn and Grace is walking through the church gate towards us, a newspaper under her arm.

'I'm just telling Katy what a fine man Michael was,' says Annabeth.

Grace smiles. 'Never a finer. I count myself very lucky to have been married to him for all that time.'

'How long?' I can't help but ask.

'Well, let's see. Our lovely Molly's coming up for forty-one and she was conceived on our honeymoon. So we'd have been celebrating our forty-second wedding anniversary next year.' She smiles broadly at the achievement and Annabeth leans over and gives her a squeeze.

'Right, I'm just nipping into the post office, ladies,' says Annabeth. 'Lovely to catch up with you, Katy.' She gives me a hug and disappears.

'And how are you?' asks Grace, sitting down on the bench beside me. 'I was saying to Annabeth it's going to be strange for you having your sister back living at your mum's.'

I frown. 'Tell me about it.'

'It'll be fine. You'll sort it out.' She reaches over and takes my hand.

The gesture, from the down-to-earth Grace, is so unexpected, it brings a surge of emotion and my eyes fill up.

'Hey, hey, I didn't mean to upset you,' she says, turning towards me and squeezing my hand in both of hers.

'You haven't. I was just thinking how close Sienna and I used to be. Like you and Annabeth, I suppose.'

Grace nods. 'Well, my sister and I got through our troubles and came out the other side as friends. So maybe you can, too.'

I shake my head. 'We obviously never had the special bond you two have. I can't see us weathering this.'

Grace smiles. 'It wasn't easy for us, either, you know. I take it Annabeth told you about Michael? I saw you with your heads together.'

'Erm, well . . .' I don't know what to say. I don't want to betray Annabeth's confidence.

'I expect she said she was in love with Michael?' She says it matter-of-factly, without even a hint of bad feeling.

I nod.

'And did she also tell you that Michael loved her right back?'

TWENTY-EIGHT

I stare at Grace. 'Annabeth and Michael? They had an *affair*?'

She gives a sad smile. 'Well, if they did, it was only in their heads. Neither of them would ever have betrayed me, I know that much. But for a time, I really hated Annabeth because Michael was in love with her. Even though I knew nothing had ever happened between them.'

'I can't believe you can talk about it so calmly,' I tell her, shaking my head. 'I'd have thought something like that would destroy a relationship. And yet you seem as close as you could be.'

Grace nods. 'We are. Michael died more than ten years ago. I miss him all the time, and I know Annabeth does, too. But time is a great healer and the emotional scars from my fallout with my sister faded a long time ago.'

'So how did Annabeth and Michael grow close? If you don't mind me asking?'

'No, I don't mind at all.' Grace smiles. 'We ran a newsagent's together, Michael and I. It was terribly hard work. Up at dawn to see to the papers and not finishing until late. Then when I was pregnant with Molly, Annabeth offered to help out at the shop. It was coming up to Christmas and really hectic, so of course I said yes straight away. And it worked really well. She and Michael had always got on, and it turned out they worked well together, too. It was only much later, of course, that I realised they were quietly falling for each other.'

'So did Annabeth carry on working there after Molly was born?'

Grace shifts her position on the bench, sitting back to catch the sun on her face. 'She did and I was really grateful, although by then I was starting to suspect their fondness for each other. Michael was just as kind to me as he'd always been, but a woman's intuition told me he was becoming a little more distant and distracted. He spruced up his wardrobe as well and started being quite jolly on a Monday morning, as if he couldn't wait to get to work, whereas before he always said he wished Sundays could last all week.

'Annabeth was behaving oddly, too. We used to go to the cinema together most weeks but that all petered out. When I asked if anything was wrong, she just kept saying she was busy and making excuses. It was almost as if she didn't want to chat any more. I knew something wasn't right.' Grace frowns. 'And then the fire at the newsagent's happened.'

'The fire?'

She nods. 'That's when I knew for sure that Michael cared for my sister.'

I stare at her, aghast. 'What happened?'

'Well, that particular day, Michael was out at a dental appointment and I'd said I would help Annabeth at the newsagent's. Molly was with a babysitter. We used to close up for an hour at lunchtime, so we did that and we were in the back having a cuppa when we smelled burning. I rushed through to find that somehow – we never found out exactly how – a spark had set the newspapers alight. They were in a wooden rack right by the door and of course, the whole thing went up, blocking our exit.'

'Oh God, how awful.'

She nods. 'I was panicking there, I don't mind admitting. I really thought we were goners.'

'Wasn't there a back door?'

'There was, but we'd just had a big delivery and all the boxes were stacked in the passageway, waiting to be stored. We started trying to move them but the fire was spreading all the time and soon it reached where we were. Luckily Michael arrived in the nick of time. He smashed a window and got us out. There was nothing left of the shop.'

'So how come the fire made you realise Michael was – er – fond of Annabeth?' I'm hoping I'm not upsetting Grace by asking. But I don't think I am. She seems quite calm and matter-of-fact about the whole thing.

She looks at me, a touch of wistfulness in her intelligent grey eyes. 'I knew because he rescued Annabeth first.'

My heart does a queasy little flip when Grace says this. I can almost feel the distress she must have felt. 'But that's awful,' I begin. 'He should have—'

'It was an action born of pure instinct,' says Grace simply. 'If Michael had had time to think, it would probably have been different. But he did what he *felt*.' She shrugs. 'I saw then how it was for them.'

'But it must have destroyed you.'

'It did. For a while. But I didn't challenge them about it and they never said anything. We all just carried on as if nothing had changed.'

'But how could you do that?' I ask, shocked.

How can Grace be so calm and rational about it all? If it had been me, I'd have been livid at both Michael and Annabeth.

She shrugs. 'I didn't want things to change – and they would have if I'd said anything. The thing that pulled me through was knowing that Michael would never leave me and Molly. I knew he loved us and that that would never change. And I also knew that neither he nor Annabeth would ever betray me.'

'So they never . . . ?'

Grace shakes her head. 'I asked Annabeth, years later, and she

255

admitted they'd been in love and that they'd kissed just once. But then they'd agreed it was never to be.' There's a tear in Grace's eye. 'In a way, I got by far the best deal. I was married to the man I loved and we had Molly and he never gave me any reason to doubt he was faithful to me. Whereas poor Annabeth . . .'

We sit in silence for a while, the sun hot on our faces, and I'm thinking how heartbreaking it must be to love a man who loved you back. But all the time, knowing you could never be together.

'Refreshment, ladies?'

We look up and Annabeth is walking quickly across the grass, brandishing ice creams. Passing a cone to me, she says, 'Didn't know what you'd prefer, Katy, but you can't go wrong with vanilla.' She hands the other ice cream to her sister. 'Mint choc chip. Naturally.'

Grace smiles. 'You know me so well.'

Annabeth winks. 'Oh, don't I just.'

'It's very *slow*, this computer of yours,' Mallory complains loudly. 'And where the *hell* is the question mark on this keyboard?'

'Right where it's always been,' I remark dryly, glancing at her across my desk in the conservatory.

Her own computer gave up the ghost last week and I – very kindly, I thought – offered to let her use mine to take care of Vintage Va-Va-Voom orders. I also, foolishly as it turns out, thought a bit of Mallory's company might help to pick me up off the floor. Because when I'm on my own, Gabe flits into my thoughts the whole time, whether I want him there or not. But the mood Mallory's in today, I'm rather regretting I suggested she come over.

'So tell me again why that idiot, Gabe Harlin, doesn't want to see you again?' She shoves her large, purple-framed reading glasses further up her nose and peers critically at me, as if it's all my fault I've been ditched.

Which, actually, it is.

A panicky feeling overwhelms me. It feels like I'm sinking in quicksand, and I experience it every time I think of Gabe and the cold, incredulous look he gave me when he found out I'd lied to him.

I raise my eyebrows at her. 'Firstly, Gabe is *not* an idiot. And secondly, I just told you his ex-fiancée got him into lots of financial trouble. Weren't you listening?'

'Of course I was listening. I just don't see what her being frightfully bad with money has to do with you, that's all.'

I shrug. 'He's just being extra cautious, I suppose.'

She frowns. 'And idiotic. As I said.'

I shake my head and get back to my accounts.

'Oh, and by the way, darling, I can't do the woodland wedding after all.'

'You can't?' I stare at her in dismay. 'Why not?'

I'd been counting on Mallory's support, knowing that Gabe will be at the wedding and I'll have to face him for the first time since he walked away from me.

A feeling of panic surges up at the thought of going myself.

She leans closer to the keyboard as if she's still trying to hunt down the elusive question mark. 'Oh, some boring but necessary accounts course.' She waves her hand dismissively. 'I'll have to stay over in London on the Friday night and do the course the next day. Pain in the arse, really, but I'll learn a lot.'

I stare at her bent head, thinking. The woodland wedding is a month away, in early September. At least I've got time to find someone else to assist me in Mallory's absence. Not sure Harry will be on my list of possibles, though, after last time.

The doorbell breaks into my thoughts.

It's Bryony, of all people. My woodland wedding bride. She's really lovely, and with her tangle of thick blonde hair and shapely figure, she's going to look sensational in her simple white dress and floral crown.

'Hi, I was just passing so I thought I'd drop in the next instalment.' She laughs and waves a cheque at me. Bryony is always laughing. She laughs when things are funny. And she laughs when things really aren't funny in the slightest – such as when she confided in me that her granny couldn't be at the wedding because she was in rehab getting treatment for sex addiction. Under normal circumstances, at the sight of that cheque, I'd be joining Bryony in a good old chortle. But these days, I find I can barely raise a smile.

She joins us for a cuppa and we chat about the wedding.

'How exciting,' exclaims Mallory when she hears about the hay bales in the forest clearing where guests will sit to hear Bryony and Mick take their vows.

I glance at her suspiciously. Is she being sarcastic? It's not like her to go into ecstasies about a wedding. But she looks genuinely fascinated and even asks Bryony a string of pertinent questions.

'The costs have really escalated, though,' says Bryony, laughing uproariously. 'And there was us thinking forest would equal cheap.'

When I go in search of biscuits, Bryony calls, 'Oh, Katy, what's this?'

I go through and she's waving the December wedding story I scribbled.

'I hope you don't mind me reading it, but it sounds so lovely.'

I smile at her. 'I don't mind at all. It's a service I'm thinking of offering clients as a little extra. You know, the story of their day so they'll always remember the details?'

'Oh, what a fab idea,' she giggles. 'Could you do that for us?'

'Well, I *could*. But aren't your costs rising too much already?'

She waves her hand dismissively. 'Oh, so what! It's our wedding day, for goodness' sake,' she says, creasing up. 'And I want to remember every single thing about it. Ah-ha-ha-ha! So will you do it?'

By the time she leaves, our jaws are aching from so much smiling. At least Mallory's mood isn't quite so grouchy.

'Hey, didn't you say your mum's invited to the wedding?' says

Mallory suddenly. 'Couldn't she help you out a bit while she's there?'

I frown at her, thinking. 'Maybe. It's a thought. I'll ask her.'

Later, when Mallory's gone home, I open up my laptop to do some work. Mallory hasn't switched it off. A website selling camping gear is still on the screen.

I stare at the display of ridge tents and calor gas stoves.

That's weird. Mallory is to camping what Victoria Beckham is to smiling broadly for the camera.

And the only camping taking place at Newington Hall as a rule is Rupert camping it up in a dynamic new shirt . . .

TWENTY-NINE

The next week passes in a blur of work punctuated by bouts of energy-sapping heartache. I've never been so grateful for my demanding work schedule. Having a head full of all things weddingy is seriously keeping me sane.

Not that the irony of my job is lost on me. In fact, it's excruciatingly, horribly clear.

I'm working my hardest to ensure my couples enjoy the whole wedding photography experience and end up with a beautiful, romantic album to cherish for the rest of their lives. (Or until their next wedding day rolls around, as Mallory is fond of pointing out.) But all the while, my own romantic life is as dead as a bunch of Valentine roses in March.

As I blunder through the days, it starts to seem more and more as if Gabe and I almost getting together was just a lovely, incredible illusion. The happiest dream I'm ever likely to have.

After he called and said he'd have to take a rain check on our date, I kept hoping he might still phone to suggest we meet up.

But as the days passed and I heard nothing, I realised he was just being kind and letting me down in stages. Instead of just coming out with it and saying he didn't want to have anything more to do with me, he'd allowed me to entertain the vague possibility that things might still turn out well. But now that hope has finally trickled away. When the phone rings, I no longer leap up, heart banging, thinking it might be Gabe. Instead, I let it go to answer machine because I'm terrified it will be Sienna. There's also the worry it could be Dominic, phoning to turn the knife a little more. In my misery, I've allowed my focus on paying off the debt to start slipping. So now, with little over a month to go until D-D-Day (as in Dominic Deadline Day), I'm suddenly aware I need to pull my finger out.

Delivering leaflets locally produced a flurry of enquiries that resulted in three firm bookings. Their deposits are now tucked away in the bank and – along with money that's trickling in from selling clothing and other stuff online – I'm about three-quarters of the way to my goal.

I phoned the Greshingham yesterday to see if the weddings co-ordinator had recommended me to any clients, but although she was really nice and positive, she admitted she hadn't got round to looking at it yet.

The only other solution that springs to mind is to do another leaflet drop in some neighbouring villages. I'll need to act fast, though, if I want to secure some business – with deposits banked – before D-D-Day.

So today is being spent cursing my ancient printer, trying to cajole it into churning out three hundred leaflets. The print cartridges are eye-wateringly expensive, but if I can get some bookings in the diary, it will all be worth it.

The doorbell goes, just as I'm yelling at the damn machine for stopping – for no good reason I can fathom – in the middle of a print run of one hundred. Still full of murderous frustration, I fling the door open.

A bolt of shock zips through me.

It's Sienna.

'Hi, Katy,' she says, her green eyes full of uncertainty. 'We really need to talk. Can I come in?'

I stare at her, a weird floaty sensation in my head. Thinking I might faint, I clutch at the door for support.

Seeing her face, a hotchpotch of memories – good and bad – tumbles into my head, swishing around crazily and filling me with emotion. The way a song can blast you right back to a particular time in your past, dredging up all those old feelings.

Time has etched a few faint lines on the fair skin around her eyes. And her hair colour is slightly different. She's got the same cropped style but it's now more golden than white blonde. Briefly, I wonder if it's darkened with the years or whether she's tinted it. The slightly wide-apart green eyes and slender figure are exactly the same.

She's looking at me with a questioning, almost pleading expression.

'Can I come in?' she repeats gently. 'Please?'

I stare at her for a few seconds longer.

Then calmly, without even deigning to reply, I shut the door in her face.

I walk back to my desk, my legs like jelly, my heart beating so furiously it feels like it might actually pop out of my chest.

How dare she pitch up at my door like this! Didn't she get the message loud and clear when I hung up on her last time?

The letter box rattles and the breath catches in my throat.

Then Sienna's voice, calling through. 'Katy! I know I'm the last person in the world you want to see. But I really do have to talk to you. It's about Mum.'

My heart pings with alarm.

Mum?

What's wrong with her?

Ever since Sienna got back, I've been dragging my heels going over to see Mum. I've been telling myself it's because I'm too busy, but deep down, I knew it was just an excuse because I couldn't bear the idea of accidentally running into my sister.

But I need to know what's happening.

I march to the door and wrench it open. 'I hope this isn't a trick to get me talking.'

She takes a step back.

'What *about* Mum?' I bark, and she flinches.

'It's awful, Katy. I mean, really bad.'

She looks genuinely upset and my alarm ratchets up a hundredfold.

I signal for her to step over the threshold. 'What's happened? Is she ill?'

'No, but she's got herself into a terrible situation. I think she's going to have to leave Clandon House. There's no other way.'

'She's *what*? What are you talking about?'

Sienna swallows. 'It's this woman. She's scarpered now, of course. But she convinced Mum that Dad wanted to give her a message and the only way was through her because she could communicate with the other side. And Mum fell for it all.'

My heart starts thudding uncomfortably fast. *Bloody Venus! I knew there was something fishy about her! Even Grace said so.* I glare at Sienna's left shoulder, not even wanting to give her the satisfaction of eye contact. 'But that woman. Venus. She's gone now, right?'

'Well, yes. But that's not the worst of it.'

My eyes flick to her face in alarm. 'What do you mean?'

Sienna smiles grimly. 'She took all Mum's savings. Every last penny. And now Mum's two months behind with the rent.'

I stare at Sienna, barely able to believe what she's telling me. This is our mum she's talking about. The same woman who mocks things like complementary therapies and horoscopes in magazines. And who's always declared that people who claim to be psychics are dangerous fakes, who prey on people's emotions. Yet she's allowed Venus to empty her savings account in the name of channelling 'the other side'? It doesn't make sense.

'I haven't got a penny to my name,' says Sienna, 'to pay Mum's landlord. The move over here cleaned me out. We're going to have to find her somewhere cheaper to rent.'

I shake my head. 'No! She's not leaving Clandon House. Not if I've got anything to do with it.'

I surprise myself with the force of my reaction. But I feel so strongly that the Clandon House community is exactly where Mum should be. It's where she belongs, where she's found happiness at last, among friends.

But with a sinking heart, I realise that keeping her there will involve money.

Money I don't have.

Sienna looks anguished. 'But I don't know what else we can—'

I stare at my sister for a second. Then I make up my mind. 'I'm coming over.'

Sienna shakes her head. 'No. I made her take one of her old sleeping pills – the ones the doctor prescribed for her after Dad died. She'll be out for the count until morning, so there's no use you coming over tonight.'

'Tomorrow, then. I'll be over at ten. Please make sure you're out.'

She nods. Then she glances over at the hall table and frowns. 'Your daffodil brooch. The one Dad bought you.' It's lying there in two pieces. She picks them up, fits them together and clicks her tongue. 'What a shame. It was your favourite.'

I nod.

'Perhaps it could be fixed?'

'I doubt it.' Even if it *were* fixable, I'm not about to agree with her. On principle.

My phone starts to ring and I turn away to answer it. As I'm talking to what is potentially a new client, I open the door and hold it pointedly.

Sienna takes the hint, gives me a brief smile and leaves. As I close the door, I see her hurrying over to her beloved old Mini, as if she can't wait to get away from me.

And that makes two of us.

* * *

265

After a night of barely any sleep, I step into the shower next morning feeling surprisingly alert and determined. There is no way Mum is leaving her home. She was a mess when Dad died but moving to Clandon House turned her life around.

Maybe Sienna was exaggerating the seriousness of the situation. I need to find out for myself.

True to her word, Sienna has left in her car by the time I pull up outside Mum's at ten o'clock. When she opens the door, I'm shocked by her appearance. Her face is pasty white, her eyes red-rimmed and puffy, and she's wearing her old pink dressing gown, which has what looks like a coffee stain down the front. She looks like she's aged ten years since I last saw her.

We hug and I lead her into the living room. She's avoiding my eye, but I take her hands when we sit side by side on the sofa and make her look at me.

'I should have been there for you, Mum,' I murmur, feeling utterly wretched that I failed to save her from Venus's clutches. I'd known something wasn't quite right, but caught up in work and Gabe, I'd persuaded myself it was to do with Sienna's return back and that once Mum had her back, everything would be all right.

'Tell me what happened with that – *witch*.' I was going to call Venus something much worse but I don't want to upset Mum any more than she already is.

Mum swallows hard. 'Oh, Katy, I'm such a stupid, stupid fool to have believed her. That night she did the séance with Annabeth and Grace and me, she claimed to have contacted the spirit of your dad. She said he had a message for me.'

I pass her a paper hanky and she dabs her eyes.

'At first, I didn't believe a word of it. But then later, I couldn't stop thinking about it. What if Dad really was trying to contact me? What if I was turning my back on him when he needed to tell me something? I couldn't bear the idea of that.' She gives me a wry little smile. 'I know it sounds daft, but I convinced myself

266

that even if there was only a tiny chance that I could somehow communicate with your dad, I owed it to him to try.'

I rub her hands gently. 'It doesn't sound daft at all, Mum.'

She shrugs. 'Well, anyway, so Venus – if that's her name, and I doubt it very much – gave me this tale about how contacting the spirits always took a toll on her, health-wise, and that there needed to be an exchange of energies in order for it to be an easier experience for both of us.'

'An exchange of energies?'

Mum smiles grimly. 'Money.'

Anger rises up inside me at the thought of that woman cheating my poor mum. But I swallow it down because right now, it won't help at all.

'So I paid her – I daren't tell you how much – and she said Dad had a message for me. She said it was about a life insurance policy he'd taken out that he'd never told me about. And that the policy was in the apartment somewhere.'

'He always said he was planning to get life insurance,' I murmur.

She gives a bitter laugh. 'Yes, and afterwards, I remembered mentioning that to Venus when she was over at Grace's for tea one time. I clearly remember saying he never got round to it. Of course, it didn't occur to me at the time. Only later. So then, of course, we had to have another "exchange of energies" so that she could contact him to find out where the policy was. Because Ralph was apparently desperate I should have the money to make my life easier now he'd gone.' She shakes her head despairingly. 'Honestly, Katy, it all sounds so ridiculous now. But at the time, I was so utterly beguiled by the notion that your dad was still there in some way, trying desperately to reach me, that I went along with the whole damned thing. Once I'd handed over that first lot of cash, it seemed silly not to carry on . . . and now, of course, she's disappeared without a trace.'

I swallow hard, determined to remain upbeat for Mum's sake.

Underneath, though, I'm absolutely livid at what that cow has put her through. A widow, still mourning the husband she loved so much, was probably easy pickings for someone in her line of 'work'. I'd like to race out now and find her, and demand to know how she can live with herself, conning decent people like my mum. But for now, I need to know what the financial damage is.

'What a bitch, eh?' I say, keeping my tone breezy. 'These people are so cunning, they can make you believe anything they want you to.' I scrunch up my nose and ask, as gently as I can, 'So how much did she get away with?'

Mum heaves a great sigh. 'Everything, love. And more besides. I haven't been able to pay the bills for the last two months.'

I nod my head, remaining upbeat, although inside I'm in total despair. So Sienna was absolutely right in her assessment of things. Mum hasn't only lost her savings, she's also gone into debt to pay that bloody woman. *If only I could find her . . . ! But she'll no doubt be long gone now she's bled Mum dry.*

I draw in a big breath, exhale slowly and tell Mum what we're going to do. There's no way she's moving away from here, I tell her. I will simply not put her through that.

I'm going to sort it out.

I sit with her for a while longer to make sure she's fine, batting away her frequent attempts to apologise to me for her stupidity. Only when she's sitting chuckling away at a box set of her favourite comedy show do I feel it's all right for me to go.

When I leave, I see Sienna's car parked a little way off.

She gets out and hurries over, and my heart sinks. I'm really not up to facing her right now.

'Is she all right?' Sienna looks anxious.

I give her a curt nod and get into my car. 'She's fine.'

'Can we talk? Please, Katy?'

I stare straight ahead, stony-faced, but I leave the car door open.

'I understand why you wouldn't read my letters.' Her voice is soft and pleading. 'But please, I really need to tell you my side of the story.'

I turn cold eyes on her. 'Yes, well, surprise, surprise, I really don't want to hear it.' Then I shut the door and drive off.

My legs are shaking so much, my foot slips off the pedal and I crunch the gears. I refuse to look at her in the rear-view mirror. I know she's standing there watching the car disappear, but I can't deal with her right now.

I drive home, thinking about poor Mum all the way, my heart like a sack of potatoes in my chest.

I know what I must do.

To ensure she can stay at Clandon House, I've told her I will make sure her rent is up to date. I've also told her that paying it is no problem for me whatsoever. She will never know any different because I won't tell her.

The money I will use is the cash I've been saving to pay back Dominic . . .

THIRTY

I don't know what I'm going to do now about Dominic's money.

My head might possibly explode thinking about it. (Which could be the perfect solution. If a little messy.)

I transferred the money to Mum's landlord as soon as I got home, so he's happy now and Mum gets to stay at Clandon House. Then just as I was sitting there in a daze, thinking about poor Mum and all she's been through with that cow, Venus, and that things couldn't possibly get any worse, I became vaguely aware of someone trying to rattle and force their way through my gate. On my way to the door, I glanced out of the window and registered that there was a white van parked right outside.

Still wrapped up in plotting Venus's sticky end, I opened the door and the instant I saw the man standing there in his work uniform and helpful name badge, my entire body screamed, 'Meter man!'

A small, bespectacled person, thinning on top, he smiled amiably at me. 'Good afternoon, madam. I'm here to read your meters.'

I gulped with suppressed horror – thinking, *okay, the game's up* – and ushered him through in a daze.

He made a joke about me being the only customer at home today, which only added insult to injury, and I attempted a smile, then darted about trying to locate the meters. (The clerical error that had given me breathing space meant they hadn't been read since I moved in, so how would I know?)

The meter official observed my near-hysterical antics patiently, obviously used to batty customers. The poor man clearly had no idea he was driving the final nail into the coffin of my disastrous finances.

I didn't dare imagine the amount I'd accrued, thanks to the previous owner's thriftiness and her correspondingly meagre monthly direct debit payment.

Happy days . . .

Several days later, I'm on the phone to Mum, discussing Bryony and Mick's wedding, when there's a ring at the bell.

Bryony's mum has sent her an invitation, and I was asking her if she could possibly help with the photography, since she'd be a guest there anyway. Mum said of course she would; it was the least she could do, considering how wonderful I'd been rushing to her rescue, sorting everything out with her landlord and making sure she didn't lose the flat.

'Got to go, Mum. There's someone at the door,' I say, heading into the hall. 'But listen, I'd only need you for the big group photo, to help gather everyone together. So you'll still have loads of time to kick back and enjoy yourself.'

I end the call and open the door.

It's Sienna.

I can't quite believe the cheek of her, turning up at my door again when I've made it so obvious she's not welcome. She's determined, I'll give her that.

Stepping forward, she pushes something into my hand.

I stare down. It's my daffodil brooch. And it's been mended.

What with everything that's gone on, I hadn't even noticed it was missing. But Sienna must have taken it with her when she left here that last time.

Speechless, I peer at it more closely. I can still see a very fine hairline crack running down the middle, but somehow, it's been fixed.

'I thought you'd need it. For your weddings,' she says. 'I remembered how superstitious you were about it.'

I clutch the brooch against my heart, emotion welling up inside.

But I swallow it down and say stiffly, 'Thank you. But if you think this is going to make up for what you did, you're sadly mistaken.'

'But Katy, it all happened so long ago,' she says, raising her voice in frustration. 'We need to talk about it. Get it out in the open.' She shrugs. 'You can yell at me as much as you want. But then we can *move on.*'

My mouth tightens. 'I *have* moved on. My life is different now. And there's no room in it for people who care so little they'd betray me at the drop of a hat.' I laugh harshly. 'Or a skirt.'

She sighs. 'For God's sake, Katy, will you stop acting so holier than thou, as if you're the martyr and I'm the eternal villain of the piece.'

'Well, aren't you?'

'None of us is perfect. Even you.'

'I know that. But I'd never, *ever* have hurt you the way you hurt me. I just wouldn't. End of.'

She hangs her head. 'But surely you know I never meant to hurt you. It was all just a horrible mistake. And I've regretted it every single day since.'

'Good. Well, you can go on regretting it every day in the future, as far as I'm concerned,' I say, trying – but failing – to keep the wobble from my voice.

'But I'm your *sister.* I absolutely worshipped you when I was a kid. And then later, you were my best friend in all the world.' Her chin quivers. 'Helping you set up the business was honestly the best fun I've ever had. I could never have believed we'd end up like this. Don't I at least deserve a *hearing*?'

I shake my head, willing the tears to stay put, clamping my mouth shut to stop it trembling. I start to close the door and she gives an odd little shriek of anger.

'You think I behaved abominably. And you're probably right. But has it ever occurred to you that the way you're behaving now is a hundred times worse?'

'*Worse?*' I bellow. 'What twisted thought process brought you to *that* ridiculous conclusion?'

She shrugs and says tearfully, 'I did wrong but I never denied it. And I'd do *anything* to make things right. But you . . . your bitterness and your total inability to forgive is not only harsh, it's also incredibly sad. Because I know I'm not the only one to miss the amazing bond we used to have – and all you're doing in being so stubborn is cutting off your nose to spite your face. I know I hurt you but don't you think it's high time we put it all behind us?'

I pounce on her words and throw them back at her. 'Yes. You hurt me. And you wrecked my life. Do you really think that's so easily forgiven?'

She nods. 'If you want to.'

I laugh incredulously and shake my head.

Seeing I'm not going to budge, Sienna throws her hands in the air. 'Please yourself, Katy. If you want to stay wrapped up in your anger forever, that's up to you. At least I've tried. Do you know how hard it was for me to come here? I was dreading it because I knew how you'd react. But I came anyway because our relationship is worth fighting for and I hate that I've made you so bitter and unhappy.'

I laugh scornfully. 'Oh, really?'

How can she stand there, like butter wouldn't melt, and say all this stuff? After what she did . . .

'Yes, *really*. Because I'd never dream of treating you as harshly as you've treated me these past few years. Cutting me out of your life and not even giving me the chance to explain.'

Her criticism of me raises my blood temperature to boiling point.

'Oh, you're so *good*, aren't you?' I yell. 'So *patient* with me. Putting *my feelings* first!'

She takes a step back, eyes flashing with horror at my anger.

I send up a bark of laughter.

'Well, answer me this, baby sister. Were you *really* thinking of me when you were getting down and dirty, shagging Dominic? The day after we split up? *In my bed?*'

THIRTY-ONE

When I met Dominic, it was love at first sight.

For both of us.

It was two days after my dad's funeral.

When Mum broke the news over the phone of Dad's fatal heart attack, I'd told my boss and quietly left the office. I don't remember anything about the train journey home. I was in a state of complete shock.

We huddled together, the three of us, completely grief-stricken, managing to organise and get through the funeral – but only just.

Afterwards, the thought of leaving Mum when she was so vulnerable and going back to my life in London, seemed really hard. But I knew I had to do it. My job was there and so were all my friends. It wasn't logical to contemplate giving all that up just because I was still devastated over the loss of my dad.

Mum would cope. She still had Sienna living at home, after all.

Then a few days after the funeral, I had an urge to get out of the house. Get some fresh air. I thought I'd go into the village and visit the graveyard, talk to Dad a bit, and maybe that would make me feel better.

I remember walking along and getting really annoyed because it was a beautiful day. The sun was shining but Dad had gone. It didn't make sense somehow. So instead of going into the graveyard, I dived into the cool depths of The Bunch of Grapes. It was practically empty, which was fine by me, and gloomy after being out in the sunshine. I ordered a glass of wine and sat at a table in the far corner, where no one would bother me.

It was around lunchtime and two guys came in and sat at the bar, drinking real ale. I tried to ignore them, but the sandy-haired man – Dominic, as it turned out – kept looking over at me and trying to make me laugh. He wasn't being creepy or anything, just friendly. But I was in no mood for jokes.

Then a song came over the sound system. A heart-rending aria by Luciano Pavarotti. Dad always loved that kind of music. Suddenly the tears were rolling down my cheeks and I couldn't stop them.

When his friend left, the talkative guy came over and asked me if I was all right and would a drink help? Two brandies later and I'd told him my life story and we were getting on like a house on fire.

I told him I hated the thought of leaving Mum and Sienna and returning to London.

He looked straight at me and said, 'So don't.'

'Sorry?' I laughed.

'Don't go back.'

'But I have to. My job's in London.'

'So get a job here.' He snapped his fingers. 'What about that plan you were telling me about?'

'What plan?'

'To set up your own wedding photography business.'

I laughed again. 'Well, yes, but I wasn't planning to do it right *now*.'

He shrugged. 'Why not? There's no time like the present.'

And right then and there, the idea was born.

I'd leave my job at the agency and set up on my own, right here in Willows Edge.

By the time that I'd worked out my notice, Dominic and I were together and planning a future. And my world was starting to look very rosy indeed . . .

Dominic was good-looking, funny and very charming. He had a bit of a wild streak and I never quite knew what he'd do next, but that was all part of the attraction. He was also very generous. When I bought my new house, he helped with the decorating. Most of my spare cash had gone towards the deposit and I'd been planning to buy furniture a stick at a time and renovate it gradually, room by room. But Dominic offered to lend me a few thousand so I could do it up straight away.

At first, I refused his offer, knowing it would take me a while to pay him back. But he said it didn't matter. What was his was mine. I should just go ahead and get the house looking the way I wanted it.

So, foolishly as it turned out, I accepted his offer.

It meant I could do up the second bedroom for Sienna, who would be moving in and paying half the mortgage.

Everything was wonderful.

Dominic and I were madly in love.

There was only one fly in the ointment. His ex-girlfriend.

They'd remained friends. But Jodie didn't act very 'ex' at all. She always seemed to be around, monopolising Dominic's attention, laughing at private jokes and smirking at me as if she knew something I didn't. She'd wag her finger at him and tell him he was a very bad boy, and I couldn't help thinking she was trying to tell me something.

Dominic said I had nothing to feel jealous about. He and Jodie were just friends, that's all.

Then one day, I was walking back from the supermarket when I saw the two of them coming out of a house, laughing and joking, arms casually around each other. I knew Jodie lived around there, so I assumed that was her home. And that's when I knew there was still something between them, even though he swore blind there wasn't.

I was past the first flush of romance by then anyway, and getting glimpses of the real Dominic. He could be horribly selfish and narcissistic at times, and controlling, too. Whenever I was out with a girlfriend, he'd need to know exactly what time I'd be back. And if I were late, he'd sulk for days. I'd heard about women who ended up in the thrall of controlling men and I didn't want to be one of them.

The shine had well and truly worn off. My instinct told me I'd never be able to really trust Dominic. So I plucked up the courage and ended the relationship. It was so hard to do because I still had feelings for him. And I knew Sienna would be gutted. Her boyfriend, Dan, had ended their relationship about a month earlier and Dominic had been great, inviting her to places with us, including her in everything and refusing to allow her to sit at home and mope. He was like the big brother she never had. I knew she'd miss him terribly.

The day after I ended the relationship, Dominic phoned me, sounding really upset, wanting to talk. I'd agreed to meet an old friend for a drink straight from work, but I told Dominic I'd be back home by ten and I'd phone him then to talk things through. Not that there was anything more to say, really. My mind was made up. But he sounded so desperate.

It was a little after ten when I got back home. The lights were on in the living room but Sienna, who'd moved in the previous month, was obviously in her room. I ran upstairs, calling out that I was back, and burst into my own room. The scene that confronted me is etched forever on my brain.

Dominic and Sienna, lying in my bed, arms wrapped around each other, fast asleep. The covers half off so I could see Dominic's bare chest. Sienna waking at the noise, seeing me and struggling to a sitting position, the strap of her skimpy nightwear slipping down.

As long as I live, I will never, ever forget the look of panic and guilty horror on my sister's face . . .

THIRTY-TWO

It's Friday, the day before Bryony and Mick's woodland wedding and I've just realised Mallory has my second-best camera, which I've promised Mum she can use tomorrow.

She was trying to get out of going to the wedding but I laid it on thick about needing her help. She hasn't been herself for a while and I really think it will do her good to get back out in the world again and have some fun.

But I need the camera for her.

Mallory won't be at home because she's in London tonight, before going to her accounts course tomorrow. But when I phoned her, she told me Rupert would be home, so I could collect it from him.

Not that it's the best time to have to venture out and drive to Mallory's. I don't need to look through the curtains to know that it's blowing an absolute gale out there, rain lashing against the windows, sounding like an angry monster is trying to batter its way in. It really doesn't bode well for the wedding tomorrow.

When I get there, the house is silent, so it looks as if my journey has been in vain. I'm kicking myself for not making sure that I had the camera before Mallory left. Without it, Mum won't be able to take any of the relaxed, informal shots that can really lift an album.

Think, Katy, think!

Rupert's probably at his studio.

Ah yes, his studio . . .

A minute later, I'm on my way back to Willows Edge, hoping I can remember which studio I saw Rupert entering that time Mallory and I were heading back from our walk.

Luckily, his car is parked right outside the unit that I recalled him going into. I knock but no one answers, so as the door is slightly ajar, I walk on into the small reception area. Vivaldi's 'Four Seasons' is being piped loudly through wall-mounted speakers.

I call out but there's no reply, so I try one of the two doors leading off reception.

It's a small room with large windows letting in lots of natural light. The perfect space for an artist. There's an easel at one end with a half-finished sketch perched on it, and the walls are dotted with framed watercolours.

Rupert's been busy.

I wander over to the easel to take a look and my mouth drops open. There are about a dozen more canvases stacked against the wall nearby and they're all of the same subject.

If I'd been hoping for lots more sludgy watercolours (with or without heather), I'd have been sorely disappointed.

These pictures of Rupert's are rather more – erm – *intimate*.

I stare, wide-eyed, at a sketch of a naked man displaying very impressive musculature. Moving on, there's another. And yet another.

They're all of the same man, in slightly different poses. They're good, too. This is clearly Rupert's forte.

'Katy?'

I jump guiltily, as if I've been caught up a ladder, peering through someone's bedroom window.

'Rupert!'

He looks marginally more guilty than I do.

282

There's a man with him. A man I vaguely recognise. I screw my eyes up, trying to place him.

'Katy, lovely to see you,' says Rupert, recovering his composure and bounding over.

I give him a hug and apologise for just walking in. 'Mallory's got a camera I need for tomorrow,' I explain. 'I can call for it in the morning, on my way to the wedding, if that's more convenient.' I look pointedly at the man.

'Er, Katy, this is my – um – new friend, Hans.'

Hans and I smile awkwardly at each other. He's a solid mountain of a man. A very tall, well-honed mountain . . .

My eyes slide to the sketches. That's why I vaguely recognised Hans. I've been studying him in these pictures for the last wee while – and it wasn't necessarily his face I was focused on, if you get my drift.

'Hans is a tailor. Of bespoke suits. In London,' explains Rupert, looking decidedly shifty.

'Oh, lovely,' I exclaim, aware of a peculiar tension in the room. 'A tailor.' By the way Hans is gazing fondly at Mallory's fiancé, I'd hazard a guess he's well familiar with Rupert's inside leg measurement.

I frown at Rupert. 'Does – erm – Mallory know about these?' I nod at the nude sketches.

Slowly, he shakes his head.

'But you will tell her. Won't you?' We lock eyes and stare at each other for a long time. You seriously could hear a pin drop. Finally, he draws in a slow breath and his shoulders droop as he exhales. 'Yes, I will.'

My head is spinning. I feel utterly distraught for Mallory. How's she going to feel when Rupert confesses the truth? It doesn't bear thinking about.

'Right, well, I'll see you tomorrow morning for the camera?' I say, heading for the door, desperate to get out of there.

I leave them standing, shoulder to shoulder, watching me go.

It all makes sense now. Rupert's 'theatrical' style and manner, the trip to Brighton, his colourful friend, Terry, the frequent sleep-overs at his studio, and now these sketches. I suppose I knew, deep down, a while ago. I just didn't want to face up to the truth because I knew how badly Mallory would be hurt.

I just hope to God he breaks the news to her soon. Otherwise I might have to tell her myself . . .

Mum phones later, saying she hates the thought of letting me down but she really can't face the wedding tomorrow. She's trying to sound normal but I can hear the panic in her voice. It's clear that the business with Venus has really knocked her confidence, and it makes me so angry.

For the millionth time, I wish that I could track that woman down and confront her for what she's put Mum through. I'd thought about calling the police but I suspected we probably didn't have a case. No real crime had been committed, after all. Mum had handed her money over willingly.

When she's gone, I peer out of the window at the torrential rain and wind buffeting the garden, tugging furiously at the branches of the hawthorn tree. Looking at the weather, I'm wondering if I'll actually *get* any photos, apart from in the marquee.

Bryony and Mick's big day has been giving me palpitations all week. And not just because the weather is so lousy.

Gabe will be there.

Every time I think about this, my heart starts to hammer so fast, I think this must be what it's like to have a panic attack. I haven't been able to face food for days. My stomach just churns constantly, like a demented cement mixer. Part of me wishes Gabe won't turn up, because then I'd be able to get on with the job without any distractions. But he will be there. I know he will. He's a good friend of Mick's. Although what I'll do if he turns up with a woman on his arm, I really can't bear to imagine.

But while part of me might be hoping he'll stay away, if I'm really honest, there's a much bigger part of me that desperately wants to see him again. If only so I might get the chance to talk to him and explain that I'm not the irresponsible near-bankrupt he seems to think I am. I mean, obviously I have got debts and there's no shying away from that. But if only I could explain how I got into such a dire situation, there's a chance he might understand . . .

An Autumn Wedding

THIRTY-THREE

The weather the next morning is no better.

I drive up to Newington Hall to collect the camera, a gale force wind buffeting the car, rain battering against the windscreen.

Motoring up the drive, I'm shocked to see Mallory's car parked there.

Oh, God, she must be back. How can I act normally with her when I know Rupert is about to drop the biggest bombshell ever? My insides shift uneasily. I wasn't expecting to have to face her today.

But I pull my rainproof around me and make a dash for the house.

'Hi! What happened to the course?' I ask when she opens the door.

'Decided not to go,' she replies brusquely. She doesn't usher me indoors but stands there with her arms folded, wincing at the heavy rain that's bouncing off the porch roof. She looks flushed, her eyes red-rimmed. Oh God, maybe Rupert's already confessed.

'I – er – called round last night for the camera but you weren't here.'

'Did you? Right.' She frowns, avoiding my eye for some reason. 'Ah, yes. I nipped to the shops.'

'Where's Rupert?' I ask, casually.

She shrugs. 'Probably at his studio. I tried to phone him last night to let him know I was here, but I couldn't reach him.'

'Are you okay?' I peer at her, concerned. 'You seem out of sorts.'

She heaves a sigh and kicks at a section of loose skirting board. 'I'm bloody brassed off.'

'Because of Rupert?' She looks confused.

'Rupert? No, no, never mind.' She folds her arms and peers out. 'Lord, the weather! Bloody abominable! Where's your mum? I thought she was helping out today.'

I shake my head. 'She's not up to it, bless her. That bloody Venus has a lot to answer for.'

Mallory's face softens. 'Too right, darling. That mother of yours is an absolute poppet. She didn't deserve any of that bollocks.'

'Listen, I don't suppose—?'

Her eyebrows arch. 'You want me to help?'

'Would you?'

She nods. 'I'd rather be doing something than moping about here. Just give me a minute to search out my posh wellies, darling, and I'll be with you.'

The rain continues to lash down as we drive to the venue – Wilkins Farm, about ten miles from Willows Edge.

And most of the way, I'm thinking about when to break the news to Mallory about Rupert. He assured me he'd tell her himself, but what if he doesn't? I suppose I need to give him some time to act before I wade in and reveal all myself.

By the time we arrive at the farm, I've got myself back into wedding mode.

It all sounded so marvellous when Bryony was regaling me with how the day would go. The guests sitting on hay bales in a forest clearing to hear her and Mick take their vows, followed by music and a hog roast in the open air and lots of opportunity for some glorious photographs among the beautiful old oak and beech trees.

Now, I'm not so sure.

'Thank heavens for tents,' murmurs Mallory, as we drive up

the farm track, branching away from the rambling old farmhouse itself and heading towards a white marquee, just visible on the edge of the small wooded area where I assume the wedding will be taking place.

Guests have already started to arrive, although they're all sitting in their cars, protecting their finery until the very last possible moment, before having to brave the torrent of rain that's falling relentlessly from a stormy sky.

Mallory stares glumly out of the window. 'Fuck's sake. The poor bloody bride. Hope it doesn't rain like this for *our* day.' Her voice is almost drowned out by the battering of the rain on the car roof.

I swallow hard, filled with dread at the thought of what I'll soon have to tell her.

I peer around, checking for Gabe's black Audi.

No sign yet.

My guts grind round relentlessly, reminding me I should have at least tried to force down some breakfast before I left.

'Right, better get this show on the road.' I slap the steering wheel, trying to be cheery.

When I open the door, a gale lashes in several gallons of water.

It's not a good omen.

We plodge across the mud in our wellies, slipping and sliding, and hanging onto each other and the gear for dear life. In the space of ten seconds, we're drenched from head to foot.

In the marquee, Mick and his best man are setting out the chairs theatre-style for the ceremony, helped by close family members in their morning suits and fascinators.

I can't help thinking these hard, folding chairs are not quite the romantic prospect Bryony had envisaged when she excitedly planned that guests would sit on hay bales. But Mick seems remarkably chipper about the weather and says that the hog roast is being prepared at the farmhouse and will be sent down in a van after the ceremony.

And I have to admit, the inside of the marquee looks lovely. Trestle tables covered with starched white cloths are ranged around the room, ready for the buffet. They're dotted with church candles, that pierce the gloom with a lovely romantic glow.

Mallory and I change out of our wellies into shoes, then we pitch in to help arrange the chairs, as the guests start to filter into the marquee, examining their muddy heels with amusement and making the most of a soggy situation.

'The best laid plans, eh?' A familiar voice reverberates through the chatter and my heart misses a beat.

'It's Gabe,' mutters Mallory, with a worried glance at me. She knows the whole story and how much I was dreading seeing him today.

My face aflame, I fiddle about with the two chairs I'm straightening, so that I can keep my back to the door a moment longer. 'Is he with anyone? *Don't stare!*'

'Blonde. Petite. Pretty,' she murmurs out of the side of her mouth. 'She's got cankles, though. *Really bad* cankles.'

'*I said don't stare!*'

'How in heaven's name can I give you a description,' she huffs, 'if I'm not allowed to look?'

Fair point.

I don't know whether to laugh or cry. But I've got to get a look at Gabe. And the cankle woman. I turn, pretending to scan the chairs, my eyes eventually drifting over – and there's Gabe, looking utterly, completely gorgeous.

He's talking to Mick and a small blonde woman, and my heart leaps so high at the sight of him, it would be a seriously good bet for the next Olympics.

He's wearing a dark suit and a white shirt, and his hair's a little shorter than when I last saw him. It really suits him.

At that second, he looks directly across at me. Our eyes meet and hold, and I'm hit by a huge pang of longing.

I can't decipher the look on his face.

Is it surprise, because he'd forgotten I'd be here? Shock because he's remembering the last time we saw each other and Dominic's terrible revelations? Or could it be a look that's tinged with regret?

I swallow hard.

That last one is purely wishful thinking . . .

Then he looks away, frowning down at the floor, and my heart feels like it's tumbling down a mineshaft.

After a moment, the blonde touches his arm, and he looks up and gives her a smile.

She *is* pretty. So pretty, in fact, that you barely notice the cankles. She's standing next to Gabe, gazing up at him like she's stumbled upon a little slice of heaven.

It was so stupid of me to cling to the hope that he'd come to the wedding alone. Of course he wouldn't. Not a man like him. It's only workaholic saddos like me who go to these things on their own because they can't dredge up a 'plus one'.

'You okay?' whispers Mallory.

I nod and try to put on a brave face. But inside, I'm devastated. With the blonde here, I'll have no chance to talk to him . . . to try to explain things so he'll understand.

Gabe will never be mine and I've only got myself to blame . . .

THIRTY-FOUR

'Oh look, here's your dear mama!' Mallory smiles and waves. Then an expression of shock comes over her face. 'Oh!'

'What?' I swivel round.

'She's with *Gareth*!'

Sure enough, Mum, looking lovely in a cerise two-piece, is chatting to Bryony's mum and smilingly turning to Gareth to do the introductions.

Gareth, it has to be said, has scrubbed up rather well.

'He's really quite handsome out of his gardening gear,' I murmur to Mallory.

She frowns. 'Hm. If you like 'em old enough to be your father.'

I stare at her. What the hell's she talking about?

But I haven't got time to wonder because Mum's hurrying over. I'm so delighted to see she's had a change of heart and decided to come along after all.

We hug and she says, 'Sorry about letting you down before, love. I felt terrible about it but I just couldn't face it.'

'Don't worry, Mum. Mallory was here after all. I'm just really glad you're here.' I smile. 'And it's nice you invited Gareth along.'

She laughs. 'Actually, *he* persuaded *me* to come. And when I said I didn't want to go on my own, he offered to be my "plus one".'

'Very charitable of him, I'm sure,' murmurs Mallory, as Mum turns to talk to Becky's mum.

Puzzled, I'm about to ask her what she means, when the marriage official announces that the bride has arrived and the ceremony is about to begin.

Everyone bustles about finding seats, and Mallory and I position ourselves by the marquee door, waiting for Bryony.

Her arrival brings out the sun. Well, not literally. It's still pissing it down relentlessly. But her smile of perfect happiness as she steps out of the car – in her simple white dress and garland of flowers in her hair – is so joyful, the mood in the room soars.

Everyone starts chattering excitedly, and Mick blushes bright red with sheepish delight at the first sight of his bride. Holding her skirt aloft and revealing green wellies beneath, she's ushered into the marquee by her dad under a large white umbrella. A quick change of footwear and she's ready to walk down the aisle.

The storm might be wreaking havoc outside but in the cosiness of the candlelit marquee, there's only warmth, love and laughter . . . Along with a slightly damp feel and the smell of wet grass.

I sneak a glance at Gabe. He's sitting near the back, next to blonde thingy, chatting to a woman in a large red hat on his other side.

I grit my teeth and focus on the job, making sure I get a good variety of shots. Mallory and I prowl round the sides of the marquee, being as unobtrusive as possible, clicking away as the happy couple take their vows and sign the register.

I try very hard not to keep glancing in Gabe's direction. But I can't help feeling his gaze upon me. He's obviously casting his professional eye over me, watching the way I work, which of course makes my hands sweat and my fingers fumble clumsily. I almost drop the camera at one point and when I glance in Gabe's vague direction, of course he's watching me.

I glance over at Mallory to see if she noticed my fumbling. But she's staring into space, a vacant look on her face, as if Bryony and Mick's wedding is the very last thing on her mind. Maybe she's brooding over Rupert, wondering why he's spending so much time at his studio these days. I really wouldn't blame her.

When the ceremony is over and the tables are being set out for the wedding breakfast, Bryony bounces over, all red-cheeked and giggly with champagne, and says please will Mallory and I join them for the hog roast.

I tell her we've sandwiches in the car but she won't hear of it, so hog roast it is. Although to be honest, I was quite looking forward to escaping for a while to the safety of the car. If nothing else, it would put an end to the fairly exhausting business of *not* stealing glimpses of Gabe and his date.

We sit at a table near one of the windows and eat in silence, watching the raindrops flooding down. I'm horribly aware of Gabe sitting on the table behind us. So near and yet so far. I can't believe I actually thought I'd get a chance to talk to him and explain about everything.

Mum seems to be enjoying herself, though. She's at a table near the door with Gareth and a few other friends of Bryony's mum and dad. I turn round to see how she's getting on. And Gabe just happens to be looking directly at me, so it looks as though I was seeking him out.

While the speeches are being made, the rain dies down and the clouds part to reveal the first patch of blue sky that day. Bryony makes happy thumbs-up signals over at me, clearly desperate to get some shots outside among the trees. Which is presumably one of the reasons she wanted a woodland wedding in the first place.

But lo and behold, no sooner has the coffee been drunk, but the heavens open once more and this time, it's actually a hailstorm.

Yes, tiny little chips of ice are actually peppering the roof and ricocheting off the sides of the marquee.

'Holy shit,' breathes Mallory. 'We're about to be snowed in.' Bryony makes her way over and crouches down by our table. 'I think we'll make the record books for the most bad weather at a wedding!' She laughs loudly but I can tell her natural optimism is waning slightly.

Mick joins her. 'You're not trying to persuade Katy to go out there in *that* for photos, are you?' he chuckles.

Bryony attempts a smile. 'No, of course not. I just thought maybe later, if it fairs up?'

'Not much chance of that, is there, love?' says Mick. 'Perhaps we'd better stick with photos in here. You'd get soaked going out there. Your lovely dress and everything.'

Bryony's chin wobbles.

I smile at her. 'Well, I'm game, if you are.'

Her eyebrows shoot up. 'Really? Go outside? For photos? Now?'

I shrug. 'Why not? Let's just get some group shots in here first, then we can go out there and climb trees . . . do whatever you want.'

She grins broadly and leaps up to start rallying everyone for the group shots.

'Well, *I'm* not going out there,' says Mallory firmly. 'You are on your own.'

I laugh. 'Chicken! What's a bit of water, anyway? You can see how much it means to Bryony.'

'I don't care.' She purses her lips. 'That is way beyond the call of duty. You could catch the most ghastly dose of pneumonia.'

I stare at her for a second, wondering what the hell has got into her, but then I'm swept up in the group photos, which – rather like the rest of this wedding – are charmingly haphazard, but great fun anyway.

Then it's out into the blizzard for who knows what.

Actually, when I peer out, the hailstones have stopped and it's now just a steady stream of raindrops. And at least the raging wind has calmed down. But when we venture out, everyone gasps at the lake that has pooled right outside the marquee door.

'Ha! Well, that settles it,' hisses Mallory in my ear. 'No way, jose!'

'Shhh!' I turn and glare at her, worried Bryony might hear.

'Ah, it's just a bit of water,' says Gareth, and I turn and grin at him.

'Quite right. Thank goodness for the voice of reason.'

Mallory gives a scathing laugh.

Undeterred by the lake, Mick picks up his bride and wades across, to the cheers and shrieks of all the guests gathered at the door to watch.

I'm just thinking of going back in to change into my wellies again, when suddenly Gabe is at my side, saying, 'Let me do the honours.'

Before I can say a word, he whisks me up, so I'm held aloft in his lovely strong arms. The total surprise of it makes me shriek, and the crowd joins in.

'My hero,' I laugh, as he carries me over to dry land. It feels so incredible to be in his arms again, I never want him to set me down.

'Just call me Mr Darcy,' he jokes.

'Your shirt's certainly wet enough – and that's without a dive in the lake!' It's true. Having removed his jacket earlier, his pristine white shirt is already plastered to his chest, the rain is lashing down so hard. But crushed against him, I can feel only the lovely heat of his body.

It's all over so quickly. He sets me down but keeps one arm around me, making sure I don't drop my camera.

'It's really good to see you.' Gently, he brushes a lock of wet hair from my eyes. 'That's better.'

My heart leaping at the touch of his fingers, I smile up at him.

'You too.' The rivulets of water running down my face feel like happy tears.

Then I remember his blonde partner. Where is she? I glance over at the marquee but I can't see her.

I'm just getting over the shock of being carried by Gabe, when Gareth – clearly loosened up after several glasses of bubbly – takes it upon himself to transport Mallory across the great divide. He hoists her rather less smoothly than Gabe lifted me, at which point she shrieks and shouts, 'I say, put me down! Put me down this instant, you rotter!'

And then, to the horrified amusement of everyone watching, Gareth does exactly that. He sets her down unceremoniously in the middle of the enormous pool. Disorientated, Mallory staggers slightly to the side, then trips over her own feet and lands on her bum in the water.

There's a stunned silence.

Then someone shouts, 'She's just done a Mary Berry!'

There's a roar of laughter from those who clearly know their Great British Bake-Off.

Gabe frowns at me.

'Mary Berry. Soggy bottom,' I explain, trying not to laugh at poor Mallory. Gareth's grinning down at her and holding out his hand. But she ignores him huffily and gets up without his help.

Gabe laughs at the soggy bottom and pulls me under a tree where the torrent is a little less fierce. I lean against him, feeling happy and exhilarated, so grateful that the tension between us appears to have vanished. It's as if I've spent the past few weeks in the desert, parched and only half alive, and now Gabe is here, I'm joyfully making up for lost time.

Bryony, meanwhile, is scampering about in the rain, hooting with laughter, finding gnarled old trees to pose beside and dragging Mick after her. I'm already as wet as I'm ever going to get, my fringe plastered to my face, so I'm happy to oblige, shooting the very soggy side of Bryony's wedding.

Gabe fetches his camera from the marquee and rejoins me in the rain.

Someone shouts, 'You're bloody mad, you lot!'

To which Bryony shrieks, 'It'll be a lot more interesting to show the grandkids than boring old group shots!'

'She has a point,' grins Gabe, snapping away beside me.

I suddenly catch sight of his date standing on the other side of the pool staring over at us, and my heart sinks.

Oh well, she can have him back once we've taken the photos . . .

Bryony is climbing a tree now, shouting for Mick to give her a push from behind. Her dress is clinging to her curves, her hair streaming down her back, and she looks like she's having the time of her life.

I take a few shots from down below. Then Gabe suggests I'd get a better perspective perched on the branch of a nearby tree. I laugh at him but he's clearly not joking. And before I know it he's helping me up onto this branch and holding me firmly while I click away, as the happy couple adopt a variety of romantic and hilariously dramatic poses.

I'm not great with heights. But I feel rock solid and safe with Gabe's hands around my waist. I'm all too aware, though, that after the photos, he'll be going back to his date.

When we've finished and Bryony has climbed down, Gabe takes my camera and puts it in the case he's been carrying for me. Then he reaches up and helps me down, holding me firmly so that just for a moment, as I slither to earth, my hands are pressed against his soaked shirt, feeling the hard muscles of his chest beneath.

Our eyes meet and something flares in his that I know I didn't imagine. For a glorious moment, the whole world disappears. It's just Gabe and me, our bodies moulded together and the pelting rain, running in rivulets down our faces . . .

Gradually, I become aware of cheering and clapping. And we move apart.

Mallory comes over to join us, while Bryony and Mick say

they're heading up to the farmhouse to dry off, and would we like to join them?

But Mallory shakes her head. 'I need to get home. Coming, Katy?'

Reluctantly, I thank Bryony, but say we really have to be going.

'I hope you're off somewhere hot and dry on honeymoon,' grins Gabe. He's standing so close to me, I can actually feel the heat from his body.

'Mauritius,' says Mick with relish.

'Oh, how lovely,' I squeak, feeling really excited for them. 'Sun, golden sands and cocktails on the beach. Can I come with you?' I joke. 'I'll put it on my credit card and to hell with it!'

Too late, I realise what I've said and glance at Gabe.

The shutters have gone down. His eyes are as bleak as the storm.

Whatever precious contact we might have re-established I've wiped out completely with one careless remark . . .

THIRTY-FIVE

In the days that follow, I try my best to put Gabe out of my mind. But it's impossible.

I keep thinking if only he hadn't gone to Bryony and Mick's wedding, stirring all the old feelings in me. If only he hadn't picked me up and carried me across the floodwater, laughing and joking, and making me think there was still something between us.

If only I could get him out of my mind . . .

Gabe isn't my only problem.

I can't stop fretting about Mallory either.

When I challenged Rupert at his studio, he agreed he'd come clean about his sexuality and his 'friend', Hans. But I really worry that he's just going to let it slide, while Mallory goes on having wedding dress fittings and planning her future with him.

She needs to know the truth. Without delay.

So, a week after the wedding, when it's clear Mallory's still in the dark, I phone Rupert at the house when I know she won't be there.

He's instantly wary when he realises it's me, and straight away, he says he's planning to tell her the truth when the time is right.

'When the time is right?' I repeat. 'But Rupert, isn't that just an excuse for delaying it?'

'No, honestly, Katy,' he protests. 'I've been thinking about nothing else since you came to the studio the other night. I'm going to tell her. Trust me.'

'Make it soon, then,' I tell him sternly. 'Or *I'll* have to do it.'

'I will,' he agrees. 'But Katy, let *me* be the one to tell her? *Please?*'

I heave a sigh. This is all just so horrible. 'Fine,' I tell him. 'But I'm not waiting forever, Rupert.'

So then, of course, every day after that I'm on tenterhooks, expecting a distressed call from Mallory at any time, telling me the wedding is all off . . .

When I first wake up, the late September sun is already peeking through the curtains.

Then I remember what day it is. And a cold fist grips my insides.

It's D-D-Day. Dominic Deadline Day.

And all I've managed to scrape together is a few hundred pounds.

Last night, when I was feverishly going over my options (which turned out to be none at all, barring getting on the next plane to Brazil), I thought about transferring what little cash I had into Dominic's account. But I knew that wouldn't be good enough for him. In fact, he might even interpret such a paltry sum as an insult. Like I was saying, *Fuck you, Dominic! That's all you're getting from me!* Which isn't the case at all.

I really want to pay him back, then I can put the debt behind me and move on. It's just that thanks to Venus Bloody Flytrap defrauding Mum of her savings, I can't do that. I really would like to wring that woman's neck.

There's no point phoning Dominic and trying to reason with him. He's not going to listen. So all that's left for me to do is wait for him to contact me, like I know he will . . .

The heavy slab of dread in my stomach makes it impossible to concentrate on work, so finally, in desperation, after trying and failing to focus on my paperwork, I put on my trainers and leave the house.

I head towards the village with no plan in mind, just wanting to walk and walk and hopefully try to make some sense of everything. Visions of Dominic taking me to court keep flashing through my mind and my heart is pumping much too fast for comfort. I find myself walking up to the monument where I took Mallory the other week. It's a gentle slope but the view from the top, looking out over the village in the valley, is a lovely, peaceful one. I sink down on a bench and hold my face up to the sun, drawing some comfort from the warm rays. If only I could go back in time, I'd do things differently. I'd save up to renovate the house, instead of borrowing from Dominic, then none of this nastiness would ever have happened.

'Penny for them?' says a voice.

I open my eyes.

It's Andrea. I haven't seen her since the day of her wedding to Ron, but marriage clearly suits her. 'What a gorgeous day!' she sings, plonking herself down next to me.

My heart sinks. The last thing I want to do is make polite conversation.

'It is. Lovely,' I agree.

'Oh dear, is something wrong?' she asks, detecting the trace of despair in my tone.

'No. Why?' I try to smile.

Her smile is gently sympathetic. 'You sound like you've lost sixpence and found a penny, as they used to say in the old days.'

The irony of this almost makes me laugh out loud. But when I open my mouth, all ready to deny it, no words come out.

'Oh, poor you. There *is* something wrong.' She takes my hands. 'You can tell me, you know. After blubbing my eyes out to you in the ladies' loos on my wedding day, you now know all my secrets. Maybe it's *my* turn to help *you*?'

Her caring smile brings a lump to my throat. I look down at our hands. 'To be honest, I don't think anyone can help. Not really. I've got myself into such a *stupid* mess and no one but me can sort it out.'

'Yes, but a trouble shared and all that?' Gently, she moves a lock of hair away from my eyes. 'Is it about Gabe?'

I look up in shock at the mention of his name. 'No. Why on earth would it be about him?'

She sighs. 'My cousin is a lovely, decent man. As straight and honest as they come. Far too good for that Caroline creature he was saddled with. So when I heard that you and he looked like you might hook up, I was . . . well, I was thrilled.'

I gaze at her through a blur of tears. 'You were?'

She nods. 'But then I saw him the other day and he refused to talk about you. He looked hellish, to be honest. I don't know what on earth's happened between you, but couldn't you maybe sort things out?'

I shake my head.

I'd been clinging to the slim chance that after seeing me at Mick and Bryony's wedding, Gabe might have a change of heart and get back in touch. But he hasn't. And I'm kicking myself for not grabbing the chance to talk to him when I had the opportunity, at the wedding.

'I've ruined everything,' I say in a small, choked voice.

Andrea frowns. 'But how? It can't be that bad, can it?'

'Oh, it is. Believe me. As far as Gabe is concerned, it's the worst.'

'Tell me.'

And because she seems like she genuinely wants to help, I find myself pouring everything out to her.

I tell her about my money problems and how Gabe could never be with someone like me. Not after all the trouble he had with Caroline. I even tell her about Sienna. I've never told anyone about finding my sister in bed with my ex, the day after we broke up – not even Mallory – but somehow it all just comes tumbling out.

She listens in silence, squeezing my hands encouragingly when I can barely get the words out.

Finally, talking about Gabe, the tears start falling and simply won't stop, and Andrea pulls me into a firm hug.

It's quite surreal. I barely know this woman, and yet here I am pouring out all my anguish, feeling so grateful to her for just being here, listening, and not judging me.

After I've calmed down, she passes me a tissue and waits until I've mopped myself up. Then she says, 'Right, best foot forward, Katy. I bet that awful Dominic won't turn out to be half as nasty as you think he will. Ask him to wait a bit longer for his money.' She pats my knee. 'I'm sure you can talk him round. And in the meantime, I'll mention to all my friends that I know the most brilliant photographer who just happens to have a few openings in her diary. They'll be queuing round the block, you'll see.'

I paste on a smile, touched by her determination to make me feel better.

'How are you and Ron, anyway?' I ask, suddenly aware the conversation has been all about me.

'Oh, we're fine. We fight sometimes but so do all couples. Even celebrities.' Her eyes twinkle. 'The best news is that Chloe is on her way to becoming a superstar actress.'

'Really?'

'Well, of course I'm exaggerating just a teeny bit. But she's just been signed up to play the Fairy Godmother in our local panto. I'm one of the organisers but I made sure I kept well away when the casting was being done.' She smiles. 'Wouldn't want anyone to think Chloe got such a brilliant part because of her mum being in charge.'

'Of course not. And that's – erm – really great news for Chloe.'

Andrea nods. 'I've got high hopes for that girl. High hopes.' She smiles brightly. 'Are you coming down now?'

'No. I think I'll just stay here for a bit. But thanks, Andrea.'

'Okay. Well. Chin up!' She winks and sets off jauntily down the path.

I watch her go, wishing I could somehow find a bit of that bounce in *my* step . . .

I'm at home later, restlessly flicking through the channels on TV, when the doorbell rings. Mustering all my courage, I slowly get up to answer it.

All the same, my heart is in my mouth at the thought of facing Dominic's anger.

But face it I must . . .

'Sienna?' I'm so relieved to see my sister standing there, I laugh out loud.

She looks surprised at my reaction, as well she might, since last time she was here, I was yelling at her for getting down and dirty and shagging Dominic.

'Are you all right?' She smiles uncertainly.

'I'm fine,' I tell her coldly.

She nods and starts backing away. 'Good. I just wanted to make sure you were okay and he hadn't come round to bother you.'

'*He?*'

She looks puzzled. 'Dominic. I transferred the money you owed into his account last night, so that should be an end to it, but he's such a bloody snake, I couldn't be sure he wouldn't come round here and pester you again.'

My mind is whirling. 'What do you mean, you *transferred the money?*'

'I sold the Mini.' She shrugs. 'It was my only capital. But I had to make sure the bastard didn't hurt you any more.' She gives me a timid smile. 'Anyway, see you, Katy.'

In a daze, I watch her walk down the path and start wrestling with the garden gate. *Sienna paid off the loan to Dominic? It can't be true. How did she know about it? And why on earth would she do that?*

'Ow, bloody fucking hell!' yells my sister, sucking her bleeding thumb and rattling the gate furiously with her other hand. My sister . . . who never, ever swears.

I walk over and calmly jiggle the catch the right way so the gate opens. She gives me a half-smile and turns to leave.

'Wait a minute. How did you know I owed Dominic money?'

Her eyes are wary. 'I didn't. Not exactly. But Mum told me she heard you on the phone to him one time, telling him you weren't interested. She had a feeling he might be trying to get back with you. I knew that would be the last thing you wanted, so I went to see him the other night.'

I stare at her. 'But why?'

She shrugs. 'I always suspected him of trying to get back at you that night.' She looks away. 'The night you found us together. And it was true. He came right out and admitted it. He said he wanted you to suffer the way he did when you finished with him. He admitted he set you up so you'd get home and find us together.'

I stare at her. Can it be true?

She swallows. 'There was never anything going on between us, you know. He only wanted you to *think* there was.' She gives me a sheepish look. 'I never imagined he could be so horrible. He always seemed so funny and caring.'

We look at each other across the gate. And across the years of hurt and heartache that have kept us divided.

Sienna's 'revelation' has left my head reeling.

She's really asking me to believe that Dominic set us both up? To get some kind of twisted revenge on me for ending our relationship?

But surely even Dominic wouldn't stoop that low?

And thinking about it, Sienna has had two long years to conjure up a tale like this. How do I know she hasn't just made the whole thing up?

She stares at me, her eyes brimming with tears. 'It's true, Katy.' Then she raises her hand and walks away.

I stare after her, full of conflicting emotions.

At the time it happened, I could never have believed Dominic capable of something so horribly calculating. But having seen his true colours lately, I now think he's capable of anything.

Could Sienna be telling the truth?

THIRTY-SIX

I can't quite believe this turn of events.

After all the months of endless worry over Dominic and his demands. After the constant, stomach-churning dread that has been hanging over me like an inky black cloud, making me feel vulnerable even in the sanctuary of my own home. After all of that, the pressure has vanished.

I float through my normal routine that night, feeling light as a wisp of cotton wool. It's as if Dominic himself has been sprawled across my shoulders, weighing me down all these months, sapping the very life in me. Then out of nowhere, a rescue helicopter has arrived and winched him off, far away into the blue yonder, out of my life for good.

And Sienna made it happen . . .

That night, for the first time in ages, I sleep deeply and undisturbed. Even thoughts of Gabe seem less desperate in this dazzling feeling of freedom I'm experiencing. After all if *this* can happen, then surely *anything* is possible . . .

When I wake in the morning, my first thought is of my sister. Already, my 'fairy-tale rescue' of the previous night has assumed more human and mundane proportions. The pressure is off as regards Dominic. But now, of course, I will have to speak to Sienna and sort out arrangements to pay her back.

I've also got to work out how I feel about Sienna's revelation of the night before.

She says she was duped by Dominic, but that's not how it looked to me. That's not the image that's burned on my mind. Sienna waking to find me there, both of them semi-naked, wrapped around each other. Even if it's true and Dominic did contrive the whole scenario, there's no escaping the fact that Sienna got into bed with him.

Soon after nine, I take a deep breath and pick up the phone.

Sienna answers. She sounds surprised to hear my voice. 'Katy? Are you all right?'

'Yes, I'm fine.' I hesitate, then add, 'Thanks to you.'

There's a taut silence. I picture her face, full of surprise at my admission.

'Look, I just want to say how grateful I am to you for digging me out of the hole I was in with Dominic. You really didn't have to do it but I'm so glad you did.'

'It's fine. Really.' Her voice sounds small and far away. 'I was glad to do it.'

A brief silence.

'I know how hard it must have been for you to sell that car.'

She laughs. 'Like having my right arm amputated, but hey, what's a classic Mini between . . . ?'

She breaks off, the word left unsaid.

A longer silence.

Then Sienna's voice again. 'Do you think . . . how would you feel about meeting for a coffee? On neutral ground. To talk.'

I swallow hard, still unsure.

There's been so much water under the bridge.

But then, what harm could it do? The close bond we once had may have gone, but now that Sienna is back, it's surely better that we try to be civil towards each other. For Mum's sake, if nothing else.

'Okay. Coffee,' I say at last.

'Great!' She sounds relieved, as if she's been holding her breath. 'What about Rosa's in the village?'

'Good. Yes. She – erm – even does lactose-free these days.'

'Oh, brilliant. I hate taking hot drinks black.'

'Unless it's Earl Grey tea, of course,' I say, remembering.

She laughs. 'Unless it's Earl Grey.'

We arrange to meet the following morning at ten-thirty.

I wake soon after four a.m. and know immediately I won't get back to sleep. So I throw on my dressing gown, make a pot of tea and settle at my desk. But the invoices and bills start blurring into each other.

So I take my tea and sit in a chair by the conservatory window, turning off the light and staring out into the silvery dark garden, thinking about what I will say to my sister.

I keep thinking about the piano she bought me. I remember arriving back with the leaflets that day and her greeting me excitedly in the hallway, thrilled at the surprise that was waiting for me in the living room.

I'd loved that piano so much – even though it was a bit drab-looking and riddled with woodworm – and I actually took lessons for a while. Then Sienna left and the piano gathered dust. I couldn't bear to play it. All my enjoyment was gone.

But now, as I sit watching the dawn come up, it plays on my mind what Sienna will say when she finds out I sold her gift a few months ago, to keep my head above water.

At the time, I'd thought good riddance to that piano. Because all it did was sit there, taking up room, reminding me of happier times that would never, ever return, thanks to Sienna and Dominic's betrayal. Now, I find myself wishing I hadn't let it go so easily.

Does that mean that I'm thawing towards my sister?

I wrap my arms around myself, suddenly aware of the autumn chill in the air.

The problem is, the passage of time might have taken the edge off the hurt. But it will never be able to wipe that shocking scene from my mind. Dominic entwined with Sienna.

Sienna is probably hoping our meeting at the café later this morning will be the first step towards a reunion.

For myself, I really don't know what to think . . .

It's a day of bright autumn sunshine with a definite nip in the air.

I wait in Rosa's at a table by the window, watching the dust motes curl in the air and breathing in the comforting aroma of fresh coffee and newly baked muffins.

The door opens and Sienna comes in, flicking back her neat blonde bob and giving me that quick, dimpled smile that shows the slight gap between her front teeth. I smile up at her as she removes her jacket and slings it over the back of her chair. 'I've ordered you the usual?'

She nods and sits down.

'Is that okay?' I'm suddenly unsure. We haven't met like this for well over two years now. Perhaps her tastes have changed while she's lived in Paris. I point over at the counter. 'There's still time to—'

She shakes her head. 'Earl Grey with a slice of lemon.'

We smile warily at each other.

I take a deep breath. 'So . . .'

She flicks her eyes up at me then looks down at her hands, which she's massaging together. 'It's good to see you,' she says, looking up again. 'I don't blame you for sending my letters back. I just need you to understand that I've regretted what happened every single day of my life since I left for Paris. And if I'd known what depths he'd sink to, I'd never, ever have let Dominic in the house that night.'

314

I give a harsh laugh. 'I wouldn't have minded you letting him in the house. It was the bit where you got into bed with him that I find a little hard to understand.'

She groans and rolls her eyes to the ceiling. 'But you don't understand. Like I said, nothing happened, I explained it all in the letters . . .'

'Well, I didn't read them, did I?' I snap. 'So why don't you try and make me understand now?'

Slowly, she nods.

'I was gutted when Daniel broke up with me. I never told you, but I was actually planning to propose to him on Valentine's Day.' She smiles sadly. 'I even bought a ring. A cheap thing, just in case a miracle happened and he said yes.'

'He was crazy about you,' I say, remembering how the two of them had seemed joined at the hip.

'Not crazy enough, apparently. But anyway, you and Dominic were brilliant, taking me everywhere, not minding me playing gooseberry, and helping me through one of the worst times of my life.'

The waitress brings our drinks. I absent-mindedly tear open a small packet of sweetener and stir it in, before remembering I don't even take sugar.

'Where was I?' asks Sienna, when we're alone again.

'Going through one of the worst times of your life.'

'Ah, yes.' She gives me a sheepish smile at the irony. 'So anyway, that night when Dominic called at the house, in a real state because you and he had just split up, I couldn't just turn him away.'

'I understand that,' I say coolly.

She sighs. 'So he came in and I gave him a whisky. Then another one. And he told me you'd been contacted by a client who wanted to see you urgently. And as she lived near London, you'd said you'd go to the meeting and then just stay over at Abby's instead of coming home.'

'Abby's? My friend Abby Fisher, from school?'

'Yeah. And I had no reason not to believe him. So he just kept going on and on about how lovely you were and how he didn't know how he was going to survive without you – all that stuff. He sounded so unbelievably cut up. But then he was going to drive home and I just couldn't let him.'

'Couldn't you have given him a lift home?'

She shakes her head. 'I'd been drinking, too.' She frowns. 'I drank far too much after Daniel left. We were two sad, lonely drunks together, I suppose.'

I give a dismissive snort but say nothing.

'So then he went into your room. I didn't think you'd mind him sleeping there.'

I shake my head. 'I wouldn't have.'

'Then he shouted through that he needed a towel because he wanted to have a shower. I'd already got changed for bed so I put my robe on and took one in for him but he was lying face down on the bed sobbing his heart out.'

I swallow hard, remembering how badly he took my decision that we should go our separate ways. I remember thinking, at the time, that I'd injured his pride and that this probably accounted for a fair amount of his anguish.

'So then I'm not exactly sure what happened next,' continues Sienna, picking up her spoon and playing with the slice of lemon in her tea. 'But I think I put my arms around him, just to comfort him. He'd taken his shirt off for the shower but I didn't think anything of it because he seemed so utterly distraught. I was crying about Daniel and he was sobbing over you. And I suppose we just clung to each other like that for ages and then we must have drifted off.' She looks up and her eyes are red-rimmed and full of anguish. 'In your bed. I'm *so sorry*, Katy. I can't imagine what it must have seemed like when you came in.'

'Not pleasant, I grant you,' I tell her stiffly.

Beneath my calm, rather stunned exterior, my mind is whirling with thoughts as I try desperately to match Sienna's sequence of events with the version that's been running in my head for the past two years.

From what I'm hearing now, Sienna was practically blameless throughout.

How the hell could I have got it so wrong?

A tear slides down my sister's nose and drips onto the table. 'Afterwards, I thought he'd just got the wrong end of the stick about you staying overnight at Abby's. I had no idea he'd just made it up.'

We sit in silence for a while, deep in our own thoughts.

'What a bloody mess,' I breathe at last.

Sienna picks up her paper napkin and blows her nose noisily.

I look at her and smile. 'Crikey. I'd forgotten about your elephant-like trumpeting.'

She laughs through her tears and I laugh with her. Then she lays her hand over mine and whispers, 'Are we friends again?'

I shrug, removing my hand. 'I don't know. Maybe. I'm not sure.'

She nods quickly, holding herself together, and I get up to go.

I walk home in a daze, going over the details of our conversation in my head. It's such a lot to take in. But the shocking revelation that Dominic deliberately set us up has turned everything I thought on its head.

If Sienna is to be believed, she was totally blameless in all this. And I do believe her . . .

THIRTY-SEVEN

I arrive home, knowing that I'll never be able to settle down to my accounts, as I'd planned. My head is far too full of conflicting emotions to start wrestling with a financial spreadsheet.

I need to see Mallory.

No sooner does the thought occur than I'm on my feet, grabbing my coat and heading out to the car.

I need to talk to her about everything that's happened today, with Sienna, so I can get the whole thing straight in my head.

I really need my best friend.

For the past few weeks, I've been deliberately avoiding Mallory, giving Rupert time to break his devastating news to her. Every day, I've been expecting a call from her to tell me the wedding is off, but so far, I've heard nothing. Which obviously means Rupert hasn't plucked up the courage to tell her yet.

When I arrive at Newington Hall, to my utter frustration, her car isn't there. There's a red Fiat Punto parked outside, though, which I know belongs to the family's long-time cleaner, Mags. Maybe she'll know where I can track Mallory down.

Mags is clearly upstairs when I ring the bell because it takes her several centuries to answer the door.

'Mallory?' She pats her tight grey perm and wrinkles her nose to think. 'Now, what was it she said she was off to do?' She taps her front teeth to aid her memory. Then a light goes on. 'Camping! That was it!'

I laugh. Rather raucously. I couldn't have been more surprised if Mags had said, 'Oh, she's hitched a lift on a spacecraft heading for Mars.'

'You must be mistaken, Mags,' I say, still chortling. 'Mallory thinks tents are nasty, smelly things. I believe she said, and I quote, "Anyone who thinks sleeping on the ground is fun was in all likelihood dropped on their head in infancy".'

Mags looks puzzled. 'Well, I'm sure that's what she said. All loved-up she was, too. Couldn't wait to get there. Packed her best underwear specially.'

I stare at her. 'Was Rupert with her?'

'No, she's meeting him there. He's driving down later this afternoon, I think she said.'

Bloody Rupert!

What the hell does he think he's playing at, deliberately prolonging their relationship by taking Mallory away for a romantic weekend?

I said I'd give him time to tell her, but he's totally taking the piss now!

'Hang on, she had a pamphlet,' Mags says. 'Wait there, love.'

She goes away for hours and comes back with a leaflet in her hand. 'There you go. South Downs. She showed me pictures of the campsite.'

I stare at a photograph of two happy campers standing proudly outside the tent they've obviously just erected.

I shake my head. 'No way.'

But then I remember the time Mallory was using my computer, and I discovered she'd been looking at a camping website.

'Right, thanks, Mags.'

'No problem, love. When you see her, tell her we need new bags for the hoover. I'm sick of patching up old ones with tape.'

In the car, I study the leaflet. The campsite is about an hour's drive away. If I set off now, I'll be able to have a good chat with Mallory before Rupert arrives. I should have told her about Rupert and Hans the minute I found out, instead of trusting that her fiancé would do the decent thing.

Well, Rupert's period of grace has come to an end.

I'm going to tell her myself . . .

I'm not great with maps and directions, but the place is just off a main road and fairly easy to find. There's a man at the gate and I tell him I'm only visiting, not wanting to pitch camp myself. When I mention her name, he says, 'Oh aye, I remember her. Posh voice. Sounds a bit like the Queen?' He scratches his head. 'Aye, she wanted to know where she could plug her hairdryer in. When I said the nearest place was probably the public baths down the road, she wasn't best pleased.'

'I bet she wasn't. Which tent is hers?'

'Ah, well, it's the one right in the corner of the field.'

I look over and there's a really luxurious, top-of-the-range thing that's just one step down from a proper house.

'Thanks.' I grin at the man and start bumping the car over the grass towards it. But when I get near, I begin to realise that unless Mallory is sharing this impressive piece of canvas with a family of sporty cyclists with three kids, it's clearly not hers.

That's when I spot the small ridge tent behind it, right in the corner of the field, just as the man said.

I get out of the car, chortling away to myself at the very thought of Mallory spending the night in that thing. How on earth has Rupert managed to persuade her?

I bend down to the zip at the front. 'Er . . . Mallory?'

No reply. Perhaps she's off trying to find a hairdryer socket.

'Mallory? It's me. Katy.'

There's a ripping sound as the zip is pulled up about a quarter of the way, and Mallory's head appears. To say she looks dishevelled would be a bit of an understatement. Her cheeks are rosier than a pair of Gala apples and it would be fair to assume she's been unable to locate that hairdryer socket.

Plus she doesn't appear to be wearing a top.

She slaps her arms over her chest. 'Katy? How in God's name did you find me?'

'Mags gave me the pamphlet,' I say, regarding her warily.

She disappears for a second and I'm sure I hear her giggle. Then she's peering up at me again, through the very small opening, her cheeks an even deeper shade of red than before. There's something odd about this.

'Are you going to let me in? Or are you just going to sit there grinning up at me like a demented Cheshire cat?' I ask. 'Oh, is Rupert in there?'

'Rupert's not here, no.' She looks at me sheepishly. 'But there *is* someone else you might recognise.'

There's a bit of a scuffle.

And another head appears.

Gareth?

THIRTY-EIGHT

'You and – *Gareth*?'

She twists her mouth up at the corner. 'Me and Gareth. Yes.'

I've dragged her off to a local greasy spoon café to have it out. (Eye contact with Gareth was brief and rather uncomfortable on both sides.)

'But how long has it been going *on*? And what about *Rupert*?'

She points at her lips and continues munching on a huge mouthful of egg, bacon and sausage.

I eye her archly. 'The outdoor air obviously does *wonders* for the appetite. Poor Gareth's probably *starving*.'

She colours up and sort of smirks. Then she swallows. 'Remember when I was ill with that hideous flu virus? And Rupert spent all his time at his studio?'

I nod.

'Well, Gareth, bless him, put those broad shoulders of his to good use and let me sob all over them. He could see Rupert was a useless nurse and that I was slowly dying of snot and boredom, so one day he pitched up with some chicken soup he'd made.' She laughs. 'What a lark! No one's *ever* made me soup before.'

'A bowl of broth is hardly a reason to fall madly in lust with someone, is it?'

'Well, apparently it is.' She beams at me.

'It must have been bloody cordon-bleu standard. Was it chicken soup for the soul?' I still can't quite believe what I'm hearing.

She considers. 'No, it was pretty shit, actually. But that's not the point. We ate his soup and we talked. And we found we had so many things in common.'

'Like camping out in a ridge tent on a regular basis, presumably,' I remark dryly. 'There's still a bloody twig in your hair, for Chrissakes.' I grab a handful of her wild bird's nest and extract the bit of forest.

'Well, I have to say, darling, the prospect of an outdoorsy sort of life didn't appeal at all at first,' she says. 'I mean, Gareth's so *fit*. He goes hiking and climbing all the time. The man's a total maniac.'

'Hence the sudden desire to get active yourself, I suppose,' I say, remembering her ill-fated stagger up to the monument with me that time.

She grins. 'I've got fitter since that walk with you. And if this is camping, all I can say is *bring it on*! Because I was having a *whale* of a time.' She grins. 'Until you showed up.'

'I bet you were!'

I feel I should be annoyed at her and Gareth but I'm not.

I don't think I've ever seen Mallory this happy, and I guess Gareth is the reason.

Her face clouds over. 'I think I'm in love, darling. Which poses so many problems, I can't even bear to think about it.'

She wipes someone else's lipstick off her mug with the edge of her sleeve and takes a slug of brick-red tea from the other side. 'I'm marrying Rupert on the eighteenth of December.'

We stare gloomily at each other.

'Don't you love him any more?' I ask. 'Rupert, I mean.'

She gives an agonised sigh. 'Yes. I do. He's kind and funny and I know he really cares about me, but the thing is, it's more – I don't know – *real* with Gareth.' She frowns. 'I mean, I never set out to make this happen with Gareth. But it *did* happen, and now, I wouldn't change it. It's so hard to explain.'

'Try?'

She shrugs and shakes her head, glancing around the greasy spoon for inspiration. Then she takes a deep breath and says, 'Okay. It's like Rupert and I are this glamorous couple in a novel who've found each other and have this whirlwind romance that ends in a beautiful wedding and happy-ever-after.' She stares at me, her eyes full of despair. 'And that would be lovely if I felt that we were really meant for each other.'

'But you don't?'

She frowns again. 'No, if I'm being honest, I don't. You need to know someone inside out to marry them, don't you? But sometimes I feel I don't know Rupert at all. It's like he goes off to his studio and has this whole other life that I'm not a part of . . .' She trails off and stares at me sadly.

I nod slowly. 'I like Rupert. But he's – um – not right for you. In fact, there's something you need to know.'

'What?' She frowns at me, puzzled. 'What do I need to know?'

So I tell her about seeing Rupert coming out of the shop for cross-dressers, and finding him with Hans at the studio and feeling there was something going on. All the little things that when you added them up meant marriage plans were not a good idea . . .

She nods as I'm talking, not seeming terribly surprised, and when I'm finished she gives a weary sigh. 'I sort of knew.'

'You did?'

She shrugs. 'You're right. The little things that didn't quite add up. Like we might be openly affectionate with each other, but the sex has never been that great.'

I frown. 'But I thought . . .'

She grins. 'I know. You assumed we were at it like rabbits twenty-four seven? Sadly not.'

'So no sex behind the garden shed or on the kitchen table?'

She looks at me guiltily and shakes her head.

'But why lie about it?'

'I just didn't want you to find out the truth. That our physical relationship was the very opposite of sizzling.'

'But why?'

She smiles sadly. 'Because I knew you'd start questioning whether I should actually be marrying Rupert if there was no real spark between us. I suppose I wanted you to think things were great. If you'd known I was having doubts about the whole proposal/marriage thing, you'd have forced me to talk about it. And then I'd have had to end it.'

I put my hand on hers. 'But obviously, that's what you'll have to do now. Isn't it?'

She gulps and stares at me in despair. 'But I can't.'

'What do you mean? If it's not working, surely you have to break it off. It will be best for Rupert, too, in the long run.'

Her eyes sparkle with tears.

'You deserve the chance to find real happiness,' I urge her. 'And so does Rupert.' *Possibly a move to Brighton with Hans? A new career as a nude artist? And a whole new wardrobe full of jazzy shirts?*

She swallows. 'Yes, but you don't understand.'

'What don't I understand?'

'The thing is, I know it probably sounds ridiculous, but I wouldn't just be breaking it off with Rupert,' she says in a tight little voice.

I frown at her, still not understanding. Has there been some sort of *ménage à trois* going on that I was unaware of?

'Don't you understand, Katy?' she wails. 'I'd have to divorce *his family as well.*'

As the penny drops, Mallory – who never cries – shoves her plate aside, puts her head down on her arms and starts sobbing as if her heart will break.

THIRTY-NINE

On the drive back to the campsite and Gareth, she cheers up a bit.

'Gareth's nice, isn't he?' she says, flicking a slightly nervous glance at me.

I smile at her, flattered that my approval is so obviously important to her. 'Gareth's lovely,' I say firmly. 'In fact, if he wasn't clearly so besotted with you, maybe *I* might be thinking about – you know . . .'

'I say!' she protests. 'Hold on there!' But she's grinning.

'Joke! But honestly, he's great. You could do a lot, lot worse.'

'I know he's older than me. Well, quite a bit older. Twenty-two years, actually. But it doesn't seem to matter somehow.'

'Age is just a number.' I shrug. 'Whoever floats your boat and all that.' I can't help thinking Gareth's maturity could actually be part of the attraction for Mallory. She clearly thought she'd found a substitute family in Rupert's relatives, especially in her close bond with his mum and sister. And I feel her pain now it's ending. But if Gareth can provide her with the love and support she's always craved, but received in paltry supply, from her own mum and dad, then how great would that be?

'Do you remember I couldn't do Bryony and Mick's wedding because I was on a course?' She darts a mischievous glance at me.

'Yes. But then you decided not to go on the course.'

She purses her lips. 'There *was* no course. Gareth had invited me to go hiking with him for the weekend.'

'So what happened?'

'I got cold feet and couldn't go through with it. Gareth was desperate for me to break it off with Rupert, but I was still so horribly unsure.'

'I guess that's why you were a pain in the arse at the wedding.' I grin at her. 'And why Gareth dumped you in the floodwater.'

She giggles. 'I was so mad at him for doing that. He did it deliberately, you know, because he was fed up with my indecision.'

'*No!*'

'Oh, ha ha! I made him pay for it later, though. You should have seen his face when I got him on the bed and said I was going to—'

'Stop right there!' I shout. 'No details! Now, I'm dropping you off at the gates here, okay? Because I'm really not up to facing Gareth just yet. In fact, I doubt I'll ever be able to look him in the eye again!'

She gives a guilty grimace and I smile at her.

'Listen, I'm really pleased you've found *lurve* with Gareth, but you need to think about what you're going to tell Rupert, okay?'

She nods. 'I know. I should have broken it off ages ago.'

'Well, do it soon, for goodness' sake.'

That night, my head is all over the place.

I'm slowly getting used to the idea of 'Mallory and Gareth' instead of 'Mallory and Rupert'. But I still can't believe she kept it all to herself and I never suspected a thing. It just shows that you can know someone so well and yet not have a clue what's going on in their head. You make snap judgements about people all the time, often regardless of whether they're based in solid fact.

A prime example being me and Sienna. If only I had read those letters she sent me, instead of angrily sending them back to her, unopened, each time. And if only she hadn't buggered off to Paris instead of staying to face the music, maybe we'd have talked things out long before now . . .

In the end, knowing Sienna's probably stewing at Mum's after our meeting in the coffee shop, waiting to hear from me, I call her.

'Hi,' she says, sounding wary. 'It was great seeing you this morning.'

'Yes. You too,' I say, surprised to find it's the truth. 'Listen, I just need to ask you one question.'

Quickly, she says, 'Nothing happened between me and Dominic, I swear.'

'No, no, not that. I want to know why you ran off to Paris. Because that's what confused me. It sort of confirmed your guilt to me. I thought that if you felt you had to run away, you *must* have had something to hide.'

She sighs heavily. 'Look, if I'm honest, I suppose I did feel guilty. Nothing happened. I'd never have done that to you. But when you walked in on us and I saw your face, I felt so terrible. And then when you refused to listen to my explanations, I knew you hated me and you'd probably never forgive me. So I reasoned it would be better for you if I just left.'

'I didn't hate you, Sienna,' I mutter. 'I could never hate you.'

'I think I thought that the adventure and the excitement of living in Paris would help me to move on and fill the big hole in my life. But of course it didn't. I missed you and Mum so much, and I wanted to come home but that vision of your face – full of shock and betrayal – haunted me and made me afraid of returning. Especially when I kept having my letters returned.' She pauses. 'I should have come home a long time ago to face the music.'

'And I shouldn't have sent back your letters.' I sigh heavily, full of regret. 'I'm just as much to blame. I should never have cut you off like that without giving you a chance to explain.'

'But I shouldn't have stopped writing. I should have kept on

329

sending them because, eventually, you would have opened one and read how I was feeling.'

'I guess we both got it wrong.' I smile sadly. 'I just wish to God you hadn't buggered off to Paris . . .'

A few days after my ridge-tent shocker, I'm about to pick up the phone to call Mallory when it starts to ring.

There was a time not so long ago when I hated answering the phone. I was so afraid it would be Dominic. Or Sienna.

Things have changed. Now, I pounce on it like it's a jam sandwich and I haven't eaten for days. But each time, it turns out to be the wrong person.

I so desperately want it to be Gabe.

Getting so unexpectedly close to him again at Bryony and Mick's wedding was a dream come true. Maybe it was my imagination, but I could have sworn by his reaction to me that he felt the same way. But then of course it all turned to dust so quickly. So the chances of Gabe actually ringing me are minimal.

I've relived over and over again my stupid throwaway comment about hammering my credit card to splurge on a holiday. *As if I would.*

If Gabe knew me better, he'd have realised I didn't mean it. And if his ex hadn't crushed him financially and emotionally, perhaps he'd have been able to see the joke.

So many 'ifs' . . .

But that look on his face when I said it, I will never forget. It's fair to say, it will haunt me for a long, long time . . .

As I suspected, it's not Gabe on the phone. But it might just be the next best thing. At last, the weddings co-ordinator at the Greshingham Hotel has come through for me! She wants to have a meeting with me next week and will be putting a lot of work my way soon.

I hang up, my heart beating deliciously fast. This is just the boost I need. More work means less worry about money and even more importantly, less time to mope about Gabe.

But when I sit down and start thinking about the nuts and bolts of it – how many extra weddings and how much extra help I'll need – I realise I've got a problem on my hands. It's great that Mallory helps out when she can, but if I'm to be scaling up the business, I will need to put a more formal staff structure in place. I definitely can't struggle on alone.

An hour later, after sitting in the conservatory, staring out at the burnished autumn leaves on the hawthorn tree, an idea has taken shape.

Five minutes later, I'm on my way to Mum's.

She's overjoyed to see me and I know why. She's been longing for ages to have her two daughters with her in the same room. And Sienna will have told her that we met for coffee and that things are looking more hopeful.

As I hug Mum back, though, I want to tell her not to jump the gun. I still can't help feeling a little bit wary. I suppose I'm scared in case too much time has gone by and that it mightn't be so easy to pick up where we left off before all this happened.

Sienna emerges from the kitchen, wearing Mum's apron and bringing with her a delicious waft of baking. She smiles at me. 'Just in time for a scone. Grace and Annabeth are coming over.'

Sure enough, a minute later, the pair of them arrive.

They fall on me happily, and Annabeth looks from me to Sienna and back again. 'Two peas in a pod.'

Grace frowns. 'Well, not really. Katy's hair is a much darker blonde and their face shapes are entirely different.'

'Oh, trust you to split hairs,' chides her sister. 'And anyway, I wasn't just talking about looks. I meant their *natures* are similar.'

'You should have said so, then.'

Annabeth digs her in the ribs. 'Stop being so grumpy.'

We all sit down in Mum's living room to sample Sienna's scones.

'We've just been to visit Michael and I picked some of those glorious white Michaelmas daisies to take over,' says Annabeth, dipping a spoon into a pot of Grace's homemade strawberry jam. 'They were absolutely his all-time favourite flower.'

'No, they weren't,' says Grace, rather predictably. 'He loved calla lilies best.'

'Yes, well, they're not in season.'

'I didn't say they were. I just said they were his favourite.'

'Ooh, these scones are lovely. Clever girl, Sienna,' says Annabeth. 'Grace, put one in your mouth, dear.'

We all laugh, even Grace, and I tell them my good news about the Greshingham Hotel.

'Oh, well done, love.' Mum beams at me, looking much more like her old self. 'I knew it was just a matter of being patient.'

'That's really cool,' smiles Sienna.

'You'll be busy, though,' points out Grace. 'Won't you need extra help?'

I nod. 'Mallory's great but I'll need someone full-time, someone with the right experience, who I can trust.'

Grace nudges Annabeth. 'You could help out. Those royal connections of yours would open doors all over the place.'

Annabeth bats this away with her usual good-humour.

It suddenly strikes me how close this pair are. They're always bickering and taking the mickey out of each other, but none of it is ever malicious. It's just sisters who are very different but who know each other inside out.

Their relationship could so easily have ruptured forever over their love for Michael. But it hasn't. They've weathered the storm and now, they're almost like an old married couple themselves.

I glance at Sienna, who's getting up to pour more tea.

Family is so important. And if Annabeth and Grace can survive such an enormous test on their relationship, there's no excuse for me and Sienna. I know what I want to do. And there's no time like the present.

'You're right, Grace. I will need extra help,' I say, launching right in before I can change my mind. 'It would be great if this person was already familiar with my annoying little foibles and knew how many sugars I don't take in my coffee. That sort of thing.' I smile. 'And it would be so much better if they knew the wedding photography business and could hit the ground running, so to speak . . .'

Sienna is staring at me now, wide-eyed, clearly wondering where I'm going with this.

'Those eyebrows have got a life of their own, little sis,' I laugh. 'Yes, I do mean you!'

'Really?' Her brows shoot even further into her fringe. She looks stricken, as if she doesn't know whether to believe me. 'But are you sure?'

I'm nodding.

But she still doesn't seem convinced. 'What if you regret it?'

'I won't.'

'But you might. You don't know that.'

I laugh. It's like she's trying to talk me out of it. Or that she can't quite believe this turn of events. (I'm struggling to believe it myself, but it definitely feels right.)

'Listen, nothing's sure in life. But I'd definitely be prepared to take a gamble on this,' I say, my voice catching. Then I grin. 'And anyway, I'm fed up with people asking me why on earth I called the business Sister Act Photography!'

Her shoulders relax and she smiles broadly. 'It would be just like the old days.'

I'm still nodding, like a Churchill dog.

When we hug, I'm sobbing and hiccupping at the same time. And over Sienna's shoulder, Mum, Annabeth and Grace are regarding us with fond pride. Even Grace's eyes are glistening . . .

FORTY

It's the first week in November and Sienna and I are slowly starting to relax in each other's company.

For the first few weeks, we sort of stepped around on eggshells, asking polite questions, gradually filling in the two-year gap in our knowledge of each other's lives. But generally avoiding the subject of Dominic like the plague. We even sat through a really awful melodrama on TV about sisters who'd fallen out because one of them had shagged the other's boyfriend. It was so awkward. And it was obvious we were both trying desperately hard to be nonchalant about it, pretending we couldn't see the parallels with our own situation. Towards the end, I bit the bullet and said, 'Fuck's sake, he even *looks* like Dominic with those little piggy eyes that get even meaner when he's angry.'

There was a shocked silence.

Then Sienna added, 'And that ridiculous swagger when he thinks he's being watched.'

We looked across at each other and burst out laughing.

'We should have had a good slagging-Dominic-off session years ago,' I said, between guffaws.

'Yeah, well, we can make up for lost time now,' chortled Sienna.

'What about the way he used to sulk for days on end when he couldn't get his own way . . .'

I can laugh about Dominic now because he's finally out of my life. I haven't heard a thing from him since Sienna paid back his loan, and the relief is enormous.

Talking about him ended up being very therapeutic. And against all the odds, I think the rift between Sienna and me is well on its way to being healed.

Bryony came over especially to thank me for the 'wedding story book' I made for her. She loved the little touches I'd written about (mainly involving howling gales, torrential rain and scarily animated trees) and I'm optimistic that as an extra service to offer my wedding couples, it could well prove popular. Also, we already have three more bookings in next year's diary, thanks to the Greshingham Hotel referrals.

I've wasted no time in getting Sienna back involved in every area of the business and it is, as she said, a bit like old times.

I confessed to her about Gabe and how his traumatic experience with his ex-fiancée scuppered any chance of a relationship for us. She was really concerned, but I brushed it off as just one of those things. As if I didn't really care. Which, given time, I know I won't.

I played down my feelings for Gabe to Sienna. So she has no idea of the nights I lie awake, going over every conversation we ever had. Every look, every touch, every little joke when our eyes would meet and I'd melt . . .

In our spirit of renewed closeness, Sienna told me all about going to see Dominic to hand over the money I owed him.

'He was cool and very off-hand,' she said. 'I think he was annoyed I was paying him back. He probably fancied having you under his thumb for a while longer yet.'

I shivered. 'We both had a pretty lucky escape there and I'm in debt to you forever for saving my bacon.'

She shook her head. 'No, you're not. I ran off to Paris without a single thought for how you'd keep the business going without me. I hate myself for doing that. So paying back Dominic was my way of making it up to you.'

I smiled at her, thinking how destructive it could be to a relationship when the lines of communication are severed. But somehow, I don't think Sienna and I will be making that mistake again . . .

My sister says the ladies at Clandon House are in mourning.

Gareth – the subject of much idle speculation on the romance front – has been snapped up. And by a woman almost half their age!

They're not too down-hearted, though. Apparently, a single, eligible bachelor in his fifties – called Hamish – has moved into the apartment next door to Mum's, along with a huge library of classical music CDs and a nifty vintage sports car. (Mum's fed up already with Grace's raised eyebrows and nudge-nudge comments.) Although according to Sienna, it's Annabeth who Hamish has his eye on. Apparently, Mum came down from Annabeth's the other day all tight-lipped because she disturbed the pair of them having a very cosy chat.

So who knows?

Sienna says she's now my eyes and ears at Clandon House and will keep me informed at all times. I have a feeling she's trying to keep my spirits up.

But frankly, my spirits are lower than a river level after a long dry spell. As November slides into December and Christmas is fast approaching, I'm trying desperately to pretend otherwise. I really don't want to think about the most romantic of all seasons (ha ha).

I keep telling myself I'm fine.

I'm absolutely fine.

Gabe Harlin? He's just a brilliant photographer I snogged a couple of times. No big deal.

And in fact, I'm so busy with work, I barely have time to think about him . . .

Only when I wake up.

And when I switch out the light at night.

And when a song reminds me of him and I have to swallow really hard on the painful lump and try to think of something funny instead.

And when . . .

Okay, so I *never* stop thinking about Gabe. Not really. I might be busier than ever, but he's always there in the back of my mind, watching what I'm doing – especially when I'm taking photos.

But I'm fine.

I'm absolutely fine.

It's two weeks before Christmas and I'm in the village doing some shopping. As I'm coming out of the post office, I happen to glance over the road and my heart stops.

Gabe is coming out of The Bunch of Grapes.

I freeze on the spot and a man behind bumps into me, muttering an expletive. I let him past and step back into the doorway so I can see and not be seen. Gabe's wearing jeans and that shirt of his that's the colour of cornflowers – the one that brings out the intense blue of his eyes. His hair is a little longer than when I last saw him at Bryony and Mick's wedding, and as I stand there, barely breathing, he runs both hands through it.

I must be brave and walk over there to talk to him. But just as I'm psyching myself up, a blonde woman emerges from the pub and joins him. It's the woman he was with at the wedding.

He says something to her and she laughs and nudges him. Then they turn and start walking along the street together.

Despair floods through me.

That's when I know I'm definitely not fine.

I feel sick and my legs are so shaky, I have to slip into Rosa's café and order a coffee just so I can sit down and try to get myself under control. I'd convinced myself the blonde woman was simply Gabe's 'plus one' at the wedding, nothing more, but I'd obviously been fooling myself. They were clearly an item . . .

I can't face the coffee, so when the assistant's not looking, I nip to the next table and empty it into the four used cups there. (I'd hate Rosa to think her refreshments were going downhill.)

Then I walk home, let myself in and flake out on the sofa, still in my coat. I just need a few minutes on my own to clear my head of all these horrible, jangly thoughts about Gabe and that woman . . .

A second later, Sienna bursts into company headquarters, with a jolly, sing-song 'Hello-o!' and my heart sinks into my boots. I try to summon up an equally upbeat greeting but all that emerges is a forlorn squeak.

Sienna comes into the living room. 'Oh, you *are* back. You'll never guess who I just bumped into,' she says, uncurling her scarf and flinging herself down in the chair. 'Andrea and Chloe. Hadn't seen them for ages. But they both recognised me.'

'Ah yes, I did Andrea's wedding back in March,' I say.

'Oh, right. Interesting. Well, anyway, Chloe's heart is set on becoming a star and Andrea's obviously one of those pushy mothers who's determined to give up her own life in honour of the great cause. So guess what she's done?'

I try to look interested.

'She's set up an amateur dramatics group in the local community centre so Chloe can hone her skills as an actress.'

'Yes, I know.'

'So anyway.' She stops and peers at me. 'Are you all right? You're really pale.'

'Just knackered, really,' I murmur.

'Right, well, early night for you, then. Anyway, I promised we'd go to their dress rehearsal on Friday. They're doing *Cinderella*? Chloe's playing the Fairy Godmother.'

'Hm.'

'Did you hear what I said?'

'What? Yes. *Cinderella*,' I mumble. 'Great.'

I escape to my room as soon as I can, playing on the early night suggestion. I can't believe how sunk in misery I am, obsessing about Gabe and that woman.

I'd convinced myself I was getting over him.

But it's *so* not true . . .

A Winter Wedding

FORTY-ONE

Mallory and Gareth are madly in love.

And I'm delighted for them. *Absolutely cock-a-hoop*, to use an expression of Mallory's. But frustratingly, I'm finding it almost impossible to pin her down for a face-to-face chat. I realise she's in the first flush of romance and that she's probably off somewhere with Gareth doing the things lovers do. But I'm really missing my best friend.

Finally, on Friday morning, she returns my calls, apologises profusely for not being in touch and asks me if I'd like to pop round later as Gareth is doing the gardens at Mum's place.

I'm working on an album that needs to go off in today's post, so it's late afternoon by the time I arrive at the back door of Newington Hall.

'I'd almost given up on you, darling,' says Mallory. 'We've only got an hour because I've got to go out.' Her piled-up hair is falling down messily and her trousers are creased. Not like the old Mallory at all. But she looks radiantly happy. She peers into the early evening gloom. 'Where's Sienna? I thought she'd be here.'

I frown. 'Why would she be?'

'Oh, no reason. Come in.'

'I've been frightfully busy, darling,' she exclaims, as she leads me into the kitchen.

I grin, thinking of Gareth. 'Yes, I can imagine.'

She shakes her head and says, 'No, no, other things.' And then she doesn't tell me what, which I find a little odd.

Instead she confirms that she and Rupert have finally had *The Talk* during which they confessed absolutely everything and had a jolly good cry. But although they were both upset at the dissolution of their marriage plans, they both knew it was for the best and have happily agreed to remain friends. This is great news because it means Mallory can still stay in touch with Rupert's mum and sister, which I know she's delighted about.

Her parents actually came home for a flying visit earlier in the week, and they really like Gareth. (They weren't convinced Rupert was right for her, apparently, and I find myself reflecting that maybe they've got a modicum of sense after all.)

It feels like I've only just arrived when Mallory is on her feet, saying she hates to push me out into the cold but she has to get moving or she'll be late.

'Are you meeting Gareth?' I'm reluctant to leave the cosy kitchen and brave the chill outside.

'Sorry?'

'Gareth? Are you meeting Gareth?'

'Oh. Erm – yes! That's it. I'm meeting Gareth.'

I'm in the car heading down the driveway when my mobile goes. It's Sienna, so I pull in to answer it.

'Where are you?' she shrieks.

'At Mallory's.'

'But we're meant to be at the community centre in an hour.'

'What? *Why?*'

'Andrea's am dram club dress rehearsal? *Cinderella?*'

My heart sinks. Oh God, I vaguely remember agreeing to go along, but I'm *really* not in the mood. I'd been hoping for a good long chat with Mallory but she's more or less chucked me out, so she can see Gareth. I can't blame her, of course. But I'm feeling emotionally fragile anyway, especially with Christmas just round the corner, and it's really dampened my spirits. Now, all I want to do is go home and open a bottle of wine.

'They won't mind if we don't go, will they?' I say, hopefully.

A brief silence. 'But that would be rude, Katy. I promised.'

'It's not as if the show won't go on without us.'

'Oh, come on, Katy. You've got to go with me. Please,' she begs. '*Pretty please?* I'll do all your invoices tomorrow. And I'll address all those envelopes for your advertising mail shot.'

I laugh. 'Sounds good. But why so desperate, little sis?'

'I *love* pantomimes. You know I do.'

She does.

'And *Cinderella* especially. *Please.*'

Honestly, I feel like I'm fifteen again and she's six, and she's begging me to take her to the ice-cream van.

But I was really dreading doing all those envelopes. So I tell her I'll see her back at mine, and I'm just about to start up the engine again when Mallory's little green Citroën hares past me, shrieks to a halt at the end of the driveway, hurtles into the traffic and disappears.

She must be late for Gareth. I don't think she even noticed me parked in the shadows.

An hour later, I'm walking into the community centre with Sienna. Andrea's am dram group have taken over the hall and we've arrived at a rather nice bit – the ball itself. Lots of women in colourful gowns, and men in odd pantaloons and stuck-on sideburns are whirling grandly around the hall in time (or for the most part, wildly *out* of time) to some rather stately music.

We stand near the door to watch. It's not just us. Chloe and Andrea have clearly invited quite a few of their friends and family along to watch the dress rehearsal. Eventually, we find some uncomfortable seats and sit down.

Chloe is great as the Fairy Godmother, playing her with a real mischievous twinkle in her eye. Cinderella is a bit too melodramatic, and sadly, the prince is as wooden as a cricket bat. Beside them, Chloe shines even brighter.

'This is great, isn't it?' whispers Sienna, looking far more excited than she should. I glance at her, puzzled. She needs to get a life if this is her idea of great entertainment of a Friday night. Mind you, mine's hardly any better.

It's warm in the hall and I find myself closing my eyes and drifting off, totally missing Cinderella running off at midnight and losing her slipper. A glass of wine. And sleep. That's all I need, really. Once this is over, we can go home . . .

Sienna nudges me.

Opening my eyes, I find a commotion going on. 'What's happening?'

I catch sight of Chloe bombing over towards me, her face wreathed in panic. 'You've got to help us out, Katy. Please. Cinderella and the prince have buggered off and we can't find them. But we have to finish the rehearsal. The Quallingham Quilters need the hall in twenty minutes and there'll be hell to pay if we're still here.'

I shake my head, wondering if this is a joke.

Chloe wrings her hands and stares at me pleadingly. Talk about melodrama!

Feebly, I point out that there must be someone else who can do it. My eye lights upon Sienna. 'What about you?'

She was, after all, the one who dragged me here in the first place.

Sienna shakes her head.

'Why not?' I demand.

'It's – erm – I've got a sore foot,' she says seriously.

'No you haven't.'

'Yes, I have. Look.' She presses her calf muscle. 'Ow.'

'That's not your foot,' I point out, but she's already up on her 'sore foot', trying to heave me off my chair.

Then, oh God, Andrea comes over and starts helping.

'Come on. It's just the wedding scene,' she urges gaily, yanking my other arm so that I've really no other option but to give in.

'Have I got to read from a script? I'll need my glasses.'

'Since when do you wear glasses?' asks Sienna in surprise.

I nudge her in the ribs as Chloe gives me an 'oh dear, found out' reprimanding sort of look.

'I suppose we could just make it up,' says a deep and very familiar voice.

I spin round and almost faint with shock.

Gabe is standing there, looking quizzically from me to his cousin and back to me again.

'No, you have to say the actual lines, *Prince Charming*,' laughs Andrea. 'Otherwise the others won't know when to come in.' She thrusts a script into his hand and one into mine.

I'm gazing at Gabe like I've crossed the Sahara Desert on foot and just spotted my first watering hole. Oh God, he's so gorgeous, I just want to wrap my arms around him and feel his warmth and get my fingers in his hair and—

Get a grip, girl! He's attached! You saw him the other day with that blonde girl!

All the same, my heart is thundering so loudly at his nearness, I'm relieved there's music playing in the background to drown it out.

My head is whirling with confusion. Where the hell did Gabe appear from? Did he just arrive? I bloody well hope so, otherwise he might have seen me slumped in a chair, napping. And, God forbid, dribbling . . .

'Katy, if you could pop along to the kitchen, we'll get your veil on,' Andrea says, rushing off before I have a chance to refuse.

Gabe smiles at me. It's one of those full-on smiles that crinkles the corners of his eyes and makes me feel like my legs will give way any second. 'Did I just walk into a parallel universe?' he murmurs. 'Or has my cousin been on the wine? What the hell's going on?'

'Mystery to me.' I smile back, my heart thumping frenziedly. It's so good to see him. And he appears fairly pleased to see me, too. I'm starting to warm to the idea of playing Cinderella to his Prince Charming. Maybe it won't be such a hardship after all . . .

'Okay, Cinderella,' trills Andrea, hurrying over and taking my hand. 'I'm afraid I'm going to have to temporarily part you from your Prince Charming. Come along.' Still holding my hand, like I'm seven and can't be trusted not to run away, she leads me over to the little kitchen area. There, she arranges a veil made of cheap netting on my head, fussing until she gets it looking just right, which seems a bit excessive considering I won't even be playing Cinderella in the real performances.

'There.' She steps back to admire her handiwork, clasping her hands to her chest and smiling like a proud mother-of-the-bride. 'You look perfect!'

I smile obligingly.

'Right, when the music starts, I want you to walk *slowly* back up the aisle to Gabe.' She tweaks the veil one last time as the sound of singing reaches my ears. It's 'Let It Go' from the movie, *Frozen*.

'Right, off you go.' Andrea gives me a little pat and I head out of the kitchen and start making my way up the aisle, between the chairs, fighting an alarming temptation to laugh.

'Don't gallop,' hisses Andrea, so I slow it right down.

I catch sight of Gabe waiting for me at the 'altar' and the irony of the situation suddenly hits me full force. I'm walking up the bloody aisle to 'marry' the man of my dreams – but it's all a bloody act!

I focus on my feet, avoiding Gabe's eye, not sure if I want to laugh or cry.

And then it occurs to me. I've been to three weddings this year which Gabe was also present at – and this is our fourth.

Four weddings. But this one's nothing but a bloody fiasco!

Halfway up the aisle, a giggle surges up out of nowhere at the lunacy of it all, and I glance directly at Gabe, wondering if he's also finding it funny. Or whether he's just tolerating it because obviously, the last woman he'd want walking up the aisle towards him is *me* . . .

But when I catch the look in his eyes, I almost falter to a standstill.

He's gazing straight at me, a tender – almost vulnerable – look on his face, as if I really am a gorgeous Cinderella in a fabulous dress.

I swallow hard. It's impressive. The man can definitely act. He might even have missed his vocation.

I smile at him, but it's like he's in a weird sort of daze, just staring at me as if he's never seen me before. So I pull a face at him to provoke a reaction.

He blinks a few times, as if he's remembered where he is. Then he clears his throat and runs a hand through his hair. At last, a smile breaks through. That gorgeous, crinkle-eyed, knee-trembling smile that actually makes all this ridiculousness totally worthwhile. And everyone else disappears. There's just Gabe. And me. And my frantically beating heart.

I join him at the 'altar', just as the song is reaching a crescendo.

'You do realise we've been set up,' he says, leaning close.

My eyes widen in surprise.

'Look at Andrea and Chloe.'

I turn and see them standing together at the back of the hall, grinning broadly. And suddenly, I get it. Oh my God, Andrea's been doing a spot of matchmaking.

But why would she? Unless . . . unless she's set her heart on us getting together. Which would be lovely, except I'm not sure Gabe or his blonde girlfriend would agree.

The 'vicar' steps forward as the music stops, and Gabe murmurs, 'Let's have some fun with this.'

My heart lurches at the warmth in his eyes as he smiles down at me. Our parting at Bryony and Mick's wedding was so cold. It felt horribly final. But today, it seems as if things might be different.

I smile back. 'What do you mean?'

'Just follow my lead.' He holds up his hand. 'Sorry, vicar, could you wait just a sec.' He turns to me and says sternly, 'So what about this fella, Buttons, then? You really expect me to believe that nothing happened between you?'

I look at him, bemused, as a ripple of surprised laughter runs round the room. I glance down at the paper in my hand. I'm pretty sure that's not in the script.

'Well?' grins Gabe.

'But it's true,' I say, catching on. 'Buttons and I are just very good friends. Ask the mice if you don't believe me.'

'Yeah, right. So you share a dingy basement and a coal scuttle, pour out all your deepest feelings to him, and yet you're telling me he never tried it on? Not even once?'

'Not even once. And anyway, what about you and Dandini? I've heard the rumours, you know.'

'What rumours?'

I camp it up with a haughty look. 'Well, that those daily rides in the magic forest aren't entirely in aid of fresh air and exercising the horses.' I wink lasciviously. 'If you know what I mean.'

People are openly laughing now, even Andrea, despite the fact that her dress rehearsal is descending into chaos.

'What are you saying? That I don't care about you?' he demands, and I shrug.

He grabs me round the waist and pulls me against him. 'Because nothing could be further from the truth,' he murmurs, gazing into my eyes with a fiery passion that makes my heart turn a series of somersaults.

'Really?' I croak, placing my hands on his chest, unable to tear my eyes from his.

'Yes, really.' He says it so softly that someone shouts, 'Can't hear you at the back! Speak up!'

'Right, folks, we'll have to stop there.' Andrea hurries up the aisle and addresses the group. 'The quilters are here and spoiling for a fight. Thanks to Katy and Gabe for filling in so brilliantly. Let's give them a big round of applause.'

The clapping and cheering breaks the spell we were under.

Gabe turns me round, takes my hand and bows to the audience. And after a second, I join in.

I'm stunned by what just happened between us. It felt so real. But of course I know it's just a play. Gabe was acting, that's all . . .

But he hasn't let go of my hand. Even though the show is over and everyone's packing up to go.

I catch sight of Sienna in the crowd. She's smiling broadly and cheering, and I know instantly she was in on it. I point at her and flash an 'I'll get you!' look. No wonder she was desperate to get me here tonight. She must have planned it all with Andrea and Chloe when she bumped into them the other day.

Andrea beckons to Gabe and he lets go of my hand and wanders over to speak to her. I can't hear what she's saying to him, but it's obviously something to do with her matchmaking scheme because he's grinning and shaking his head in disbelief at her.

Clearly, he thinks the whole idea of he and I being set up is nothing less than hilarious.

My heart plummets into my shoes.

Everyone is chatting and gathering their things, and moving towards the door

Gabe comes over and says, a little awkwardly, 'So. We need to leave. Before we get savaged by the quilters.'

I laugh but inside I'm panicking.

After all of Andrea's efforts, what if Gabe and I part company now and never see each other again?

I've *got* to say something. Even if I make a total fool of myself. 'I – erm – expect you've got something nice planned for tonight,' I blurt out.

He grins broadly as if I've said something really witty. 'Funny you should say that, but yes, I do.'

My heart sinks. I don't want to ask. But I'd rather know once and for all that there's no hope for me. Then I can get on with my life.

351

So I say, 'Dinner with your girlfriend, maybe?'

He looks surprised. 'Girlfriend?'

'Yes, that pretty blonde girl at Bryony and Mick's wedding?' I'm blushing furiously now. I'd never make a spy. Everything shows on my face in full glorious technicolour.

'Oh, Gill? No, she's a friend. She knew I was dreading going to the wedding, so she offered to go along to cheer me up.'

'Oh.' A spark of hope flares within. Casually, I ask, 'Why were you dreading the wedding?'

He smiles down at me and murmurs, 'I think you know why.'

'Oh.' My heart is racing so fast, I feel quite breathless.

'I wanted to see you. But at the same time, I didn't.'

I nod, thinking *snap!*

'My head was telling me you were bad news but my heart . . .'

'Your heart?'

'My heart was telling me to forget all that and dive right in.'

I swallow hard, caught in the heart-stopping wonder of those intense blue eyes, which right at this moment are so full of tender emotion, I can barely breathe.

'Come on, you two, get a move on!' Andrea's shrill tone reaches us from the door. 'We need to go.'

'Yeah, come on. We need to go,' says Gabe and heads abruptly for the door. The curt way he says it breaks the mood entirely. I follow him, hurrying to keep up with his long strides. What the hell is going on? After all he said to me, it now looks as if he can't get away fast enough . . .

Stumbling into the raw December evening, I pull my coat tightly around me, and start following the crowd. They all seem to be walking in the direction of Willows Edge green and shops. The Christmas lights, strung across the street at intervals, light our way and there's an excited feel in the air that only happens when the festive season is in full swing.

I'm walking beside Gabe in silence and we keep brushing

against each other, but it only makes me feel lonelier than ever. I want to talk to him. Tell him how I feel about him. But we're part of the crowd now, surging along, and I doubt I'm going to get the chance . . .

It's such a Christmassy scene. There's a huge tree on the green, shimmering with lights, and the shops look so warm and inviting, with their jolly decorations. It's late-night closing, specially for Christmas, and shoppers are making the most of it. There's a man selling hot roast chestnuts on the green and I can even hear live music coming from somewhere. The song is 'It Had To Be You'. And the instrument I recognise all too well. It's an accordion, or squeeze box as it's sometimes called.

I smile sadly, remembering those Sunday lunchtimes in the pub, Sienna and I drinking coke and listening to Mum and Dad and their musician friends, holed up in a back room, playing all the old favourites.

'Look.' Gabe takes my arm and points over at the Christmas tree on the green.

And suddenly I realise that's where the music is coming from. There's a woman sitting on a stool, playing the accordion.

I stand stock still.

Is it . . . ? It can't be! She hasn't played that thing in years. Swore she never would, after Dad . . .

But it bloody well is!

Crossing the street, I hurry over to her. 'Mum! What on earth are you doing?'

'You'll find out, love,' she says with a twinkle in her eye.

The song draws to a close.

At which point four people step out from behind the Christmas tree, form a line in front of me and start singing their hearts out to a soundtrack that's begun playing.

My mouth drops open.

The song is 'Love Is In The Air' and they're belting it out like good 'uns. Grace and Annabeth, wrapped up in their winter coats, red tinsel in their hair. And Mallory and Sienna, with big grins on their faces.

Then Gareth appears out of nowhere, performing a spectacularly dramatic dive onto one knee at Mallory's feet. Laughing, she pulls him up, and he joins in with the singing.

They're all moving in time to the music, swaying their hips in unison, slowly moving their arms up in the air every time the music rises to that classic crescendo. 'Love is in the air! Da-da-da. Da-da-da. Love is in the air!'

Then, just as I'm thinking this night can't possibly get any more bizarre, Bryony and Mick step out from behind the tree. Followed by Andrea, Ron and Chloe, all gyrating in time to the song. I giggle. Ron in Christmas jumper and reindeer antlers, shaking his booty, is a real sight to behold.

The music swells as the crowd behind start joining in.

Gabe appears, grinning down at me.

'Did *you* know about this?' I demand laughingly.

He nods. 'Andrea let me in on it just before we left the hall. It's their version of a flash mob. Quite a surprise, huh?'

'They're good.' I smile up at him, my heart pounding.

'It's all in our honour. Andrea and Chloe have been planning it for weeks apparently. She said she owed you a favour.'

'A favour?'

'You saved her marriage? In the Ladies at her wedding?'

I laugh. 'Oh my God, she gave me one of her favours and said it was in lieu of a proper favour. I wasn't expecting her to follow through.'

He snakes his arm around me and a delicious shiver runs up my back. 'Are you glad she did?'

Snuggling closer, I gaze up at him. 'Extremely glad.'

'I'm going to kiss you now,' he murmurs in my ear. 'Got to give them a finale.'

I giggle as my ecstatic heart soars to the top of the Christmas tree and beyond. 'Yes, let's give them what they want.'

He pulls me round to face him and bends to kiss me.

'Just one thing.' I place my hand gently over his mouth. 'Before, when you said your head was telling you one thing and your heart was telling you to just dive in?'

He nods.

'Which did you go with? Head or heart?' There have been so many uncertainties up to this point. I have to know for sure.

He smiles. 'Our pasts are no longer an issue. It's the future that counts. And I've finally realised I want you in it.'

He pulls me closer and I melt against him, slipping my hands beneath his open coat, so we're locked in an embrace that makes me see stars – and they're not just the ones on the Christmas tree.

'Is that okay by you?' he murmurs.

I smile up at him. 'It's absolutely, tremendously, one hundred and ten per cent all right by me. But do you think you should be kissing me? In front of all these people?'

'Absolutely, tremendously, one hundred and ten per cent yes,' he says firmly, as his mouth comes down to crush mine.

The sound of whistling and cheering mingles with my heart-beat and his, as he leaves me in no doubt whatsoever of the strength of his feelings.

I should be holding back in view of our audience, but for once, I really don't care what people think.

This is one fiasco with a *very* happy ending . . .

Epilogue

One year later . . .

'Aren't you ready yet? You've been in there a lifetime.'

I rap on Mallory's bedroom door and she calls, 'Don't come in, darling. You'll spoil the surprise.'

'Okay, but please hurry up. I can't wait for the big reveal. And you don't want to keep Gareth waiting.'

Finally, the door opens and Mallory emerges, closely followed by a smiling Sienna, snapping her from all angles.

Mallory's dress is a stunning, silk creation, with delicate crystal beads on the bodice. It fits her slim figure like a glove.

I knew emotions would run high. But I wasn't expecting the giant lump in my throat at the first glimpse of my best friend on her wedding day.

'Don't cry. You'll ruin your make-up,' she laughs, doing a little twirl for my benefit.

'Stunning,' sighs Sienna, snapping more photos. 'Right, come on, the two of you together.'

So we pose.

I've taught Mallory all about squinching so we really ham it up for the camera.

'Gorgeous,' says Sienna, grinning at me. 'I can't believe you're taking a back seat, today of all days.'

'Yes, well, I've got – erm – other things to concentrate on. Like getting this one to the church on time. Come on, the car's waiting.'

Sienna is the chief photographer today and I have absolute faith in her to do a brilliant job. It's so good having her back, working alongside me. We've photographed close to fifty weddings together so far and the bookings are increasing all the time. It's hard to believe we spent two years at war with each other. Our relationship is back to being as close as it ever was. Maybe even closer, because we don't take our sisterly bond for granted any more.

Mallory still helps us out from time to time with the weddings, but Va-Va-Voom is also booming, so that takes up much of her time. That and Gareth, of course. They're still blissfully happy one year down the line. She says she keeps expecting the romance to wear off but it never does.

They still go on their camping trips – although these days, thanks to Mallory's subtle persuasion, it tends to be more glamping than ridge tent. Gareth actually proposed to her in a tent, which is why we're en route to their wedding right now . . .

At the church, we step out to gasps of delight from the assembled guests.

I spot Mum waiting for me in her lovely lilac suit and fascinator, her face softened into a goofy smile. She was at Mallory's earlier but she hitched a lift to the church with Hamish, Annabeth and Grace.

Mum and Hamish have been getting on like a house on fire. I remember the day Sienna told me she'd disturbed Hamish having a cosy tête-à-tête with Annabeth. We all thought he had designs on her. But it turned out he was trying to find out how the land lay with Mum. They were just friends for the first year and I knew Mum was racked by feelings of guilt over Dad. But we had a long talk and I told her Dad would have wanted her to be happy. She cried a lot. But I think that was the point at which she turned a corner.

I have high hopes that Sienna and I might photograph another happy event before too long.

And as for me . . .

I love Gabe to distraction and the feeling, I'm happy to say, is mutual.

I still have a tendency to spend beyond my means and he can still be a bit mean when it comes to splashing out on things we don't really need. So we balance each other out beautifully.

He asked me to marry him on a trip to Paris. We'd gone there with Sienna and her new boyfriend, Phil, so she could show us the sights, and one night, Gabe took me to this gorgeous place in Montmartre and got down on one knee in front of a whole restaurant full of people, as the band played 'Love Is In The Air'.

I was crying so hard, I couldn't speak. So I just nodded.

I link arms with Mum, who's walking me down the aisle.

She wipes away a tear and we wait for our signal, watching Mallory gliding down the aisle on the arm of her father.

Gabe turns and catches his first glimpse of me. He looks so handsome in his morning suit, my heart feels like it might explode with joy.

Then Mum squeezes my arm.

And I start walking down the aisle towards him . . .

Q&A with the Author

Where do you write your novels?

I write most of the time on my trusty old laptop at a desk in the spare room, surrounded by books galore. But I like to ring the changes. So often, I'll decamp to the public library (no kettle or fridge-type distractions there!) and sometimes, if I'm in the mood to treat myself, I'll head for my favourite coffee shop. It's the perfect place to people-watch over a cappuccino or two . . .

Can you describe a typical working day?

I'm definitely a morning person, so it's no hardship rising early to get my son off to school. I start work around eight, usually reading over what I've written the day before and crossing my fingers it doesn't need too much altering. I then 'down tools' at eight-thirty for breakfast and one of my guilty pleasures – 'Lorraine' on TV! A writer is always on the look-out for story ideas – and what better source than a magazine programme like this one. That's my excuse, anyway . . .

I then start work 'proper' and aim to write at least a thousand words by early afternoon. When the creative juices are flowing, that's easy – but other days, it's painfully slow and you start to wonder if you made a Big Mistake thinking you could be a writer. After a break for lunch, I'll get some fresh air (my best ideas tend to arrive when I'm out walking) or I'll spend the rest of the afternoon catching up on emails and surfing the net (for research, of course!).

What is your most vivid memory?

Apart from the birth of my son, the memory that always stays fresh in my mind is when my agent phoned to tell me I finally had a book deal with Avon, HarperCollins. It felt truly surreal, but the frustrating thing was, the house was empty so there was no-one around to hear my squawks of hysteria. So I went for a long, fast walk in the woods to try and get my head round the fact that finally, *finally* all my years of hard work were paying off. I had so much elated energy, I just had to burn it off otherwise I might have spontaneously combusted!

What was your inspiration for Four Weddings & A Fiasco?

I've always loved the film, *Four Weddings and a Funeral.* It's such a brilliant concept for a movie – a romantic relationship slowly developing over the course of four very different weddings, with lots of great humour along the way. So I suppose I felt inspired to try something similar. It helps that – like Katy, the book's heroine – my lovely friend, Victoria, is a very successful wedding photographer, so I didn't have to venture too far for inspiration and the answers to various technical questions. I've helped her out on occasion, as her assistant, so I can actually claim first-hand knowledge of what my heroine gets up to during an average wedding day!

When Izzy Fraser's long-term boyfriend walks out on her, she's left in a bit of a pickle . . .

A funny, heart-warming tale, full of the joys of summer. Perfect for fans of **Jenny Colgan** and **Lucy Diamond**.